THE SEVENTH GRACE

TALES OF THE NEPHILIM BROTHERHOOD

AUGUST ARREA

VII
PUBLISHING

First Printing 2022
First Edition 2022

ISBN: 978-1-7371661-5-3
Library of Congress Control Number: 2022902224

10 9 8 7 6 5 4 3 2 1

To request permissions, contact the publisher at:

VII
PUBLISHING
VII Publishing
P. O. Box 1272
Clovis, CA 93613
www.viipublishing.com

Book Cover Design by: Diana Chituleska

For my sisters, Alison and Andrea;
two of the many Graces with which I have been blessed.

Table of Contents

CHAPTER ONE

THE WHITE CIRCLE

Jacob couldn't recall ever before seeing Anahel looking quite as grim as he did the moment a trumpet call, deep and rumbling, reverberated through Eden just as morning unfolded in full bloom over the Garden. Whipping the air with his mighty wings, Anahel was carried from his balcony skyward with unbroken swiftness. He was followed by the other Guides—Zuriel, Eksel, Thaniel and Damiel—all of whom wore equally grave expressions. As he watched them in their swift departure, Jacob caught sight of the unmistakable shapes of several more angels silhouetted against the gold and lavender dawn sky far in the distance approaching from the south. "What's happening?" he asked Gotham.

"Anahel has summoned a meeting of the White Circle," answered Gotham.

"About me?"

The visible angst in the angel's face mirroring a sense of growing alarm that was beginning to spread through the Garden like a fire through a dry corn field since the incident at Lions Bite was something he could not readily hide.

"You have had a long and no doubt confusing night. Try and get yourself some rest until we return," suggested Gotham.

"You're joking right?"

Nothing about what was taking place, however, was worthy of a laugh; not to Gotham nor the Guides, and certainly not to Jacob. It was a far cry from the afternoon earlier which found Jacob and the other Shrikes at Lions Bite enjoying a rather amusing show by Ethan demonstrating his Jedi fighting abilities during a duel with Balantine while the rest of the group took a break from practicing their own sword fighting skills. Suddenly, there came a loud wounded cry from Balantine as he dropped to the ground. Jacob didn't need to see the blood that began to seep from between Balantine's fingers while clutching his thigh to know what had happened and rushed to his side. The commotion that followed remained a blur to Jacob, beginning with Ethan running off in search of help once he spied the deep gash he had unintentionally set into Balantine's leg, and ending with Damiel suddenly appearing at his side gently urging Jacob, who had diligently been applying pressure to the wound, to remove his hands from Balantine's leg so he could get in and assess the injury. What remained crystal clear in Jacob's memory, however, was the shared look of ice-cold shock from both Damiel and Gotham when Jacob stepped back and revealed to everyone's surprise the wound Balantine suffered had miraculously and mysteriously healed. Before Jacob knew what was happening, Gotham was in his face outside Lions Bite where he had dragged the boy by the neck out of earshot from the others demanding an explanation for whatever witchery had taken place. Jacob had no idea what to say, but he was certain any answer he gave would not suffice easing an almost fear-filled look fixed upon the angel's face. And even now, standing on Anahel's balcony, Jacob wasn't sure if the dense fog he now found himself swamped inside which refused him any clarity on the matter was one he wanted to be lifted.

"How long will you be?" he asked Gotham.

"As long as it takes," came the elusive reply.

And before Jacob could press him further, Gotham was gone like a passing gust of wind leaving Jacob alone on the balcony to watch as the angel met up with the others and sailed the skies over Eden toward the high-reaching cliffs beneath Broken Earth where what appeared to be a pair of large glowing eyes in a state of perpetual watch over the Garden could be seen peering out from behind the sheer curtain of the mystical waterfalls.

~ ~ ~

When the band of Guides came in reach of the cool spray coming off the main column of the falls wafting through the air like a feathery, misty fog, Anahel made a subtle gesture with his hand and the raging shower of water began to part like a theater curtain. Slowly, the source of the mysterious, fiery orbs seen aglow—particularly under the cover of night—coming from behind the sheet of thunderous, white frothy water like a pair of baleful eyes peering out from the precipitous face of the mountain was revealed. They emanated from two caverns burrowed deep into the cliff rock. But they were indeed eyes; fierce-looking eyes belonging to a sculptured face of a bird of prey protruding from the wet, sleek rock of the mountain. Massive in size, it looked to be like some ancient monument set in the mountain side by an unknown civilization. And yet any eye could see it had not been chiseled by hand, human or angel, but somehow spectacularly formed by the natural carving powers of the water.

Anahel swooped down toward a hook-shaped canopy of rock forming the beak of the bird-shaped facade leading the way to a large platform just inside. There was a rustling of feathers as the angels shook themselves free of the water beading their wings before they made their way to an immense chamber lying beyond a stunted arched entrance just inside the mouth of the rock-sculpted bird. The cavernous cavity was spacious in size and lit by both the warm, orange glow flickering from several balls of fire hovering high above in the air, and two large shafts of bright white sunlight streaming through two portals high above the cavern, which from the outside appeared as the illuminated eyes of the bird face fixed to the side of the mountain.

The floor was rock, but polished to a high gloss so that it gleamed like marble. At the center of the chamber was a large round table chiseled from the mountain rock and also polished to a marble-like sheen. So too were the ten intricately carved chairs positioned around it. As Anahel and the other Guides made their way to their assigned spots, Gotham quietly retreated to the left side of the chamber where there was arranged a row of seats, also made of stone, though smaller in size. The unspoken tension inside the chamber was palpable, but nowhere was its simmering presence more noticeable than in the troubled look on Gotham's face, despite his best efforts to mask it. His thoughts kept drifting to Jacob, whose nervous restlessness he'd felt throughout the night continued to stir at his side like some phantom even as he sat alone.

"There's nothing to be nervous about," he had told the boy more than once throughout the long night in his best reassuring voice.

"I'm not nervous," Jacob would argue, even as the boy quietly tried to make sense of the graven expressions he saw shared by the angels surrounding him. Now, suddenly, it was Gotham who found himself struggling to steady his own nerves as the revelation of what had occurred at Lions Bite, which had quietly, and not so quietly, been debated inside the private confines of Anahel's quarters under the cloak of night, was about to be revealed in the light of this sacred chamber.

It wasn't long before the five remaining members of the council arrived and entered the chamber in single file. Leading the way was Haniel, whose rare presence was often relegated to the forests of the Garden where he served as Guardian of the Tree of the Life. Only when Gotham cast his sights upon the last in line did he feel a semblance of comfort. It was Johiel, not donning the old, withered visage of caretaker he wore on Akdamar Island amongst mortals, but in the image of the mighty, virile angel he was. The serious expression fixed on his face was broken briefly by a friendly smile which passed subtly across his lips when he glanced with his kind, warm eyes to the far corner of the chamber where Gotham sat quietly and nodded. When he and the others had taken their places at the large stone table, Anahel rose from his chair.

"I hereby call to order this gathering of this White Circle," his voice echoed through the cavern. Then, with a wave of his outstretched hand, there was a burst of light and from the center of the table rose up a large flickering white flame.

He then went around the table and lent a greeting to each of the angels seated. To his immediate left was Haniel looking every bit the capable winged warrior in whose hands the welfare and well-being of Eden, and all living things residing within it, had been placed without worry. His face, fair and vibrant, and framed by the loose, wavy curls of his chestnut-tinted hair, possessed the classic profile often cast in marble of Roman emperors long-past. Yet the hard edge seen in the outline of most conquerors had been softened with Haniel in a way most becoming as only nature itself could lend to one so in touch with the heartbeat few were able to detect deep within the earth.

Next to Haniel was a venerable figure by the name of Dalquiel, whose fullness of strength, evident from the loose, open shirt of woven gold he donned and matching his long-braided locks, was even more apparent in the way his body poised itself in the relaxed yet self-assured manner in his seat. Following him was Jabniel and Rabacyel, both dark- haired and equally as postured and eminent at first glance. The three together served under Anahel as ruling subordinates of Eden, with Dalquiel overseeing the East, Jabniel the South, Rabacyel the West, and Anahel all of Eden as a whole, but particularly the tempestuous northern realm. Continuing around the table to the left and seated directly across from Anahel was Johiel, Eden's longtime sentry, for as long as Eden has had a need for a gatekeeper, followed by Thaniel, Zuriel, Damiel and finally Eksel, who looked to be the most dour amongst the other Guides while sitting slumped deep in his seat wearing upon his face a prominent scowl of discontent.

"If you please, Anahel," Jabniel jumped in once the greetings were concluded, "I'm most anxious to learn why the convening of this council was called with such pressing urgency."

"I'm most appreciative, Jabniel, of the haste with which you and the other members of this governing body have answered my beckoning to assemble here in short order. I, in return, will be forthright in getting to the issue at hand," replied Anahel.

He stepped away from his chair, pensive in a moment of silence that settled upon him briefly as he slowly began circling the table with his eyes to the floor as if searching for words absent from his tongue. And then, finally, he began.

"Late yesterday afternoon, as the sun was growing weaker and the winds that emerged from the Forest began whistling through the trees as it usually does with the approach of dusk, there was an urgent knock at my door. When I opened it, I found Gothamel standing at the threshold with one of our Fledglings at his side. Both had the same troubled look on their face, and yet strangely different. There's something of extreme importance that needs to be brought to your attention,' Gothamel informed me, even before I had the opportunity to invite the two inside. 'Very well,' I replied, motioning them in from the hall. 'Let us go out onto the terrace where we can sit a spell and discuss whatever is on your mind.' But as I began to lead the way, Gothamel stopped me. 'I'd rather talk in here if you wouldn't mind,' he said. 'I don't want the risk of what is about to be shared to inadvertently fall on unsuspecting ears.' I knew not what was about to be told to me, but whatever it was I could hear in the tone of his voice an unmistakable urgency. 'As you prefer,' I replied warily while gesturing for the two of them to have a seat. It seemed to take Gothamel a moment or two to find his voice, as if what he had to say was too great to be uttered. And when finally he did speak, the reason quickly became apparent. Which is why I feel what was told me, and must now be revealed to the rest of the White Circle, be passed through his lips and not mine."

The waterfall, whose parted seam had closed when the last member of the Circle had passed through, cloaked once more the entrance to the side of the mountain with its rushing curtain of water which rumbled loudly outside. Yet strangely its pounding presence did not drown out the deathly silence which presided over the chamber. Those seated at the table whose attention had remained steadily fixed on Anahel now shifted their gazes in union to Gotham who looked visibly unprepared by the gesture to address the Circle. Clearing his throat, he rose to his feet and approached the table.

"Because I understand the seriousness, not to mention gravity, of what I am about to say, I will attempt to be as precise in my recollection as I was with Anahel," he began. "Yesterday I was accompanying Damiel to Lions Bite. He has been notably impressed with how well the latest brood of Fledglings were faring in their training thus far and wished to share their progress with me, and I was more than happy to accept the invitation. We were about halfway there when we saw one of the Fledglings running full speed toward us. He had his sword gripped in one hand and was calling out to us for help. We hurried to him and when we reached him Damiel asked what had sent him scurrying across the grass like a jackrabbit, or rather banshee to use his words. It took a moment for the boy to catch his breath, but when he did he managed to sputter something about one of the Fledglings being badly injured during a sparring match. I then took notice of the boy's sword and what was undoubtedly blood coloring the blade and I knew he was not exaggerating. Immediately, Damiel took off towards Lions Bite like a bolt of lightning and I quickly followed at his heels along with the boy.

"When we reached the clearing, Damiel pushed his way past the other Fledglings found gathered in a tight circle around the injured boy who was lying on the ground, his face grimacing with pain. Another boy was kneeling beside him clasping the injured leg at the thigh with one hand placed on top the other and firmly applying pressure to the wound. There was a panicked look in his face and we could instantly see why by the amount of blood coating his hands as well as soaking the injured boy's pants."

"I'm sorry, but I fail to understand the direness with which you tell your accounting," interrupted Dalquiel. "Numerous Fledglings have come to be injured at one time or another during the course of their training. Fortunately, it's only a momentary affliction before one of the Guides are at hand to remedy the situation. I hardly see it as a reason to call forth this Council."

"If you'll allow Gothamel to finish," said Anahel, "it will become clear as to why you've been summoned." He then nodded to Gotham to continue.

"You are quite correct, Dalquiel, injuries are par for the course when training Nephilim, and even with a wound as serious as this particular one appeared to be there was nothing to indicate the boy wouldn't be up and running around in mere moments as any other Fledgling who has fallen lame in the past," said Gotham. "Damiel moved quickly calling out for water as he dropped to his knees and instructed the boy attending to the injured Fledgling to remove his hands so he could lay his own upon the wound. But when the boy moved his hands away from the Fledgling's leg, there was no wound to be seen."

Gotham paused suddenly and glanced over to Anahel with a look revealing the magnitude of the words he had just spoken.

"Did I hear Gothamel correctly?" Jabniel asked, after a brief moment of quiet settled itself on the chamber, while focusing a quizzical gaze across the table to where Damiel was seated. "There was no injury to the Fledgling's leg?"

Damiel's hooded eyes peered out from behind his almost stone-like expressionless mask of a face.

"That is correct, Jabniel," he replied. "No wound."

Jabniel appeared briefly taken aback before a smirk tickled the corners of mouth.

"Is this some sort of riddle?" he asked. "How does one bleed forth where no wound is present?"

But Jabniel's smile was quick to fade when Damiel declined an answer and instead cast his eyes downward once more to where his finger was mindlessly tracing an invisible shape on top the table.

~ ~ ~

"What exactly is it you're implying, Gothamel?" asked Rabacyel with a growing tenor of suspicion heard clearly in his voice.

"I'm not implying anything, Rabacyel. I'm stating the facts to you outright as Damiel and I witnessed them," answered Gotham in a matter-of-fact manner. "The wound on the boy's leg had been healed, but not by the hand of an angel."

"By who then? The boy?" asked Rabacyel almost jokingly.

"He was the only one whose hands touched the wounded leg," said Gotham.

For several weighted moments, a whispered hum of perplexity was exchanged amongst the five angels to whose ears the surprising news was reaching for the very first time.

"I don't believe it," stated Dalquiel emphatically.

"It is not for you to believe or disbelieve, but what it is and nothing less," replied Damiel. "The sooner you accept that as the rest of us have come to, reluctantly and otherwise, the quicker we can try and weave some sense of it."

"Make sense…but do you realize what it is you're saying?" argued Rabacyel. "Such a thing, if it were to have any bearing of truth, could only be achieved by—"

"One who possesses the Grace of Healing, or as all who sit at this table know him to be called, the Light Bearer," said Anahel, completing Rabacyel's sentence. "The Nephilim long ago prophesied to bring mortals and angels together and do battle in the coming war against the Darkness, yes I know. And now you see why your presence here was bidden with the urgency in which you received it."

Dalquiel opened his mouth to speak, and without looking at him Anahel held up his hand to hush his voice before the angel could mutter a syllable.

"I sense as I look around this table, Dalquiel, you are not the only one to feel a sharp tug at your tongue," said Anahel. "But I ask that you indulge me just a little while longer before taking to task the absurdity of my words. For there is more to this story, and it is of utmost pertinence that I share with all of you what occurred in the hours after I had learned what had unveiled itself at Lions Bite."

~ ~ ~

When Anahel completed a full revolution around the table, he began anew and the measured pace of his footsteps against the stone floor ticked off like the slow count of a metronome. The chamber once again fell silent.

"My initial reaction when Gothamel had finished telling me the news was to state with unequivocal certainty, 'You must be mistaken.' But I've never known Gothamel to be anything but cautiously bluff in such manners and knew well enough a pronouncement of such consequence would never pass his lips unless he had exhausted all doubt in his mind. Still, I found myself searching for some unseen reasoning temporarily lost to me at that moment to somehow fit an explanation of what had been laid at my feet."

"I left Gothamel and Jacob to themselves—perhaps rudely—and retreated to a corner of my quarters to ponder this most extraordinary of claims. The wind was coming in gentle, soothing gusts through the trees and across the terrace like an ocean tide rolling along a sandy beach. It carried in its currents the sounds of night birds frolicking in the silver-tinted moon-lit darkness. But they were all but drowned out by the chatter of my dueling thoughts which seemed to carry the echo of a thousand different voices. I sat in silence with those voices and after a few moments—though I suspect it was much longer—I got up and returned to my guests. 'I take it you will want to call upon the White Circle,' Gothamel smartly inquired while rising to his feet in preparation of issuing the summons. But I held him to his spot. 'In due time,' was my reply, with no due disrespect intended toward the members seated at this table. There remained a few more hours of night before the East would open her golden eye, and in that time left there was a great measure of suspicion gnawing at me that I first wished to attempt to quell. And so I instructed Gothamel to summon first the Guides quick haste, but in particular Zuriel."

"And might I ask what counsel had you hoped to receive from Zuriel that you felt you couldn't receive from the full council?" asked Rabacyel.

Anahel detected a note of offense in the angel's voice but chose to ignore it, realizing the issue at hand was far more pressing than a momentary disjointing of ego.

"The Apocrypha which speaks of the coming war to be waged against the Darkness is murky at best," said Anahel. "But in its telling of who shall lead forth that war—the one to be known as the Light Bearer—it is without mystery. He will carry mortal blood in his veins and clutch all seven Graces in his fist. But when the boy of whom we now speak was brought to the Crescent Scar in his first days here in Eden, he left without a single Grace revealed."

A look of puzzlement crossed Dalquiel's face as his gaze shifted from Anahel to where Zuriel sat several seats away. "I'm not sure I follow. He refused to be read by the Blackstone?"

"The refusal lied with Blackstone," explained Zuriel. "It made several revolutions around the boy before casting itself clear of the Crescent Scar. I wasn't sure at first what to make of it. In the past, it has been the rare case of a Fledgling whose Grace is slow in being recognized. And in those few instances, the Blackstone when thrown ended up dropping to the ground like a dead weight, but never tossed aside in such a manner as I just described."

"Which is precisely the reason I chose to confer with Zuriel before calling forth this council," said Anahel. "I felt it imperative to remove all question to why the Blackstone behaved as it had that first day and the subsequent days that followed. And so I took a seat with Gothamel and my fellow Guides and we all looked on in silence as Zuriel set out to test what Graces, if any, the boy might unwittingly possess. Seeing the boy was confused by what was understandably a confusing situation in which he felt hopelessly in the dark, Zuriel attempted to ease his nerves. 'We shall begin with something fairly easy,' he said to the boy before instructing him to change his shape as he had observed in class from others with the Grace of Cloaking."

"Fairly easy?" remarked Rabacyel while turning his gaze to Zuriel. "A rather cavalier comment to make to someone lacking the Grace to make any such transformation, wouldn't you say?"

"Except I knew he could," answered Zuriel much to Rabacyel's surprise, and those seated on either side of him.

"I'm sorry to say you have already lost me," said Dalquiel. "First you report this Nephilim to be without Grace, and then moments later proclaim his ability to navigate the ways of Cloaking. Which is it?"

"Both," answered Zuriel, lending to more confused looks. "You see, the boy came to me soon after his initial reading with the Blackstone and told me something quite intriguing. It seems he was helping a fellow Fledgling—one who was bestowed with the Grace of Cloaking, himself—make his first transformation and in the process discovered quite by accident—and I venture to say even greater surprise—that he had managed to change his form to that of a lion, albeit briefly. The boy he was helping witnessed it, as did his three other roommates. And so, too, did I when I asked him to repeat it before my own eyes. Afterward, the two of us made our way to the Crescent Scar in hopes that with this revelation the Blackstone would logically correct its earlier fluke."

"And?" inquired Jabniel eagerly.

"The Blackstone acted exactly as it had before."

"Well, then?" barked Rabacyel with a heightened tone of impatience lacing his tongue. "How did you account for such a thing?"

"I couldn't," Zuriel answered simply. "While it was obvious the boy possessed the Grace of mimicry, I assumed the Grace itself to be late-coming to the boy and undetectable by the Blackstone in its infancy stages."

"When has any Nephilim showed the ability to take the shape of a lion, briefly or not, without the full strength of given Grace fully in his grasp?" asked Jabniel.

The puzzlement on Jabniel's face was equally shared amongst Dalquiel, Rabacyel, Haniel and Johiel, while those of the Guides grew visibly more troubled in the following silence before Anahel cleared loudly his throat.

"If I may continue, perhaps I might lend some light on this strange circumstance, though you may end up debating me whether it is a guiding light I attempt to offer up," he said. "Despite what Zuriel had already informed me regarding this rather unusual discovery, the boy's attempts at first to change his form last night in my quarters were met with no success. Perhaps it was the anxiety of performing before the Guides whose skeptical glares were focused on him with the intensity of ten burning suns. He certainly wouldn't be the first Nephilim to have failed under the weight of such pressure. I can tell you I found myself growing more certain as I sat quietly watching the demonstration from my chair that the only shift in form the boy would ever reveal would be from boy to man, and then it would be due to the Grace of nature over the course of several years. But then we were brought to the edge of our seats when his shape did, in fact, begin to change and morph before our very eyes. The transition was rough and awkward, as would be expected from a Fledgling attempting to exercise a skill so new and foreign, but surely the boy before us eventually disappeared and a chimpanzee was left standing in his place."

As Gotham sat listening in his seat off to the side of the chamber, he couldn't keep the corners of his mouth from curling slightly upward.

"And why, may I ask, of all the animals did you choose a chimpanzee? Why not a lion as you had managed before?" he recalled asking Jacob in a quiet moment afterward.

Jacob shrugged. "I was nervous. I figured if I got stuck and couldn't change back, at least I wouldn't be so far removed from being human as say if I chose to turn myself into a fish."

But the levity of the memory was short-lived when Anahel's voice retook command of his drifting attention.

"Afterward, Zuriel led the boy out onto the terrace and into the silvery night outside," continued Anahel as he once more resumed his stroll around the table. "There he turned his eyes to the heavens above where the moon loomed large in all its marbled glory to which he pointed and instructed the boy to blot it from sight."

"Another fairly easy task, I see," remarked Haniel, sarcastically.

"It was not intended to be easy," said Zuriel with a glare. "For a Nephilim born with the Grace of summoning the forces of nature, darkening the moon should be no more difficult than blowing out a candle. If indeed he had the gift, I wanted there to be no doubt."

"And was he able to perform what you asked?" asked Rabacyel somewhat impatiently.

"Despite several attempts, the boy failed, just as he had when attempting to changing his shape," answered Anahel and bringing a sense of dismissive relief to the faces of those hearing for the first time the events being shared. "But Zuriel proved patient and, some might say, a tad relentless in exhausting all question of the boy's abilities, or lack thereof. His frustration becoming more and more apparent, the boy attempted the task over and over again until those of us watching were about ready to surrender to the growing doubt that could be seen slowly moving across each our faces. But then, a remarkable thing happened. The boy made one last effort, and to the surprise of us all an ecliptic shadow began to pass over the face of the moon. The look on the young

Nephilim's face was beyond disbelief, but it was nothing compared to Zuriel's and that of the rest of us as we watched the moon slowly being nibbled away. And when the last bit of moonlight drew its final gasp before being smothered from sight, I looked to the boy who had been rendered a silhouette of shadow set against the face of utter darkness suddenly cast upon the Garden, and I silently wondered if I was bearing witness to the possible rebirth of a prophesy long-thought dead. Then again, it is not uncommon for a Nephilim to be gifted with two Graces. Was this boy one of those few? And could it have just been a lucky coincidence that the first two tasks chosen for him to perform happened to be the two Graces handed him?"

~ ~ ~

No one spoke a word, and all eyes followed Anahel as he continued his circling trek around the table.

"One by one, Zuriel led the boy through each of the six Graces," the angel continued. "And while he struggled with every one—some much more readily than others—I'm here to tell you with no uncertain stretch of the truth or lingering doubt of my vision that the boy proved himself in possession of all of them."

"And just exactly who is this boy whose name I have yet to hear be mentioned?" asked Rabacyel.

It was evident Anahel had resisted this moment, and now that it was suddenly upon him and could no longer be stalled he clenched tight his jaw and returned to his seat at the table. Instead of answering, however, he turned his gaze to the fire burning in the center of the table before him and his eyes illuminated from within to a bright blazing gold and suddenly an image revealed itself amid the flickering white flames. It was Jacob. He was lying on his bed staring out the window while deep in thought trying to rest as Gotham had instructed him but finding it impossible to fall asleep.

"His name is Jacob," said Anahel.

"Ah yes, I remember. The boy who made a rather impressive

showing at the Illumination," remarked Jabniel as he along with Dalquiel and Rabacyel leaned in for a closer look. For some time they studied the image inside the dancing flickering of light, and if any had a sudden revelation with what they saw they didn't show it, at least not immediately, much to Anahel's relief.

"I cannot deny what you have shared with us about this boy Jacob is quite fascinating, to say the least," said Dalquiel, after a while. "But again I must voice my skepticism and ask the one and obvious question for which we have yet to hear an answer, and that is how is such a thing possible? The obvious answer is the Apocrypha which tells of the coming of the Light Bearer, as you yourself have touched upon, Anahel. But as far as any of us here are concerned, the prophesy has already come to pass with Gothamel's son, and with his death went unfulfilled."

"I wish I had an answer to your question. Unfortunately I do not," answered Anahel with an exhaustive sigh sounding as though he had spent countless hours going over and over in his mind the same gnawing concern. "Unlike civilians, we are not hampered by arrogance that keeps us from firmly accepting those things of which we are not meant to understand; things which reside far beyond the boundaries of what we are able to even minutely comprehend, even with everything we know as angels."

"If I may, Anahel. Did I mishear you to say earlier you believe it is possible the Apocrypha in question to be...reborn?" asked Jabniel.

Anahel paused a moment. "Despite whatever doubts I may find myself wrestling with in my existence as an angel, there are few things of which I am unwavering in my certainty. One is this: A prophesy—like the laws governing over nature and the vast universe itself—eventually finds a way of fulfilling itself despite even the most successful efforts to alter its course," he said.

"And yet—if I may be so presumptuous to remark—despite what you've revealed to us regarding the boy, you seem most conflicted about what it is you're suggesting," said Haniel.

Anahel offered a weak smile and reached over to clasp warmly the hand of the angel seated beside him. "You have always been, if nothing, keenly perceptive, my dear Haniel."

"Perhaps your concern, like most of ours seated at this table, lies not in the prophesy itself, but the vessel in which it chose to resurrect itself, if, of course, it indeed has," blurted Eksel suddenly from Anahel's opposite shoulder in the smuggest of manners.

"Mind yourself, Eksel, not to attempt to analyze what may or may not be troubling me," scolded Anahel, coldly. "It is a delicate matter of which I was about to touch upon. I will not have you trample forth over it like some frothing bull leading a stampede."

"Well, I should hope you should touch upon it quickly. I have been sitting here amused for some time watching the look on Rabacyel's face grow more perplexed the longer he stares at the image of the boy you've revealed to him; the same look of familiarity which greeted all of us here at this table when we first cast our sights upon him."

Indeed, the expression on Rabacyel's face was one of frowning puzzlement. His eyes, which held the reflection of the fire burning at the center of the table within the frames of his golden pupils, were fixed unblinkingly upon the licking flames, studying with the keenest of focus the vision of Jacob seen in the smoldering white heat.

"I know exactly what it is you're thinking, Rabacyel. You're wondering to yourself, am I seeing things? Could it possibly be true what I hear my mind's voice whispering to me? So let me be the one to tell you, no...your eyes are not playing tricks on you," continued Eksel, stirring the curiosity of Jabniel, Dalquiel and Haniel who now joined Rabacyel in narrowing their gazes on the flames, and particularly the unsuspecting Jacob still peering out in thought through his window, to see what exactly Eksel was referring.

"That's enough, Eksel," Damiel hissed under his breath while leveling a disapproving glare in Eksel's direction.

"Enough what... truth? Disclosure? Goodness knows it would be high-time we had a heaping helping of both," Eksel shot back. "Come now, Damiel, you know as well as I this discussion of tricks being performed and an Apocrypha rising up for a second coming, as Anahel would have you believe, is meaningless while fellow members of this

White Circle are kept in the dark about just who exactly is performing such tricks."

"What is it you're trying to say, Eksel?" inquired Dalquiel with growing suspicion.

Before Eksel could utter another word, Anahel was up on his feet.

"Eksel is quite correct, despite his boorish manner in which he chooses to express himself," he said while casting a long, withering look down upon Eksel. His eyes radiated his ire in a flash of gold, but it did nothing to erase the contemptuous smirk on Eksel's face. "There is something of utmost importance of which you must all be made aware. Something of which I was just about to bring to your attention."

"No," a stern voice rang out in an echo through the hollowed mountain rock. Anahel and the rest seated at the table turned to see Gotham rise from his chair.

"This is a matter requiring my tongue," he said in a tone challenging any attempts of argument, "and it is with my tongue it will be addressed to this council."

Reticent at first, Anahel acquiesced with a nod.

"Very well then," he said. And as he slowly sank back into his chair, the eyes of everyone inside the chamber came to rest on Gotham as he made his way to the table.

~ ~ ~

When the name Samael was finally uttered, a jarring and uneasy silence settled itself upon the chamber. Gotham, in a clear and unfaltering voice, proceeded to recount at length his great, vengeful battle with his dark nemesis, just as he had the night he returned to Eden before the Guides in the privacy of Anahel's quarters. He told of Samael's shackling by the Herrinsu vine and his promised eternal banishment to an unspoken desert prison. But no prison cell, no matter how fortified its construction might be, is absent the eventual discovery of a fracture within its walls to lend itself to escape. Such was the case with Samael, for he remained an angel, despite the fact he was Fallen, and as such still held in his possession the powers given all angels, including that of Drifting, which in its many forms allowed one to venture outside its physical being. And while the wielder of such power gained nothing more than limited movement outside its physical self, Samael managed to find a way to shape his wanderings, powerless as they were, into an unexpectedly sharp weapon, and it was with this weapon that would eventually lead to Jacob's birth.

To several seated at the table, the story was wholly new. Those, however, who already knew it quietly watched a shared pall emerge from those hearing the details for the first time just as they themselves had experienced. And when Gotham had finished, a noticeable gloom made itself present, and for a long while no one spoke. When the silence was finally broken, it came not from one voice, but a fiery chorus of voices which rose up as one within the cavernous walls of the mountain chamber. No longer did the debate shape itself around whether or not the Apocrypha long-thought buried had arisen. Suspicions abounded that dark forces were at play, and even Gotham, Fallen angel that he was, was accused in none too polite terms of aiding the dark angel Samael by bringing the boy into Eden. And in the heat of the visceral back and forth a call was put forth to denounce the supposed resurrection of the Apocrypha as nothing more than a scheme by the Darkness and to immediately cast Jacob out from Eden's lands.

"I'm not sure we have that right to denounce such a thing," argued Gotham steadfastly. "Can we honestly say we have the authority to act so brazen?"

"Forgive me, Gothamel, if my words sound harsh, but what right has a Fallen in questioning the authority of those of us who are not?" asked Zuriel.

"Fallen or not, Zuriel, behold I am still an angel," said Gotham, casting an icy look Zuriel's way while still managing to hold the burn of the sun belching forth a solar flare from the depths of his pupils. "And you'll forgive me when I say I often find myself questioning if as angels we sometimes mistake our place as guardians with that of the one who made us."

"And what, exactly, are you inferring by such a statement?"

"Do we dare allow ourselves for a moment to think we have the right to deem what is or is not prophesy and who is worthy of carrying its mark as we see fit rather than what has already been decided by our father?" said Gotham.

"With all due respect, Gothamel, as you yourself have pointed out, we are guardians," said Haniel. "And as guardians it is our rightful duty to ensure any suspect prophesy that shows its face to us has indeed been sent forth by our father and not some nefarious trick of the eye set in play by the Darkness."

"Perhaps if we had been a bit more vigilante in our authority we could have prevented the unnecessary unpleasantness that traitorous excuse of an offspring you sired brought upon us," Eksel was then heard to remark sourly.

The chamber grew quiet under the weight of the insult. Gotham's face darkened and the hateful stare he turned on Eksel flamed bright and vengeful.

"Eksel, my brother," Gotham began in a calm tone holding within it a lethal venom itching to be jabbed into the angel's veins as if by a pair of fangs bared by a poisonous viper, "since returning to Eden I have done well in keeping a civil tongue toward you while in your despicable presence. So I shall gift you this warning I shan't repeat: Speak ill of my son once more and the power to speak will no longer be yours to have as I will permanently relieve you of the use of your tongue. Do we understand one another?"

Anahel, who had been sitting quietly looking more and more troubled as he listened to the bickering taking place around him, turned his eyes to the chair on the far side of the table directly across from him where Johiel sat, almost forgotten in the silence he had held over the course of the meeting.

"Johiel, you've been particularly mute during the course of this heated gathering; you who have served to greet each and every Nephilim to have passed through Eden's Gate. Surely you must have some thoughts regarding this dilemma before us."

Respected and admired amongst angels, Johiel was not rushed to speak, even as those seated about him who held great interest in what he would say leaned forward in their seats.

"I have been sitting here listening with great curiosity to all that's been put forth here today," said Johiel finally in an almost quiet, contemplative voice. "What has struck me particularly is the one possibility no one here seems ready or willing to consider. And that is the boy may, indeed, in fact, be the one long-awaited."

Johiel's words appeared to wash over the others seated at the table like a wave of arctic ice water, but no one seemed more offended by the suggestion than Eksel.

"You can't be serious," he seethed, almost furious at the idea.

An expected disgruntled rumbling rose up inside the chamber to which Johiel readily ignored and patiently waited to die out.

"I cannot remember much of a time where I have not served as Guardian of the Gate," he said once quiet had returned while continuing to watch the fingers of his right hand lightly drum the hard, cold stone surface of the table before him. "My servitude began when I was long ago sent down to enforce the exile of man from this garden paradise. Since then my time has been spent as a sentinel of Eden cloaked in a weathered, mortal frock on a rock in the middle of a vast dead lake. It is a lonely, solitary existence I have been tasked to endure, but one I do so willingly and without complaint except, I admit, the rare moment a brief sigh of despair inadvertently escapes my lips.

"What Anahel says is true; I have been the one to shepherd through Eden's Gate the countless scores of Nephilim brought here over the past many millennium. It is I who first sets eyes on these boys in the last throes of their naivety before being ushered into this wondrous realm that had existed to them only as biblical lore. In many of those faces I've seen great promise and hope and, like that of an expectant father, I eagerly awaited the day I might at last catch a glimpse of the one promised to unite angel and man and lead forth an army to the dawn of the next Great War. My wait ended the day Gothamel introduced me to his son David. Or so I believed.

"And now you see how wrong you were," Eksel remarked sourly. "The son of a Fallen—"

"Don't mistake one's fall from grace as having never been in possession of grace in the first place," Johiel interrupted sharply while shooting a silencing glare across the table at the angel. "I tell you all, it did not surprise me one bit when David was brought before this council and the question of the Apocrypha was raised. For I can recall strangely being overcome by an inexplicable sense when I first laid eyes upon him. What it was I did not know, only that it was something I had never before come across with any other Fledgling. And while I kept my musings to myself, I knew without question this fair-haired boy was no ordinary Nephilim."

The angel fell silent for a moment, and his face suddenly revealed a weighted anguish. Taking a deep quivering breath, he continued: "It's been nearly fifty years since his tragic end, so disappointing, so unfair. And with his passing, there has never been a glimmer of reason in all this time to believe the brief life of the prophesy foretold was anything more than a smoldering wick of a doused candle. That is, until Gothamel's return to Akdamar since that dark day past. Even before I knew of his presence, I was hit by something...something I hadn't felt but just once in my existence. It unnerved me. And then I saw him— Gothamel—standing in a corner of the church. At first all I could see were his golden eyes radiating as two orbs of flame from behind the shadows within which he lurked. But then upon seeing me he stepped forward and his glorious face came into view and it was like witnessing one of the images painted upon the church walls stepping out of its stone confines and take on a life form."

"But what exactly was it you felt?" asked Haniel.

Johiel thought a moment.

"I wish I could explain it, but alas I fail to find the words, except to say it was exactly the same as when I first met David, yet more profound. It ignited a fire beneath my feet and sent me off in a short run out of the cathedral to the grounds surrounding the church until my eyes finally rested themselves on this one," Johiel explained, offering a nod to the image of Jacob in the flames of fire at the center of the table.

"It was then I knew what it was I was feeling."

"What is it you're saying, exactly?" questioned Zuriel, his face fixed with a look of confusion to match the tone heard in his voice. "You believed Jacob to be the Light Bearer from the moment you met him?"

"I did not say that, Zuriel," said Johiel. "My words were only an attempt to express the inexplicable feeling I had regarding the boy. I can't fully describe it except to say I found him to be much unlike other Nephilim I've come to know on their journey to Havenhid."

"Perhaps what you found to be so inexplicable was the fact this…Nephilim, if I can call him that, was, is and will continue to be a spawn of the Darkness," said Eksel in his continuing berating of Johiel. "A simple enough fact that seemed to have escaped your senses when you made the decision to allow him entry through the Gate."

"No, Eksel, it did not escape my senses, as you so put it. Quite to the contrary, it may have been the one contributing factor that allowed me to clear passage for the boy from Akdamar to the Gate beyond."

Eksel looked as though Johiel's words might topple him from off his seat. "You explain yourself in a manner as if your words should lend comfort to those of us who sit here listening to you," said Eksel, "when all the while I find myself more and more baffled by the presence before me whose questionable judgment has befouled Eden…twice, mind you."

"Am I to take it by the snide bend of your tongue you wish to now call into question my competence in the role given me as Guardian of the Gate?" Johiel inquired with a raising of an eyebrow.

"I'm sure Eksel meant nothing by the words he finds getting away from his mouth," offered Anahel in an attempt to quell the signs of ire beginning to surface in Johiel's face in bubbling flashes, but Johiel paid him no mind.

"I can see, Eksel, you wish for me to express remorse for what you clearly see as a mistake on my part. Well, I can assure you such apologies will not be made this day," said Johiel firmly. "The decisions I made— both in regard to Gothamel's son David, and more recently Jacob— concerning who is allowed entry through the Gate into Eden are not done so on a whim. Nor are they ones I would rethink, even at this moment. As someone once reminded me in the shadow of the church I have come to call home on Akdamar, a Nephilim may be a product of his father, but his father he is not."

With those words, Johiel gave Gotham a knowing glance, and Gotham was instantly reminded of the conversation he had with Johiel in his attempt to persuade the angel to consider the most unfathomable of requests: allowing the son of Samael passage through the Gate.

"That is not to say my decisions have not left me conflicted, for indeed I have been," continued Johiel. "So, too, have I found myself pondering at great length, for whatever the reason, the first time not so long ago we were all gathered together here in this chamber to discuss the matter of the Apocrypha. You asked me, Zuriel, if I believed Jacob to be the Light Bearer from the moment I met him, and my reply was I did not. That said, I also expressed to you and the other members of this council how I was not surprised when David was brought before this council when it became known he possessed all seven Graces. So, too, do I tell you now it surprises me not that I find myself brought here by a similar summons regarding the Fledgling Jacob Parrish."

With those words, silence once more fell upon the chamber. "Johiel, you have always been one whose words have been guided by great wisdom, unrivaled instinct and thoughtful reflection," said Damiel finally with unmistakable reverence. "Are you saying we were mistaken in believing David to be the Light Bearer?"

"I'm saying the path leading to the promise made by the prophesy may have required the service of two Fledglings to pave," answered Johiel, bringing a murmur of whispered voices to be exchanged amongst the gathered angels.

"Then we are correct in hearing you declare outright that you believe the boy...Jacob...to be the Light Bearer?" asked Thaniel, who had been relatively quiet through the proceedings while taking in all that was being said.

Johiel gazed heavily into the white flames holding Jacob's image and seemed to ponder carefully the answer being formed on the tip of his tongue.

"There is much truth in what Anahel said about the Apocrypha being reborn," he said. "What passed from the world with David may quite possibly have now taken up anew with Jacob in its quest for fulfillment. If you're asking me what it is I believe, it is that, without question."

"Through the son of Samael?" Rabacyel gasped with marked horror. "Do you realize what you are saying?"

"Why not the son of Samael? Or the Dragon himself, for that matter?" countered Johiel fervently. "Who are we to decide in what manner God will choose to vanquish the Darkness, and when he chooses to do so. All of us thought our brethren who fell during the Great War were of good, loyal stock, resistant to the turn of the dark worm. Is it so hard to fathom the same betrayal of the Dark by a prick of Light?

"Damiel said it best to Rabacyel; it is not for you to believe or disbelieve, but what it is. Whether we who are seated here choose to believe it or not is of no consequence in the realm of reality of what has come to be."

Johiel's words draped itself across the chamber like a blanket woven from lead bringing an almost palpable, pensive silence to the council.

"I hear and appreciate what you have said here today, Johiel," said Anahel, eventually cutting through the quiet. "It is a difficult task we now face in deciding whether or not we chose to accept, as has been put forth, the rebirth of the Apocrypha. I only wish for the rest of us here that we could have been blessed with this feeling, this unknown sense you have seemingly tapped, that allows you to be so certain in your declarations regarding the boy. Then there's the fact half of us here were not privy to witness what was demonstrated last night in my chambers, and even less still who were present to see what occurred at Lions Bite. Not to say what both Damiel and Gothamel have told us should be questioned or distrusted in any way. But when it comes to a matter of such importance and consequence as this, seeing with one's own e tends to lead to belief."

"Perhaps there's a way," Thaniel chimed in quietly.

"What do you mean?" inquired Daquiel curiously.

"A way for all of us to shirk the doubt that clings to us."

"What are you proposing? That we have the boy hop up on the table before us and perform an encore like some circus monkey? Or perhaps we should venture to Lions Bite in hopes a Fledgling gets carried away with his sword again," Eksel sounded off in a voice dripping with sarcasm.

"At this point, I'm not sure even the healing of a wounded leg would fully dissipate the doubt that has taken up company with us in this mountain chamber," replied Thaniel. "No, there is one way, and one way only, to prove or dispel the notion the prophesy has indeed been reborn."

Muddled whispers made their way around the table as confused looks came to the faces of the other angels. All that is, except Anahel, whose eyes came to settle their focus heavily on Thaniel with both clear understanding and heavy concern as his lips parted to utter a single word, "Azrael."

"Azrael," repeated Thaniel in agreement.

~ ~ ~

The name brought an instant hush to the White Circle, not to mention looks of noticeable uneasiness to those seated at the table. It was the same unease that had shown itself with the mentioning of Samael's name. And in the unsettling silence that followed, Anahel rose from his chair once more. Instead of circling the table as he was apt to do, he turned his back and stared blankly to the far side of the chamber.

Haniel was the first to speak up. "I agree on the face of what Thaniel has proposed. But we mustn't be hasty in overlooking the dangers associated with calling upon him for such a task."

"Certainly the gravity of what we're facing far outweighs any danger," argued Eksel.

"You speak far too quickly than you should, Eksel," said Johiel with a rebuking tone. "This is a decision not to be taken lightly and carries with it numerous ramifications."

A contemptuous smirk formed itself on Eksel's lips. "Forgive my imprudent ways, Johiel. I know how thoughtful and cautious you can be when it comes to decisions of such heavy a caliber. But what ramifications, may I ask, could outweigh those with which we could soon find ourselves wrestling should this idea about a prophesy being reborn prove itself to be nonsense, as I believe it to be, and the boy revealing himself to be nothing more than a black plague let loose upon Eden?" he asked.

"There is always a grave danger when willfully summoning the one who holds the reins of death," answered Johiel. "Azrael would have sole discretion in determining what task would be suitable for what we seek, with all of Eden at his whim to do with as he pleased."

"But what is more urgent to consider is the boy himself," Anahel quickly broke in while turning back to those at the table. "For someone to challenge Azrael—and worse, wrestle away that which he has laid claim to—is to forever draw his wrath. I'm not sure we have the right to wade forth into such risk, especially with one whose welfare we've been charged with overseeing, prophesy or no prophesy."

"That I agree, Anahel," said Johiel. "But in the same breath I hasten to caution you, do not underestimate this one. For trust me when I tell you within this Nephilim a flame pure in its burn smolders. Even Azrael would find it a challenge to extinguish it."

The weight of the proposal furrowed itself in Anahel's brow as he stared off in thought at the rushing curtain of water hanging at the chamber entrance.

"Ironic, is it not, if indeed it proves itself true?" he said releasing a heavy sigh. "From the Darkness is spit forth a son swaddled in a promise of more Darkness. Yet from him a brigade will soon be birthed that will usher forward a charge of Light from which the Darkness will find no escape, even in the deepest pit of Hell."

No one at the table could put forth an argument. Not even Eksel.

CHAPTER TWO

With Mist at his side, Jacob headed to the Hall of Light where the other young residents of Havenhid were already gathered eating dinner. Somehow he'd managed to sleep a couple hours, but it was a restless sleep and instead of fighting the endless tossing and turning he took to writing in his journal, hoping the thoughts his pen transferred to the page would somehow quiet the babble of voices inside his head, but it didn't. In fact, it only seemed to incite the chatter until, finally, it drove him from the serenity of his room.

As he entered the Hall through the huge arched doorway and his presence became noticed, heads turned, eyes shifted, and the lively chatter filling the cavernous room quickly diminished to a blaring silence. Everything became as still as the giant angel statues positioned on both sides of the Hall standing guard over the boys seated at the tables. Not even the scraping of a utensil against a food-filled plate could be heard.

With the rubber soles of his sneakers squeaking loudly against the smooth, wood floor, Jacob did his best to ignore the sea of eyes closely following him as he made his way to the left side of the long, divided table and slipped into a vacant seat he spied between Max and Ethan.

"Crikey Moses, but you look terrible!" exclaimed Max.

"Thanks, I thought I looked worse," mumbled Jacob wearily.

"Couldn't sleep, I take it."

Jacob shook his head while catching sight of his ghostly disheveled reflection distorted in the gloss of the empty porcelain plate in front of him.

"So…what's happened?" asked Max, barely able to contain his eagerness.

"What do you mean?"

"The last we saw of you, Gotham was rushing you off in the direction of Anahel's room like he was a Pinkerton guard and you were a sack of money."

"I really don't want to talk about it," answered Jacob.

"Then this morning we find out there's an emergency meeting of the White Circle," continued Max, ignoring his friend. "It's been hours and hours now and they still haven't returned."

"What can they possibly be talking about for so long, that's what I'm curious to know," Leos piped in from his seat on the other side of Max.

Just as Jacob began thinking maybe it would have been best if he had stayed put in his room and suffered through the unrelenting voices of his thoughts, he glanced up and noticed the curious eyes and ears belonging to the roomful of fellow Nephilim remained focused on him.

"Why is everyone staring at me like I've gone and sprouted a second head?" he asked under his breath with a growing edge of irritation.

"You're kidding, right?" answered Ethan. "After what happened yesterday at Lions Bite with Balantine? You've become a bit of an overnight celebrity around here. You know that, don't you?"

"What are you talking about? Celebrity...that's ridiculous!" Jacob muttered with growing discomfort. His eyes roamed across the aisle separating the two sides of the long table and caught sight of Balantine who gave him a friendly, yet timid nod.

"Call it what you want, but where I come from, healing a person, that's some pretty major stuff," said Kairo, taking a breath from inhaling the food piled high on his plate. "Next thing you know you'll be raising people from the dead."

"Not funny," said Jacob unamused.

"Forget Guadalupe. Pretty soon people from all over the world will be making pilgrimages to you," wised Ethan. "You'll be a modern-day Jesus Christ."

"Bite your tongue," snapped Leos sharply. "That's sacrilegious."

"You're right," Ethan replied apologetically. "How about saint then? Saint Jacob. I can see it now, a tiny image of you dressed in your Chuck Taylors and hoodie replacing statues of St. Christopher on car dashboards all over the w—"

"Will you just shut up about it already, Ethan?" barked Jacob angrily. "I don't want to hear your stupid cracks. Just drop it and talk about something else."

A soured look replaced Ethan's smile.

"Alright...sheesh...you don't need to take my head off about it. It's not my fault the only thing anyone is concerned about is whether you're—" He stopped himself abruptly mid-sentence, and while staring past Jacob to Max, the look on his face was suddenly overcome with that of a small child who'd just been scolded for dumping milk on the kitchen floor.

"Whether I'm what?" asked Jacob.

When Ethan began to stammer, Jacob followed his gaze to Max who was returning a tongue-silencing glare. "What is it? Whether I'm what?"

"You've got some pie hole on you, Ethan, you know that?" reprimanded Max. Then giving a quick glance around, he leaned in closer to Jacob and spoke in a quiet manner so as not to be overheard. "I guess it's only right you should know. There's been a lot of whispering about what happened at Lions Bite with Balantine and...well...some are speculating whether you're... you know...."

"Whether I'm what?" asked Jacob, looking as oblivious as he felt.

Max struggled with the words, and for moment it looked as if he might actually be afraid of finishing his sentence. Then taking a deep breath he managed to spit it out. "The Light Bearer."

Jacob felt a wave of nausea climb up inside himself.

"You don't have to say one way or the other," said Max. "In fact, my gut tells me maybe you don't even know the answer yourself. Either way, you've got four of us in your corner."

"I don't need anyone in my corner, because it's a ridiculous idea," said Jacob. "Besides how could it even possibly be the tiniest bit true? Or did you forget the most important piece of the puzzle you're trying to put together: that there's already been a Light Bearer?"

"Then...how do you explain what happened at Lions Bite yesterday?" asked Ethan hesitantly.

"Or why the urgency of the White Circle meeting?" Leos chimed in. "They've been tucked away out of sight behind the falls all day and they're still not back. What else could they be talking about for so long?"

Jacob couldn't fault his friends for speaking aloud the exact same questions that had been churning around inside his own head. Yet hearing those same concerns coming from the mouths of those around him for some reason brought an unsettling reality to what was happening. And while a part of him desired more than anything he could ever before remember wanting more in his life than to rise from his seat and escape the curious eyes that continued to stare his way, he feared drawing any further unwanted attention his way.

"I told you I didn't want to talk about it," Jacob said quietly under his breath. "It's all just some weird fluke, that's all. You'll see.

"How can you say it was a fluke?" asked Ethan. "A fluke would be buying a scratcher at the 7-11 and winning the lottery. Or the tail fin of a whale, depending how you use the word."

Jacob could feel himself losing a grip on his patience.

"Fluke, chance, coincidence...pick your word. But that's what it is. I can't explain why or how. Who can explain half the things that happen around here? And if it's all the same to you I'd just as soon forget it ever happened."

"Well...that might be easier said than done," began Max as he sat back in his chair and enjoyed a bite of his food. "Fluke or not, you've shown yourself able to do something no one else around here can do, or is supposed to be able to do, and everyone here's just trying to figure out the why and how. As for stuff that happens here in Eden, we might not be able to explain it but we do know there's a reason for it and where it comes from. You might just find out soon enough you're one of those strange mysterious things, so you better start getting used to it."

"Don't you understand? This isn't something I want to get used to," Jacob snapped loudly, sending his voice echoing through the Hall and leaving Max momentarily taken aback mid-chew. Recognizing his outburst, Jacob closed his eyes and gave his friend an apologizing squeeze to his shoulder. "I'm sorry."

Max could see there was something troubling Jacob and he leaned in to whisper out of range from the other prying ears, including those of his own roommates. "What's happened?"

Before Jacob could answer—not that he would have spoken of what had taken place in Anahel's room before the White Circle scrambled to meet, at least not there at the table—there came a familiar, and most unwelcome, voice from above.

"That's what I'd like to know."

Jacob and Max glanced upward, along with the rest of the table, and they found the presence suddenly looming over them belonged to none other than Creed Maggert.

"So is it true?" asked Creed in a manner that was instantaneously accusatory.

Jacob hesitated a moment. "Is what true?"

"Don't play dumb with me, Weed, you know what I'm talking about."

That word again: Weed. Jacob could feel a look of hate shape itself on his face in the finest of detail.

"I warned you about calling me that."

"What's the matter, Weed, the truth hurt?" Creed continued with his mocking.

"Why don't you shut your north and south and get lost maggot," said Max, drawing an instant scowl to Creed's face.

"It's Maggert," corrected Creed with a hiss of annoyance.

"I'm sorry. Must've been a Freudian slip," said Max, feigning remorse. "My apologies creep."

Creed's eyes narrowed themselves on Max.

"Uh, that would be Creed," noted Ethan.

"Yeah, I know," replied Max without so much as a smirk yet drawing the chuckles from those seated around him which Creed did his best to ignore as he once more leveled his attention on Jacob.

"The word being passed around is that you healed Balantine over at Lions Bite of a bloody gash to the leg caused by this doofus over here," said Creed with a nod in Ethan's direction.

"For the hundredth time, it was an accident," Ethan shot back.

"Personally, I think it's a load of hogwash," said Creed. "We all know the power to heal is reserved for angels, and angels alone. We also know what it would mean if a Nephilim somehow acquired the gift, don't we? And it certainly wouldn't be you, would it? I mean look at you—" Creed's contempt-filled eyes slowly raked themselves over Jacob in a way that made Jacob want to send two forks into both sockets. "You're still the only one here who remains wingless. Heck, even Ethan here has you beat, and that's saying a lot."

Jacob felt himself begin to rise up out of his chair when Max firmly clasped his shoulder and directed him back into his seat.

"You know *Creee-eed*, I've just about had a gut full of you, and I think I speak for pretty much everyone when I say with all due seriousness, you're about as welcome here as a turd in a swimming pool. So why don't you do us all a favor and go flush yourself?" said Max with a pleased-as-punch smile.

"And why don't you, Kelly, quit feigning to stick up for your so-called friend when I can see written all over your face the same desire the rest of us have—whether we all care to admit it or not. And that is for this Weed to prove or disprove this nonsense once and for all," spat Creed before narrowing his eyes again on Jacob. "Well I admit it, and I'm here to get to the bottom of it."

And with that he reached across the table and grabbed hold of a knife from Jacob's place setting and brought it to his forearm. A look of shock came to Jacob's face as he watched Creed slowly drag the sharp edge of the knife across his skin bringing forth a stream of bright, red blood.

"Alright healer, let's see you defend yourself and your name by fixing this," demanded Creed while at the same time thrusting his bleeding arm across the table toward Jacob. As he did a hand suddenly shot out and seized a crushing hold of Creed's wrist. Creed grimaced in pain and when he looked to see who it was who had grabbed him he was met by Anahel's flaming eyes searing down at him from above.

~ ~ ~

"What kind of nonsense is this?" the angel seethed with restrained anger. "Do you harbor such disregard for faith that you chose to mock it in such an open fashion?"

Creed attempted to stammer forth an answer, but Anahel quickly silenced him.

"You'd do best by yourself to return to your seat before you discover even the healing power of all Heaven's angels wouldn't be enough to allow your backside the enjoyment of a chair again without wincing."

He released his hold and Creed stumbled awkwardly backward a couple of steps or so. The withering fierceness seen in Anahel's face, which until then had only glowed with a warm kindness and stoic strength, was astonishing to behold. And yet Creed somehow managed to conjure up the courage to offer up the injured arm he cradled. "But I'm bleeding."

"So you are," replied Anahel indifferently. "And I suggest you hurry off and get it bandaged. Perhaps it will serve as a reminder to you of the foolishness you've shown here."

Seeing from the look harbored in the angel's eyes there was little hope mercy would lead Anahel's healing hands to settle upon his bleeding cut, Creed slowly retreated from the shadow of Anahel's presence and slunk back to his seat. Anahel then turned to Jacob and held the boy briefly in his gaze. The fiery furnace that had been his eyes returned to their natural warm glow, and the anger that had momentarily

He said nothing but took a collective breath before he slowly made his way to the center of the Hall between the two table halves.

Standing beneath the mural-covered ceiling which was slowly being pieced together by the coming together of tree branches as the sunset-colored skies began to fade and darken, Anahel's eyes wandered up and down each table to focus upon the inquisitive faces staring back at him. Yet even as they sat in their silence, Anahel could hear the feverish chattering going on in their heads.

"Your mortal penchant for rumor-mongering I see is in full flourish. Normally, as you've come to learn, I would rebuke such unbecoming behavior. However, tonight I make an exception. If anything, it will serve me from having to speak longer than need be after such a long and tedious day," said Anahel, looking as weary as he sounded. "I hear in your clandestine whisperings that you are all well aware of the happenings at Lions Bite day before today. And just to assure there is no more foolishness like that which Mr. Maggert so grandly demonstrated just now, let me attempt to ease whatever doubting notions might be swirling around in some of your noggins by telling you what occurred did indeed, in fact, happen."

A grumbling of hushed voices rose up and Jacob felt all eyes in the Hall once again suddenly settle themselves upon him. So uncomfortable was it that he contemplated using his Grace of Cloaking to vanish completely from sight.

"You are also well aware what it means for this to have happened," continued Anahel. "Of that I caution you all to mind your tongues. What has come to reveal itself to us here is as startling as it is delicate—and I dare say equally unforeseen. But it has also showed itself in a murky light that bears as much caution as it does clarity, and as such the White Circle—myself included—must tread lightly in making an outright declaration regarding something of such vital significance and importance. Which brings me to the reason I've come here to speak to you tonight, and it's with the upmost urgency I ask each of you to pay attention to the words which are about to pass from my lips."

The Hall became as still as a tomb as bodies shifting in their seats leaned forward anxious to hear what Anahel was about to say. None, however, sat as tensely still as Jacob. What now? he wondered uneasily as another wave of queasiness churned inside his stomach.

"In a few hours, when the moon hangs over the vicinity of the Silent Forest, a trumpet will sound," began Anahel. "When you hear it, you are to retire to your rooms immediately. There you are to remain without exception until the morning sun rises. There will be no lights, nor talking, nor ruckus of any kind, and especially no venturing outside of your rooms under any circumstances. Do I make myself clear?"

So clear was Anahel, especially in the direness heard in his voice, that the boys sat stone-still listening without so much as a breath escaping their lips. Even the birds which flew in and out of the ceiling's decorative murals at will came to a standstill.

"I don't mean to alarm you," continued Anahel. "But in this case I find it to be necessary. Because sometime in the hours to follow a shadow will pass through Eden—that which belongs to Azrael."

Jacob noticed a restless hush move through the Hall and, as he gave a quick glance around, he noticed by the expressions of some of the boys the news was troubling.

"What's Azrael?" he whispered to Max suddenly alarmed.

"Not what, who," Max answered grimly. But before he could explain who, Anahel once more called for quiet with the clearing of his throat.

"I take it many of you are already acquainted with the name I've just spoken," said Anahel. "For those of you who are not, he's an angel...the one appointed the duty of separating the soul from the body. You most likely know him by another name—the Angel of Death."

An unpleasant chill cut through Jacob at the muttering of the name, and without shame he sank down into his chair knowing wasn't alone.

"I'm heartened to see a look of fear shared by many of you at this moment," said Anahel. "Unfortunately it's the kind of fear often accompanied by a voice of intrigue. Turn a deaf ear to it. When the hour comes, as it will before you know it, keep tight to the shadows the night is gracious to lend you for cover. More importantly, steer clear of the windows, even as you find them beckoning to you to steal a peak. Quick on our feet as I and the other Guides may be should your screams call out to us, Azrael, I assure you, will be quicker."

Anahel then suggested to the boys that they hurry along and finish their dinner before turning in for the night. It was clear, however, the news Anahel had delivered of Azrael's expected visit—and more specifically the possibility of screams which may or may not at some point be involved—had completely spoiled whatever appetite any of the boys may have held. Once it was apparent Anahel had finished speaking, Jacob hopped to his feet. He had hoped to have a moment to speak with Anahel alone. After all, if anyone was to be concerned most about a pending visit from the Angel of Death it was him. Before Jacob could reach him, though, Anahel was gone, after exchanging a half-hearted, if not sympathetic smile with the boy and then quickly disappearing through the scrum of bodies of Nephilim as they got up from their seats and prepared to close themselves up in their rooms for what would undoubtedly be a long and unsettling night.

CHAPTER THREE

Within a few short hours, the task of ensuring all the Nephilim were following Anahel's imposed curfew and had locked themselves in their rooms came and went, and a noticeable, if not strangely unnatural, quiet made its presence heard as Thaniel walked the vacant halls until he came to a seldom-visited corner of Havenhid. There, he found Gotham standing alone in the frame of an archway overlooking Eden with only the warmth of the flickering firelight keeping him company in his solitude.

"I was wondering where you might have disappeared," remarked Thaniel as he crossed to where the angel stood to share in the view of the Garden whose beauty even the nighttime could not dim. "Coming upon you just now, I wasn't sure if you had secured yourself a spot to stand guard over the expectant shadow that has been called to visit Havenhid, or a moment to be alone with the jumble of thoughts we all, no doubt, are wrestling with this night."

Gotham smiled weakly. "A little of both, I suppose."

"You also are well aware of the fact that Azrael has a deep-seated aversion to gazing eyes that might bear witness to him at the hour he chooses to make his presence known. Not just curious Nephilim, but his own brothers as well."

"Trust me, Thaniel, I don't relish the opportunity of catching sight of our grimly cloaked brother like some child spying the skies for flying reindeer on Christmas Eve, and will make leave of this view long before his arrival."

Thaniel breathed deeply the night air as his eyes searched the moonlit darkness. "What do you expect he'll do?"

"What he always does: claim the soul of that who is touched by his shadow," answered Gotham. "Who or what will find themselves unexpectedly in its shade is what unnerves me this moment."

"Like it or not, you know as well as I what's to occur this night must, if any of us ever hope to have peace of mind on this matter," said Thaniel, drawing a heavy sigh from Gotham.

"I know this, Thaniel. But it doesn't make this moment now upon us any easier," said Gotham. "Peace of mind, however, is an entirely different thing that I'm less certain, with each tick of the clock, will be gifted any one of us when the light of dawn marks the morning's arrival."

The two angels stood in silence staring out across the Garden when Gotham turned and focused his gold-glinting eyes on Thaniel.

"You were unusually quiet at the meeting today of the White Circle," noted Gotham. "I'm curious to know what you think about all that has suddenly unfolded itself to us concerning the boy."

"It is the rare moment when the depths of my wisdom, if you so choose to call it that, reveal a stretch of shallows. But, alas, what I came to witness last night in Anahel's quarters has left me befuddled; so much so that my thoughts regarding the boy continue to fail me this very hour," replied Thaniel, after careful pondering.

"And your gut?" pressed Gotham.

"You understand me better to know the assessments I make when gazing upon the prism of life come not from the gut, but rather logic," said Thaniel. "From that perspective, I think the words that became lost to my tongue earlier this day smartly found their way to be heard from Anahel's: it is quite possible the prophesy of the Apocrypha has found a way to travel twice through the womb."

The angel's words seemed to come to a heavy rest upon Gotham's shoulders.

"Then you believe it's true…that the boy may quite possibly be the Light Bearer."

"In the first few days each young scion is brought here to Eden, we spend a great deal of time convincing them that what is beyond the realm of believability in their eyes is in fact real. Now, suddenly, we each of us find ourselves on the precipice of our own Broken Earth and are being told to take a step into the abyss," said Thaniel. "I don't know if

Jacob is the Light Bearer resurrected. Only the light of the day to come will shine forth some semblance of an answer. What I can tell you is I've come to have a genuine endearment of the boy. Just as Johiel pointed out today, I, too, have come to recognize a certain uniqueness about him I can't find words adequate enough to express. When I look upon him, I don't see the son of Samael. Oh, sure, the obvious resemblance he bears is not lost to my eyes. But there's a certain light that radiates from within him that blinds me to such progeny in the same way a bird is lost to the sky when it passes directly across the face of the sun."

"And yet there is not a light capable of burning bright enough to erase the fact that, indeed, he is the son of Samael. Even one shone forth by our father," Gotham stressed firmly before his eyes closed themselves tight as if in a grimace at hearing the words pour forth from his mouth. "Listen to me, you'd think to find Eksel standing in my boots rather than myself."

Thaniel studied Gotham closely and took notice of a quiet angst in the first throes of blooming that had taken hold of the angel.

"The boorish words that have a habit of escaping our brother's tongue can be overlooked, forgiven even; he has not allowed himself to come to know Jacob as you have," said Thaniel.

"I wonder sometimes how well I actually do know him," remarked Gotham.

"And yet I'm suddenly reminded of the night you first brought Jacob to Eden," said Thaniel. "You took me and the rest of the Guides into Anahel's chamber to make your case for why we should welcome the son of Samael into Havenhid, a case I might add which you put forth with as much conviction and heart as you laid down for your own son."

"Don't misunderstand the trepidation that makes itself heard in my voice, Thaniel," said Gotham. "The boy has managed against all odds to bore his way inside my hardened heart. I have come to care about him nearly as much as my own departed child, and as much as I may have tried to resist such feelings I find myself looking upon him as such."

"What, then, may I ask has changed since then except, perhaps, our father, for reasons unbeknownst us, has decided to anoint this child with the Grace most rare?"

"I wish I could say," Gotham answered, with a heaviness in his voice. "All I know is I'm oftentimes struck in a most discomforting way when I look upon the boy and how the image reflected back becomes more and more similar to that of my son."

"Perhaps it's because you, knowingly or not, have held up the same mirror to both boys," said Thaniel.

Gotham leveled a quizzical gaze at Thaniel. "What do you mean by that?"

Thaniel, at first, held his tongue, careful in choosing his words before he spoke them.

"Love and trust more often than not exist intertwined with one another. I doubt you would find me remiss in saying the vine of trust that once grew healthy in you atrophied greatly when Heaven and you parted ways," Thaniel surmised. "One could argue what residual of credence you once had left within you suffered its final death throes along with the passing of your son. For what cutting could ever possibly take root to soil that has suffered such a thorough salting of betrayal, especially when said betrayal blossoms from one's own flesh and blood."

Gotham opened his mouth to reply but, instead, it was a heavy, burdensome sigh that escaped his lips at hearing Thaniel's pinpoint reading of his innermost turmoil.

~ ~ ~

"What a great offense of sin I must have committed to have garnered the wrath of our father as I have," Gotham, turning away to face the night to prevent Thaniel from reading any further whatever tea leaves his angst-filled face might be revealing, pondered. "You'd think it was I who had led the rebellion against him in Heaven."

"You were his favorite, his shining beacon of pride," said Thaniel.

"It was a role not of my choosing, I can assure you," Gotham rebuffed, in an almost offended manner.

"No, but it was to your relish you came to be gifted such a position, as it would be to any one of us. Is it then so hard to deduce that the debt for causing him displeasure would be as lofty as the exalted heights you came to enjoy your view should your feet ever muddy the pedestal upon which you were placed?"

"But even you would agree, Thaniel, the most insuperable of debts is eventually paid off," argued Gotham, "and does not become an eternal show of retribution."

Thaniel cocked his head ever so slightly as a look of curiousness came to him. "You sound almost as if you believe what has taken place in regards to Jacob to be a form of punishment put upon you."

"The prophesy of the Light Bearer has made itself seen in my eyes as an unsightly changeling which has once more been left at my front door," said Gotham. "Am I to believe this current manifestation, if indeed it has been birthed, to be some queer coincidence? And if not, even you would agree it most certainly wouldn't come forth with an offer of salve to soothe my wounds, not while wearing the face of my enemy."

"Don't take this the wrong way, Gothamel, but I would find it hard to believe our father would waste something as precious and important to the world as the prophesy of the Light Bearer just to stick another thorn in your side," said Thaniel. "But it seems you've managed to answer my next question."

"Which is?"

"The same thing you asked me just moments ago: Do you believe Jacob could actually be what we all thought had been lost to us more than half a century ago?"

Gotham took a pause and the labored breath that left him conveyed instantly the hours he had spent wrestling over the very question.

"I can honestly tell you I haven't the foggiest notion what to think anymore at this point," came his reply.

"Then what about your gut?" pressed Thaniel.

"My gut?" Gotham took a moment to ponder the question as if the words themselves were a foreign utterance. "My gut is something I've made a conscious effort to ignore at the moment, even as I feel it champing away at my insides."

"I don't fault you for being heedful, as we all find ourselves to be at this hour of unease," said Thaniel. "And just perhaps a punishment, as you so put it, is indeed forthcoming, yet with its eyes set not on you but the one for which it was long-ago promised. Since the meeting of the White Circle I've been left pondering rather intriguingly a remark made by Anahel mulling the irony of the Darkness' downfall coming from within its own ranks."

"From your mouth, Thaniel," said Gotham with a smile, brief though it was. "One thing is certain: whatever the answer in return, we will come to know it sooner than any of us are ready to hear it."

Thaniel's gaze shifted to the night outside and a stark seriousness came to him.

"The hour is drawing ever nearer," he remarked. "Come, and let's walk the halls to ensure there are no curious-minded wandering about to meet it."

~ ~ ~

The hours that followed were the quietest—not to mention the longest—Jacob could ever recall while staying at Havenhid. Not a peep could be heard coming from any of the neighboring rooms, and the minutes seemed to stretch themselves into hours.

"How long has it been?" whispered Ethan, who was sitting motionless on the floor next to his bed with his knees tucked up against his chest and his eyes fixed on the window looking out to the settled night.

"About five minutes from when you last asked," mumbled Jacob also seated on the floor at the foot of his bed and petting his beloved wolf companion Mist, who was stretched out beside him looking unusually alert and guarded. "When you ask again in another five minutes, it will be ten minutes."

But Ethan couldn't help himself. The seconds could almost be heard ticking themselves off ever since the unseen trumpeter sent his ominous cry across Eden marking the start of the curfew which brought the last of the Nephilim to the confines of their rooms as they had been instructed.

Also huddled on the floor was Max, while Leos and Kairo chose the comfort of their beds to sprawl out across. Sleep, however, was the furthest thing from their minds and like the others their eyes, too, remained fixed on the window on the far side of the room.

"You know what this reminds me of...in a strange, twisted sort of a way, that is?" asked Kairo after a while. "Christmas Eve when I was growing up."

"Oh, yeah?" said Leos, "And just what kind of scary-ass Christmases did your family celebrate?"

"I can just see it," said Max with a demented chuckle. "'The children were nestled all snug in their bed, with visions of Azrael dancing in their heads.'"

But Kairo ignored the snickering.

"My cousin Dontae and I would sneak out of our beds once everyone had gone off to sleep and tiptoe downstairs to where the Christmas tree and presents were and we'd wait, determined this would be the year we'd finally catch Santa Claus in action. Closest we ever got was once when there came this loud sound...almost like the jingling of a bunch of bells being dropped on the ground. Made us almost jump clear out of our pajamas. This was it, Dontae and I thought, and with adrenaline pumping through us we rushed to the window certain that what we heard was Santa landing his sleigh outside. It didn't take long to realize the bells we thought we heard had actually been one of those large silver ball ornament hanging on the tree that had fallen off and shattered on the floor." Kairo paused while reliving the rekindled memory inside his head, and he breathed a disappointed sigh.

"We never were successful. Every Christmas morning Dontae and I would wake up curled up on the floor next to the tree where we eventually wound up falling asleep, and when we saw our presents nearby we realized we'd been bamboozled one more time by that sneaky, jolly fat guy."

"What do you think he looks like?" asked Ethan.

"Same as always," answered Leos. "Red suit, white beard, a nose like cherry."

"Not Santa doofus, Azrael."

"My guess is he's skeletal in nature, wearing a long black robe and carrying a scythe," said Max. "And of course at the ends of his long bony fingers there would be razor-sharp claws shaped like daggers. You know, so he's able to rip open a person's chest in order to retrieve the soul."

He couldn't hold silent the chuckle of amusement fighting for release when he saw the look of dread creep its way across Ethan's face.

"Ha, ha, very funny," said Ethan. But his wide eyes were unable to mask his ardent desire for the night to pass as quickly as possible and make way for the return of the sun and the safety which resided in its light. Humorous as it was pulling at the threads of Ethan's unraveling nerves, Max couldn't help take notice at how quiet Jacob was being.

"You okay?" he asked, and his voice seemed to break through whatever dense fog of thoughts Jacob was lost inside.

"Sure," said Jacob not too convincingly.

"Maybe a little nervous?"

"Why should I be nervous?"

Max gave a shrug. "I think I might be, if I were in your shoes, knowing Azrael was being called here on my account."

If Jacob was harboring such nerves, he did well hiding it.

"What's the big deal? Anahel said as long as we stay in our rooms there would be nothing to worry about."

Such assurances did little to assuage Ethan. "Really? Then why did Anahel order all the lights to be doused at a certain time so that we're left sitting here in the dark. And why did he warn us to keep away from the windows like he did, and especially not to look at him?"

"What are you getting so freaked about? The lights haven't even been put out yet," said Max, motioning to the two flickers of flame holding back the nighttime shadows as they burned in two corners of the room.

Ethan ignored him. "You want to know the thing I really can't get out of my head, no matter how hard I try? When Anahel said he and the other Guides might not be quick enough in getting to our rooms should one of us scream out to them. Why would there be screaming?"

"He was just trying to put the fear of God into us so we'd do what we're told, right?" said Max looking to Leos and Kairo for backup.

"Sure," both boys answered in unison, though the glances they exchanged held looks far less certain.

Ethan, however, wasn't buying it. In fact, his eyes suddenly widened as if he'd been stuck by a most unpleasant thought. "What if Azrael comes here...to our room?"

"And why exactly would he come to our room?" asked Max.

"Why wouldn't he? You said it yourself, he's coming here because of..." Ethan's voice trailed off as he gave a look in Jacob's direction.

"What if he does?" said Jacob in as nonchalant a manner as he could muster.

"That doesn't make you a little...you know...?"

Jacob didn't answer, fearing his voice would be lacking the fortitude to make his answer completely believable. Instead he grabbed for his bag which was lying within reach and pulled from it a book he had buried beneath some of his clothing. It was his copy of "Paradise Lost" that he brought along with him on his trip which he had long-finished while in Eden. He opened it and began earnestly flipping through the pages. When he found what he was looking for, he turned the book around and thrust it toward Ethan.

"What is it?" asked Ethan leaning forward while squinting down at a black and white illustration showing an angel fair and strong with long, wavy hair standing in the shadow of towering trees amid lush fern and hanging palm fronds.

"It's Satan, shown hiding right here in Eden," said Jacob. "Look at him. Does he look like some big, scary demon? No, he looks just like Gotham, or Damiel or any of the other angels here."

"That's nothing but a stupid story book," said Ethan dismissively. "And who even said anything about Satan? We're talking about the Angel of Death. D-E-A-T-H, death! Besides, it's not so much what Azrael looks like that I'm so concerned about than what he can do. And if you ask me nothing good can come from anything named the Angel of Death."

"Where I come from, death isn't something to be feared as it is in other parts of the world," Kairo spoke up from his bed as his eyes traced the formation of branches shaping the ceiling above him in the dim firelight. "The whole purpose of life is to reach that moment when one comes face to face with death and crosses its threshold into something beyond our imaginings. One should not recoil from it, but embrace it."

"Yeah, well, when it gets here you can be my guest. Embrace it, tickle it, dance the tango with it, do whatever you want, just keep it far away from me," said Ethan, drawing a gaggle of snickers from the others.

~ ~ ~

A hush of wind swept suddenly across the room kicking up papers resting on a desk in the corner before rustling the pages of the book Jacob still held in his hand. It circled about carrying a faint chorus of whispers with it before extinguishing the warm firelight that had served as some comfort to the nervous boys and allowing the moonlit darkness outside to suddenly rush forth and flood the room.

"What's going on? What's happening?" whispered Ethan who was teetering on the verge of panic. "It's Azrael...he's here, isn't he?"

"Relax Ethan, it's just the start of the blackout," said Jacob.

"Yeah? How do you know?"

"Because, you dope, Anahel said it would take effect when the moon hung over the Silent Forest. Take a look," answered Jacob, nodding to the window where the moon shone through and reflected brightly in his eyes.

Ethan followed Jacob's gaze, angling his head downward until he saw firsthand the moon hanging in the sky like a hunk of glowing marble whose light strangely was unable to illuminate the dark, shadowy shape of the Silent Forest beneath it.

"Oh, so it is," he said with a dismissive laugh. "Just like I thought."

"You're a real credit to Jedi geeks all over the world, y'know that, Ethan?" said Leos. "First you nearly hobble a fellow Shrike and now, Darth Vader hasn't even landed on Eden and your Hershey factory is already in full production mode."

Jacob managed a chuckle before he noticed Mist had jumped up from where she had been laying on the floor with the dousing of the light, and was now sitting close beside him looking even more alert.

"Don't tell me you're a big fraidy cat like Ethan over there," said Jacob.

"Who's a fraidy cat?" challenged Ethan, stirring a pointed bark from Mist.

"It's amazing how she's taken to you like she has, how protective she is," said Leos, watching from his bed as the wolf hovered close to Jacob.

"I feel just the same about her," said Jacob before scrunching his face when he was suddenly given a slobbery lick from Mist.

"Do you think maybe she knows?" asked Max.

Jacob shrugged. "I'm sure she senses something's going to happen tonight."

"No, I don't mean that. Do you think she senses that you are...I mean, that you might be, you know...special?" Max, stammering over the words he found suddenly tangled on his tongue, asked. "You know, wolves are known over all animals to have an innate, highly-tuned instinct. Maybe that's why she latched on to you like she did."

Jacob stared deep into Mists's eyes and he couldn't deny there was something lurking in the icy blue tundra peering back at him.

"I think she just recognizes a good back scratcher when she spots one," he said with a smile.

"I hope you know what happened earlier tonight in the Hall...what Creed implied...it isn't true," said Max. "I mean, naturally I'm curious as everyone else about whether what's been said about you is true or not. But not the way he implied it."

"Don't give it a second thought. I can't say I wouldn't be wondering the same things if we swapped shoes. Heck, I can't really even fault Creed much either."

Max's brow furrowed. "What do you mean?"

"I mean, Creed may be a jerk, but there's a lot of truth to some of what he said earlier tonight in the Hall. Just look at me, for Pete's sake," said Jacob who would be the first to point out the ridiculousness of any such idea that regarded him being some promised anointed one. Just the simple act of looking in the mirror made the prospect laughable at best, especially considering his wing-barren back failed to make him look like he even belonged in Eden much less walking the halls of Havenhid with other Nephilim who had been blessed with their plumed appendages. "To be honest, I think come tomorrow we're all going to share in a big laugh when we find out all of this trouble was much to do about nothing."

"But what about what happened with Balantine's leg? I was there at Lions Bite. I saw what happened, just as everyone else did," said Max.

"I don't know what happened at Lions Bite," Jacob sighed with frustration. There was a part of him that wished he'd not been so valiant in coming to Balantine's aid. "As far as I know it could have been the water from the River that was used to clean his cut. It's well known it carries with it a special force. I mean, I watched Gotham splash the water on his face the day we got here and saw the cuts he received by the Infectors who attacked us disappear right before my eyes."

The fixed look on Max's face showed he was unmoved by the argument.

"Besides, can anyone in this room honestly say they can entertain the idea of me being this 'Light Bearer'?" Jacob added with a laugh.

The room became quiet as his eyes slowly moved their focus from Ethan to Leos and then Kairo, who sat in silence looking conflicted as they mulled the question.

"Yes," answered Max, drawing a look of surprise from Jacob.

"Really...you can?" asked Ethan with noted surprise before turning quickly back to Jacob and offering an apologetic: "No offense."

"Don't ask me to try and explain why. I can't," said Max. "Just an instinct I feel, really. Like Mist there."

"But how is it possible?" questioned Kairo. "Have you forgotten Gotham's son was already found to be the Light Bearer?"

"Stranger things have happened, especially here in Eden," answered Max with a shrug. "And why then are we all sitting here like a bunch of nervous nellies waiting for whatever's about to happen tonight? Obviously, Anahel and the rest of the Guides believe it's possible as well."

"If only I could make the leap from Broken Earth, then this whole matter would be so easy to prove, or better disprove," Jacob contemplated with a sigh.

"What has Broken Earth got to do with anything?" asked Leos.

"Last night, in Anahel's room, when the Guides were arguing over whether or not it was possible I was...well, you know...Thaniel said the Apocrypha detailing the prophesy made note that the Light Bearer would carry a mark on his wing—a single white feather."

"Maybe subconsciously that's what's kept you from jumping," Kairo offered.

"But I don't believe I'm the Light Bearer," Jacob stressed emphatically. "If anything, it makes me want to jump just so I can get my wings and prove it once and for all."

"And just what if, on the off chance, it's proven otherwise?" asked Leos. "What if you find out you actually are the Light Bearer?"

Jacob hadn't allowed himself to ponder such a possibility. Even considering such a thought was enough to make the blood drain from his face and cause his skin to break out in a nervous sweat, just like at the moment Leos raised the question.

"Well, there's no use wearing ourselves out about such things, least of all tonight," Max stepped in as he noticed the tense angst take hold of his friend, even in the dark of the night. "I just want you to know whatever ends up happening, you can count on me to support you as your right-hand man. Mark or no mark."

Jacob reached out for Max's hand extended his way. And as the two smiled warmly at one another and locked hands to symbolize the close bond they had formed, he knew Eden had given him at least one thing he would cherish: a true friend.

"Get a room already," Ethan cried out, cuing a laugh from Leos and Kairo.

"What's the matter Ethan, you gettin' your panties in a jealous bind?" teased Max before playfully tackling Ethan.

~ ~ ~

For several minutes they forgot themselves—and the ominous visit Eden was expecting—as they wrestled and rolled about on the floor in attempts to best the other through fits of laughter. Jacob watched from the sidelines giggling with amusement when his ears suddenly pricked to a strange sound causing his body to freeze. He cocked his head and strained to hear what sounded to be coming from outside, but the ruckus was too loud and he feverishly motioned Max and Ethan to quiet down.

"What is it?" inquired Max, trying to catch his breath while remaining sprawled across the floor.

"Did you hear that?" whispered Jacob.

"I don't hear anything," said Leos.

"What did it sound like?" Ethan gasped as he rolled himself over and revealed a renewed look of concern that had been momentarily forgotten.

Jacob didn't answer. And as the quiet still holding firm its reign over the darkness returned to the room, the boys each turned a focused ear to it and listened hard for what could have possibly caught Jacob's attention. Mist, who remained sitting at attention, looked to the window and let out a small whimper.

"You heard it too, didn't you?" asked Jacob.

Again he strained his ears and soon a curious frown came to his face. He moved forward onto all fours and crawled his way over to the open window formed by the bending and twisting branches of the trees. Ignoring Ethan's whispered reminder of Anahel's warning to steer clear of all windows, he peeked out into the night.

At first, there seemed to be nothing unusual when he peered out over the Garden. Except for the strange stillness, it looked as beautiful as it ever did while bathed in the silver spray of light cast down from the massive full moon. Yet there was a definite strange presence Jacob had never felt before in the Garden. Whatever it was, it was lurking close by, unseen, and causing Jacob's arms to come alive with goose bumps. And then he saw it—a vast and far-reaching shadow, like the black tide of a solar eclipse, only much darker. It moved slowly across the Garden, as if a giant blanket was being pulled over Eden, swallowing everything in its path. Glancing upward toward the sky, Jacob saw nothing—literally nothing, and yet most definitely something—as the sea of stars and the moon itself were slowly doused one by one from sight by the same approaching smothering blackness stretching itself wide to the furthest corners of Eden like a funeral shroud. The soothing breeze instantly fell still as did the fluttering leaves of the trees, and the expression on Jacob's face suddenly soured sharply when the heavenly perfume from the blooming night flowers scenting the night air turned and took on the rotting fragrance of decaying, diseased flesh. His attention was then quickly pulled away from the putrid stench when he again heard the strange, mysterious sound that had before caught his ears.

Clip. Clop. Clip. Clop.

The sound was like that of hooves, distant at first and carrying a flat echo, as if coming from some unseen horse strolling with a slow gait down a damp cobblestone street choked by a dense, ghostly fog. Again Mist whimpered, only louder.

"Do you hear it, now?" whispered Jacob, looking back over his shoulder at the others.

The strained look on their faces told Jacob they were still trying to lock in on what he was hearing. Max was the first to perk up.

"I think I hear it."

"Me, too," whispered Ethan, sitting up straighter. He took on a hard look of concentration as he stared past Jacob and out the window. "It sounds like...it sounds like a..."

Ethan found himself unable to reveal his guess when his mouth slowly unhinged itself, and the color in his face drained to a pale whiteness that even the moonless night couldn't hide. He became frozen with wide-eyed fear and before Jacob could inquire from him what was wrong he noticed Max, too, was overcome with the same look followed by Leos and Kairo. Then his ears picked up the sound of snorted breathing that could only come from one big-nosed creature, and Jacob knew something was behind him. A chill unlike any he'd ever known ran through him, but he managed to gather what courage he needed to slowly turn his head back around. As he did, his eyes grew wide when they came in contact with the front half of a big black horse which had passed into view from outside the thicket of tree branches and stopped in front of the window. Its eyes were as dark as its wiry mane and its ebony pelt was the color of the same moonless night that had descended upon Eden, and it stood there breathing hot gusts of air through its flaring muzzle.

Jacob felt his heart buckle in his chest as he knew instantly what he was seeing was virtually impossible, especially since the view from the window he was looking out of was a good four or five stories high from the ground below, and even in Eden he had yet to see a horse with wings like the mythic Pegasus. Yet there was no dismissing the fact that he was staring straight into the face of a horse standing just outside this same window, and the horse seemed to be staring sideways right back in his direction. Jacob's eyes shifted ever so slowly to the long black robe donned by the rider draped across the horse's side and a heavy booted foot peeking out from beneath the hem line. At that precise moment, Jacob didn't know for which he was most thankful: the fact the rider sat so high up on the horse to disallow being seen any further past his waist, or that the window where Jacob remained crouched was too low for the rider to peer inside. Either way, Jacob was unable to see the rider's face unless he were to stretch his neck forward and poke his head through the window for a look, and he certainly wasn't about to entertain such a notion. In fact, he dared not move, not even to breathe, for fear the rider, seemingly oblivious to his presence, would spot him in a squat position just inside the window cloaked in a veil of shadow. And only when the horse was nudged by the booted foot to continue forward did Jacob exhale heavily a grateful breath.

Clip. Clop. Clip. Clop.

~ ~ ~

"Is it him?" Ethan gasped nervously. However, before any reply could be given, he immediately began muttering an answer to his own question. "Of course it must be him. What a stupid question. I mean, who else would be on a black horse right outside our window several feet above the ground?"

When he felt the coast was clear, Jacob quickly sprang to the other side of the window and slowly, with great caution, snuck another peek outside. His eyes once more found the rider who was descending to the Garden grounds below. And while the rider appeared to be little more than a darkened figure against the shrouded night, Jacob was able to make out a large pair of wings folded across the back of his robed body. Like the horse beneath him, they were smooth and shiny and black as pitch as if acquired from a giant raven.

"It's Azrael," said Jacob quietly. Squinting his eyes which fought to focus through the murky darkness, he spotted much to his surprise the silhouette of an unmistakable curved weapon clutched in the angel's left hand, and he swallowed nervously. "And believe it or not, he does have a scythe."

"Get out!" blurted Ethan, his voice quavering on the brink of panic.

Clip. Clop. Clip. Clop.

Jacob then found his gaze drawn to the hooves of the black steed upon which the angel rode, and to his shock he discovered them to be treading on nothing but the empty air. And yet, somehow, they continued to carry the sound of a paved path.

Clip. Clop. Clip. Clop.

"What's he doing?" asked Leos anxiously, though like the others not daring to go to the window to see for himself.

Jacob waved at him to keep quiet while his eyes remained fixed on the shadowy, mysterious figure descending his way slowly from the trees as if making his way down an invisible flight of stairs leading to the grounds just outside the entrance to Havenhid. There the figure came to a stop and dismounted from his horse, scythe in hand.

"He's getting off his horse," said Jacob, sounding like a sports announcer describing a game on-air while fighting a bout of laryngitis.

"I knew it...he's coming up here," cried Ethan, grabbing for his sword he made sure was in his reach.

"SHHHHH!"

Even cloaked beneath the flow of his black robe, it was evident to Jacob as he continued to peer outside that the angel was an entity of considerable size. And if there was any doubt to his intimidating presence, it could be heard in the heavy footsteps even the grassy earth was unable to muffle. Making his way to the banks of the River, the angel lifted the scythe in hand toward the sky before powerfully impaling the handle deep into the earth, leaving it to stand upright out of the ground like some planted flag. Then, as he approached the water he reached across his chest and under his left arm into the plumes of his black wings and drew forth a mighty sword.

"Well?" asked Ethan impatiently. "What's he doing?"

"I don't know," replied Jacob. "He's just standing by the River clutching his sword."

"I thought you said he had a scythe."

"He has both."

"Of course he does," Ethan muttered under his breath before swallowing nervously.

For some time the angel stood motionless at the River's edge with his head bowed toward the water, almost as though he were praying. Then something seemed to capture his attention, as if some stray sound not snuffed out by the surrounding quiet had pricked his ears, and he slowly turned his head. As he did, Mist, who had positioned herself in an unusually protective stance beside Jacob with her large ears perched high and eyes fixed unblinking on the dark figure below began to rumble with a deep and low growl.

"Shhhhh, keep quiet," scolded Jacob, not so much because he was afraid the figure might hear Mist, but because he suddenly found himself struck by something eerily familiar about the figure and was now struggling to concentrate on what exactly that was.

As he continued to focus hard on the figure, it came to him and he was suddenly transported back to the memory he held inside his head of the night his mother died. He had been jolted awake suddenly after nodding off in the middle of studying while stretched out on his bed. What exactly jolted him suddenly back to consciousness, he had no idea; but somewhere in his grogginess, even before he awakened, he had become aware of the hollow, clacking echo of horse hooves tapping a slow cadence of a walk upon cobblestone—the same clacking sound he heard come from the horse of the dark, faceless rider. At first, Jacob thought it was the remnants of a dream until he realized the sound, which remained in his ears when he finally opened his eyes, was coming from his TV he had earlier turned on, hoping the ambient noise would help keep him awake and focused on his reading.

Fumbling around the tangle of sheets beneath him, he found the remote and aimed it at the TV, extinguishing the lonely, yet eerie, image of a horse pulling a dark carriage through the narrow, fogged-in streets of some turn-of-the-century town in a scene from some old horror movie being played. With the plodding horse silenced, Jacob then took notice of the whirling wind outside that was rattling loudly the blinds as it blew through the open window on the other side of his room. He swung his legs over the side of the bed and sat himself upright with a strenuous groan. His eyes immediately focused on the hole in one of his dingy white socks that he noticed had grown larger, exposing more of the big toe of his right foot which he wriggled and stretched about inside.

The hardwood floor creaked slightly when Jacob stood up and side-stepped the littered remnants of dirty clothes that had formed various piles around the room as he made his way to the window. It was really kicking up, he thought to himself as he peered out into the darkness through the slats of the blinds and saw the nearby trees swaying and moving about in the whistling bluster as if they were alive. The noticeable, unexpected nip in the air moved Jacob to close the window to ward off the familiar prickly sensation of goose bumps beginning to rise up on his arms. He was just about to shut the blinds when something else caught his eye. A figure. It was standing on the opposite side of the street directly across from the house beneath a lamppost, the light of which strangely was not working, even though Jacob saw plainly the other lampposts operating normally as he took a quick glance up and down the rest of the street.

Jacob squinted trying to force his eyes to see more clearly through the dense ink of the night. The figure was oddly tall and appeared to be wearing a long-hooded cloak of some kind, which only made the figure appear even more shadowy and ominous. And even though Jacob couldn't make out a face, it was obvious the gaze hidden within the dark folds of the draped hood was fixed on the house. For all Jacob knew, the figure could have been staring directly back into the window from which he was looking down onto the street.

"Who the hell is that?" Jacob muttered to himself.

He then noticed the figure wasn't alone, but standing beside an equally black and shadowy horse. The strange sight made Jacob give his eyes a vigorous rubbing to remove whatever thin film of sleep may have lingered to play tricks with his vision. When he then proceeded to peer through the slats of the blinds once more, the cloaked figure and the horse were nowhere to be seen. Stranger still, the lamppost under which he spied them was now working and its light illuminating the now vacant spot where he could have sworn the vanishing apparition had stood just a second earlier.

~ ~ ~

"It was him," Jacob muttered to himself when the vision receded from sight back into the vaults of his memory. It was then he suddenly realized the dark, menacing figure lurking near the River and the one he spied outside his home who would become the uninvited guest who would steal away from him the one important thing in his life—his mother—were one and the same.

"It was him," repeated Jacob as a swell of anger moved through him

"Who are you talking about?" asked Max.

"The Angel of Death," said Jacob hatefully.

The dark angel below suddenly turned and gazed over his shoulder toward the grove of trees where Havenhid resided hidden in its cradle of branches. It was then Jacob was given a look of the dark figure's face, and it made him shrink back further into the shadows. It was not skeletal as Max earlier joked, nor was he monstrous or grotesque as one would expect the Angel of Death to be. Yet neither was he beautiful and pleasing to the eyes as other angels. Unlike them, his severe face was a pale, lifeless mask of porcelain white skin made more stark by the mane of long black hair framing it. There was no hint of kindness to the thin-lipped mouth, and the eyes hooded beneath a sloped brow were vacant of the golden fire burning in those of other angels. But burn they did, though with a white cold flame, encased in an even more chilling, icy hardness. And as they penetrated the surrounding night and slowly turned their focus to the tree tops where Havenhid resided, Jacob felt his breath catch in his chest when the figure's searching gaze appeared to settle itself upon the window at which he was crouched.

Mist began to growl with a growing fierceness while baring ever more her fangs.

"He's looking this way," Jacob, barely able to find his voice, gasped. "I think he sees me."

"Are you crazy? Get away from the window," Max whispered urgently.

Jacob, though, was frozen tight in his spot, and his eyes grew wider as they watched the figure below slowly raise his arm and level a pointed finger in his direction. Then suddenly from inside the draping sleeve of the angel's robe a dark plume burst forth.

"He's released something," said Jacob, his voice climbing.

"Released?" echoed Ethan, looking as if he was about to faint on the spot.

"What do you mean released? Released what?" asked Kairo.

It suddenly became too much for him not seeing what was happening, and he leapt from his bed to crouch beside Jacob. When he peeked over the ledge of the window, his eyes grew large and wide like Jacob's at the sight of the angel and the mysterious black cloud being spilled forth from the confines of the figures black robe. At first it looked like a trail of black smoke shooting forth. Massive in size, it ascended as a swirling pillar high into the sky. The rumbling growl coming from Mist instantly fell silent, and the wolf suddenly turned on Jacob. She took a firm hold of Jacob's jeans with her teeth and tugged with all her might in a desperate attempt to pull Jacob away from the window.

"What is it?" Leos pressed with a growing anxiousness.

"Don't ask me. For all I know, its death," whispered Kairo. "Black death."

Ethan's already strangling grip on his sword grew even tighter. "Black death?"

Watching motionless the black mass take to the night sky, both Jacob and Kairo were together at the same time seized by a heightened look of fright when suddenly the dark shape swooped back down and came barreling toward the trees at a great speed.

"And now it's heading straight toward us," cried Kairo in a last-ditch warning to the others as he abandoned Jacob's side and bounded back across the room like a spooked gazelle to find safety somewhere within the confines of his bed.

Max and Ethan followed suit with skittish swiftness, diving beneath their tangled covers with the desperate hope it would provide a safe sanctuary from whatever sent Kairo running from the window in fear. Jacob, however, remained firm in his spot despite Mist's continued efforts to yank him away; not because he was unable to find function in his feet to flee due to the overwhelming sense of terror rising up inside him, but rather a strange sound coming from within the approaching black cloud his ears had suddenly locked on to; a high-pitched buzzing amid a rustling of what sounded like millions of fluttering wings. Foreign as it was to him, it was also a sound oddly familiar at the same time, one that had met his ears not too long ago. The noise came in louder waves, and as it did he focused harder on it while feverishly searching his brain for when it was he had last heard it. And only when the black mass had nearly reached the trees did his memory flash to an especially tedious afternoon in his biology class back in Cain's Corner where he struggled to stay awake during a video of the most destructive forces on Earth. One of those forces was shown to be prevalent in the fertile farmlands of India. Not only did it carry the same marked sound now buzzing in his ears, but it also moved through the air in the shape of a massive cloud of blackness.

It was then, suddenly, Jacob knew what was headed his way and his wide eyes reflected his sudden fear..

"Locusts," he whispered, struggling to dislodge his voice which had become caught in his chest.

"IT'S LOCUSTS...."

With only a second to spare, he managed to dive away from the window just as the cloud burst through with a terrifying force and began swarming the room consuming it whole in a frenzied, chaotic darkness filled with the thunderous drone of furious wings and gnashing teeth.

And screams.

CHAPTER FOUR

DEATH IN EDEN

When he finally came to, Jacob felt the comfort of his bed beneath his body. How he got there he was unsure, and as he forced open the heavy lids of his eyes, he was surprised to find the soft light of morning coming through the window and bathing the room with its golden tint.

The window...

Last he remembered, it was the dead of night and he was dodging for cover from a plague of locusts sent his way from the dark angel Azrael, whose face he hoped to never set eyes upon again. Now, thankfully, the darkness had been cast away and the screeching winged insects were nowhere to be seen. Had he dreamed the whole thing? he found himself wondering. Yet there was a definite presence in the room with him. He could feel it looming just behind him and he quickly rolled himself over to see who—or what—it was.

"Anahel," he exclaimed with relief at the welcoming sight of the angel. Yet he found the face staring down at him, usually fixed with the cordial curl of a comforting smile and friendly glimmer in the eyes, was overcast by a tense seriousness.

"I must say, I'm surprised coming to your room and finding you still asleep," said Anahel. "Of anyone, I would have thought you would be the one I would not have to rouse from bed this morning."

Behind him stood Max, Leos, Kairo and Ethan looking strained on their feet as though they had only moments earlier been plucked from their own comfy beds.

"To tell you the truth, I don't remember even getting into bed, much less falling asleep," said Jacob pensively. "In fact, the last thing I remember is..."

He quickly silenced himself from speaking further.

"And what would that be?" implored Anahel.

"Nothing," answered Jacob, though it was clear from the raised eyebrow serving to punctuate the angels' scolding glare that Anahel was already the wise.

"I'm not so sure I would call a swarm of locusts nothing," said Anahel.

Jacob shifted his gaze to where the others lingered nearby and one glance at Ethan was all it took to know who fed Anahel's insight.

"It kinda slipped," admitted Ethan.

"You just couldn't help yourselves could you? Even after I gave you implicit instructions last night," Anahel reprimanded sternly. "Well, you can count yourselves lucky locusts were the only thing to rain down upon you last night. Azrael has about as much patience for the living as I do for Nephilim who blatantly choose to ignore one of my directives."

"Is he gone?" asked Jacob.

Anahel took a calming breath before answering.

"Since before the sky saw the approach of the dawn, I imagine. Azrael has never been one with a fondness to wander in the company of his own shadow." Anahel then turned on his heel and crossed the room to the door. "And now it is time you rise up, Fledgling. The others have already been gathered and are waiting for us outside to see what mark has been left on the Garden."

Looking somewhat wrinkled and disheveled in his clothes from the previous day, Jacob sat up and shuffled his feet into his sneakers that had been discarded on the floor next to his bed. When the other boys had filed out of the room, Anahel looked to Jacob only to find him still sitting on the edge of his bed looking noticeably troubled and burdened. His heart immediately grew heavy inside his chest as he realized whatever anxiety he had for what awaited outside, it was the boy who had been left to quietly suffer the brunt of this unknown and most confusing situation.

"Go on ahead with yourselves," Anahel instructed the boys patiently waiting in the hallway outside the door. "Inform the Guides we'll be down shortly. We just need a minute or two, if you please."

"Something the matter?" asked Max, directing a concerned look past Anahel to where Jacob sat. "He buggin'?"

"Buggin'?"

"You know, freaking out? I'm not sure I wouldn't be if I were in his shoes…a little bit, at least."

"I'm sure your friend will be quite fine after he's allowed a moment to collect his…bugs," Anahel awkwardly assured Max. "Now, run along with you all."

With some reluctance, the Fledglings did as they were told and, with the sound of their feet growing fainter as they scurried their way down the hall, Anahel quietly closed the door behind them.

"I suppose now would be as good a time as any to apologize," the angel said once he had crossed the room and taken a seat on the bed next to where Jacob sat staring off into space.

"Apologize? For what?" inquired Jacob, breaking free of whatever deep, trancelike thought had momentarily taken hold of him and looking somewhat taken aback to find anyone still in the room with him.

"Oh, I don't know; many things, I suppose," Anahel replied with a deep sigh. "First and foremost, I would say for not checking in sooner and seeing how you were handling everything that has happened in this short span of time."

"Everything's just been just so confusing," said Jacob. "Here I was waiting on pins and needles for you to return from meeting with the White Circle, and then when you did you looked so…I don't know…upset. I thought maybe I had done something to anger you without even knowing it. And when you then disappeared like you did from the Hall of Light after informing everyone about Azrael without even talking to me to explain what was happening, well…it's left a bad feeling in the pit of my stomach."

"I guess the only excuse—if you care to call it that—I have for my brusque display is finding myself grappling with the same overwhelming sense of confusion you, yourself, are experiencing," said Anahel. "This is a most unique and strange circumstance I and the rest of the Guides find ourselves confronted with that I can remember. Unfortunately, in my bafflement I chose to turn inward in a search for answers and in the process ended up closing the door on you. And for that, Fledgling, I am sorry. It was not my intention."

The angel's apology was warming to Jacob. At least Anahel wasn't angry with the boy, which is what Jacob had feared to be the case.

"Well, at least one good thing came out of it," said Jacob.

"And that would be?" asked Anahel.

"The look on Creed's face when you cut him down to size in front of everybody," Jacob replied with a glimmer of satisfaction peeking through his grin."

"Ah, yes, Creed—son of Sandel. He is his father's son, if ever there was one," remarked Anahel. "I wouldn't take too much stock in what Creed has to say. He is more rattle than snake. But be assured, if the chips should ever fall and you should find yourself in need of a helping hand, you might surprise yourself to find his to be the first extended your way."

A quiet descended upon the room as Anahel and Jacob stared blankly at one another before a smile crept up on both their faces at the same time.

"Or maybe not," they said in unison with a chuckle.

"There's a lot a whispering going on with the other guys," Jacob said once the moment of levity wore off.

"And what is it they're whispering?" asked Anahel, though the tone in his voice held a hint he already knew the answer.

"That I'm...the Light Bearer," Jacob replied timidly as if uncomfortable even uttering the name.

"Boys have a propensity to be gossipmongers, even more so than their female counterparts, I have found," said Anahel. "No doubt your ears will prick to more such consorting before the day is through."

"But is it true? Am I?"

A look heavy in weight, the same Jacob recognized from when the angel returned from meeting with the White Circle, emerged and settled itself upon Anahel. "That, my dear boy, is the elusive answer we're all hoping is revealed today, and the reason Azrael was summoned last night."

"So what happens now?" asked Jacob as Anahel rose to his feet.

"We find out if, indeed, the seventh Grace resides within you," answered Anahel.

"And if it does?"

Even though it was a question Anahel could not stop pondering since the night the incident at Lions Bite was brought to his attention, it was one he could not, or would not, lend an answer to, at least not at that moment.

"Let's confront one thing at a time, shall we?" said Anahel with a meek smile.

He then motioned Jacob to his feet and as they were about to step out into the hallway Jacob paused suddenly in the doorway.

"Have you looked already?" he asked.

Anahel shook his head in a disturbing manner. "Not yet."

"I saw him you know," Jacob confessed. "By the River."

A curious look came to Anahel's face.

"The River?"

For a moment it was as if Anahel was unfamiliar with the existence of the channel of water that had paved an unhindered path from the Garden to the furthest corners of Eden. Placing a hand on Jacob's shoulder, the angel guided the boy through the doorway.

"The River," he repeated quietly to himself sounding more and more puzzled with each utterance.

~ ~ ~

The rest of the Nephilim were already gathered in a tight grouping just outside the hollow which served as the entrance to Havenhid when Jacob emerged into the warm sunlight with Anahel close to his side. They were standing motionless, staring out in the direction of the River, and, as they turned around, Jacob took notice of the dour expressions on their faces and knew instantly something horrible had taken place. Perhaps sensing a strong desire within the boy to retreat back to his room, and to his bed, the hand on Jacob's shoulder gave a knowing squeeze while guiding the way firmly through the throng.

The morning, bright and clear as any other to greet the Garden, was occupied by a strange uncomfortable stillness. Absent from the trees was the rustling of leaves from a tickling breeze. Nor could the familiar chirping of the birds be heard, or the bubbling of water usually heard coming from the River. Most noticeable and odd, however, was the sound of the waterfalls whose distant presence was markedly absent. After a few steps more, Jacob and Anahel were met by Zuriel.

"There's nothing I can say to prepare you," he said. "It's the River."

He appeared strong and reserved, but there was a sorrowful presence in Zuriel's eyes he could not shield. It was the same shared by the other boys, only much more pronounced, and when he stepped aside to allow Jacob and Anahel a path to the River behind him, it became clear why.

A deafening silence made itself heard. Jacob felt Anahel's hand slip limply from his shoulder. The angel slowly came around him, his strong, stout face stricken with a horrified look, and his feet guided him warily to the River's edge where he stood for some time disbelieving and silent. The serpentine channel that had once etched a winding pathway of crystal blue water through all of Eden was now a black and fetid soup. Its flow had been brought to a standstill and it's bubbling heartbeat of life silenced. Fish that lived in its currents, as well as frogs, turtles and other water creatures, could be seen floating dead in large numbers all along the murky surface. Their bodies were already in stages of decay and rot, and overpowered the scents of nearby blooming flowers, filling the air with a sickening, unmistakable stench of death.

Anahel turned his gaze to the north where the absent sounds of the thundering waterfalls had not escaped his ears, and when he found to his great dismay the spectacular downpours of rushing water that fed life into the River below had vanished, he stared blankly upon the dried up mountain face and released a heavy, wounded sigh. All that remained to be seen were the falls' paths staining the bare dried rock of the mountain cliffs that had once shaped their beauty. The angel's face grew tense, mirroring both a profound sadness and anger, and for a brief moment beyond his control, his eyes did what was rarely seen amongst angels; they welled with tears. Before a drop could breach the brim of his eye and streak across his cheek, he managed to regain his steely composure when he heard the rustling of wings and caught sight of Gotham and Damiel sweeping down from the sky and finding footing on the ground beside him.

"Look what sacrilege has been committed on our fair Eden," Anahel remarked woefully. "I thought he'd fell one of the creatures who roam this sacred place. Perhaps an entire herd, leaving their motionless bodies scattered as a challenge to the one who dares defy his edict by attempting to stir life back into their hollowed-out corpses. But to take the Sword of Death and plunge it to the hilt into her very soul..."

His quivering voice fell silent as his eyes continued to search the looming mountains, as if in the hope of miraculously spotting a trickle of life to suddenly burst over the barren cliffs.

"How far does it go?" he asked the two angels, knowing they'd been out surveying the damage.

"We followed her path through the Urgon Meadows and Changeling Hills and further south to the Emmaus Corridor," answered Gotham. His jaw suddenly tightened, and in his moment of pause, a pained look flashed across his eyes. "The River lies dead all the way to the Dilmun Sea."

Anahel closed his eyes at the news and clenched his chest with his right hand.

"Unfortunately, I wish that was the worst we had to report," Damiel added with a great deal of trepidation. His hesitation only drew a fiery glare from Anahel.

"Yes? Go on then. Out with it!"

"Death is not contained in her channel," said Damiel.

"What do you mean not contained?"

"It spills over the River's banks, just as it did with life when she flowed unspoiled. It creeps slowly for the most part, the blackness you now see the River to be, but in some areas we spotted it has already inundated and infected large swaths of land."

The sigh which escaped from Anahel was almost too burdensome to breathe forth, and the forlorn look on the leader of Eden's face was the same shared by any father who'd just received news beyond their imaginings that their child had been stricken by some tragic end. There was also anger, a great unbridled anger which brewed hotter within the wells of Anahel's eyes with each new unsettling detail he was given about this most grotesque assault he stood bearing witness to.

"Well then, I guess we'd better move this along," he said turning on his heel. "Fetch the boy!"

As he retreated back to where the Nephilim remained huddled, Zuriel, who had been standing nearby listening along with Thaniel, stepped in front of him blocking his way.

"You can't be serious," he said incredulously.

"About what?" asked Anahel.

"The Fledgling, naturally."

"Correct me if I am wrong, Zuriel, but that is the whole point to all this, is it not? answered Anahel, motioning to the angel before him to steer clear from his path. Zuriel remained firmly footed.

"The boy is untried," said Zuriel. "We don't even know for sure if he possesses the ability to reign in death. All we've heard is the tale of a bleeding wound being healed."

"Then I expect this exercise shall remove all doubt and silence indefinitely from even the most hardened of skeptics amongst us if he's able to reverse the dark tide that is slowly strangling Eden, won't it?" Anahel replied before impatiently pushing his way past Zuriel.

"To leave something this serious in the hands of a Nephilim is nothing short of irresponsible," charged Zuriel as he shadowed alongside Anahel.

"Irresponsible as some may find it, I fear it may be necessary," Thaniel, who was quick to follow beside Zuriel, argued. "A claim has been made. A lofty claim at that. And whether you believe it or not, none of us will be allowed to rest until that claim is substantiated or proven false. That hour is now upon us."

"No offense to Thaniel, but I have to agree with Zuriel about this," said Damiel, who was to Anahel's left walking closest alongside the blackened River. "Even if the boy does have the Grace—and that's a very big if at that—I question highly it'd be of the strength he'd need for something of this magnitude. As it is, it would take many of us positioned at different points along the River working in unison to attempt to reclaim her at this point, and it becomes more of an impossible task with each passing minute we choose to argue the situation. How do you expect a mere boy to manage such an unfathomable feat, Grace or no Grace?"

"Oh, Damiel, the constitution of your faith is revealing itself to be surprisingly weak at this moment," said Anahel. "It makes me wonder should the boy rise up to the challenge and finally quiet this fervor of skepticism if we will still find you tripping over your tongue weighted with excuses over how what we have witnessed was merely a mirage or a trick of light brought about by the sun."

"Of course not," replied Damiel. "But—"

"No buts, Damiel. Lest you forget, this is the second time we have been visited by the supposed birth of the prophesy ushering forth the Light Bearer, and as of today I plan to lay to rest for good the Apocrypha that has shadowed us, as I have no intention of making this a yearly event we celebrate like Illumination," said Anahel firmly. "Azrael was well aware of the reason for which he was summoned. And despite an overwhelming amount of choler I hold for him at this moment, I know he would not have laid down an obstacle which could not be cleared by the one for whom it was designed. If the boy truly is that which we are being forced to entertain, he will, after this moment, leave us no room to further question the matter."

As he spoke these words, Anahel's gaze found Jacob whom he spotted ahead standing beside Gotham staring long-faced at the stricken

River before him. And while the boy didn't appear capable of breathing life into any one of the numerous fish floating lifeless on the water's surface much less the River itself, Anahel felt a curious stirring of hope rise up inside him as he held the boy in his sights, and strangely the idea of something as miraculous as resuscitating miles and miles of the elixir that once fed Eden its life-force no longer waded outside the realm of possibilities in his mind.

"I can't believe this has happened," said Jacob, when Anahel approached him. "Why would Azrael do something like this?"

"So that you can undo it," answered Anahel.

The angel's brazen suggestion brought a scrunched-up look of disbelief to the boy.

"You're joking."

"Comedy, I think you would agree, is not exactly my forte," replied Anahel.

"But…there's no way," insisted Jacob.

"Well, then, at least you're keeping good company on that point," said Anahel turning to Zuriel. And for the first time that morning a subtle smile returned to Anahel's face.

~ ~ ~

"This is ridiculous. I'm telling you, what you're asking is impossible," lamented Jacob for the countless time as Anahel walked him downstream out of earshot from the other boys who stood on the tips of their toes craning their necks in an effort to keep the two in their sights. They were already wise to the rumors circulating through Havenhid, and if any held truth to the fact an "anointed one" lurked amongst them, they were going to make sure they lay witness to the unveiling.

"Balantine. Is it not true you healed his leg?" Anahel questioned Jacob once they were far enough away from the prying ears.

"No...yes...I don't know," stammered Jacob in his struggle to respond to the question he had grown weary of trying to answer or make sense of. "He was bleeding when I placed my hands upon him, and when I removed them he was not. That's all I know."

"Then you possess the power to heal, it's that simple. And you will now do to this River that which you did to Balantine's leg," said Anahel confidently.

"But why me when you can easily do it yourself?" asked Jacob.

"You don't need me to provide an answer you already know to your question," answered Anahel as the expression on his face suddenly grew more stark in its seriousness. "I understand the fear you feel hovering above you, truly I do. A moment of great uncertainty and trepidation is suddenly upon you, Fledgling. You are being called upon to prove something you obviously doubt to be true, perhaps even hope isn't. Fail if you will. In that, there will be no shame. The same cannot be said if you do not rise up and meet this challenge Azrael has put to you, not when Eden has made to suffer such a wound in your name."

Jacob nodded knowingly, yet reluctantly, for he knew despite how ridiculous the idea of the Grace of Healing lurking somewhere inside him was, suspicions had been raised—perhaps even his own—and the only way he'd ever quiet them would be to take crack at the insane task he was now being asked to attempt.

"But how?" asked Jacob. "I didn't even know what I was doing with Balantine. I certainly haven't a clue what to do here."

"That is precisely why I am here to guide you," answered Anahel.

He then directed Jacob to kneel down at the water's edge and gently place his hands upon the black murkiness. Jacob did as he was told, and as he did his face soured when his nostrils were instantly assaulted by the putrid stink rising from the brackish water.

"Ugh...it reeks!" complained Jacob.

"Never mind that," snapped Anahel.

Easier said than done, thought Jacob, as he stretched forth his arms until the palms of his hands were resting upon the surface that now felt more like a thick sludge than water.

"Now what?" he strained while trying to keep from breathing in the foul air suddenly smothering him.

Concentrate," came Anahel's voice. "The River is no different than Balantine's leg. Imagine it as it was, its waters flowing clean and blue and full of life, and force the wound you feel gurgling blood beneath your grip to close itself."

Jacob did as the angel asked, but after a few minutes he opened his eyes and found himself staring down into the same gross, blackened water.

"It's useless," he said with a defeated cock of his head. "I'm telling you this is pointless!"

"And you will fulfill your self-proclaimed prophesy by continuing to doubt yourself," Anahel was quick to scold. "You aren't making hot chocolate through the simple task of stirring cocoa into a cup of warm milk. This is going to require you to tax every last bit of strength you can muster and nothing less. Now, you must concentrate!"

Jacob heaved a heavy breath of frustration before he finally submitted to Anahel's appeal to try once more. Again he stretched forth his arms and floated his hands upon the unsettling muck and fought hard to focus. He conjured up in his mind an image of the River as it was, just as the angel instructed; peaceful and bubbling, it's clear waters creating rushing cascades as it rolled down the descending slopes on its way out of the Garden before settling in a smooth snaking calm while journeying across Eden's vast stretches. He recalled the numerous animals brought to the River to drink and bathe and a smile gradually came to his face. It just as quickly faded when he wriggled his fingers and felt them still wading in the now familiar frothy gunk.

There came a flapping of wings to his ears and he saw in the black foulness of the water the reflection of a figure passing overhead. Looking up, he found Gotham kneeling upon one leg on the River bank opposite him where he had come to land. And when the angel looked into the boy's eyes beginning to tear up with the pained frustration often hinged to the dreaded weight of failure, Gotham lent forth a look of confidence.

"Get in," he instructed.

"You're kidding me with this, right?" The grossness of immersing himself in such foul water immediately made Jacob's face tighten at the idea. "Forget about it, I'm not going swimming in that!"

Gotham proved insistent, and when Jacob realized arguing the matter was as futile as he believed this whole embarrassingly public exercise was, he begrudgingly removed his shoes and socks. Then, glancing back at the many eyes fixed upon him in the distance where his fellow Nephilim and the other Guides stood watching, he gritted his teeth and proceeded to the water's edge. He had only made his way knee-deep into the foulness when he was overcome by an even stronger, stomach-turning stench that could only be described as raw sewage which brought forth a tide of overwhelming revulsion. Yet somehow Jacob managed to find within himself the strength and will to push forth and wade further out until he stood waist-deep in the wide River where he was again instructed to stretch forth his arms so the palms of his hands rested upon the water's dirty surface.

"Alright…what now?" grumbled Jacob in a tone most unhappy.

"Think of Christopher," came Gotham's answer in a voice at once firm in its command and at the same time percolating with immense sympathy.

The mention of Jacob's childhood friend whose brief life ended tragically when he was struck by a semi-truck while acting a good Samaritan in the commission of trying to save an injured duck he spied flapping about helplessly in the middle of winding rural road caught Jacob off guard.

"You expressed once how you believed you could save your friend when tragedy struck him. Now's your chance," noted the angel. "Better yet, think of your mother. Rest your hands upon them, not the River."

Jacob appeared blank at first, dumbstruck even that such a request would be made of him, but then a look of understanding seemed to sweep over him, one that appeared to give him the spark of optimism that had remained so elusive to him since he was guided down to the River's banks. Once again he closed his eyes and Gotham, after trading a quick look with Anahel, leaned forward anxiously and watched closely the boy. For some time nothing seemed to happen, just as before, but then after what seemed a long angst-filled moment of silence when not even a bird could be heard to tweet, Gotham noticed a most unusual thing. Jacob's veins—first in his hands followed slowly by the tendrils weaving their way up his arms—began to darken and reveal themselves beneath the skin. A blackness began to flow through them sure as blood, and it was as if Jacob's body had suddenly become a sponge and was attempting to absorb the deathly poison choking the River.

A tense, almost disbelieving look settled itself upon Gotham. He soon felt the earth give a brief shudder beneath him, startling him further. It was quickly followed by another and then an even sharper trembling. For several moments the ground rolled and quaked as if stirring from a deep sleep before settling back into silence. Taken aback some, Gotham looked to Jacob who remained fixed with his hands over the water and eyes shut tight as if oblivious to the passing series of quakes. Then came a mighty rumbling in the distant northern edge of the Garden and all eyes turned to the mountains where the waterfalls once reigned supreme. Another roar sounded, as if made by some unseen beast caged within the rock itself stirring, and from it a deluge suddenly burst forth and a thunderous reawakening of water reclaimed its stained path upon the rocks with magnificent splendor.

The reappearance of the falls brought forth a clamor of cheers from the Nephilim and stunned silence from the Guides. For Gotham and Anahel, it was a promising start to a task which remained a long way from being completed, and they returned their attention to the River before them which remained black as the deepest and coldest of nights waiting for the first stirring of ripples to come from the approaching water being spewed from the mountain. When it finally came, Jacob felt the water beneath his hands stir with the swirling of a cool current. Slowly, he opened his eyes and at first both his heart and the look on his face sank with the weight of disappointment when he saw the River remained in its deceased state.

"I tried," he muttered to himself, oblivious to the sound of the reawakened falls. "I swear I tried."

As he removed his hands from the surface, however, he did a double take when he saw the first signs of the blackness begin to crack. It was subtle at first, so much so that Jacob wasn't sure exactly what he was seeing. It began like a drop of condensation leaving a clear trail on a frost-covered window as it trickles down across the pane of glass. Soon what appeared to be tears in the shroud of murky darkness began to form and they gradually grew larger and wider until the blackness was reduced to thin ribbons that were quickly washed downstream.

"It's working!" Jacob gasped in disbelief.

~ ~ ~

Yet while the River once more trickled with the sound of life, he noticed the fish that continued to float lifeless upon its surface, and for a brief moment his perked spirit became dampened. And then he caught sight of the gills of one of the fish begin to move, slowly at first, and then with increased gusto. Its tail soon wriggled with life and with a splash it dove down into the River's depths.

"Did you see that?" Jacob cried out to Gotham and Anahel while pointing to other fish whose gills could be seen undulating with movement. Soon the River was alive with the plopping splashes of the numerous fish, as well as frogs and turtles, as they awoke from their sleep and slid one by one off their watery death beds in schools of little resurrections to disappear beneath the surface.

"They're alive...the fish...the River. They actually came back to life!" Jacob yelled loudly with great excitement while sending up splashes of water into the air with his flailing hands.

The sound of Gotham's wings once more brushed against the air and carried him back across the River to where Anahel stood.

"Well done, Fledgling," said Anahel. "What you have done is no small feat, even for an angel."

The praise was noticeably restrained as was the joy that had returned to the angel's face with the healing of the River. And as Jacob's gaze shifted from Anahel to Gotham, and then to the other Guides standing a short distance away looking more troubled than ever, the pride which had beamed forth unabashedly from his smiling self gradually began to recede. For the subdued expressions staring back at Jacob sent him a wordless reminder of why the River had fallen victim to death's hold in the first place. It was to seek an answer to a most important question. And now that question had been irrefutably answered, for good or bad.

"So now what?" asked Jacob.

Anahel's brow arched itself inquisitively. "What now, indeed? That is the question now upon us, isn't it?" he said. "But for the moment, let us gaze out and watch the River of Life as it turns out its one dark enemy from its tide."

And as they turned and cast their eyes to the south, they could see the dead and stagnant River snaking like a black ribbon through green grasslands and dense forests to the furthest reaches of Eden slowly being revived by the clear renewed flow sweeping its way from upstream. The blackened patches of land creeping outward from the River banks slowly began to recede with the arrival of the fresh water, and the lush grass and plant life overcome by a withering death quickly sprang back to their former glory.

"Keep the memory of this moment tucked inside you. I venture to say you will remember it to be one the easier tasks called upon you," Anahel said to Jacob, as the sound of cheering could be heard coming from the other Nephilim racing along the River bank toward them.

CHAPTER FIVE

By the next day, the River flowed clear and alive with no sign Azrael had ever kneeled at its banks. Yet where the River had washed itself clean of the stilling black death which had infected its tranquil waters, a newfound gloom seemed to settle itself over Jacob. He became visibly troubled and withdrawn, and decided to shrug off going to his classes despite the cautious objections of his roommates who he asked to lie to the Guides, should they inquire about his absence, and tell them he was feeling under the weather.

"They're not going to like it," warned Max. "This isn't like back home where you can skip class every now and then when you're not in the mood to hear about the Spanish-American War or dissecting 'The Odyssey' line by line."

The consequences of his truancy were the last thing on Jacob's mind as he watched until the other Shrikes were out of sight as they hurried on their way to the Crescent Scar before he and Mist headed off in the opposite direction toward Broken Earth. Only there was he assured the distance and solitude he sought to be alone with his conflicted thoughts and attempt to make some semblance of sense to the unexpected twist his life had taken. Yet sometimes, as he sat staring out over the gaping ravine watching a tide of clouds stream in from the Northern Lands and spill into the vast open void of space like an immense waterfall of white, misty vapor, the solitude which Jacob had sought in the high reaches of the mountain was often intense company.

Now and then, when the voices dueling inside Jacob's head grew intolerably loud against the blaring silence, he would allow himself a moment of distraction by toying with his new-found talents whether it was spinning his finger over the ground to conjure up a whirlwind that would dance around him before spinning itself right off the ledge and dissipating in a cloud of dirt and dust, or changing his shape into different creatures from the animal kingdom as though trying on a new outfit while Mist looked on with her head curiously tilting from side to side watching the unusual performance. Jacob couldn't deny it was fun and exciting experimenting with these wondrous Graces, and he would readily admit, if only to himself, the empowering feeling he experienced knowing he possessed all seven of them. Mostly, though, his momentary demonstrations were to reassure himself he did possess them, and that what was happening was, in fact, real and not, as he once tried to explain away, a fluke.

"I'm glad to see you are at least exercising and not at leisure in the cool shade of a tree."

Startled, Jacob spun around at the sound of the familiar voice and found a mythic-looking figure perched high on a nearby crop of rock with wings outstretched and silhouetted against the brilliant light of the sun.

"Anahel!" he said with surprise in his voice. "How long have you been there?"

"Long enough to check the sharp scolding eager to lash forth from my tongue," the angel replied coolly. With a flap of his great wings he came down off the rock and landed feather-like on the ground.

"I guess you're wondering what I'm doing up here instead of in class," said Jacob, knowing all too well some kind of reprimand was about to befall him.

"An explanation would be nice," said Anahel, "but I reckon I already know the reason."

"So, who was it who decided to squeal on me?" asked Jacob sourly.

"Well, Fledgling, you are having yourself a red-letter day, aren't you. First, playing hooky, and now questioning the loyalty of your friends," said Anahel. "But if you must know, it was Zuriel who came to me earlier wondering if there was some reason he was unaware of as to why you were not in class today. Needless to say I was even more surprised when I went to Thaniel to inquire about your whereabouts only to find out you were absent his class the day before as well."

Jacob felt his face redden for jumping to the conclusion his friends had ratted him out.

"I'm sorry, I didn't mean to have you searching all over Eden for me."

"Believe it or not, this is the first place I chose to look, as I had a hunch this is where I would find you," said Anahel, sighing heavily as he took a seat on the ground beside Jacob and cast his eyes out over the daunting abyss stretched before them. "Strange is it not, for one seeking comfort to be drawn to the one place which, for you at least, is anything but comfortable?"

They sat together in silence for some time basking in the tranquility that seemed to ripple unseen about them like the edges of a calm lake lapping gently the shores enclosed around it. The afternoon sunlight was beginning to thin and deepen with an orange tint signaling the throes of its waning hours were fast approaching. Ragged shadows cast from the surrounding cliffs began to grow and slowly slink their way across the mountains.

"You know, Jacob, you cannot hide from what's settled itself upon you," said Anahel finally.

"I'm not hiding!" Jacob shot back defensively as if he had expected such an assertion to be lobbed at him. "It's just...everything was coming at me at an overwhelming pace. I just needed some space to breath...and to think things out. I don't know...this just reminds me of a place back home where I used to go frequently to unwind and be alone with my thoughts."

"I imagine them to be quite jumbled at the moment, hmm?" Anahel, in his wise, knowing way, inquired. "You are not the first—nor do I expect the last—who has come to discover that hidden away within the beauty and wonder found in plenty here is an equally overwhelming presence that can prove confusing and, yes, even taxing. You think the other Fledglings have a leg up over you, and in some regards I guess they do. They grew up knowing who and what their fathers are, and in turn who they themselves would eventually become. They've been groomed for this moment in their lives. But in the end they are each one a child of man, and as such are not immune to the struggles that oftentimes arise from the life they grew up knowing through mortal eyes and the jarring reality which exists here in this place—in this Eden."

"You're not really suggesting what I'm dealing with at this moment is anything remotely close to what anyone else here has faced, are you?" asked Jacob.

The boy's directness caused Anahel to smile.

"I suppose that would be reaching, wouldn't it? No, what you now find yourself struggling with is something of a most unique nature," said Anahel. "It can be quite discombobulating to realize the dream one thinks he is treading while waiting to awaken is, in fact, no dream at all. The problem you face, however, is mistaking the dream in which you now find yourself immersed to be something in the shape of a nightmare."

"Well…isn't it? A nightmare, I mean?" asked Jacob. "Because it sure feels like one to me."

"Only if you allow it to become one," answered Anahel.

Jacob opened his mouth, then immediately closed it again, drawing silent for several moments as Anahel looked on patiently as he watched the boy struggle to carefully choose his next words before his lips parted once more.

"Do you remember the night of the Illumination…when you told us we had the choice to stay here and continue with our training, or go back home, without any shame, and live life as we did before coming here?" asked Jacob.

A troubled look of concern slowly descended upon Anahel.

"You want to leave?"

"I think with everything that's happened it would be best…at least for me."

Anahel became still as a stone before looking off into the distance and leaving Jacob feeling as if he'd somehow offended—or worse, wounded—the angel with some unintentional insult.

"So…I was mistaken about you," said Anahel, finally. "You're not hiding; you're flat out running."

"That's not true," Jacob shot back.

"No? Then what pray tell would you call it?"

Jacob became stymied, as if his tongue had suddenly enlarged itself by three times inside his mouth.

"I don't know...how about trying to wake up from this dream, as you call it, that I don't care to be in anymore for starters?" said Jacob. "I just...I can't make myself understand any of this. I mean, why me?"

"Maybe the better question is, why not you?" countered Anahel.

Jacob was in no mood for ponderous philosophical banter, and his agitated state that had been bottled up inside him since the morning he found himself doing things no mere Nephilim should be capable of doing by breathing life into the River made murky and dark with death made him suddenly leap to his feet in desperate frustration.

"Look at me," he cried out stretching his arms out wide. "Would anyone ever mistake me for being this...this...Light Bearer I have suddenly been deemed to be?"

"You tell me," argued Anahel. "What do you envision the Light Bearer to look like?"

"For starters, someone with wings," cried Jacob, stepping dangerously close to the ledge of the sheer cliff and staring down into the wide gulf of emptiness at his feet. "Do you know for the past two days that I've come up here, I've stood right here just as I am now praying while teetering on this very edge that I might find whatever it is I lack to take that less than half a step jump? And I cannot do it, no matter how much I want to or how hard I try. And it's not because I'm afraid of heights. I can't tell you how many times I've made similar jumps back home. Granted I had a parachute strapped to my back. But supposedly I have something even better than a parachute on my back, only last time it failed me and refused to open."

Anahel could see the visible angst overwhelming the boy and he rose to his feet.

"Yes, I'm quite aware of your first experience jumping from this ledge," said the angel. "Of course, Eksel didn't much help matters, did he? But give yourself some credit, Fledgling; at least you have not let what was a terrifying experience keep you from returning to this spot and attempt to face down the fear that holds your feet fast to the mountain beneath them."

"Big deal. A coward is a coward is a coward," said Jacob. "If I can't find the courage to take one step, how can I even begin to accept and be at peace with this burden which now rests on my shoulders?"

"Be careful not to mistake courage with faith, Fledgling. Courage serves to guide one's hand to un-sheath his sword against a foe far greater than himself. That you've plenty of, as I've seen it brimming in copious amounts deep within your eyes on more than one occasion. What guides one without pause into the heart of darkness with only a solitary light offering its protection against the tempest is something entirely different that many claim to have and very few possess," said Anahel with a narrowing of his brow. "A very difficult thing to fully embrace, faith is. If it were not the case, the mortal world would be teeming with it. Even within some of us who have looked into the face of God, it has run dry. That is why they call it blind, and that is how it will come to you Fledgling. In time."

"How can you be so sure?" asked Jacob.

"Because, Jacob, in that *I* have faith," replied Anahel with a serene smile. And it was within his eyes aflame in twin pools of molten gold that Jacob caught an inexplicable glimmer which sent through him a tingling warmth of comfort, and even a sense of confidence that what Anahel said was true.

A familiar high-pitched screech wailed in the distance drawing Jacob's attention to the sky above where he saw what had become the familiar sight of the snake eagle whose sole intent seemed to keep him in its watchful eyes hovering in circles above.

"So I guess what you're saying is I'm saddled with this Light Bearer thing either way, right?" he asked as his gaze continued to follow the eagle's flight.

"Saddled, as you so put it, yes, I suppose," said Anahel. "Of course, what I offered the night of the Illumination applies to you as well. You have the option to turn your back and refuse that which is your destiny. You can go about a life you began when you were first brought into the world, and the prophesy detailed in the Apocrypha will quietly die with you. But so, too, will any hope for the world of man to escape perishing in the Dragon's smothering shadow when he eventually emerges from his lair."

"Well then…so long as there is no unneeded pressure or guilt placed on me," Jacob remarked sarcastically. Finally, after kicking at the ground with his feet, he looked again to Anahel and offered a somewhat defeated shrug of his shoulders. "Looks like I don't have much of a choice."

"Choice is the one gift we've all been handed," countered Anahel. "The question is whether the decision you ultimately choose is one you can live out the rest of your days at peace for making."

Jacob looked again to the sky to the circling eagle, and even though the chorus of voices he had been wrestling with continued to sound off inside his head, they had become noticeably quieter and much less urgent.

"You know, I have a strange feeling that eagle has been following me," said Jacob, pointing to the majestic creature gliding effortlessly upon the breeze seen ruffling through its outstretched wings. "My mom used to tell me if each person in life paid close attention they'd realize a particular bird was always shadowing them no matter where they went or what they did. She said they were called Beacons; and their job was to watch over a certain soul from the time they were born until the moment they died. Then they'd guide that soul to Heaven."

"An enlightened woman, your mother," said Anahel, and as he held the boy in his contemplative gaze he found his own struggling doubts concerning Jacob and the most questionable fate that had been handed down to the boy had begun to recede. In fact, for the first time, he found himself ashamed he had ever quietly questioned Heaven's wisdom on the matter.

"Come," he said stretching his hand toward the boy. "I wish to show you something."

~ ~ ~

Anahel's wings once again unfolded, and began to beat against the air lifting Anahel and Jacob up off the ground. They flew high over the yawning mouth of the mountain gorge where the misty clouds settled deep below had begun to stir and rise up from the bottomless abyss in wafts of smoky whiteness like awakening spirits taking to the sky. And for the first time, Jacob was finally able to look down into the ravine in a way his feet—and will—had refused him.

Over the gorge they flew to the highlands on the other side, climbing higher and higher skyward until they reached one of the towering peaks. There they came to rest and Jacob was greeted with an endless plain of mountains stretching far to the north for as far as the eye could follow. Yet the view, while breathtaking in scope, was immediately greeted by a strangely curious fix from Jacob's eyes. Perhaps because it was the only place he'd looked upon in Eden since his arrival which revealed a scar to its beauty.

Greened with clusters of trees scaling the sleeping behemoths of rock and whose peaks were capped with snow and ice, the mountains were almost sea-like, rolling along endlessly to the far-off horizon where they met the sky. Yet the further away the eye followed them, the more unappealing they appeared. The trees and other signs of life clinging to them slowly withered from sight leaving behind only bare rock, marred and desolate and encased in a frozen tundra of a bitter and endless winter. In many ways, it was like bearing witness to the face of a beautiful woman succumbing to the cruel ravages of age.

"It's known as the Barrens, the Northern Lands forbidden to all to enter," said Anahel.

"The Barrens," repeated Jacob. "I'm not sure I see a reason to deem it forbidden. I don't know why anyone would be inclined to want to step foot there. It doesn't seem at all hospitable. I'm surprised something so unappealing even exists in Eden."

"It doesn't," said Anahel. "What you gaze upon lies outside its borders. It is where Paradise ends and the pit which houses the Darkness begins."

The angel's words made Jacob's eyes widen and, perhaps fearfully, he refrained from speaking the four-letter name more commonly used to refer to the place where the fires of damnation burned, especially while standing within eyeshot.

"I don't have to rest my hand upon your shoulder to know you tremble, and understandably. Eyes more steeled than yours have flinched at the sight of these two realms residing so close to one another, like a husband and wife sleeping side by side," said Anahel.

The angel wandered ahead to the edge of the precipitous cliff upon which they stood. And even though it was but a few steps, the small gap of distance made Jacob uncomfortable while staring out into the far-off distance where he imagined countless lost souls writhing in pain in the fiery confines of the prison hidden from sight somewhere in the bowels of the deadened landscape.

"It is a fine line which separates Heaven from Hell; or as it is better known here, the Underneath," said Anahel. "And while the distance between the two may appear greater, it is but just a step; one that cannot be retraced with the same ease with which it's taken. If any words from my lips were to seed themselves in your memory, may it be those I have just spoken."

Jacob couldn't help but think of Gotham's son David at that very moment, knowing his own end came after venturing inside the forbidden border he was now gazing out over.

"Are you saying you fear I may take that step? Betray Eden?" asked Jacob, his voice noting offense.

The angel seemed hesitant in answering the question, at first.

"The Darkness has a way of swallowing mortals whole. Angels, as well," he said quietly.

"It will not swallow me," Jacob replied in a tone both firm and defiant.

The angel, however, looked back over his shoulder and leveled an unsettling look upon the boy.

"It will try," he said without pause, and the three simple words which settled themselves upon Jacob's shoulders as both threat and promise made the boy swallow nervously.

Anahel then turned away from the cliff and came toward the boy. "I say this not to trouble you, but to lend warning. It is a daunting and perilous road you will eventually venture down as both hunter and hunted, of that you can be certain. And it is here your journey is destined to eventually return you."

The angel moved behind Jacob placing his hands on the boy's shoulders. And as the two looked out into the vastness before them, Anahel leaned down and continued speaking his words into Jacob's ear. "A day is fast approaching when the hounds of darkness caged deep within those dead hills will be unchained and set loose and the skies will turn red from the heat of the Dragon's breath. When that time comes to pass, you will find yourself standing once more where your feet are now planted. What you look upon now is poised to become your battlefield. But know you will meet it with all the power of Heaven, and legions of angel and man will be at your back."

"I don't know if this is your attempt at making me more at ease with all this," said Jacob somewhat meekly, "but you should probably know it's actually having the completely opposite effect."

Anahel smiled and circled back around the boy until they stood face to face. "Only because you lack the confidence needed for one who stands in your shoes. Changing that will be our first order of business as we push forward."

"And how exactly do you plan on doing that?"

Anahel paused a moment in thought. "For starters, a strenuous training program; one I would heartily propose to begin as soon as possible."

"Correct me if I'm wrong, but isn't that what I've been doing with the Guides since I got here?" asked Jacob.

"You've been training to become a Nephilim," answered Anahel. "Now it's time for you to train as the Light Bearer you are, and in doing so become learned in a heightened set of skills. And while the Guides are masters of their craft, you will require the guidance of one unmatched in his expertise and abilities."

"You?" guessed Jacob.

"I thank you for even entertaining the notion, Fledgling," Anahel replied with a grin. "No, the one I had in mind has already proven himself more than capable for such a task. And let me assure you now, he will not be one to test with truancy."

Whoever Anahel had in mind he did not let on, but it was quite apparent from the grin he tried to hide the idea tickled him leaving Jacob to wonder all the more what he was in for as the two headed back across Broken Earth and down to the more pleasant hospitalities awaiting at Havenhid.

CHAPTER SIX

TRAINING A LIGHT BEARER

The next day when Jacob came trudging out of Lions Bite with Mist at his heel sweaty and spent from an especially exhaustive day of sword play and physical combat with his fellow Shrikes, he found Gotham waiting for him in the shade of a giant soursop tree with its prickly looking fruit hanging from its branches overhead like strange, whimsical-looking Christmas tree ornaments.

"Come, and follow me!" the angel instructed the boy.

Without knowing the where, or the why, Jacob took after Gotham, shadowing his footsteps south through the lush landscape of the Garden while the other boys continued along the path that followed in the direction of the west-drifting sun toward Havenhid.

Gotham and Jacob walked without words for several miles, passing through brief patches of forest that now and again encroached on the open grass land whose borders it shaped. They soon came upon the River and walked along its bending banks, crossing over gentle slopes of green through which the clear flow of water had carved out its serpentine path. The loud screeching cries of ovenbirds competed loudly with one another, filling the foliage of the surrounding trees with their avian symphony. Mist's crystal eyes reflected the birds' flitting movements, watching keenly as they dove from the tree tops, buzzed playfully past the great wolf before taking wing in a skimming glide across the River's surface.

It wasn't long before the land began to bow down in rows of ever-deepening slopes and the chatter from the feathered creatures began to recede, being drowned out by the growing roar of the River. The calm, peaceful flow of the water suddenly quickened. The currents began pounding like a stampede of spooked stallions, racing around and over boulders of protruding rock along the channel and sending the water cascading downward in the form of numerous waterfalls in its surging descent to Eden's lower valley where a renewed calm awaited. There, Gotham led Jacob to a large tree rooted at the River's bank, its branches stretched wide over the water. Nearby on the ground was seen a long wooden pole fashioned from an arm of the tree, and tethered to both ends of it by thick, strong vines were hefty blocks of rock.

"Take it up," instructed Gotham, "and rest it across your shoulders."

Jacob stared blankly at the strange, medieval object and then at Gotham.

"And why exactly?"

"If you have any hopes of going up against malevolent forces that is the Darkness and coming out the other side intact, there is much you still have to learn, beginning with the basics, which rests on the ground in front of you," answered Gotham.

It was then Jacob realized the teacher Anahel had spoken of the day before at Broken Earth was Gotham.

"You're going to train me?"

"Anahel convinced me it would be in your best interest if I were take on the role, yes," said Gotham. "Unless of course you have reservations."

"No, no, of course not...I think it's great!" said Jacob quickly. "It's just..."

"Just what?"

"I've been training all day already, and Damiel really put us through the paces. To tell you the truth, I'm kinda beat."

A sadistic kind of grin found Gotham.

"Merely a warm up to your real training, which starts now," he said. And before Jacob could whine any further of his exhaustion the angel again instructed the boy to pick up the rock-laden branch.

~ ~ ~

Jacob sounded a tired groan as he picked up the branch. After a bit of a struggle to get the contraption resting across his back behind his neck, and looking none too comfortable in the process, he looked to Gotham for further instruction and found the angel pointing to a low-lying branch of the tree stretched out over the River which Jacob then clumsily managed to maneuver his way out onto until he stood over the water. Moving just his eyeballs for fear any other movement might upset his already delicate balance, he glanced down to find the tree limb upon which he was precariously perched to be extremely narrow; so narrow he questioned at first whether it would eventually snap and send him plunging headfirst into the River. It was a fleeting worry when almost immediately he realized the more pressing concern lied with his own footing as he quickly found it wasn't the weight of the rocks hanging from either end of the branch laid across his back that caused him strain, but the struggle in retaining his balance

"From Damiel, you have learned how to wield a sword, and quite well," said Gotham after a while of watching the weighted rod teeter on the youngster's back like a shifting scale. "However, to be a truly impressive warrior takes more than just strength. Balance—and more importantly focus—go hand in hand with one's blade. A lack of either would most certainly assure you defeat."

It didn't take long before Jacob's face reddened and became awash in multiplying beads of sweat. His legs began to quiver and burn with a fire that was only matched by the flames in his arms. Keeping his body straight and still grew more and more difficult until, finally, it took every ounce of strength he could muster to keep from toppling over one way or the other and plunging below into the waiting River. Glancing out of the corner of his eye, he saw there was no immediate sign from Gotham that he would soon call him off the tree limb, for he had relaxed himself on the soft grass beneath the cool shade of the tree.

"How much longer do I have to do this?" Jacob, unable to camouflage the breathless strain heard in his voice, eventually inquired.

"Until you look sturdy enough to survive, at the very least, a light spring breeze from sending you off your mount and into the bath that's waiting for you below, Light Bearer," answered the angel.

"In case you forgot, I've been training my butt off every day for I don't know how many months now. I think it's fair to say it's going to take a little more than a breeze to send me over," grumbled Jacob through clenched teeth before adding gruffly, "And don't call me that name."

With that a devilish grin came to Gotham's face. Pursing his lips together he blew forth his breath in Jacob's direction and it took the form of a gentle gust of wind. The leaves of the tree soon stirred and flapped about in the breeze. Jacob's teetering immediately became more pronounced until his body swayed too far to one side for him to correct, and his feet, shuffling wildly, slipped from the branch and sent him careening down into the River with a splash.

When he surfaced, he found much to his chagrin Gotham momentarily lost to laughter. Even Mist, who was sitting nearby on the bank watching intently, looked to be tickled at the sight.

"So you think it's funny, too?" questioned Jacob with mock offense to which Mist offered up an enthusiastic and gleeful bark in return. "Traitor!"

"You can hardly fault her. I suspect she might have thought you were trying to regale us with a friendly game of charades," Gotham snickered. "I for one thought you captured perfectly the grace of a spooked bullfrog charging belly-first into the water, albeit with a far more joy-filled-sounding splash."

"Ha, ha...very funny," Jacob mumbled sourly under his breath in his best—though unintentional—Ethan impersonation while doing his best to hide his embarrassment.

"Alright then, Light Bearer," said Gotham as he worked to make straight his face once more, "shake yourself off and climb back upon your lily pad where hopefully you can redeem yourself or, if it so pleases you, entertain those of us who remain dry with more bumbling animal imitations."

Unamused, Jacob remained where he stood, immersed in the River, looking more like an overgrown drowned rat than water-loving amphibian.

"Can you explain something to me?" he asked finally. "Why that name?"

"What name?"

"Light Bearer. Ever since I first heard it when Johiel explained the Apocrypha that night on Akdamar Island, there was something…I don't know…oddly familiar about it," said Jacob. "It finally came to me when I remembered something from when I used to attend Bible studies when I was younger: Lucifer."

"Lucifer," repeated Gotham while showing no sign he was quite following the boy.

"The name the devil was originally known by before he rebelled against God and fell and became, you know…Satan," said Jacob. "If I remember correctly, the name Lucifer translated from Latin to mean 'light bearer' or—"

"The bringer of light," Gotham was quick to finish.

The boy was a smart one, of that there was no doubt.

"You're right about the name. But the creation of Lucifer was one spawned by man not Heaven, that I can assure you," continued the angel. "How or why such a bestowment of a moniker and all of the irony woven into it came to be, I could not tell you. Man has always had an attraction to extremes. Or, perhaps, it was an effort on the part of the dark powers to foul the wind of prophesy long before it took its first breath. But this I can tell you: The one who would become the Dragon was no more a bearer of Light than the sands of a dry desert could be the bearer of a cool, flowing spring to a man parched by thirst. A creature of the night, that one was and always will be, and as such bears as much light as one would find warming the dark side of the moon."

It seemed a simple enough explanation, but the truth was Jacob found the immense amount of prophecies and biblical history he'd had to confront and dissect since coming to Eden far too riddled with riddles and hidden meanings to fully grasp and comprehend. Still, he gave Gotham a slow nod of understanding and proceeded to fish out of the water the weighted balancing instrument that had sent him toppling off the tree limb stretched out above him and into the River.

"Let's give this another go, shall we?" Gotham suggested with a faintly wicked grin once Jacob had emerged soaked and dripping with the despised device in hand and looking none too happy to attempt a repeat performance.

~ ~ ~

And so began an intensive regimen Jacob would find himself following under Gotham's tutelage. With the Guides, he continued his regimen as he normally would. Then, at day's end, when the other boys would be left the few remaining hours of daylight free from their studies to engage in the mindless fun and play demanded of most energetic adolescents their age, Jacob would find Gotham patiently waiting for him.

One day, when Jacob reached the bottom of the pathway which wound its way up the mountain to the Crescent Scar, he found Gotham mounted on the back of a Snowdrift stallion. Looking around, he saw there was no sign of any of the other horses from the herd.

"Where's mine?" he asked.

"You won't be needing one for what we'll be doing today," answered Gotham. And with that he gave the white horse a gentle nudge to its side with his heel and the neighing beast launched into a full gallop leaving Jacob in a passing cloud of kicked-up dirt and the sharp command of the angel's voice trailing over his shoulder to follow.

They raced at great speeds across Eden's vast open lands, ducking into patches of forest and clearing streams of different sizes which had veered off vein-like from the River. The steed upon which Gotham rode moved with a swiftness and speed which made it appear almost phantom-like. And struggling to keep up with a growing gap of distance separating them was Jacob. When they reached the base of a rather steep mountain side, there was no pause. The horse's hooves pounded their way unrelentingly up a narrow winding path carved into the side of the granite and shale behemoth before it. With his lungs on the brink of collapsing, Jacob persevered onward until he was greeted with the sight of the mountain summit and the horse upon which Gotham rode, motionless and still.

"Not too bad," the angel offered, "For a first try."

"What do you mean first try?" Jacob managed to heave. "How many times do I have to do this?"

"Until you reach this summit before this horse does," the angel replied matter-of-factly.

Other days, the angel would lead the way on a long, yet much less tiring, walk to a pocket of green, wind-swept meadowland tucked away in a secluded recess of the Garden. There the peaceful roar of rushing water coming from the River in its descent to the lower-lying yonder Valley served as a buffer to any distraction that might steal Jacob's concentration as he was put through what he found to be the most intense part of his training: developing his seven Graces. The days spent at Crescent Scar had become something Jacob had particularly looked forward to in his curricular schedule in Eden. And while Zuriel could be a difficult teacher, Jacob had come to enjoy learning how to use his newfound abilities. It was not the same enjoyable experience he looked forward to under Gotham's thumb, and it soon became the one part of his training Jacob came to detest most. The rigorous, and often times draining, sessions more often than not left him frustrated and doubting his own capabilities. Then again, Gotham's tactics were designed not for the common Nephilim, but for the one destined to one day take lead of them all. His goal was simple: to help the boy hone his amazing gifts into an arsenal of celestial weaponry. In his eyes, Graces weren't just tools which allowed one to perform impressive feats, but raw steel to be hammered and sharpened into the shape of invisible lances. Forging such weaponry, however, was far from simplistic.

The hours were long.

The days grueling.

And the painstaking patience required from both angel and student were stretched to the breaking point on more than one occasion. Frustrations mounted for both, but none so much than for Jacob. When he wasn't silently cursing his failure to perform as instructed, he found himself begrudging in a most potent and feral way Gotham's turn at becoming a relentless taskmaster. And his resentments only grew when his keen hearing picked up the sounds of carefree fun and freedom coming from his friends at the other end of the Garden as they were released from their day's lessons. Jacob's grumbling grew especially sour one particular day after forty seemingly eternal minutes of standing before a towering oak tree with his hands pressed against its trunk. What point was there in being in paradise, a world outside his own—in this case a heaven—only to be held to a grindstone of constant study? And worse, being shackled to this winged slavedriver of a teacher.

While Jacob kept his grumblings of frustration confined to an angry echo inside his head, it did not escape Gotham's attentive ears.

"I didn't bring you to Eden so you could vacation and lollygag in the sun," Gotham remarked as he slowly circled Jacob with a patient pace.

"Lollygag," mocked Jacob under his breath with a roll of his eyes.

"You can rest assure this has been no day at the beach for me neither," said Gotham. "But I intend to help you transition successfully into your new role, as it has been asked of me."

"Even if it kills me," muttered Jacob sarcastically.

"You can gladly have at that disdain and contempt you hold for me now," said Gotham as he continued circling Jacob and the tree he faced with growing disdain. "Perhaps it will aid you in your concentration, of which you sorely lack."

Jacob said nothing. His face masked with great tension and frustration became suddenly even more intense. His gaze narrowed, burning its focus into the scaled armor of bark until finally the rim of his glaring pupils erupted and glimmered with circling flashes of light. Jacob felt his breath catch itself suddenly in his throat when the tree suddenly began to creak and groan. Its massive roots snaking along the ground began to stir with movement before starting a slow retreat from deep within the earth in which they were burrowed. At the same time, the tree itself appeared to retract its outstretched branches and began to shrink in size. Instinct made Jacob want to jump backward, but Gotham was quick to coax the boy in keeping his hands firmly in place against the trunk and retain his concentration. Smaller and smaller the tree became, surrendering in a matter of seconds a supremacy of height and stature that had taken centuries for it to cultivate. When it finally vanished from sight, a look of disbelief came to Jacob's face. Standing frozen in his place afraid to move a muscle, even slightly, he turned his eyes to his hands, which had come together prayer-like. Slowly he opened them and his eyes widened at the sight of a single acorn found tucked away in his palms.

"I did it," he gasped in an incredulous whisper. Then turning to Gotham he held out his hand to reveal the seed of what had seconds before been a giant of the Forest and again exclaimed, "Look, I actually did it!"

"And so you did," said the angel with an approving nod.

"Amazing," mumbled Jacob staring wide-eyed at the acorn.

"What's so hard to believe? A boy who resurrected the River of Life from the clutches of Death is now awestruck at his ability to return a tree to the brink of its birth?"

Gotham then motioned to Jacob to pick up his sword and follow him out to the middle of the grassy meadow.

"What was the point?" asked Jacob.

"The point?"

"Of doing this," said Jacob, holding up the seedling before carefully tucking it away in his shirt pocket.

"To demonstrate that you can," answered Gotham. "You might do well by yourself in remembering this moment the next time you pay a visit to Broken Earth."

A light came on in Jacob's eyes. "Ah, I get it. This has to do about my wings, or my obvious lack of, doesn't it? Well, you're mistaken about what it is you're thinking."

"And what exactly is that?"

"You don't think I have the faith needed to get them."

"Then tell me," argued Gotham, "where are they? Why do you continue to lack what all the other Fledglings now have?"

"Look, I tried, alright," Jacob, who was becoming more flustered, answered. "I made the jump off Broken Earth. On the first day. And nothing happened. No wings, almost no rescue, just lots and lots of falling."

"So you've sat on the sidelines ever since," noted Gotham.

"Better than fulfilling my destiny at becoming a bloodstain at the bottom of Broken Earth while Eksel and his so-called life preservers with wings looked on," argued Jacob.

"Hmm…" Gotham muttered in reply as he quietly turned on his heel and walked off.

"What's that supposed to mean?" asked Jacob, trailing after him.

"All I said was 'hmm'."

"Yeah, but there was so much to that 'hmm'."

"Just something I've come to notice about you, that's all."

"What's that?"

"How truly fleeting your faith is," answered Gotham. "Oh, it's present, what there is of it. But when it fails to materialize in the precise manner you wish it to, when you wish it to, oh then how easily you throw it aside."

"That's not true!" balked Jacob.

Even before Jacob could finish, the angel stopped suddenly in is tracks and turned to face the boy. He then reached into his pocket and pulled from it something that immediately and abruptly silenced Jacob from uttering any further denial. It was a rosary. Not just any old rosary, but one which had once belonged to his mother; the same one Jacob had thrown blindly into a rain-soaked meadow in a fit of rage and sorrow the morning he learned she had died.

"That's my rosary," Jacob said in disbelief. "How did you…"

He didn't need to bother finishing with his question. Nor did he pull back his arm when Gotham returned the rosary to the palm of his hand.

"The key to your survival against the Darkness—to the survival of any Nephilim—rests not only in the knowledge of what you can do, but more so in that which you cannot, and then, with that knowledge at hand, continuing onward in a forward march toward whatever obstacle resides in your way, no matter the danger or fear you feel gnawing away at your insides, because you have blindly put the safeguarding of your being completely and wholly in the hands of divine providence. For in your mind, and more importantly in your heart, you've come to know without question such faith, blind as it may be, is the keyhole to the door leading to sanctuary, particularly in the face of defeat by death," said Gotham. "Only then will you truly come into the light illuminating your existence."

As he spoke, Gotham's golden eyes stared deeply into those of Jacob. "Always remember, the Light Bearer is not simply born, he is made."

Suddenly the boy began to understand, and the frustration and resentment that had built up inside him began to disappear along with the puzzled look on his face.

"Can I ask you a question?" he asked the angel somewhat hesitantly. "Where do you get yours…faith, that is? I mean, after all you've gone through between what led to your Fall and what happened to your son; I would think you'd be royally pissed off at God."

Gotham smiled slightly before his expression sank somewhat as if it was the first time he ever pondered such a question.

"There was a time when I spent many a day and night royally pissed off at God, as you so tactfully put it," said Gotham after a short moment of quiet reflection. "But he is my father, and I am his son. And while sons are often times given to moments of anger at the ones who brought them into the world, the love that binds the two is absolute. Such a bond is not absent with me.

"Even if it were," he continued, after a reflective pause, "I know what is right and what is wrong, and I have looked into the heart of darkness and have witnessed the cold decay of the insidious malevolence it holds. No amount of anger or hate could ever see forth my allegiance, or even blind eye, to the maelstrom of evil that seeks to snuff out the light of salvation. Even if my face is to forever be denied the warmth of such light."

~ ~ ~

Again, Gotham called for Jacob to pick up his sword. "The day has only a few more gasps of breath left before it surrenders to the coming twilight."

Jacob grabbed his sword which rested amid the blades of soft, feathery grass.

"I guess now would be a good time to say I'm sorry for being a bit of a pill since we started coming here," he said when Gotham unsheathed his sword and began twirling it in his hand. The blade became a blur, much like a started propeller of an airplane, and it cut through the air with a deadly whoosh of sound.

"A bit?" answered Gotham, curiously raising an eyebrow.

"Alright, alright, the whole bitter pill," Jacob conceded.

They came together, crossed blades and a duel instantly ignited between the two. With an impressive showing, Jacob managed to fend off the angel's incoming jousts as well as stay one step ahead of his lightning-quick moves. The impressed look which found itself upon Gotham's face was not one of surprise but pride.

"Damiel has taught you well," remarked Gotham after being caught off guard more than a few times by Jacob's own surprising cat-like reflexes.

"So have you," said Jacob. "As frustrating as it has been, I kinda wish I would have started coming out here and learning what I needed to from you from the beginning. Heck, I didn't even know I could do that thing with the tree."

"Do not devalue what the Guides have taught you," said Gotham. "Theirs is a way steeped in success which has turned out many a Nephilim warrior."

"And yours?"

"Truth be told, this is one of the rare instances my services have been so summoned."

They continued to circle one another, each lunging now and again to bring a loud clang ringing from their swords when the blades met and tempered steel brushed against tempered steel.

"How come?" pressed Jacob.

"You tend to forget I'm Fallen."

"It doesn't seem to be an issue here."

"My brothers, for the most part, have remained most accepting of me. But I am Fallen, and that is something that is never forgotten, nor completely overlooked," explained Gotham. "I'm also known a bit too well for my penchant for not believing in rules. It comes from living amongst mortals—as well as other Fallen—for as long as I have. As a result, I'm looked upon as a liability, for lack of a better word."

"Anahel doesn't seem to think so," said Jacob.

Gotham gave a knowing smile. Lowering his sword, he stood quiet for a moment in front of the boy.

"Anahel has always been a big believer of rebirth," said the angel as he stretched forth his hand, reached inside Jacob's shirt pocket and retrieved the seedling tucked away inside. Holding it up gently between his forefinger and thumb, he studied it for a moment in the waning glow of the golden light surrounding them. "In a way, so am I."

And with that he tossed the seedling over his shoulder toward the Forest and when it hit the ground there was a thunderous, ground-jolting rumble as the oak hidden inside immediately shot forth toward the sky, unfurled its bushy limbs and rooted itself back into the earth where it had previously stood. Jacob stood spellbound, unsure which was the more dazzling to witness; squeezing the mammoth tree back into its seed or seeing its release.

"Everything changes now, doesn't it?" he muttered quietly.

Gotham turned and followed Jacob's gaze which was locked unblinking on the tree, but he knew it was not of the tree of which the boy was speaking.

"Such is the inevitability of life," answered Gotham with a sigh. "It changed the day I came to you in Cain's Corner and revealed to you who I was, and more importantly who you were. Rest assured sharper turns lie further down your path."

For the first time, words offered by the angel which usually brought comfort to Jacob in times of uncertainty failed to do just that. Even more so, they appeared to bring a noticeable heaviness to Gotham.

"What is it?" asked Jacob.

"What is what?"

"You seem…I don't know…more on edge today, even for you. Something bothering you?"

"It's nothing," answered Gotham dismissively.

"My mom used to tell me holding things in just causes the rest of your insides to curdle, like a carton of spoiled milk," pressed Jacob. "But I get it. You're probably not comfortable confiding your problems in some kid."

The angel eyed the boy knowingly. "I can see you've also adopted your grandmother's ways."

"What do you mean?"

"She also used a similar kind of bait whenever she went fishing for answers."

Gotham knew Jacob well enough to know he would not leave the issue lie there. He also knew he would have to sit the boy down before too long and discuss exactly what he was mulling in his head, and now was as good as time as any.

"Anahel came to see me this morning," he began. "After quietly observing your progress these past few weeks, he's decided it's time for your Blessing."

"Blessing…what's that?"

"A ceremony of sorts where you would be officially recognized as the Light Bearer."

"You mean like a coronation?"

"Coronations are for kings, and the head which sits upon your shoulders is hardly built for the weight of a crown," replied Gotham sternly. "Better for you to think of it more as a second baptism of sorts."

"Blessing," muttered Jacob under his breath before noting a heaviness in Gotham's face which offered the impression of a certain bitterness that existed inside such a sweet-sounding word.

"I take it you're not happy about this."

Never one to allow his inner torments to rise the surface when he could help it, Gotham was quick to shake off his visible angst. "It's nothing."

"You once called me a bad liar," said Jacob, "but, if you don't mind me saying, you're not so stellar in that department yourself."

"Baptisms are a wonderful thing," said Gotham in a quiet voice that was less than up-lifting. "Unfortunately, for me, they've come clouded with last rites."

Jacob knew instantly Gotham's inference was brought about by thoughts of his own son—the first Light Bearer who received such a Blessing—who now rested in a stone crypt on the other side of the Garden.

"I feel badly," said Jacob, following a moment of awkward silence.

"You are just overwhelmed, as any Fledgling in your shoes would be"

"No...not about that. I feel badly for you."

Gotham's brow raised. "And just what have I done to garner such sympathy?"

"I've been having this guilty feeling eating away at me as though I'm taking away something that doesn't belong to me. Something that belonged to your son."

The mention of his son instantly darkened Gotham's face with a melancholy seriousness.

"And by taking it from him, it's as if I'm taking it from you," continued Jacob. "I know how important it was to you when David was named Light Bearer. I want you to know I'm not looking to strip him of anything, especially something that was a core to who he was."

Slowly, Gotham turned around and when he saw the genuineness mirrored in the eyes staring back at him, he was for a brief moment taken hold of by a welling of emotion reserved for mortals. A smile of gratitude quickly appeared on his face and he reached out and clasped gently the back of Jacob's neck in an almost paternal embrace.

"Thank you for that, Fledgling, and I'm sure David would thank you as well," he said. "You know, it just occurred to me. In a way we are both marked, you and I. But unlike me, you must wear yours with the same unabashed pride a warrior bears a medal."

At that moment, for the first time, Jacob felt the possibility he could do just that.

~ ~ ~

With the setting of the sun came a dawn of confidence Anahel had noted as lacking in Jacob, and with each passing day that followed it began to visibly solidify itself inside him. It could be seen in the boy's stance when he went one on one with Gotham, and in the way he gripped his sword and held it before him. Most notably, it was spotted prominently in the boy's unflinching gaze, and soon the golden flecks of celestial light deep within his eyes gradually churned brighter with each strengthening demonstration of his power.

The other Guides, meanwhile, also observed closely from a distance Jacob's progress with great interest and skepticism. Yet as each day came to pass, followed by weeks, they found whatever doubt remained amongst them regarding the promise of a prophecy once believed dead resurrecting itself inside Eden's borders slowly beginning to ebb away.

They weren't the only ones watching, however, and just when it seemed as though a real threat to the future of the Darkness might finally be at hand in the shape of this wingless, teenaged Nephilim, a mysterious and unexpected presence slithered its way toward Havenhid.

CHAPTER SEVEN

THE STOKING OF DOUBT

I *think I might finally be getting the hang of this grinder of a training regime that I've suffered through now for the past few weeks. That's not to say training with Gotham still isn't a frustrating experience, to say the least. There are still days I dread when my regular instruction with the rest of the Shrikes ends knowing he will be waiting for me with his whip in hand. But as angry and annoyed as I oftentimes get with him for how relentless he can be in riding me, and even more unforgiving when I make mistakes, I know it's only because he cares about me and, more importantly, believes in me, even more so than I do in myself. If I were to be completely honest, I would have to admit it is because of him and his strenuous training sessions that I now find myself doing things I never thought another living thing was capable of doing, Nephilim or not. He's helping to grow inside me, slowly but surely, a strange yet comforting confidence I haven't experienced before. I actually find myself, at times, entertaining the possibility of what before seemed an all but certain impossibility: that maybe, just maybe, I might actually have the feet needed to fill the enormous shoes handed me called "Light Bearer."*

But then, just as I'm experiencing these brief moments that come to me where I have a spark of belief that maybe I might just be this thing everyone (mostly) around me believes me to be, I'm abruptly reminded that for all the incredible feats Gotham has taught me to perform I still lack something very big, and very noticeable: Wings.

I can't count the number of times I've stood on the ledge overlooking Broken Earth since my first failed jump, but for the life of me I can't summon the will inside me to force my feet to take that running leap again, no matter how hard I try or wish to. I don't think it's fear that's holding me back. Goodness knows I've jumped off plenty cliffs with my buddy Ty back home. But if it's not fear, then what?

One thing's for certain: I'm going to have to overcome the hurdle of Broken Earth sooner or later. It was bad enough feeling like an outcast at home because of these two humps on my back. Now, ironically, I'm feeling more and more like an outcast in the one place where I shouldn't.

~ ~ ~

As Jacob busily scribbled his thoughts down in his journal as he did every night without fail since the day he began his trek to Eden, Max sat quietly beside him reclined in the deep-seated comfort of an over-stuffed sofa before a crackling fire in one of Havenhid's many common rooms. His attention was intensely focused on the sigil branded on the inside of his wrist by the fiery point of the Illume's feather as a mark of victory for capturing the rare elusive bird in the final competition during Illumination a few weeks earlier. Slowly, he moved his arm back and forth under the silvery radiance of the moon shining its way through a nearby archway and carefully studied how the light of the nighttime sun made visible the markings of the unusual design seared into the skin as if by some glowing, iridescent blue fire still burning deep within his flesh. For that was the only way to see the badge of victory, under the light of the moon, in the same way a diamond reveals its preciousness in sparkly flashes when held up to the sun.

"You know what I wonder?" he pondered aloud to Jacob who continued writing down his accounting of the day as intently as Max was studying his arm.

"Who wrote the book of love?" Jacob muttered jokingly even as his face held its frown of concentration.

The smart-alecky reference to the rock 'n' roll group The Monotones' hit song was either ignored by Max or, which was more likely the case, sailed completely over his head.

"You think this mark Anahel branded into our skin is just some cool invisible tattoo, or do you think there's something more to it?" he asked.

"What do you mean more to it?" asked Jacob, though sounding clearly uninterested in whatever the answer might be as he continued with his writing.

"I don't know, but remember in 'Lord of the Rings' how the doorway leading to Moria could only be seen in the moonlight?"

"So, you're saying the marking on your arm is some kind of door?" asked Jacob drolly.

"Not a door, dill," said Max. "But maybe it's some kind of key."

Jacob finally aborted writing any further as his attention shifted from his journal to his own arm, which he stretched out until it was within reach of the moon's presence to reveal a near identical sigil on the inside of his wrist like the one marking Max.

"Doesn't look like a key to me," Jacob remarked unenthused.

"I'm just speaking hypothetically. What if? *What if* it was some sort of key? And what if it was something else like…?"

"Like what?"

"I don't know…maybe the symbol is like some sort of secret passcode to something?" mused Max.

"I'd say you've seen too many James Bond movies," countered Jacob.

"You know, you're about as helpful as an ejector seat in a helicopter," Max grumbled in frustration. "For all we know we may have been given some secret power or strength."

"We already have. They're called Graces."

"I'm talking about something other than Graces."

"Oh, I know," Jacob, mocking sudden enthusiasm, said. "Maybe we've been given the ability to transform ourselves into hideous creatures that can breathe blue fire just like the Illume."

"That's fine," Max replied in a huff as he sank heavily into the softness of the sofa. "Here I am trying to have a serious conversation with a fellow Illuminite and all you can do is poke fun."

"I'm sorry. I just don't think there's anything more to these sigils other than being Eden's version of a trophy," said Jacob.

"Doubtful. If there's one thing angels aren't big on its symbols of pride," said Max.

"Maybe that explains why they're invisible on our arms most of the time."

Max shot Jacob a glowering look out of the corner of his eye. "You know something, ever since you've become the Light Bearer you've been about as much fun as backing into a porcupine with me bum. What's going on with you?"

"I'll tell you what's going on with me. I get up every morning and I spend half the day training with the rest of you. Then when you are all done and are free to do what you'd like I get to start Round 2 with Gotham. If I'm lucky, when we're done, I have just enough time like tonight to cram in the reading assignment Thaniel's given us for Study, that is if I'm able to keep my eyes open long enough before finally going to bed," said Jacob with a noted sourness. "And I know I sound pissy, and I don't mean to be, but it's only because I'm one hundred percent bone-tired."

Jacob didn't need to explain how exhausted he was feeling; Max could see it in his face. It was long and drawn, especially in the eyes.

"I keep forgetting you're burning the candle at both end these days," said Max. "Old Gotham's really putting the thumb screws to you, eh?"

"You have no idea," replied Jacob with a heavy sigh.

"I guess being Light Bearer isn't all it's cracked up to be, is it?" asked Max.

"I know it's a big deal, and I'm sure it'll get better with time," said Jacob, "but right now it feels like an undeserved punishment."

"It can't be all bad, I bet."

Jacob shifted his gaze from his journal in his lap to Max and deadpanned, "You spend a day training under Genghis Khan, Patton and Attila the Hun all rolled into one and then get back to me."

"I just mean at least you must be learning a lot of cool stuff the rest of peons aren't privy to."

"I guess so," Jacob replied with a half-hearted shrug. Then as he appeared to take stock of his time training with Gotham a faint smile slowly showed itself on his face. "Yeah, I'd say he's taught me some pretty neat things."

"Yeah, like what?" inquired Max who instantly straightened up in his seat with an anxious gleam in his eyes.

"I don't know, lots of things," answered Jacob.

"Come off it, Mr. Bogart, don't make me give you a biff."

"A biff?"

"A slap upside your head," explained Max. "Out with it! I'm your platinum mate, not someone looking to dethrone you for your Light Bearer crown."

"Alright," surrendered Jacob when it was obvious his friend wasn't about to give him a moment's peace until he shared something from his clandestine sessions with Gotham. "What do you want to know? How to smell out an Infector?

Max's nose immediately scrunched itself up, as if it just caught the aroma of soured milk. "Smell out an Infector? Why in bloody hell would I want to do that?"

Every Nephilim, from the time they were old enough to learn such things, were taught what signs to watch out for whenever an Infector or Fury or any of the other inhabitants of the Underneath were close by: straying shadows, certain grotesque sounds coming from their presence, and a sudden and striking chill in the air. As Jacob explained to Max just as he came to learn from Gotham, there was another way such odious entities unknowingly made their presence known, even before the tell-tale signs to alert an unsuspecting Nephilim revealed themselves.

"It's a subtle smell and hard to detect, especially among other humans, which is why your nose has to be vigilant so to speak," said Jacob.

"So, what's the smell like?" asked Max with a growing curiosity.

"It's hard to explain. Kinda like a combination of despair and desolation," said Jacob. "One thing's for sure, once you get a whiff of it you never forget it; kinda like a dead body."

"I'll take your word for it," said a clearly disgusted Max. "Actually, I was hoping to be wowed by something a little more awe-inspiring than the bouquet of Underneath stink."

Jacob thought for a moment.

"How about this?"

Jacob cleared his throat and straightened himself in his seat before closing eyes and, for a moment, Max wondered if he was about to get an introduction to a new form of meditation, particularly when a whispered chant was heard to come from Jacob's lips like some New Age mantra. Only it wasn't so much a mantra as a calling. And with a look of growing intrigue alight in his eyes, Max leaned in closer focusing ever so closely on the words coming from Jacob's mouth, so much so that he was oblivious to the stirring coming from the branches of the trees outside a nearby open archway looking out onto the Garden surrounding Havenhid. It was through the archway one of the boughs twisted itself to reach inside the sitting room toward the sofa where the two boys sat. Max sat oblivious to the gnarled, leafy appendage that had positioned itself right above him until the branch suddenly curled back and struck him on top of the noggin.

"Ow!" cried a startled Max who quickly spun around just in time to see his assailant slither its way back through the archway in retreat. Rubbing his head, Max turned back with a pained look on his face only to find Jacob caught up in a fit of laughter. "What the bloody hell was that?"

"Looks like the tree just gave you a biff," Jacob replied through his chuckling.

"In the words of Ethan, 'Ha, ha, very funny!' " said Max, looking none too amused.

"You wanted to know the kind of things Gotham's teaching me," said Jacob. "Anyone who has the Grace of Whispering thinks it refers mainly to animals in general, but, actually, you can summon any living thing like trees. Of course, I didn't realize until just now the amusement factor that came with the gift."

"Yeah, well, seeing as neither of my Graces is Whispering, I don't rightly care about conversing with trees. But thanks for the nice crack in my skull. I owe you one," said a still-smarting Max.

"Alright, let me make it up to you," said Jacob before pausing a moment in thought. "Okay, I got something I think you'll dig. Take off your shirt."

Max threw his friend a queer look.

"It has to do with your wings," explained Jacob with a roll of his eyes. Max quickly stripped out of his shirt and proceeded to unfold his wings into view.

"Remember how we've been taught that wings aren't just for flying?" asked Jacob.

"Damn straight," answered Max with a knowing self-assured smirk.

Aside from guiding his pupils into the final transformation of Nephilimhood atop Broken Earth and training them to navigate the skies as skillfully as an Air Force pilot maneuvering a fighter jet, Eksel also schooled the boys on other more deadlier uses of their newfound appendages. While their wings were similar to that of an eagle, the deceptively soft, delicate plumage was anything but. The edge of each feather was as sharp as a razor, and one pointed swipe of a Nephilim's wing, like that of their angel counterpart, had the ability to slice deeply anything that stood in its way with the same deadly effectiveness of a hundred drawn swords. There was also a certain hardness to the plumage, similar in many respects to armor, which allowed the wings to be used as a shield to deflect a great many deadly things. Yet as durable and deleterious as these wings were, there was also a delicateness to them as Jacob demonstrated as he carefully took hold of one of Max's plumes.

~ ~ ~

"Hey, what's the big idea?" Max yelped when Jacob reached out and yanked free a feather from his right wing.

"Do you want me to show you this or not?" said Jacob.

"Not if it involves me being plucked like some Thanksgiving turkey," balked Max.

"Quit your whining already. It'll grow back just like the hair on top of your head." Jacob then glanced around the sitting room which had emptied itself of any of the other boys. When he spotted what he was looking for, he turned to Max. "You see that column over there?"

Max looked in the direction of where Jacob was pointing to a large wooden pillar on the far end of the room. "What about it?"

With that Jacob drew back his arm and sent the feather he pulled from Max's wing sailing across the room. The feather shot through the air faster than a dart thrown at a dart board and hit the pillar dead center.

"Whoa!" Max exclaimed under his breath, looking momentarily gobsmacked before both boys quickly scampered across the room to closer examine the quill whose point had embedded itself so deeply into the pillar it caused a sizable split to be seen in the wood.

"Crikey, you could really turn someone into a voodoo doll this way, eh?" remarked Max, once he had managed to pry the feather out of the column after several strenuous tugs.

"I think that's the idea," said Jacob. "And because a Nephilim gets his wings by taking a leap of faith, if you strike someone who's infected by an Infector or some other demon, it will send them fleeing from the body just like a vampire who's doused with holy water."

"That's beaut!" said a clearly impressed Max while closely eyeing the sharp point of his feather.

"At least you'll have better use out it than I will," said Jacob.

Max's gaze shifted Jacob's way and from the noticeably long look in his friend's face he knew the glumness was caused by the constant reminder that Max, and the rest of the boys at Havenhid, had the one important thing Jacob still lacked: a pair of wings.

"You've just lost your mojo at the moment," said Max, offering his support while being mindful not to sound like he pitied his friend. "You'll get it back…eventually."

"Wish I was as optimistic as you," said Jacob.

"Then why aren't you?" asked Max, though not meaning to say out loud the words swirling around inside his head."

"What do you mean by that?"

Max stood quiet for a minute, his lips pressed tightly together as if second-guessing whether to speak any further on the subject.

"Look, I'm your mate, and I want you to know that I always have your back. And being as you're the best friend I've ever had, I think it's important we're always straight with one another," he finally said. "I'm just having a hard understanding what it is you're so afraid of that's keeping you from leaping off Broken Earth."

"Who said I was afraid?"

"What would you call it then?"

"In case you've forgotten, I've already made the jump and nothing happened."

"So did a bunch of the other guys, with the exact same results. But they kept on trying."

"I'm not like the other guys," said Jacob.

"That's my point," said Max. "Getting one's wings is all about faith. You've come along and revealed to everyone to have all seven Graces. You've all but been named the Light Bearer. Diving head first off Broken Earth should be a piece of cake."

Jacob wanted nothing more than to argue Max's point, but he couldn't.

"Then why isn't it?" he asked his friend instead.

The question, at first, seemed to be as equally puzzling to Max.

"Maybe you're afraid of being the Light Bearer," said Max when he finally offered up an answer. "I hate to even say it, but maybe you don't even want to be a Nephilim."

"That's what you think?" asked Jacob, sounding slightly offended.

"I told you what I think, the night of Azrael's visit," Max replied without so much as a sign of waffling. "I'm just playing devil's advocate.

Although considering where we are, it might not be the brightest role-play choice."

Jacob's first reaction was to deny outright Max's suggestion, but something held his tongue. Not that he for one minute believed his friend's diagnosis. At least, he didn't think he did. Sure the idea of him being the Light Bearer was a bit much to take in, overwhelming really, but he was doing his best to wrap his head around it and accept it, even taking on the exhausting training regimen he'd been undergoing for the past several weeks to fill the shoes of the role suddenly handed to him. Not really the actions of someone who was fearful of such a thing. Besides, he'd grown skittish of Broken Earth long before the possibility of being Light Bearer was even a whisper on anyone's lips. As for not wanting to be a Nephilim, he may have had such feelings when the existence of such a thing was first laid at his feet. Who wouldn't? Becoming a Nephilim, however, was something Jacob had quickly come to embrace as it was the one thing that finally made him comfortable in his own skin. He loved Eden. He loved the Guides. He loved this thing that made it possible for such an astonishing world to be opened to him. Yet after what Max said he found himself second-guessing if he actually did. After all, the subconscious had a mind of its own, so to speak.

"I better head off to bed and get my rest if I'm going to make it through another day with Sergeant Gotham," Jacob said instead of further arguing the topic. "You coming?"

"In a bit. Think I'll go feed me cake hole with a snack. Maybe try my skills at spearing an apple or something," said Max, holding up his feather with an anxiousness to test out his newly discovered weapon like a kid with a new toy on Christmas morning.

~ ~ ~

While Max headed off in the direction of the Hall of Light to quiet his grumbling stomach, Jacob started back the opposite way towards his room, all the while mulling over the conversation he had just had with his friend. Turning a corner of the corridor, he was just short of the foyer and the stairway leading upstairs when a voice called out to him, stopping him in his tracks: "Starting to finally see the light, are you?"

Jacob turned and spied the orange glow of a lit cigarette being smoked by a figure coming from a darkened nook just behind him.

"What about?"

There came no answer, only a brighter glow of the lit cigarette as the figure took a long drag from it.

"You know there's no smoking allowed in Havenhid, don't you?" said Jacob.

He didn't need to wait until the figure stepped out from behind the veil of shadows to see that it was Creed; not only was Creed the only boy known to toke on a cigarette now and then—out of eyesight from any of the Guides, that is—but he also possessed a distinct voice which carried with it a uniquely contemptuous tone whenever he opened his mouth and set his tongue to wagging, even when asking the most innocuous of questions.

"So what, have you now declared yourself hall monitor as well?" snarked Creed with his usual unpleasant smile.

Jacob then watched with disgust as Creed proceeded to take a last drag from his cigarette before tossing the smoldering fag onto the floor and grinding it out with the bottom of his shoe.

"You know, it's somewhat sad in a way—pathetic, really— watching you bust your hump the way you've been doing when it's all a big waste of time," said Creed.

"How's that?" asked Jacob but not really caring about the answer, especially while doing his best to fight back the urge he had to pounce on the sneering boy and give him a quick lesson in being respectful to the hallowed halls they were lucky enough to call home and using his fists as the etiquette guides.

"Because sooner or later you're going to realize what the rest of us already do."

Jacob let escape a weary sigh. "Which is?"

"The absolute joke that is you as the Light Bearer," said Creed with a cheeky grin.

Jacob opened his mouth to tell the malcontent before him what he could do with his realizations, but he stopped himself, hard as it was.

"I'll let you get back to your midnight feeding. I think I heard a couple mice scurrying around down the hall," he said instead.

Then turning on his heel he proceeded on his way, but Creed's voice followed after him.

"I don't know why you keep beating your head against the wall about why your back's still bare. It's really no big mystery why you're still the wingless freak you are this late in the game."

Jacob halted once more and turned his head to give Creed a glowering look over his shoulder when he realized the talk he had with Max moments earlier had been eavesdropped upon. "Listening in on private conversations now are you, Creed? That's pretty low, even for you."

Again Creed smiled his weasel grin as if to silently suggest there were far lower places he would be more than willing to stoop.

"You're not going to be able to keep this sham going forever," he hurled boisterously when Jacob attempted again to walk away. "You really think you're going to come close to living up to the prophesy of the Light Bearer when you can't even make a simple jump from Broken Earth?"

"I'll make the jump when I'm good and ready," Jacob replied while facing his taunter with a defiant stance.

The answer only seemed to make Creed's smirk stretch itself wider across his smug face.

"Oh yeah? You sure about that?" asked Creed. "Because you may not like the outcome."

"What's that supposed to mean?"

Creed slowly stepped his way closer towards Jacob. "Have you ever see the wings belonging to a Weed?" he asked. "They're noticeably different than those of normal Nephilim. Some are jet black like a raven's or a crow's. Then there are some that look as if they came from a giant bat or dragon."

"Really? Then what about Gotham's son?" asked Jacob with noticeable skepticism. "From everything I've heard about him he was as normal-looking a Nephilim as anyone else."

"Yeah, well…," Creed began contemplatively, "most would argue Gotham isn't a Fallen in the true sense of the word. Of course, I'm not one of those people. Then there's the fact how far a Fallen has fallen determines what a Weed's wings end up looking like."

It was obvious by the stultifying look growing more prominent in Jacob's face that his patience with this conversation was quickly coming to an end.

"What does any of this have to do with me?" he asked with an impatient sigh.

"Are you really that dense?" asked Creed. "Or have you forgotten what happened at Illumination during the Illume hunt?"

"Of course not. I came back to Havenhid the victor, and you didn't. You don't forget something as sweet as that," said Jacob with a grin of satisfaction.

Creed couldn't help but bristle visibly at the boast.

"I'm talking about our little private talk in the forest. Where I told you the truth of who and what you are, Weed," remarked Creed with a hateful hiss. "And my gut still tells me that you are about the weediest Weed there is."

The brief moment of levity that had found Jacob quickly dissipated at the reminder of that moment during the Illumination competition when he and Creed finally had an airing out of differences (to put it mildly) and, in what became a heated physical display worthy of two nemesis with such disdain for one another, Creed let loose from his tongue a wicked revelation no Nephilim ever wants to hear about himself: that Jacob was the son of some unknown Fallen. Or in more derogatory terms, a Weed.

"I warned you about ever calling me that name again," Jacob seethed under his breath.

"I can't ignore the truth, not when it's standing right in front of me staring me in the eyes," chided Creed.

"It's not the truth!"

"Really? Then why didn't you ask my father like I dared you to?" argued Creed. "Better yet, why not go straight to the horse's mouth, Gotham, and prove me wrong?"

Jacob hesitated a moment in replying. He knew in his core Creed was lying to him (or as Max would say in his attempt to ease his second-guessing, "That knob's just shaking your tree.") The fervency, however, in which Creed stuck to this lie just to malign him wasn't just obnoxious and nettlesome, it was starting to become downright infuriating.

"I've got enough on my plate these days rather than give you the satisfaction of watching me take your bait," said Jacob, doing his best to stay even-keeled in front of the smirking dolt before him. "Besides, Gotham wouldn't keep something as important as who my father is a secret from me. And he certainly wouldn't lie about it."

"Right," Creed replied with a snide guffaw. "A low-down Fallen who cuts down his own son in cold blood, but lying? That's where he draws the line."

Jacob felt his blood beginning to boil in his veins, but he fought back the urge to get into a verbal spat with Creed. Or worse.

"Let's say your lie is true," he mused. "Why do you care one way or another as to whether I'm a Weed or not?"

"I don't. But if you think I'm going to stand around and watch you mold yourself into something you're not, especially the Light Bearer, then you've got another thing coming," said Creed threateningly. "So know this, I'm watching you."

If there was one thing Jacob liked least of all, it was threats, but he managed to force forth an unnerved smile. "I'm flattered Creed, really I am. But I should tell you you're really not my type."

"Go ahead and make your jokes, Weed," Creed said without a hint of amusement. "You may have the others fooled but not me, and you can bet sooner or later I'm gonna expose you as the fraud you are, mark my words. And trust me that's going to be one sweet day."

Jacob's mouth unhinged itself to spit back a retort but instead he took a deep, calming breath when he was suddenly stuck by something epiphanic in the mask of tenseness that shaped Creed's face.

"You're really threatened by me, aren't you?" he asked while smiling coyly.

The question seemed to catch Creed momentarily off guard.

"Threatened? By you?"

"Of course, it's so simple. Here I've been thinking you were just some nasty, entitled hater, and all along it's been nothing more than a simple bad case of jealousy. Why else would you be spending so much energy trying to burrow under my skin like some kind of annoying deer tick?"

"You've got bigger problems than I thought if you think that," Creed protested with a chuckle that was anything but. "What on God's green earth could someone like me possibly be jealous about over some nothing like you?"

"Well, for starters," said Jacob, pursing his lips into a pondering pout, "I think it's eating you up inside that you're no longer the big man at Havenhid that you thought you were when you first arrived here. That big pedestal you've placed yourself upon so you can look down upon the rest of us has little by little been kicked out from beneath you. The son of the great Sandel the Archangel has been out-shined by some fatherless nobody: first during a sparring match at Lions Bite, then during the most prestigious competition at Illumination. And now…now this wingless nothing has somehow, for whatever reason, been favored with all seven Graces to become the Light Bearer and I can almost hear the one lone question rattling around in that pea-sized brain of yours echoing repeatedly in a desperate need for an answer, 'How did this wingless nothing rise above me?' "

The hulking Creed Maggert, for the first time since Jacob came to know of the boy's existence, appeared for a moment somewhat diminutive in stature and, rarer still, speechless. It was as if Jacob had gutted the entitled giant like some fish and exposed the green ore secreted away inside like some pocket of pus in desperate need of draining. And it was through the silence that followed that Jacob knew nothing further needed to be argued, and that for all intent and purposes the back and forth that had taken place between the boys since Jacob's arrival in Eden was finally finished, at least for the time being.

Or so he thought.

"There's a log," Jacob heard Creed say when he turned and started once more to make his way in the direction of his room.

"What are you talking about? What log?" inquired Jacob, turning to face Creed once more with a confused look etched in his face.

"A birth log. You know, as in official records." The yielding moment that had settled itself upon Creed, however briefly, was quickly swept away when he stepped his way toward Jacob, and with it's passing, the familiar cold deep-set steeliness was returned to his icy blue gaze. "Supposedly it holds a record of every single Nephilim born since Nephilim existed."

"Yeah? So?"

"So? Are you really that dense that you need even the most obvious of things spoon-fed to you?" barked Creed. "We're basically talking about one huge database of birth certificates here. And if you know anything about birth certificates, you'd know there's a lot of important information that can be found in them, like who was born when and in what city and country, who the mother is and, more importantly—"

"Who the father is," Jacob muttered under his breath with a gasp of incredulousness. Was it actually possible such a simple tool existed with the ability to disperse the dark cloud of mystery that had hung over his head for as long as he could remember?

"I wouldn't get too excited, if I were you, though. It's true these records would list the father of every Nephilim born, but it's not likely to do you any good. That is, not when it comes to your kind," said Creed, quickly pricking the balloon of hope Jacob found himself grasping.

"What do you mean my kind?" he asked gruffly.

"Weeds, of course," answered Creed with his casual brand of snobbery. "As I understand it, the log only holds the records of legitimate Nephilim. Even Gotham's son wouldn't be listed in the log because his father is…well, a dirty Fallen. I give ten to one odds you'd be missing from it as well."

Jacob could feel his blood pressure rise with every ugly slight coming from Creed's thin-lipped mouth, but he did everything but chew through the inside of his cheeks to keep himself rooted to his place on the floor and his clenching fists at his side.

"If what you're telling me is true, how come I've never heard about this so-called log before? And if it exists, where is it?" he asked.

"I actually just heard about it myself not too long ago," replied Creed. "As for where it is, since Anahel's head honcho of Eden, my thinking is he has it locked away somewhere in a safe place."

"I don't believe it," argued Jacob. "If it contains what you say, Anahel, and certainly Gotham, would have shown it to me. They wouldn't let me go on wondering who my father is."

"You're making an argument based on the delusion you're a legitimate Nephilim like the rest of us here," Creed countered with visible contempt. "My guess is they want to keep you in the dark. Better for you to go on living believing in a falsehood than to know the truth, know what I mean?"

Any other time, the snide smirk accompanying the taunting words spilling out of Creed's mouth would have tried the durability of the few remaining threads of Jacob's patience. However, he was too taken aback at the prospect that such a thing as a birth log existed. And, while he had every reason in the world to be suspicious of anything that came out of Creed's mouth, this particular revelation seemed quite believable. Obvious, even. After all, if birth certificates existed to record all the births of regular babies brought into the world, naturally, it stood to argue, there would be something of equal means to keep track of all the Nephilim born.

"Look, Parrish, I don't really care whether you believe me or not. I'm just telling you what I know," said Creed. "You don't want to confront Gotham, Anahel or even my father and question them about the rumors of what you may or may not be, that's your prerogative. Go ahead and keep deluding yourself into believing something that's a total lie. Personally, I'd want to know the truth. But that's just me."

Jacob felt an ice-cold discomfort disperse itself to every corner fiber of his being. He wouldn't believe Creed if he argued the sky was blue; but the lengths and vigor with which he fought to bring life to this preposterous lie—that he was the son of some unknown Fallen—was beyond the realms of cruelty even Creed would ever be suspected of dwelling within so gleefully. And not since the day in the Forest during the hunt for the Illume when Creed first made light of the lie with his barbed tongue did Jacob find himself quietly pondering a most unsettling prospect: Could this lowly untruth actually, in fact, be true?

Such an unsettling rumination delivered upon Jacob an instant cold sweat. He was almost thankful when the sound of approaching footsteps made itself heard moments before Thaniel was seen rounding the corner in a hurried manner before stopping suddenly at the sight of the two boys.

"It's rather a late hour for the two of you to be down here socializing," he said.

"I was just comparing notes with Parrish here about today's Study lesson," Creed offered up quickly, causing Thaniel's brow to rise with aroused interest.

"Is that so?" said the angel with a slightly dubious tone in his voice.

Having observed on more than one occasion the mutually tempestuous feelings the two boys harbored for one another, Thaniel eyed the teens suspiciously knowing the odds were stacked against what would require a miracle for both of them to come together and share a friendly, light moment recapping the day's happenings, much less calling a cease fire in the name of their studies. Yet he had much more pressing business on the other end of Havenhid that he was in a hurry to tend to at that moment than to scrutinize more closely the curious come upon, and so he gave both boys a supportive nod and smile and said simply, "It's good to see the two of you getting finally getting along so well with one another."

He managed only a step or two when Jacob attempted to pull him aside.

"Do you mind if I talk to you about something? Privately?" asked Jacob. If anyone would know anything about some log of births, it would be Thaniel.

"If you wouldn't mind, could it keep for the morning? I've got another matter that demands my immediate attention at the moment," said Thaniel.

"Sure, tomorrow," Jacob muttered with a quiet disgruntlement as Thaniel disappeared down the hall.

CHAPTER EIGHT

Thaniel hurried briskly along the vast length of corridors winding their way through Havenhid's numerous halls until he reached Anahel's quarters, which was tucked away in a quiet corner of the capacious domicile created by the living trees.

"Enter," came a voice from within when Thaniel rapped the door with his knuckle.

Thaniel opened the door and stepped inside the stark, yet homey chamber warmed by the illumination of twin orbs of lights floating weightlessly in the air like two miniature suns at opposite ends of the room. A gentle breeze coming in off the large open terrace brought with it the delightful and pleasing smells of the garden grounds outside, filling the chamber with the strong, soothing fragrances released by the awaking blossoms of the many night-blooming plants making up Eden's landscape such as jessamine, moonflowers, evening primrose, orchids and, naturally, angel's trumpet. Just off the terrace was a large ornate desk where Anahel was found seated and busily at work writing amid the clutter of numerous books stacked one upon another, scrolls and parchment paper curling with age.

"I don't mean to disturb you when you are busy," Thaniel apologized, after waiting patiently for a moment when Anahel might look up for his work, which never came. "I can come back later, if you wish."

"It's quite alright," replied Anahel who remained focused on what he was writing.

"I was hoping to have a moment of time to discuss something that has recently been brought to my attention," said Thaniel.

"Which is?"

"It's in regards to the Fledgling Jacob," said Thaniel. "I understand you have come to a decision regarding the boy and the Apocrypha of which he has called into question. Namely, you have decided to perform the Blessing that will officially recognize him as the Light Bearer foretold."

Only then did the ink-dipped tip of the feather quill clutched in Anahel's hand cease its loud scratching against the parchment upon which the angel was studiously writing.

"And from whom may I ask have you come to hear such a canard of which I have not voiced publicly?" Anahel, finally looking up and acknowledging Thaniel's presence, inquired.

"Rarely does such a resolution over something as significant and consequential as this require the aid of a courier to make itself heard," said Thaniel with a smile.

"I wouldn't quite yet call it a resolution as I'm still turning over the idea in my mind," said Anahel. "But when I come to a firm decision I'll be certain to make my intentions known."

"Then you do intend to gather the White Circle to apprise them of your proposal," said Thaniel, looking slightly relieved.

"I had no plans to," replied Anahel.

The answer drew a notable pause from Thaniel. "Certainly, then, you mean to meet with the Iudicium Tribunal and advise them of what has transpired here and your…aspirations, if I may say, concerning the boy."

Anahel sat quiet in his chair for a moment or two staring stone-faced at Thaniel before opening his mouth to speak

"My aspirations, as you so interestingly noted, is to pave the way forth for the will of our father and nothing more," the angel said finally.

"Of course. I meant nothing sorted otherwise—" Thaniel hemmed before he was quickly interrupted.

"The White Circle, as you well know, has already been called together and apprised at length of the happenings we find ourselves facing concerning the mystery that is the Apocrypha," Anahel remarked in a brisk and even sterner manner. "I see no reason to involve the Iudicium Tribunal in a matter that is clearly rooted in Eden."

"True, it may be rooted in Eden, but the magnitude of an act by which one is officially recognized as Light Bearer extends far beyond the borders of this garden," Thaniel calmly reminded Anahel. "Nor do I need to remind you there is an established sequence in addressing such things."

"Perhaps, Thaniel, should a day come that the reins of this heavenly paradise pass from my hands into yours, you can make right the missteps I have made of which you continue to take note. Until that day I will risk tripping over my own feet."

"I meant nothing untoward by it," Thaniel offered apologetically. "You'll forgive my interrupting your work."

As Thaniel quickly backed his way out of the room Anahel's face tightened with contriteness and he called out to the angel before he reached the door.

"Please," said Anahel, motioning for Thaniel to return.

Thaniel hesitated a moment before once more crossing the room to the desk where Anahel sat. There he slowly sank into a large chair nearby which Anahel gestured for him to take.

"My apologies for the brusque manner in which I spoke to you just now," said Anahel ruefully. "Truth of the matter is, while the two of us have had our differences in the past, I have always trusted and found comfort in the clear and objective way you have of analyzing certain things which have a tendency of fogging those senses belonging to the rest of us. And by coming here tonight you have saved me the effort of having to call upon you for counsel on this matter that finds itself grating on me in larger measure with every passing day."

Thaniel appeared slightly taken aback by the confidence voiced by Anahel and said simply, "However I might serve to be helpful I will, as you well know."

~ ~ ~

For some time the two angels chewed on the silence that comes when surrounded by the tranquility of the night. Anahel sat drumming his fingers upon the heavy wooden desk in front of him while staring over at Thaniel who patiently awaited whatever it was the angel seemed reticent to discuss.

"You've no doubt spoken to the other Guides about the matter surrounding the boy," Anahel said finally. "Tell me, what have they to say about it, if anything, since witnessing what occurred with the stricken River now that they've had some time to ponder over it?"

"What makes you think any discussion's been had?" asked Thaniel.

"Come now, Thaniel, let's not pretend me to be anything less than acute when it comes to my brethren," said Anahel, drawing a smile from Thaniel.

"It's a difficult thing to deny what one witnesses with his own eyes," answered Thaniel. "We each of us stood on the banks of the River and watched a Nephilim resurrect life from that which death had seized, and no matter how any of us might wish or try to explain it away as some freak phenomenon there is no turning a blind eye to what had shown itself before us."

"Have they come to accept it? That's the real question," said Anahel.

Of that question Thaniel was not as quick to answer.

"It's one thing to witness such a miracle. It's quite another to reconcile in whose hand such a gift has been placed," said Thaniel. "Damiel has allowed the boy to show himself as he is, not by the shadow of his father, and as such has come to be quite endeared by the child. Zuriel has been more slow in his melt, but I can see he, too, has come to look upon the boy with a less forbidding gaze."

"And Eksel, as if I need ask?" inquired Anahel.

The question drew a heavy sigh from Thaniel. "Let's just say Eksel will be Eksel. Unlike Zuriel, he is an iceberg of which I see no imminent thawing."

Anahel nodded knowingly.

"I suspect he could be summoned before our father, himself, to be explained the mystery of his will and he would still hold tight to his disdain for Jacob. And, yet, strangely I somehow understand Eksel's unbending," he said, looking off in thought before shifting his keen gaze onto Thaniel. "And you?"

"I may find myself questioning now and then the logic to this strange and unexpected turn," replied Thaniel, "but I know there is no book among the hordes that fill Havenhid's Library which can refute that which has shown itself to be."

Anahel nodded and slowly rose from his chair to begin wandering about the room.

"I remember the last time we were all confronted with the first visit by this enigmatic prophesy," said Anahel. "Then it was Gothamel's son, David, and the idea of Blessing the son of a Fallen nearly split Eden in two. Now, here I am so many years later confronted with committing an even more brazen act that could surely cause an irreparable divide. The question now is do I ignore that which is undeniably standing before me staring me in the face, and ignore our father's wishes in the process, or do I risk setting into motion a tragedy far greater than the death which brought an end to the first Light Bearer?"

~ ~ ~

"What's Gothamel's feeling on the matter?" asked Thaniel after a quiet moment had settled itself upon the room, drawing, at first, a questionable look from Anahel. "I assume you've approached him about your consideration of performing the Blessing on Jacob."

"I have," answered Anahel. "Strangely, he seemed oddly at ease with the idea or, perhaps, not so strangely now that I think back upon our conversation. Oh, I could see an undeniable moment of disquietness take hold of him when I broached the subject. How could it not? This wondrous and beatific Blessing has already disfigured itself in his eyes as that of a coiled serpent baring its fangs, and strike it did. Only now the serpent, caged as it might be at this moment, is a far more real and threatening presence to this bearer of light who lives and walks each day naive to the slithering shadow stalking his every step. Perhaps that is why, despite his unspoken reluctance, Gothamel has yielded to my proposed consecration; if anything to help shield this still weak flicker of light from being extinguished by the storm which, undoubtedly, will come in a gale of vengeance."

Anahel turned suddenly from his deep thoughts and settled his gaze on Thaniel who remained quietly seated in his chair listening.

"I suspect I know what you are thinking, Thaniel," he said.

"What might that be?" inquired Thaniel.

"That my rush to officially declare the boy Light Bearer is based in fear; fear that the Darkness may find a way to once more smother the Light we once thought lost to us."

"Is it?" Thaniel wondered aloud.

"It's been several weeks now since the night Jacob revealed himself to miraculously hold within himself all seven Graces and the contentious meeting of the White Circle where we spent much time arguing against such a miracle," said Anahel. "Since then I have with each passing day watched closely but from a distance as the boy labors tirelessly to transform himself into this thing that until now has been but a faceless figure of legend in his mind.

"It is an undeniable challenge of great measure to attempt to hoist the mantle of Light Bearer upon one's shoulders; a challenge I might add that Jacob neither asked to take up or competed to become a victor of its spoils. And yet take up the challenge he has all while wrestling endless bouts of frustration and self-doubt every step of the way. There is determination there, a spirit of purposefulness and stout-heartedness burning deep within his eyes like some inextinguishable flame of fire that I don't recall ever witnessing before, even with Gothamel's son. It heartens me; it brings me a strange and inexplicable sense of comfort when, perhaps, there should be consternation that the promise of the Apocrypha has finally come to rest in the confines of this unexpected vault of flesh and bone and, most importantly, spirit where I pray it will remain safe from even the most darkest of forces seeking to hijack it."

Thaniel, who was listening with a quiet intenseness, remained silent for a moment or two pondering Anahel's words.

"I suspect whatever hemming continued to gnaw at you concerning the Blessing, you have now put to rest with your own words," he remarked finally.

"I suspect I have at that," replied Anahel with a slight grin of relief.

"And yet I can't help but wonder," Thaniel was quick to comment.

"About?"

"If maybe, despite your encouraging plaudits concerning the boy, you'd be better served by fear rather than the comfort of confidence. Perhaps we all would better served."

~ ~ ~

The comment drew a curious look from Anahel.

"Would you care to explain what exactly you mean?" he asked.

The angel's gaze followed Thaniel as he rose from his seat and crossed his way to the edge of the open terrace overlooking the Garden with slow, pensive steps.

"What about the Sword of Destiny?" asked Thaniel finally.

"What of it?"

"When you went to Gothamel to discuss your intentions regarding the Blessing, did you also happen to touch upon the bequeathing of the sword?"

The creases forming Anahel's furrowed brow deepened along with his puzzlement. "Should I have?"

Thaniel shot the angel a questioning look over his shoulder.

"I'd be most surprised if you didn't," he remarked. "To ignore that which in many ways is equal to a scepter held by a king when addressing a possible formal declaration of the Light Bearer would be like looking up at the sky and not acknowledging the existence of the sun."

"I would hardly equate the role of Light Bearer as that of a king," said Anahel somewhat tersely.

"Nor would I," agreed Thaniel. "For there exists no kingdom under kingly rule, or whole countries for that matter, which can survive defeat against the one in whose hand holds the one divine weapon of great power by which he himself has been anointed.

"I'm not sure I understand your point," said Anahel, sounding all the more confused.

"I only mean to convey a heightened sense of concern I feel tugging at me over the grave responsibility demanded in overseeing such a weapon."

"Concern?" Anahel questioned incredulously. "The sword has never been in safer hands since coming into Gothamel's possession."

"And I would not argue with you if it were not for the addition of the burial plot that took root next to the Tree of Life shortly after the Sword of Destiny was brought out of hiding and passed on into the hands of a new master not so long ago," said Thaniel.

Anahel stood studying Thaniel with a growing keenness. "What exactly is it, Thaniel, you are attempting to say?"

"Merely that, perhaps, the time has come to consider relieving Gothamel of such responsibility and placing the sword under new guardianship," replied Thaniel.

"New guardianship?" Anahel repeated under his breath as a look of utter conflict suddenly gripped him.

"Don't misunderstand me," Thaniel was quick to explain. "It is out of pity and regard for my brother that I even make such a proposal."

"And by what measure would Gothamel be in need of such pity?" inquired Anahel.

"Come now, Anahel! Are you that heedless, even now as we stand here discussing your plans to officiate the Blessing that would name a new Light Bearer in our midst?" asked Thaniel with a dismissive chuckle. "Surely, the thought has crossed your mind at least once what can only be imagined as a great insufferable burden confronting Gothamel over such an act. The last time such a Blessing took place he was over the moon with jollity and immense pride, and how could he not when finally he was able to place the Sword of Destiny into the hands of the Light Bearer who also was his own son. Do you think for a minute such gladness will find company with him when he is forced to relive the moment when such joy was quickly remade in unspeakable horror and tragedy?"

Thaniel watched closely as the weight of his words made itself seen in the forlorn look that gradually settled upon Anahel's face.

"I must admit, regrettably, such a thought has refrained from visiting itself upon me," Anahel muttered in a voice of lament. "What is it you suggest be done to mitigate such needless anguish."

Thaniel took a deep breath. "To put it bluntly, the sword should be placed under new stewardship," he said. "Not only would such a step help relieve our dear brother in some measure of the unfortunate trauma we would inadvertently be hoisting upon him by forcing to repeat an act that continues to fester to this day in his memory, it would also place the responsibility of uniting the sword and Light Bearer into the hands of someone with a clear mind to ensure such action takes place at the appropriate time with no unseen threat lingering in wait for such a moment."

"And did you have someone in particular in mind to take on this consequential role as overseer?" asked Anahel.

If Thaniel did, he was coy at first to say aloud any such nomination.

"I can't say I've given the matter that much of my time to ponder," he said offhandedly. "But just off the top of my head it seems to me the logical choice would be to place such a duty under the charge of the Library. After all, anything and everything of significant importance to be safeguarded concerning Eden and, in fact, beyond its borders has fallen under its conservatorship."

A heavy look of consternation slowly crept upon Anahel and he slowly stepped to the ledge of the balcony and stared out into the night while silently mulling Thaniel's proposal. When finally he spoke after a long pause it was with a quiet yet firm voice: "No."

~ ~ ~

"Your regard and sympathy for Gothamel is well-placed, Thaniel, and he would be the first to embrace you for it," said Anahel kindly. "He would also be the first to chastise you for it."

"I'm sorry?" said Thaniel, looking somewhat befuddled.

"Gothamel's role as keeper and guardian of the Spear these long years, which you well know, is not one for which he was appointed," explained Anahel. "His tireless hunt for it took him deep inside the boneyard created by the Underneath's expanding gates where the Dragon briefly surfaced into the sunlight from his lair of fire to feast upon the children of man. I don't have to tell you, Thaniel, how perilous it was for Gothamel, as a Fallen, to risk such an undertaking as walking willingly and with great vulnerability into the fog of an evil of such enormity and monstrosity. Yet into it he went unflinchingly and, with all the cunningness of a fox, swindled from the Darkness' grasp its one chance to wield oblivion at its whim. And in doing so he quietly and without fanfare changed the course of history of mortal man.

"Since then the Spear has resided, for the most part, out of sight and out of memory except for the hawkish eyes of the one who has taken upon himself the great duty of seeing through its destiny. How many Fallen, if any, would have been able all this time to resist the calling of the power residing within such a coveted instrument, especially a Fallen who undoubtedly holds unresolved grievances where his banishment is concerned? Now, you would suggest we strip from him the one business to which he has shown estimable loyalty; a loyalty to which he was not then nor is he now bound?" asked Anahel as he shook slowly his head in answer to his question.

"You say it is out of compassion and empathy for the unspeakable sacrifice our brother was made to suffer while serving as caretaker of the Spear that we relieve him of the burden his servitude has reaped," continued the angel.

"Of course it is," Thaniel insisted vehemently.

"That as it may, you and I both know it is because he was made to suffer such a sacrifice that it would take an army of great strength this side of

Heaven to force him to voluntarily resign his duty, much less an outreach of compassion from either you or myself."

Thaniel opened his mouth to further argue the point but the unyielding look in Anahel's eyes caused his tongue to twist itself in a different direction.

"I tend to forget how resolute our brother is when it comes to matters of affliction," he remarked.

Anahel offered a faint grin of agreement. "Then you understand now why it would have to come from Gothamel's own lips an appeal to be relieved of this duty he has willingly taken up upon his shoulders. He has, at the very least, earned such consideration."

"Apparently I have failed to fully think through the proposal I have laid at your feet," said Thaniel.

"Not to worry, Thaniel," said Anahel, smiling warmly as he reached out to give the angel's shoulder a friendly clasp. "I must say it is good to witness the rare occasion when you are led by the heart rather than the mind.

CHAPTER NINE

The morning started like all the others that had come before it. Havenhid awoke to the stirrings of Nephilim rising from their sleep, and soon the deathly quiet halls came to life with renewed chatter accompanying the growing patter of feet following with quickening steps the enticing aromas beckoning the advancing hordes to the Hall of Light.

There, the expectant breakfast was laid out across every open spot on the two long tables like some lavish smorgasbord, drawing the boys in like ants to a sugar cube. With gusto, they dived into the generous buffet awaiting them, loading up their plates with heaping helpings of the various dishes as if they each were dead men walking partaking in their last meal. It didn't matter that there were no plates of bacon, or platters of sausage, nor servings of ham. In fact, in a land where animals were as plentiful as they were varied, there was one place where their presence was banished and that was in the Hall of Light basted and served up in some succulent form of an entree. No, it did not matter, and their absence brought about no complaints or disgruntlements. For the dishes, strange and unfamiliar as they were, that were introduced to the boys were so satisfying and delicious in their own right that common fare cured from beasts of the land were quickly forgotten.

"Anyone besides me ever wonder where all this food comes from?" Leos pondered aloud while everyone seated around him heartily worked their way through their plates.

"What do you mean?" asked Max between bites.

"Well, has anyone here seen anything in Havenhid that even remotely looks like a kitchen? I mean, where's the stove and oven or even a fridge or pantry filled with food? Not only that, who's been making all these meals every day since we've been here?" wondered Leos. "I know the Guides are capable of doing some pretty incredible things that defies logic, but I'm not really picturing any of them wearing an apron and beating things with a whisk, know what I mean?"

"Maybe it's manna," offered Kairo after thoughtful consideration.

"Manna?"

"Yeah, you know…the stuff that rained down from Heaven for the Israelites to eat when they were wandering the desert after the Exodus."

"I know what manna is. It's bread from Heaven, right?" said Leos, looking to his roommates for a thumbs-up.

"Actually, it was more like a coriander seed," corrected Jacob who had been quietly listening to the debate as he ate.

"Seed? Who can get by on just eating seeds?" Leos scoffed.

"Newsflash, Leos: you can actually make things from the seeds," said Max. "It was probably ground up like grain and then made into bread, or cakes, or whatever."

"Okay, but even so, there's a lot more here in front of us than bread and whatever else you can manage to bake from a bunch of crushed up seeds," argued Leos.

"Maybe Heaven expanded its menu," said Kairo, chuckling under his breath.

"You know, I think you just might be on to something there," Max agreed with a wink. "For all we know this is God's take of the early bird special at Lenny's."

"Denny's," Jacob was quick to interject with a playful nudge of his elbow.

Kairo mimicked the sound of a comedy punchline rim shot and, as the group erupted in snickers over the light-hearted moment reminiscent of a bad TV commercial long past, Max went to grab another helping of "manna" when he glanced over at Ethan who he suddenly realized was being uncharacteristically quiet. "What say, Ethan?"

Ethan didn't answer. Instead, he sat unnaturally still in his seat staring straight ahead, fork in hand and held mid-air looking as though he was eating with his jaw working.

"Earth to Ethan," cooed Jacob.

"Don't mind him, he's trying to do some last-minute cramming for Thaniel's test in Study this morning," said Leos with an exasperated roll of his eyes.

The other boys leaned in for a closer, curious look. Sure enough, what first appeared to be an odd manner of chewing was, in fact, an indecipherable recitation of words coming from Ethan's mouth but uttered too quietly for any of the straining ears to make out what was being whispered with such focus. Adding to the intensity of the sight was the fact Ethan's eyes were rolled slightly upward and fixed on the ceiling above, giving the boy the appearance of being in the grips of some kind of epileptic episode.

"Looks sorta catatonic to me," Max deadpanned.

"How can you tell the difference from when he's normal?" joked Leos.

Kairo gave Ethan a couple shakes to rouse him from his trance.

"I think I finally might have gotten it," Ethan suddenly said spritely.

"What is it you're trying to memorize?" asked Jacob.

"The ranks of angels according to the Celestial Hierarchy. Thaniel's sure to ask it on his test."

"Alright, so let's hear it," coaxed Max.

Ethan's face tightened noticeably as the gears to his brain could almost be heard kicking into motion.

"It goes Seraphim, Cherubim, Thrones…" He paused to chew the inside of his lip while pondering the list. "Then there's Dominations, Virtues, Principalities and Powers…followed by Archangels and, lastly, Angels.

A gleam of victory flashed brightly in his eyes but was quickly put out at the sight of Max's disapproving shake of the head.

"So close," said Max.

"And yet so remedial," Leos was quick to chide.

"What did I get wrong?" Ethan, clearly frustrated, inquired.

"It should be Powers, then Principalities," said Jacob.

"Great," Ethan groaned. "Which means I probably have the Choir that each belongs to messed up as well."

Relax, it's not that complicated," said Jacob who couldn't help but feel somewhat sorry for his friend and the growing angst gripping him as the clock ticked closer to the start of Study. "All you have to do is keep in mind the number three. There are three Choirs and nine ranks of angels. Divide the number of ranks by three and you get three. Three ranks to each of the three Choirs. As long as you manage to memorize the ranks in the right order, you're good as gold."

"Of course, there's also the question of who came up with the Celestial Hierarchy," Leos, who couldn't restrain himself from further tweaking the clearly agitated Ethan, cut in.

"You think Thaniel's going ask that?" questioned Ethan as the troubled frown etched in his forehead grew more pronounced.

"The question is why wouldn't Thaniel ask that?" said Max.

Ethan let out a frustrated sigh and resumed his "thinking" pose with his eyes turned once again to the ceiling and mouth agape, only this time void of any whispered chatter.

"Anyone want to give me a clue?" he eventually appealed with a squeak of surrender.

"Pseudo-Dionysius the Areopagite," Max, Jacob, Kairo and Leos answered in a loud and unifying chorus.

"I'M DOOMED!" bellowed Ethan, dropping his head onto the table with a deadening thud.

"Don't fret, Ethan," said Leos, giving the defeated pile seated beside him a reassuring rub on the shoulder. "Maybe there'll be an extra credit question on the test that can save you. Like name the order of the Jedi."

"If only I had been born with the Grace of Drifting instead of Cloaking," Ethan was heard to croak.

"What good would that do except allow you another day or two to study when you should have been?" asked Kairo.

Ethan raised his head to reveal a look of hope far outside his reach. "With the Grace of Drifting, I wouldn't have to sit here worrying about what order the ranks of angels are. I could just go into the test cold and if I came across a question I didn't know I could just nonchalantly slip out of my body, go look up the answer and slip right back without anyone being the wiser. Easy A."

"You really are a walking idiot, you know that?" berated Leos. "You really think Thaniel, of all people, wouldn't be wise to such subterfuge?"

"Not necessarily," argued Ethan. "He might be smart, but just cause he's an angel doesn't mean he knows everything."

Leos could only look to Kairo, Max and Jacob and offer up a dumbfounded nod. "Gentlemen, I give you the latest installment in the Jedi Saga: 'Star Wars: A New Dope,' starring Ethan Richert."

Drawing chuckles from the other boys except Ethan, Leos then assumed his best Princess Leia impersonation. "Help me, Grace of Drifting, you're my only hope."

As the snickering grew, so too did Ethan's scowl. "Ha, ha, very funny!"

~ ~ ~

The frivolity continued as Leos and Kairo continued to rib Ethan, and no one was more amused looking on than Jacob. To him it was like watching some modern-day Three Stooges reincarnated before his very eyes doing everything but a two-finger poke in the eyes. His joviality, however, evaporated in a puff when he went to reach for his glass of water to quiet a coughing fit that all at once overtook him in the midst of his chortling, and instead his face took on the kind of ashen look one gets when struck by a sudden cold sweat.

A strange black shape—the kind of slow billowing plumes formed when drops of black ink from the tip of a fountain pen meet water— was seen swirling in his drink. It moved about with a hypnotizing slowness like some drowned shadow set adrift in the currents of some dark sea. And from within the shape there was seen the pale whiteness of a face. Whose it was Jacob couldn't tell as it remained in a constant state of blurred distortion. It had dark eyes, and they were staring back in a most noticeable way at Jacob.

Then came the voice, or rather voices as they made themselves heard to Jacob's ears in a chorus of feminine whispers overlaying one another but coming from the same mouth with the same message. They were beckoning to Jacob, but beckoning him where? Into the glass? All such logic was lost to him at that moment, as was his surroundings: the table he was seated at, the joking bantering going on in front of him, even the Hall of Light itself had momentarily ceased to exist. The only thing that remained was this strange, dark, luring figure that had turned Jacob into a statue frozen with a look of intrigue and trepidation.

"You alright there, mate?" Max's own voice managed to pierce through whatever spellbinding trance had gripped Jacob, though it was the hard jab that followed that finally tore his gaze from the glass, instantly silencing the mesmerizing voices.

"What's that?" asked Jacob, looking as though he had just been shaken awake from a brief nap.

"You're looking at that water there as if you're holding a glass of arsenic. Don't worry, it came fresh from the River like it does every morning," said Max, reaching for his own glass and lifting it in toasting fashion. "Cheers."

"Right, cheers," muttered Jacob as he cautiously eyed the glass of water gripped his hand only to find the strange dark shape no longer swimming inside much to his relief as well as consternation. Instead of taking a drink, he quickly abandoned it on the table where he continued to stare at it for several more moments.

You're training too hard, he thought to himself to help explain away the weird hallucination. *Gotham is working you ragged and now you're seeing things in your water. Tomorrow, maybe the eggs will come to life.*

When it was clear the vision was gone and only his sanity remained in question, Jacob breathed a sigh of relief and looked to Max who was cleaning up the last few bites he had left on his plate.

"About what you said yesterday," he said in low voice out of earshot from the others. "I've been thinking about it a lot and, well, as much as it pains me to admit it, I just wanted you to know that I think you might have been right."

Max's face instantly beamed with light.

"Oh, yeah?" he replied almost too gleefully between swallows of food.

The look of delight was just as quickly replaced with one of perplexity, making the beginnings of his eyebrows dip down lower to the bridge of his nose. "What a minute, you'll have to remind me what I said. So much of the wisdom I pass along on a daily basis ends up enlightening so many I have a hard time keeping track."

"You know, last night, in the common room," explained Jacob. "What you said about my wings. Or rather, why I still don't have them."

Along with clarity, a look of slow-rising remorse came to Max. "Oh yeah, about that," he began to hem. "Sometimes this pie hole is just that and should stay shut. I really didn't mean—"

Jacob was quick to quiet the backpedaling. "No, you were right…at least, I think you were. Maybe I am afraid. Whether it's this whole Light Bearer business, or fully embracing being a Nephilim, I'm not sure. All I know is tomorrow I'm going to face down whatever this fear is that's taken hold of me. I'm going to make that jump at Broken Earth."

"Well, I'll be a stoned mullet!" said Max. "But I think you've got your days mixed up, mate. Tomorrow, we'll be at Crescent Scar. You mean the day after."

"No, I mean tomorrow," Jacob said defiantly. "When I do this, there's one certain pair of eyes I want watching."

Max followed Jacob's shifting gaze to where some unseen source of amusement was drawing a row of raucous laughter from the neighboring table where Creed could be seen huddled with his small band of followers and he knew immediately which pair of eyes his friend was referring.

"As long as you got your clangers to make the jump, you don't need to worry about anything, or anyone else, trust me," said Max as he continued eating while glowering at Creed. "You certainly don't have anything to prove to that galah."

The look cemented on Jacob's face silently argued his friend's well-meaning sentiment in spades, especially as he attempted to eye with an ever-growing sense of suspicion what was causing the guffawing and sniggering coming from the bodies congregated around Creed. It was then Jacob suddenly became conscious of someone hovering close behind where he sat. Glancing over his left shoulder, he discovered it was a boy by the name of Predmore.

Jacob didn't know much about Predmore (the two had only spoken two, maybe three times during their stay so far in Eden, and then it was in brief passing conversation), but what he did know he seemed to like. Predmore was a quiet boy, some would even call him shy. Jacob saw the perceived shyness as something more along the lines of a shared kinship they both had in common: a trait of uncertainty about themselves that seemed to be lacking amongst the other boys.

"Sorry if I'm disturbing you," Predmore said somewhat sheepishly.

"You're not disturbing me," replied Jacob. "What's going on?"

"I was wondering if I might have a word with you." His voice carried the undeniable English accent of his hometown of Manchester, England in the same way Australia had imprinted itself on Max's tongue, but without the colorful and humorous choice of phrases.

"Sure, what's on your mind?

Predmore's eyes darted with hesitancy at the others seated around Jacob. "I was hoping alone."

"No need for that, Predmore. Come on and have a seat," Kairo offered politely as he scooted over to make room on the wooden bench for Predmore to sit. "We're all friends here."

Despite the friendly gesture, Predmore remained on his feet looking even more apprehensive.

"Something bothering you, Predmore?" asked Jacob.

"I'm not sure what I'm about to ask is right, and I'm not looking to offend you, especially after what happened with Creed a while back when he cut his arm and challenged you to…" He paused for a moment as if unsure whether to finish his sentence before he managed to spit out the remaining words caught in his throat, "heal him."

Now Jacob found himself intrigued.

"You won't offend me," he assured the boy. "What is it?"

Slowly, Predmore stretched out his right arm toward Jacob while pulling up his long sleeve to reveal a large makeshift bandage on the underside of his forearm. When Predmore pulled back the bandage, Jacob grimaced at the three-inch gash freshly set in the flesh.

"Ow! That had to hurt," remarked Max with a pained look. "Looks like you retreated and caught a blow when you should have gone forward."

"That's about the size of it. A really stupid move on my part," Predmore said with a weight of admonishment aimed at himself rather than a reflective comment.

"Why didn't you have Damiel take care of it?" asked Leos.

"Are you kidding me? I never would have heard the end of it making such a lame-brain mistake this far into our training," said Predmore.

"So, why are you showing me?" asked Jacob, though his suspicious tone indicated he already had a hunch.

"I was just thinking about what you did for Ballantine when Ethan here cut open his leg," said Predmore.

The unwelcome reminder drew a tired eye roll from Ethan. "It was accident," he remarked under his breath with a deep sigh.

"You want me to heal your arm?" asked Jacob as if such a thought was as foreign to him as the possibility of a green sky.

"I wouldn't ask you if it wasn't for the fact that it still kinda hurts," said Predmore.

Jacob glanced around the table and caught the stares of Max, Ethan, Leos and Kairo fixed firmly on him waiting for his response. And for a brief moment he understood what a circus animal must feel like when it's paraded out into the spotlight to perform its tricks for the waiting audience.

"Don't take this the wrong way, but maybe it's a good thing it hurts," he said finally bringing a confused look to Predmore. "We all know how Damiel is about wounds suffered during training; if it isn't life-threatening he won't heal it. He says it's better to live through the pain as a reminder so that in the future we avoid making the mistake we made to get injured in the first place. The bleeding has stopped and your cut seems to be on its way to healing on its own. I think I'd be stealing a valuable lesson from you if I were attempt to heal it."

It wasn't what Predmore was hoping for, but after allowing Jacob's words sink into his head he eventually nodded agreement and rolled down his sleeve.

~ ~ ~

"Did I call it or what?" Ethan said under his breath once Predmore left. "Oh man, can you believe it's happening already? Just like I said it would."

"What is it you're yammering about?" asked Leos.

"Uh, hello. Guadalupe?" said Ethan, reminding the table of the mysterious holy site people from all over the world flocked to every year in hopes of curing their ills.

"Uh, hello, one person is not exactly a pilgrimage, bonehead," said Kairo.

"Neither was Guadalupe until that first person went there and was miraculously cured. News like that has a way of spreading," argued Ethan.

"What news are you talking about" asked Jacob with an almost horrified look on his face. "You make it sound like I'm going to set up a corner lemonade stand when I leave here and peddle miracles."

"You have to admit it's pretty remarkable," Max chimed in.

"Not you, too," said Jacob.

"I don't mean about you being some modern-day healing deity for the masses," said Max. "But like it or not, I think they might be starting to buy into what's happening."

Jacob gave a hesitant look to the other boys seated nearby oblivious to the conversation taking place as they busily continued on with their breakfast when Max's voice once more met his ear, "One by one, they're starting to believe who you are, which is a good thing. Because eventually they're going to be the ones who make up your army. We all are."

Army?

The conversation was suddenly getting a little too real, and even more heavy, for Jacob to take in at this early hour. For all the training he had undergone the last several weeks, he had never really sat down and thought about where it would all eventually take him. Accepting he was the Light Bearer was one thing; to understand fully how, exactly, it would come to shape his life was something he had failed to allow his mind to wrap itself around. Was it because he was too scared to do so? Or could it be, more likely, he knew the pondering of such thoughts were immensely too much for a kid like him to digest? Whatever the reason, he was almost relieved when another load outburst of chuckling erupted from the small group of boys clustered around Creed ended the conversation.

"What's got them so amused?" Leos wondered aloud as he spied at the group from over his shoulder.

"I don't know, but whatever it is it's been entertaining them since breakfast started," said Kairo.

They each narrowed their eyes on the group of boys, searching for an opening in the scrum in hopes of stealing a peek at whatever hidden private joke was the cause of so much enthrallment. Whatever it was brought the exact opposite response from Jacob when he suddenly caught a glimpse of something unexpectedly familiar in Creed's clutches: a worn, brown leather-bound book that he instantly recognized as a journal. *His* journal. And what could only be described as a murderous look instantly descended upon him.

"Where're you goin'?" asked Max when Jacob got up abruptly from his seat at the table.

Jacob didn't answer, and without a word he made his way around to the neighboring table to where Creed and his bunch continued to laugh it up. As he approached, his ears captured Creed reciting with satisfying mockery the private thoughts he kept in his journal, and he immediately felt the blood in his veins begin to boil. Yet, somehow, instead of giving in to his unbridled desire to lunge across the table and allowing his hands the pure delight of securing themselves around his arch nemesis' strangle-worthy throat, he managed to stay rooted to the floor, like a burning flame to a candle wick.

"It's times like these late at night when everyone's asleep that I find myself lying awake in my bed wrestling with incredible pangs of homesickness," Creed continued to read from the journal. "Even though Zuriel is a hard nose against any of us using our Graces in frivolous manners, I have to admit there have been a couple times in those late hours while everyone's snoring away where I couldn't help but utilize my Grace of Roaming to leave Eden, if only for a few minutes, and travel back to the night of the school dance. Just to see Wray again, to have her hand in mine as she is leading me to the middle of the gymnasium, and then to feel her in my arms as we slow dance to our song…it really is 'Sanctuary,' at least the sanctuary needed to momentarily cure my loneliness. But I know it's a visit I must keep short. My place, at least for the time being, is here in Eden, and there's a lot of work I still need to do. Yet the brief moment we get to spend looking into one another's eyes and sharing our first kiss before Mrs. Braukoff painfully pulls me away by the ear has me looking forward to the day when I can return home, whenever that day comes."

~ ~ ~

Standing there listening to Creed read the words to his inner-most private thoughts out loud and with such dripping derision to an accompaniment of snickers was enough to light the burners of rage inside Jacob. However, the smug and most self-satisfied of smiles, growing all the wider like the body of a stretching cat across Creed's face, to reveal his thorough enjoyment of this blatant violation was enough to turn them on full tilt.

"I think you have something that belongs to me," Jacob managed to say in as cool and collected a manner as he could muster.

"Well, well, well…speak of the devil," Creed croaked snidely when he looked up and spied Jacob standing a stone's throw away and appearing as hot under the collar as he felt.

"Maybe one of you can help me. Anyone know who this belongs to?" inquired Creed, holding up the journal. "I found it last night in one of the common rooms before I went to bed."

"You know it belongs to Jacob," Leos grumbled surly.

"Does it?" said Creed, feigning a naivety that was anything but believable. "You know, now that I look at it more closely, I seem to remember seeing you off in a corner on more than one occasion writing furiously in a book similar to this. Sorry if I didn't put two and two together, but you really can't fault me for not thinking this belonged to anyone in this room. I mean, no offense, but keeping a journal is something my mom did when she was a little girl. Only then it was called a diary."

The snide remark drew a gaggle of chuckles from the other boys in the Hall who looked to Jacob with increased anxiousness as the air grew more tense. Yet it was Max who spoke.

"Now that you know, you'll give it back…if you know what's good for you," he said.

"Of course," replied Creed, looking anything but intimidated as he placed the journal on the table and, with a shove, slid it in Jacob's direction.

"I knew you were a lot of things, Creed, but I didn't think thief was one of them," said Jacob, once the journal was back in his hands.

"I already told you where I found it," hissed Creed, looking suddenly hateful.

"Likely story," Ethan muttered under his breath yet loud enough to reach Creed's ears.

"You calling me a liar, runt?" Creed's cold, steely gaze made Ethan shrink slightly into the protective grouping of his friends surrounding him. "If the diary—excuse me, *journal*—is so important, then maybe you should keep it under lock and key and not just leave it lying around for anyone to pick up. Besides, what interest would I have in anything you keep in that thing?"

"Then why did you make it a point to read out loud from it to everyone?" sniped Jacob.

"You're not sore at me for having a little harmless fun at your expense, are you?" Creed couldn't help but grin when he saw plainly and clearly in the angry glare Jacob had fixed on him how truly unforgivable and, better still, cutting his trespass into the boy's privacy was. "Actually, you should probably be thanking me for being snoopy."

"How's that?" Jacob replied.

"Well, now everyone knows Jacob Parrish actually likes girls. Go figure!" said Creed. "I was beginning to wonder, close as you two seem to be, if old Max here was starting to make you see little hearts dancing around your head."

"Keep it up, creep, and I'll be the maker of stars dancing 'round your head, I can promise you that," said Max while clenching his fists in a show his words were not just some idle threat.

"Forget about him," urged Jacob. "He's just trying to get under our skin."

"Yeah, like a ringworm," Kairo muttered with disgust.

With Jacob's journal returned to its rightful place, the boys turned their backs on Creed choosing not to engage any further with him and return back to their seats on their side of the Hall.

Creed wasn't quite finished.

"If it makes you feel any better, the only other parts I read were about your mom," Creed called out to Jacob, bringing the boy's feet to an instant halt. "Sad thing what happened to her, though not completely surprising seeing how she brought a Weed into the world. But if you want a little friendly piece of advice from one Nephilim to, well…you: let it go. I mean, it's been a while now since she bit the dust. Going on and on about in your little diary just makes you sound…whiny."

If rage was what Jacob felt pulsating through his body moments earlier then it was a whole newly discovered emotion that suddenly surfaced and made his mouth instantly tighten as though he was struck with an immediate case of lock jaw; but it was Max who erupted first.

"You really are a ratbag, aren't you?" he seethed, turning around and taking an advancing step toward where Creed sat in his aura of smugness, before Jacob grabbed hold of him to keep him in his place.

"He's not worth it."

Creed, however, argued differently as he allowed his mouth to continue flap like the unsecured sail of a boat caught in the throes of a storm.

"Don't get me wrong, I feel for you, Parrish, really I do," he said in that patronizing way he had mastered of allowing words to drip from his tongue like bile. "The guilt you must be carrying around must weigh like a ton of bricks."

"What are you talking about? What guilt?" Leos couldn't help but ask.

What are you, blind?" answered Creed. "If your buddy here truly is the Light Bearer like everyone assumes he is, then that means he could have stepped in and beat back death from taking his mom. He could have placed his healing hands on her and saved her at any time. Instead, he just stood around and watched her languish until they stuck her in hole six feet under. If that isn't the cruelest of ironies, I don't know what is."

The Hall became as quiet as a chapel in a church, as no one dared to speak. Creed may have had a reputation for possessing a tongue more suitable for the back end of a wasp, but the extremely personal and virulent sting of his latest goad was pointedly vicious and cruel, even for him. Even Max was resistant in allowing his eyes to slowly shift their gaze to witness the enveloping pain he expected to have settled upon his friend like some kind of unpleasant death mask.

"Like you said, he ain't worth it," Max offered quietly.

"I know what I said," Jacob agreed with a deceptively cool calmness.

Jacob quietly handed off his journal to Max and offered up a reassuring smile, and for a brief moment Max couldn't help but be impressed by the level of self-restraint being demonstrated before him; much more than he himself could have possibly mustered had the tables been turned. Then, in a moment that was quick in its passing, Max caught sight of a flare of an unmistakable fire in Jacob's eyes and any notion of a gesture to turn the other cheek was instantly incinerated. What happened next came in a flash of movement when Jacob suddenly turned and, before anyone could register what it was their eyes were seeing, he leapt across the table like an attacking mountain lion and pounced upon the unsuspecting Creed, knocking him clean off his seat and down onto the floor.

The Hall immediately erupted in a loud roar as the other boys quickly jumped to their feet to form a tight circle around the two bodies thrashing and flailing wildly about the floor like two sharks grounded in the shallows. With each punch thrown, the cheers grew louder, but the only sound to meet Jacob's ears was the pounding beat of anger pent up inside him drumming its way to all points of his body while fighting back with all his might against a force of rage coming at him with equal intensity. He suddenly found himself back home in his high school gym grabbling for domination in a high-stakes wrestling match. Only instead of focusing to pin his opponent to the floor, he fought as hard as he could to push him through it.

The growing clamor of excitement not heard since the competitions marking the start of Illumination some months earlier echoed within the Hall. And, indeed, the frenzied match taking place on the floor was every bit as rousing and gripping as the rivalries put on showcase that day at Lions Bite. Each swing of a fist or trade of the upper hand as Jacob and Creed each won momentary positions of domination over the other only to lose it in what became a constant flipping and rolling of bodies incited a spirited verbal row from the sidelines where the scrum of Nephilim looking on made their individual alliances known by the howling and goading shouted forth in a feverish cacophony of enthusiasm. Quite suddenly, though, and much to everyone's disappointment, the momentary fracas was stilled as instantly as it erupted when two large tree limbs, unnoticed at first by the riveted throng below, wriggled themselves free from the architecture shaping the cavernous Hall's high walls. The other boys, jolted by the sight, immediately scrambled out of the way as the two arboreal limbs reached down toward them and, with their finger-like branches, took hold of Jacob and Creed, both equally startled as they were pulled apart from one another and lifted into the air like two squirming mice nabbed by the tail.

A look of shared bewilderment shot its way to all corners of the Hall by the gathering of boys until quickly they all caught sight of Anahel's presence standing nearby with a none-too-pleased look on his face, and immediate silence was returned to the Hall.

"One would think the appetites of growing Fledglings had overwhelmed the breakfast menu and incited a row over the last morsel of food," Anahel remarked as he made his way slowly toward the abandoned tables and eyed the buffet of food spread out like a cornucopia worthy of a king. "But I see I would be mistaken."

He then turned his gaze to Jacob and Creed, looking disheveled and out of breath, but with fire still burning in their eyes, as they dangled limply and helplessly high above in the air in the clutches of the branches. "It's been said, 'Where jealousy and selfish ambition exist, there will be disorder and every vile practice.' I don't think I would be remiss in saying the two of you have consistently proven there to be truth in such words. And let it be known I am at my wits end."

There was a firm tone of disfavor in Anahel's voice that made Jacob chasten somewhat, even as he remained in the grip of his anger, and for a brief moment he wished the tree limb that had a hold of him would fling him through the open ceiling of the Hall and out of sight of the dismayed look the angel had fixed on him. The branches, however, offered no such favor and, instead, discarded the two sullen-looking boys back onto the floor like a couple of bowling balls where they tumbled and rolled until coming to a splayed-out rest at Anahel's feet. Then, looking a bit dazed and confused, Jacob and Creed watched along with the other boys as the two limbs maneuvered their way seamlessly back into position to become part of the structure that was the Hall of Light.

"You'll pay for this, Parrish," Creed threatened under his breath while giving Jacob a shove aside. Jacob responded in kind to the insolent gesture, but before the back and forth escalated to a second-round scrap, Anahel's voice stilled them in their place with a thundering command, "You two, come with me!"

CHAPTER TEN

SACEREL

"Don't see why I'm being pulled aside as though I did anything wrong," Creed protested the moment Anahel led the two boys into a quiet sitting room down the hall away from prying ears. "Ask anyone and they'll tell you I was minding my own business having a little breakfast before class when this unhinged freak jumped me for no apparent reason."

"Speak about my mother again and next time this unhinged freak will be standing here with your ripped out tongue in his hand," Jacob shot back.

"That will be enough!" declared Anahel, but neither boy paid any mind.

"Look, I'm willing to forgive and forget for this unwarranted attack," offered Creed. "All you have to do is apologize for being an uncivilized cretin."

"Apologize? You're joking right?" Jacob guffawed. "You can count on that when pigs fly."

"At least that will be a lot sooner than you ever will, by the looks of things," Creed replied sneeringly.

"I SAID SILENCE!" Anahel's voice roared loudly once more, ceasing instantly the verbal sparring between the two boys.

"Never have I heard such a constant squabbling between Nephilim than with the two of you," Anahel grumbled with a huff of exasperation. "From the day the two of you first laid eyes on one another, you've been at each other's throats, and for the life of me I am at a loss for the genesis of the enmity the two of you harbor for one another. Nor, frankly, do I care. But hear me now when I tell you in no uncertain terms that you will end it this day; in fact, this very minute."

The two boys stood stock still beside one another and breathed not a word, but the furtive looks they exchanged out of the corner of their eyes as Anahel walked the room about them revealed no intentions of a truce would be had.

"Rivalries have existed amongst Fledglings long before either of you added your breath to this world; no doubt they will exist after your last. But the level of disdain the two of you continue to show for one another has no place in Eden, and needless to say I will not tolerate either one of you attempting to extend the footprint of Lions Bite into the sanctuary that is Havenhid. Do I make myself clear?" The boys offered a slight, albeit obedient nod of their heads, but if they thought their reprimand was finished they quickly discovered differently as Anahel resumed his pacing of the floor. "You'd both be wise to reflect on why you and your fellow Fledglings have come to pass through Havenhid's doors. A far worse adversary lies outside Eden's gate; a true foe that you will find far outweighs any juvenile contretemps you now wrangle with amongst yourselves. Best you harness the energy you've chosen to focus on your disdain for each other and, instead, forge forth an alliance to fight your real and common enemy."

Anahel studied intently each boy's face for the faintest sign his words had managed to penetrate the tight-lipped expressions staring back his way, but if the ice between the two boys had succumbed to even a slight thawing it didn't show.

"In the meantime, for the remainder of the week, you will each of you be confined to your rooms once you are through with your lessons for the day," said Anahel, bringing a shared look of unpleasantness to Jacob and Creed. "Perhaps then you will find within yourselves a level of civility and restraint to keep you from regressing to the feral caterwauling usually found in common alley cats."

Even as Anahel spoke, Jacob could sense Creed's back slowly beginning to rise upwards.

"That's not fair," Creed protested. "I told you he jumped me. Why then am I the one being punished?"

"Fairness, by its very nature, has always managed to retain an elusive quality, even here in Eden," answered Anahel. "But, be that as it may, I've yet to come across a bear that attacks without being poked in some fashion."

One could see the slow boil Creed was coming to as his face tightened with a surly scowl. "You can bet I'll be letting my father know about this as soon as I'm able," he huffed petulantly.

"I would be disappointed if you didn't," Anahel replied with a twinkle of amusement. "And now I sense the hour is about ready to call you to your lessons."

Creed continued to hold Anahel in his withering gaze until he realized his air of intimidation had not the slightest effect on the angel and promptly stomped off.

"If you wouldn't mind, I'd like to have a word with you alone," Anahel called out when Jacob turned to follow suit.

~ ~ ~

"I know what you're going to say and you're right," Jacob was quick to note before Anahel could launch into a new round of scolding he was sure was coming. "It's just sometimes he makes me so mad everything turns red and nothing seems to matter except the desire to literally twist his head off his body."

"He is incorrigible, that one," said Anahel with a subtle grin.

"That's not exactly the word I had in mind for him," Jacob muttered sourly under his breath.

"A Nephilim though you may be, I have not lost sight of the fact that you are first and foremost a boy. And, like all boys, you come wired with boyish ways. Fighting with one another, however loutish it may be, is but one avenue by which you tend to feel your way through your early years of growth and discovery. I accept this, for it is nature's way." A mischievous twinkle suddenly alighted Anahel's eyes. "If I were to be completely honest with you, Mr. Maggert's prickly ways have admittedly forced me on more than one occasion to wrestle internally with myself to keep from, as you so tactfully put it, twisting his head off his body."

A gratifying smile slowly unrolled itself across Jacob's face.

"Now that I would give anything to see," said the boy before he and the angel shared a chuckle together over the image of a suddenly headless Creed running around wildly like some decapitated chicken.

"On a more serious note, let me stress upon you that anger can be a dangerous thing, not just for the person for whom it's focused upon but more so for the one consumed in it," said Anahel as his light-heartedness slowly gave way to a noticeable earnestness. "Where you find anger, you'll find the Darkness swarming, like mosquitoes to stagnant water. It's where it thrives; for when wrath is set alight, the doorway to the soul becomes ajar allowing for these malignant forces to slip inside with all their infectious ways. It is man's one true Achilles heel."

"Harness the beast, don't let it harness you," Jacob was heard to mutter.

"I'm sorry?" said Anahel.

"Just something Damiel likes to drill into our heads when we're training at Lions Bite," explained Jacob. "He says anger is red meat to the Darkness; that it allows one to be blinded to rationale thinking and judgment. Kinda makes sense when you hear in the news about all the horrible crimes committed by people caught up in a moment of rage."

"Damiel knows well of what he speaks. You'd do well to take his guidance to heart."

Harness the beast, don't let it harness you. Jacob quietly pondered Damiel's mantra when a sheepish look suddenly weighed itself down upon the boy. "Guess I really blew that lesson, didn't I? Not only did my anger harness me, it hogtied me."

Anahel said nothing at first. Then offering a polite, if not understanding smile, he said, "Come, and walk with me."

~ ~ ~

They strolled together, the two of them, with leisurely and unhurried steps along Havenhid's long meandering halls. As they did, Jacob couldn't help but take notice of how Havenhid, which had always held within its walls a blissful serenity, seemed even more tranquil and quiet than usual with the absence of the constant patter of feet and drone of chit-chat coming from its many teenaged residents who by now had rushed off to their daily lessons.

"I must tell you, Jacob, I've found myself becoming increasingly impressed with you with each passing day," said Anahel.

"Impressed? With me?" echoed Jacob with surprise.

"Don't misunderstand me, Fledgling," Anahel was quick to reply. "My feeling is not based on the boorish display I was made to witness this morning in the Hall of Light."

You certainly made that clear enough, Jacob thought to himself as he followed Anahel out onto one of the many large verandas offering stunning views of Eden from Havenhid's vantage point hidden high in the tree tops.

"To the contrary, it's out there where a glint of your capabilities shimmer like some evening star drawing the attention of all eyes in a sky full of twinkling stars," answered the angel as he stared out into the distance in the direction of Lions Bite. "I've been observing you now, albeit from afar, for the past few weeks now since Gothamel's taken you into his tutelage, and I've found myself quite pleased, inspired even, with the undeniable progress I've seen demonstrated by you in such a short amount of time."

Anahel snuck a glance out of the corner of his eye at the boy who remained noticeably quiet at his side. If Jacob agreed or disagreed with the assessment, he didn't say so one way or the other.

"I must say the young man I look upon beside me now is a far cry from the image of the boy I found at Broken Earth not so long ago wringing his hands in despair over what has been revealed to be his fate."

"I wouldn't go so far as to say I was wringing my hands in despair," Jacob argued. "Just temporarily overtaken by a big dose of…pessimism."

"Pessimism that has been swept aside by an even bigger dose of confidence and, I suspect, sense of purpose," said Anahel.

The words of encouragement from the angel brought forth from the boy a beam of pride, though in a manner that was noticeably reserved and not at all puffed up.

"What can I say? You were right about Gotham. Sure, he can be a royal pain in the a—…that is, in the neck," said Jacob, grinning sheepishly at Anahel over his quick catch of the tongue. "But in the time we've been training together, he's managed to push me to do things I never would have believed I had the abilities to do in ways the other Guides haven't. Still, I can't help but feel I have a long ways to go yet."

"Your instincts serve you well," remarked Anahel. "A Nephilim's training is never complete, no matter how outwardly it appears his strength has been conditioned or how masterful he wields his divine gifts. When preparing to go to battle with the dark forces, one eventually discovers he is deficient a completely impregnable suit of armor."

"I take it that means I'm stuck with Attila the Hun for the unforeseeable future," Jacob gloomily joked.

A knowing grin raised the corners of Anahel's mouth, both at Gotham's well-earned reputation as being a hard-driving teacher, and the boy's obvious regard and affection for his taskmaster despite his outward scoff to hide it.

~ ~ ~

The two stood on the veranda sharing a quiet moment as they stared out at the scenery of the Garden laid before them when Anahel asked, "Has Gothamel shared with you yet the conversation I had with him not too long ago concerning your next steps as Light Bearer?"

Jacob thought for a moment. "I'm not sure. It seems everything we talk about these days concerns it one way or another, it's hard to keep track.

"Has he made mention of a rite called the Blessing?"

"Oh, that," Jacob muttered quietly, catching Anahel curiously.

"I see he has," said Anahel. "And you're response brimming with enthusiasm answers my next question in knowing your feelings about it."

"It's not that I'm unenthusiastic about it," Jacob was quick to explain. "To tell you the truth, I was actually quite flattered to hear how confident you were in me to make such a formal fuss over this whole thing. It's just..."

"Just?" Anahel urged the boy to continue.

"Well, don't you think it's all a bit soon to be considering such things?"

"You still carry doubt you are not what the Fates have destined you to be become."

"It's not so much that anymore. In fact, I think I've come to pretty much accept this whole Light Bearer thing," said Jacob.

"Then what continues to sow seeds of doubt inside you?" asked Anahel.

"I just feel so far behind the others," answered Jacob. "I mean, after all this time I'm the only one who's still wingless. What if there is something seriously defective about me and I never get them? Have you ever thought about that? What good's a Light Bearer without wings?"

A light of clarity found Anahel's face. "Ah, so that's it. The malediction whose continuing murmur you are unable to turn a deaf ear to: Wings, wings, wings! Better for you to cast aside this niggling obsession and realize wings alone do not a Nephilim make."

"Easy for you to say. You're not the one being goofed on behind your back," said Jacob. "I think the longer I go without wings, the more some of the other guys doubt I'm even a Nephilim, much less the Light Bearer."

"And are you among those who share such doubts?" Jacob felt the angel's searching gaze resting upon him with an uncomfortable intensity that kept his lips firmly sealed tight.

"After all of Thaniel's effort to cultivate your young minds, I would have thought the simplest of realizations would have by now already taken root," said Anahel. "Whether you are the Light Bearer or just an ordinary Nephilim, it came to be from the sum whole of what I see standing before me. You are not alone a bearer of some sacred Grace, just as you are not alone a bearer of the sigil of the Illume. And you most certainly do not exist solely as a bearer of wings."

"You can say that again," Jacob mumbled glumly.

"You're wings will come in due time," said Anahel. "Surely, you would not crack open an egg to force a hatchling to greet the world sooner than it is prepared to do so."

As assured as the angel sounded, Jacob, somehow, could not completely rid himself of his nagging doubt. "But what if you're wrong? You said it yourself once: faith determines coming into one's wings. What if I'm missing the faith needed for wings and don't even realize it?"

"Trust me when I tell you the faithless have a tendency of standing out from the more...enlightened," said Anahel. "I say this as someone who has looked upon many a soul who have come to inhabit faith-barren shells."

"And? What do they look like?" asked Jacob curiously.

"Like someone standing completely naked amid the clothed with their shortcomings left to dangle in a particularly cold breeze."

"And what do you see when you look at me?" Jacob asked with noted reticence.

Anahel looked thoughtfully upon the boy and smiled.

"A boy who appears to be dressed for an early winter."

The angel's words may not have completely assuaged Jacob's worries regarding his wings, or rather lack of, but they seemed to lift his spirits and prop him up a bit taller where he stood.

"When were you thinking about having this so-called Blessing?" asked Jacob.

"Nothing is set in stone," answered Anahel. "But I thought the last day of Illumination would be the appropriate time for such a ceremony. At the very least, it would allow you time in the remaining weeks to further relax yourself into this most extraordinary and, indeed, unexpected role hoisted upon yourself. Perhaps by then the wings you now find yourself pining for will have blossomed, or perhaps not. Either way, this Blessing should be something you embrace, not cringe at the thought of, and so whether a Blessing takes place or not I will leave entirely up to you. Deal?"

Feeling the ebb of pressure and uncertainty that had been slowly building inside him ever since he heard of the Blessing from Gotham gradually begin to reside, Jacob revealed the easing of his mind with a grateful nod. "Deal."

"And now I think I've kept you long enough from you morning lesson," Anahel noted with a smile.

Jacob went to leave when he suddenly hesitated where he stood as if his feet had come into contact with flypaper. "There's just one more thing."

"There always is," Anahel sighed expectantly in that knowing way of his.

Jacob wavered for a moment in making heard what had been rolling about in his head since he and Anahel began their stroll, biting his lip before finally finding his tongue.

"Is there really a record of Nephilim births?"

"Record of..." Anahel appeared somewhat bemused at first by the boy's question. "I take it you're referring to the Descendants Archive."

Descendants Archive. The name echoed inside Jacob's ears like some bewitching spell and he felt his chest tighten slightly when he realized Creed had told him the truth. Though how much truth, exactly, Jacob found himself wondering suddenly.

"May I ask how you came to learn of it?" asked Anahel.

"Just something I overheard some of the other boys talking about," Jacob found himself lying without really meaning to, and yet brushing off his reply as one not completely estranged from the truth.

"The reason why I ask about it," Jacob continued with noticeable hesitation, "is because I understand it contains not only the names of all the Nephilim ever born, but all the important things associated with each one…kinda like a birth certificate."

"It lists the information one would deem pertinent in the birth of a child, yes," said Anahel.

Jacob wasn't sure whether the reticent manner he perceived to be suddenly wrapped around the angel like a shawl was imagined or real.

"Including fathers?" the boy asked with both reluctance and eagerness.

In the brief moment of silence that followed, Jacob felt the angel's eyes sharpen their focus on him in a manner that brought him slight unease.

"Yes," Anahel finally answered softly.

For the life of him, Jacob couldn't figure out why this conversation had taken on a feeling of pulling teeth, and how such an enlightened and perceptive vessel of wisdom as Anahel couldn't see where Jacob's line of questioning was leading.

"Then theoretically," the boy pressed on, "it should say who *my* father is, right?"

Jacob expected to see some kind of light flicker with understanding somewhere inside Anahel's vacant expression, but none revealed itself. Instead, Anahel subtly nodded his head in agreement and muttered, "Theoretically."

Whatever had momentarily appeared to confound the angel passed as quickly as it came, and Anahel seemed to emerge from the brief fog that had settled over him.

"I'm sorry, Jacob, but you're inquiry seems to have caught me to the quick," he said with a half-smile. "It's not often I'm asked about the Descendants Archive."

"So, where is it? In the Library?" asked Jacob.

"No, the book resides in my care in my chamber." A troubled look suddenly found Anahel's face once again. "I presume you would care to have a look at it."

"If I might," replied Jacob eagerly.

"Very well," said Anahel, though with much less eagerness. "I'll see to it it's made available to you by this time tomorrow."

When he turned to leave he was stopped by a tug on his sleeve.

"I don't mean to be pushy about this, but is there any way I could see it now?"

Anahel glanced outward from the terrace to the sky lit by the morning sun. "As it is, you'll have to dash out of here in a full sprint just to be tardy to your morning lessons."

"Do you really think I'm going to be able to concentrate on any lessons today knowing the possibility that the answer to who my father is might rest in some book?"

The boy was all but jumping out of his skin despite the calm demeanor in which he struggled to contain himself, and Anahel knew there would be no rest for either of them until certain long-brewing curiosities had been finally sated. What the angel found painfully impossible to convey to Jacob at that moment was that the Descendants Archive would offer no such rest. If anything, it would likely bring about an agonizing spell of sleepless nights.

~ ~ ~

"You're probably wondering to yourself why it is I never made the Descendants Archive known to you in regards to the mystery you live with concerning the identity of your father," said Anahel, when the two reached his chamber. "Truth of the matter is the document, important as it is, is one whose existence is quite easy to forget. Like the four Witnesses housed in the Library, it is self-propagating and adds to its record the births of Nephilim as they occur. In fact, I cannot tell you the last time I've cracked its binding and perused its pages."

Jacob watched silently, yet anxiously, from where he stood planted in the middle of the room as Anahel made his way to a large bookcase crammed with numerous books and scrolls. When he returned to the boy, he was carrying in his hands in an almost protective manner a large book whose worn leather binding revealed a long history in the same way wrinkles deep-set in skin betray age. There was a guarded look glistening in Anahel's eyes, and for a moment it appeared as if the angel suddenly had a change of mind about allowing the boy the look inside, but to Jacob's delight, Anahel eventually, if not reluctantly, handed the book to him.

"I didn't expect there would be so many," noted Jacob when the full weight of the hefty book rested in his hands. "Are all these Nephilim?"

"It's a family tree whose branches reach back thousands of years," answered Anahel.

Yet it was that long-documented history he keenly eyed in the boy's anxious hands by which Anahel felt himself suddenly in the grips of a feeling rarely, if ever, felt by angels: pangs of panic. For it was in that moment that he was reminded of the night Gotham first brought the child to Havenhid; the night he gave his word to keep secret the boy's own history and allow the truth surrounding his birth to remain concealed in the deep, dark folds of mystery in which it was long-ago swaddled. Now, he knew there was no shroud dense enough or tomb deep enough to keep this untold truth buried any longer. Unbeknownst to Jacob, the Descendants Archive was a sort of divining rod in his hands, and the simple act of opening its pages would finally uncover this spring of deceit.

"Before we go any further, there's something most vital, and I dare say unsettling, I must discuss with you," said Anahel with marked trepidation.

Jacob, however, had already plopped himself in a nearby seat and was eagerly flipping his way through the pages of the book. Grimly, Anahel sat himself next to the boy combing through his thoughts for how best to deliver what would undoubtedly be a shocking revelation with the ability to upend everything the boy had come to believe about himself.

"It's important I have your full attention for what it is I'm about to tell you, as it won't be an easy thing for me to say. Nor will it be, I can assure you, an easy thing for you to hear," said Anahel.

Jacob wasn't listening. Having found the year in which he was born, his finger quickly made its way down page after page in a desperate search for his name.

"Here it is!" he finally exclaimed. "Jacob Samson Parrish."

Beaming with excitement, the boy turned to Anahel who, in stark contrast, was fixed with a look better suited for a funeral.

"Jacob Samson—" the angel muttered before his voice quickly dissipated,

"I know. I've never been quite jazzed about having 'Samson' as my middle name, myself," Jacob, seemingly oblivious to the dazed and disoriented manner slowly sweeping its way over Anahel, noted. "Apparently, it was grandmother's idea to name me after an opera she was famous for performing. But what are you gonna do?"

He returned his eager attention back to the pages of the book, oblivious to the stupefied state that seemed to have taken a hold of Anahel.

"Let's see here…mother's name: Isabeth Grace Parrish," recited Jacob as his eyes slowly followed his finger across the penned notations inscribed on the page. "And now for the moment of truth…"

Anahel's eyes bore themselves into the boy with a look of apprehension that rivaled Jacob's.

~ ~ ~

"Sacerel."

The name rolled off Jacob's tongue with a simple utterance, lacking all the pomp and drama one would expect such a long-awaited announcement would hold.

"Sacerel? Did I hear you say Sacerel?" asked Anahel, looking more confused than ever.

"That's what it says here under 'Father,' " answered Jacob. "Sacerel. It has a great and important sound to it, doesn't it?"

The name was still echoing in the boy's ears, and already he was envisioning illusions of grandeur regarding the elusive father that had existed as nothing more than some phantom figure he now and then entertained daydreams about in his mind. Only now the make-believe figure was slowly starting to take on a shape, beginning with a name. Yet when he turned to Anahel, he was not met by a face that shared in his joy, but rather an expressionless mask of stone.

"May I have a look, if you please?" asked Anahel coolly before Jacob handed over the book to his waiting hands.

The angel sat in silence as he scanned the entry with a careful and discerning eye. *How can this be?* he wondered to himself while attempting to spot some small tell-tale sign of how such a crafty untruth had managed to make its mark in the pages of the book, and more importantly, by whose hand. After all, the Descendants Archive was a record of angel offspring and did not include those of Fallen. Stranger, still, was the name listed as Jacob's father.

Sacerel.

It was as foreign to Anahel's eyes as its sound was upon his tongue. And yet as he continued to study closely the questionable notation, he was careful to keep the ruminating murmurs churning about inside his head from making themselves too loud for fear Jacob would overhear.

"So, do you know who this Sacerel is? What's he like?" Jacob began to pepper Anahel with questions pent up inside himself. "More importantly, do you know how or where we might find him?"

"A great multitude, we angels are, as you yourself have become quite aware," Anahel, trying to focus past the haze of dubiety that had settled itself about him, muttered. "I'm sure you can imagine the difficulties of reciting to memory every name with every face."

"I guess that makes sense," said Jacob.

The angel didn't want to further lie to the boy, nor did he want to help foster any further hope for what had unknowingly unfolded itself as some kind of cruel hoax. Yet revealing the truth, at this point, proved even more difficult and complicated. Especially when he himself needed to investigate exactly what that truth was.

"So now what?" asked Jacob.

Anahel turned a soft gaze onto the boy. "Do you trust me, Jacob?"

"Of course I do," Jacob replied without hesitation.

The answer brought a pleased look to the angel. "Then I ask for your patience at this most impatient moment. Give me some time to sit with this and figure out which path our footsteps should mark."

At first, Jacob seemed to be low on the requisite patience to honor such a request, but he eventually offered up a reluctant nod of agreement.

"And now I think you would serve yourself well by making your way to your morning lesson; that is, while there's still time to savage what there is left of it," said Anahel.

Reluctantly, Jacob got to his feet and with slow steps made his way to the door.

"One more thing, Jacob," Anahel's voice caught the boy halfway across the chamber. "For the time being, let's keep this just between the two of us. Don't even speak about it with Gothamel until I've had a chance to discuss the matter with him."

The request struck Jacob as odd not to mention disappointing as he couldn't wait to run off and find Gotham to tell him the good news.

"But why?" he asked.

"I'm sure you would agree matters as delicate as this demand a certain amount of sensitivity in being handled. Just for the time being," explained Anahel.

"Okay. I guess that would be the right approach," Jacob agreed somewhat dourly, before a bright of gleefulness quickly made itself seen in his face. "It's kind of amazing, isn't it? All this time of wondering who my father might be and the answer was right here all along."

"Yes...quite amazing," Anahel replied, forcing forth an agreeable smile in return. However, it was quick to fade the moment the boy disappeared through the door and his footsteps were heard to grow distant as they hurried their way down the hallway leaving the angel alone in his room with a most troubled look.

"Quite amazing."

CHAPTER ELEVEN

Anyone who met Creed Maggert would rightly assume he inherited most of his looks from his mother, from the slightly upturned nose and ears that stuck out somewhat, to the full-lipped mouth seemingly fixed in a permanent pout. The sharp, cutting tongue lying in wait behind the boy's lips, however, was most certainly a gift from his father, as were the colorless twin mirrors of contempt and mischief that were his eyes. Even the carefully styled dishevelment of his mousy brown tousled hair was slowly beginning to take on the whiteness of his father's mane one strand at a time, giving Creed the appearance of someone afflicted with the early stages of premature graying (or in his case whitening).

He had a natural way about him that began almost from the moment he was brought into existence of looking down his nose at others, even from the vantage point of a small boy whose head is constantly tilted back in order to size up the rest of the world. It bred a certain unfriendliness and aloofness in the boy that didn't help in endearing him to other children while growing up in a small town in Indiana. As a result, they avoided him like a modern-day plague. And for a child such as Creed, whose father instilled fear as one of the twelve Angels of Plague, there was no greater compliment.

It wasn't that he was a bully or the neighborhood ruffian. He was simply Creed Maggert, son of the Archangel Sandel. And nothing gave him greater pleasure than being Creed Maggert and exerting what he saw in his eyes as his rightful, elevated standing in the world. There was just one problem: No one else around him—the other kids, in particular—knew anything about the existence of an Archangel Sandel, or Nephilim, for that matter. They were oblivious to this hierarchy of greatness of which Creed walked through life knowing he was one of the higher rungs, and nothing rankled him more than to observe first-hand this blindness the other kids suffered from in seeing clearly the pedestal he had rightfully placed himself upon proudly and firmly. In return for such snubbing, he often took to exercising his early abilities to spread his own brand of pestilence.

One of Creed's earliest guinea pigs was a boy by the name of Calvin Doogan, who suffered from the unfortunate geography of not only living down the street from the Maggert household, but finding himself seated in the desk right besides Creed's in Mrs. Pollard's English class as well. It wasn't that Creed disliked the boy so much as he disliked almost every child his age who crossed his path. Especially seemingly well-to-do children from well-to-do families whose fathers were climbing the ladders to pick the fruit of more well-to-do-ness. And Calvin Doogan, a high-ranking politician's son, certainly fit the mold with his preppy appearance and even preppier attitude.

So it happened one day when Mrs. Pollard's class was busy taking an exam that Calvin's concentration was broken by some strange happenings coming from Creed's desk. Glancing over, he noticed some movement coming from Creed's backside where his t-shirt met the top of his jeans. At first, it looked as if some living thing was squirming around. Then to his utter amazement Calvin watched as what appeared to be a tail wriggled its way into view and slowly slithered out into the open like some furry snake. The longer it revealed itself to be, the larger Calvin's eyes grew at the sight. His gaze then shifted and caught Creed glancing his way while wearing a smirk of utter amusement. But it quickly became distorted when Creed's eyes flashed a strange light and his nose and mouth began to morph in a most unnatural way to take on the shape of a muzzle you'd commonly see on a dog. No, make that a wolf. The most unnerving sight made Calvin instantly freeze up with fear, and with his eyes the size of dinner plates there was heard what briefly sounded to be the patter of a soft rain when that fear was released in the form of a piddle inside Calvin's pants that trickled its way down onto the floor where it created a most unfortunate and embarrassing pool of yellow at the boy's feet.

Creed, naturally, had his father to thank for the jolting visual spectacle. Sandel had acquiesced to his anxious son's desire at a young age to help uncover before its time hints of what special gifts resided inside the boy long before visiting the Crescent Scar and having the

Blackstone reveal Shifting as one of the three Graces he possessed. And while Creed was far too young and undeveloped to wield successfully the ability he would one day have at his whim to fully morph his physical self into another shape, he honed the elementary skills necessary to play his cruel trick on Calvin. It didn't matter to Creed that he didn't gain anything of substantial value from his prank except to witness the look of utter humiliation on Calvin's face when the classroom became filled with the sound of giggling over the boy's Depends moment. Nor did it matter that he had broken one of the primary rules drilled into young Nephilim heads at an early age forbidding any action or behavior that would call attention to one's true birthright; a rule Sandel, himself, would have promptly and properly disciplined his son for disobeying in such a blatant and flagrant manner.

What did matter to Creed at that instant was knowing he ceased to be just some ordinary kid in Calvin's eyes and, instead, would come to exist, from that moment forward, as something worthy of heedfulness, and prudence. And as Calvin rose to his feet with great humiliation at Mrs. Pollard's urging that he go change while doing what he could to conceal the embarrassing dark, sopping stain marking the front of his pants, Creed sat back in his seat with a look of utter superiority, as well as twisted contentment, and he smiled.

~ ~ ~

The exact same smile found Creed so many years later as he stood shirtless on the precipitous ledge overlooking Broken Earth with his wings flexed and flared behind him, like the cape of some unnamed superhero frozen in a breeze.

For the many Nephilim who would eventually make the long climb up the side of this northernmost mountain leading to the awe-inspiring gulf of vast emptiness separating Eden from the bedeviled Northern Lands, Broken Earth served as an especially sacred spot. It was here each boy would come and eventually stand and stare into the fathomless chasm as if it were a looking glass revealing the deepest crevices of their innermost selves. One by one they would each search deeply their faith and cast themselves willingly into the great maw of uncertainty awaiting them with the hope their unwavering confidence in the one great power would lift them from the churning mist shrouding the steep harrowing fall with the one final gift awaiting all sons of angels: Wings.

But this day the eyes that gazed out over Broken Earth were filled not with intimidation or fear, but vigor and spirit, as they followed several Nephilim darting and dodging about the open sky like the winged wonders they had become. Standing firmly at the cliff's edge where the mouth of the ravine began its yawn, the angel Eksel also watched intently, barking commands at his pupils like the brusque militant teacher he was, as they struggled to evade the obstacles bearing down upon them in an ever-increasingly ruthless effort to keep them from reaching their goal: a large glimmering green ring suspended in the center of Broken Earth.

The obstacles, of course, were Acruxel and Betryel, the two angels assigned as Eksel's assistants to ensure the safety of the Nephilim in training at this spot which was as precarious as it was sacred. Yet, to the group of boys watching from the sidelines, it was hard to look upon the two strong and stout figures as life preservers as they attempted with all their skill and might to wrangle and pounce upon the Nephilim struggling to avoid the relentless attacks coming at them and send them spiraling into the pit from which their attackers were entrusted to ensure they did not fall. Nor were Acruxel and Betryel the only obstacles Eksel's pupils were quick in discovering; the mist itself, which migrated from the eternally snowy mountainous peaks of the Northern Lands and spilled into the deep ravine as a continuous waterfall of icy vapors, churned with an unseen presence. Now and then it would make itself seen as some ghostly apparition shaped by the fog in the form of a clawing hand or a fierce dragon rising suddenly from within the peacefulness of the clouds at rest to take a vicious swipe or bite at the startled Nephilim before vaporizing into nothingness.

As Creed watched his fellow Harriers struggle to keep the wind in the sail of their wings, his self-assured smile gave way to an even more cocksure glint of confidence, and with an effortless dash he was sky-bound. In a flash, he sailed past Betryel and Acruxel who quickly abandoned their lesser opponents and made off after him. Creed sailed for the green shine that was the prized ring floating unguarded in the air, but claiming it proved far more difficult that it appeared when a massive beastly figure reared up suddenly from the misty soup below blocking the straight path to the ring as it opened it mouth to show its vaporous fangs and let loose a horrific roar. Creed immediately pulled upward in a straight climb with the two angels fast on his tail. All the while, Broken Earth carried the constant echo of Eksel's voice as he barked various maneuvering techniques he had spent the past many months teaching his students in an effort to school them in the ways of dominating the skies.

"Pitchback."

"Tailslide."

"Break, break, BREAK!"

~ ~ ~

Jacob made his way as inconspicuously as possible to where the other Harriers were gathered about cheering on Creed, looking equally transfixed at the sight of what was reminiscent of a thrilling dogfight taking place between three world war flying aces. As much as he may have disliked Creed, Jacob could not deny (silently, of course) that the boy knew how to fly, and he found himself staring upward from the ground in utter awe and, yes, even envy, in the breathtaking and gripping way Creed piloted the skies in a choreographed manner that was both ferocious and graceful, and in the end formidable to the two experienced winged figures in furious pursuit of him.

Escaping another phantom shape lunging from within the mist blanketing Broken Earth like a whale breaching the surface of the ocean, Creed made a climb straight upward to the highest reaches of sky. With growing frustration, Acruxel and Betryel pursued after him, and from below it appeared Creed's luck was just about to run out as the two angels quickly closed in on the boy from different directions. Just before they managed to get him in their clutches, Creed managed a twirl similar to a pirouette performed by a ballerina before falling into a flat inverted spin that dropped him out of the sky, and the angels' reach, like an anchor. Downward he careened in a mad whirling fall before he straightened himself out of his spin and with a great speed soared straight for the coveted ring which he snagged victoriously to the sound of wild applause and cheers.

While Creed celebrated his undeniable showing in a training exercise where his peers had all failed miserably by showboating across the sky in the same way a football player dances and preens in the end zone after making a touchdown, Jacob made his way over to where Eksel stood.

"What are you doing here?" snarled Eksel, at the sight of the boy. "If I'm not mistaken, you and the rest of Shrikes should be with Zuriel at Crescent Scar."

"I'm ready to make the jump, now," Jacob announced with as much conviction as he could muster, even as he eyed the daunting and terrifying obstacle laid out before him.

Even through the grin that found its way to Eksel's face, the contempt and disdain the angel held for the boy was plain for all to see.

"You're several months too late for that, I'm afraid," he replied.

"What do you mean too late?" questioned Jacob. "Anahel never said anything about any time limit. In fact, he said my wings would come when I'm ready to make the jump."

"You made the attempt already and failed, miserably I might add," said Eksel. "What makes you think you'd succeed this time 'round?"

"Because I just told you I'm ready," answered Jacob while glowering at the angel.

Just then, Creed dropped down from the sky, landing a few short feet from Jacob with his trophy proudly on display.

"Put that in your Illume pipe and smoke it, Weed!" he said nastily.

"I'm impressed," said Jacob.

His sardonic reply only made Creed's smile of self-satisfaction widened with glee. "As you should be."

He then cast the prized ring out across the openness of Broken Earth like a Frisbee, where it returned itself like a magnet to its levitating spot in the center of the deep gorge. Jacob stood with an ever-tightening grimace as he then watched Creed walk over to where the other Harriers were gathered to receive his high fives of congratulations.

"I'm ready to do this. Now!" said Jacob, turning to face Eksel once more with a look of determination greater than when he made the climb to Broken Earth earlier that morning.

"It's been my experience that a Nephilim who crashes and burns in his first attempt to rise up on his own from the depths of Broken Earth will likely continue to fail to grasp the faith necessary to reaffirm themselves in repeated attempts," said Eksel.

"Then how come a lot of the other guys failed at first and managed?" argued Jacob. "Even the great Creed Maggert did."

Eksel's gaze narrowed with scorn upon the boy. "Yes, well, then again you are no Creed Maggert, are you?"

No, I'm not, thank God, Jacob wanted to spit back, but he kept his lips sealed tight, instead.

"What you fail to recognize is the fact that I am in the middle of a training session with a group of Nephilim who have managed to successfully come into their wings quite some time ago. If you think your sudden turn of consciousness is worthy of disrupting my class, you're sadly mistaken," Eksel continued in that snide way of his. "If there's one thing I have no patience or tolerance for is remedial instruction."

It was hard for Jacob to believe that someone as outwardly hostile and dislikable as Eksel could be an angel, or anything Heaven-sent for that matter. Yet there he stood wings and all, though Jacob was sure, if he looked hard and closely enough, he'd manage to find the makings of a pair of horns concealed somewhere in Eksel's thick, stringy mane. He also knew arguing with someone as disagreeable as Eksel was as futile as it was a waste of time and energy.

"Have it your way," Jacob conceded. "If you won't spot me, I'll just have Gotham do it. Or perhaps Anahel."

He began to walk away when Eksel stopped him, though begrudgingly.

"The last thing I need is a dressing down from Anahel because I refused to partake in the duty of hand-holding with one of my pupils," grumbled Eksel. "Make your jump, and be quick about it."

~ ~ ~

Creed and the rest of the Harriers quickly quieted down when Eksel called for their attention. "Should any of you require a short breather, or a moment to amuse yourselves, now would be a good time. Mr. Parrish here is demanding my undivided attention so that he can attempt to prove that a stone, when thrown into the water, floats rather than sinks."

Eksel's belittling way at Jacob's expense drew a sniggering of support from the other boys. Jacob, however, was too ensnared by the forbidding sight of Broken Earth to pay them any mind, particularly the gaping gulf unfolded at his feet, leading the way straight down to a certain unseen doom even the wafting mist could not fully cloak and keep a boy's wild imagination from imagining.

"Any day now," Eksel pressed with an impatient sigh.

"I'm going," snapped Jacob. It seemed his words of assurance were aimed more at giving himself the push needed to move forth his feet, and the longer he studied the harrowing path before him the more his feet seemed to plant themselves more firmly into the rocky hide of the mountain beneath them. Despite his best efforts to fight it, he felt his body fall into the grips of a cold sweat, and it quickly began to chill the heated resoluteness of the purpose which led him to the top of the mountain in a charge of determination.

Eksel took note of the slow drain that revealed itself in a look of growing self-doubt glassy in Jacob's eyes with a sense of morbid amusement.

"You won't spy a safety net down there, no matter how hard you look," he chided the boy. "Then again, someone as intent as you are in proving they carry inside themselves the very thing to validate that he is, indeed, worthy of the name Nephilim wouldn't need one, wouldn't you agree?"

There suddenly came a rustling of wings, and Jacob caught sight of Betryel coming in for a landing upon a finger of rock, jutting out beyond the ledge of Broken Earth, that had served as a springboard for the angel to dive after young Nephilim who remained wingless after their jump and needed rescue from their deathly fall. Jacob then looked to the second platform and found Acruxel already in position upon their perch.

"What about them?" Jacob asked Eksel of the two angels.

"What of them?" asked Eksel.

"They still our so-called 'life preservers' in case something goes wrong? Or are they just grabbing their front-row seats in hopes of watching a big splat," said Jacob while eyeing both angels suspiciously before turning his gaze once more onto Eksel. "I'd sure hate to see you get the daylights pummeled out of you again on my account."

It was obvious the bitterness lingering within Jacob had not waned over the passing months since the day he first attempted the jump and no wings came to him. Neither did the expected rescue by either Acruxel or Betryel, as both had been given a repeated order to stand down before Damiel swept in to snatch Jacob from his terrifying free fall. If the reminder of the swift beat down Damiel unleashed upon Eksel for his fly-or-die stunt caused the angel any pause or regret over his potentially deadly lapse in judgment, Jacob got his answer with the bemused look returned his way.

"What are you worried about, boy?" said Eksel. "Damiel made clear the consequences should I allow one hair to be plucked from your head, not that his threats have ever done much in the way of sending me off to cower in a corner. But, now, my hot-headed brother Gothamel is back in Eden, and I can assure you that is one hornets nest I will resist shaking, at least while they are both just a scream away."

Eksel's awkwardly disturbing assurances, however, did as much to appease Jacob as the sight of a vulture circling the sky overhead would have to a man attempting to cross a desert.

"No worries, mate, I got yer back."

Jacob turned to the sound of the familiar voice and to his surprise there was Max, a stone's throw away, standing shirtless with his wings flared and ready like the hoisted sails of a tall ship filled with the guiding wind of the ocean.

"What are you doing here?" Jacob, sounding like a kid whose parent had just shown up unannounced at the local teen hangout, questioned his friend after quickly pulling him aside out of earshot of the others.

"Scenic photography. What do you think?" cracked Max.

"You know what I mean. The reason I came up here today while the rest of you were at Crescent Scar was so I wouldn't have the pressure of you and the rest of the Shrikes watching in case I go down like an anvil like the last time," said Jacob.

"Yeah, well, let's just say I thought it was a bit selfish of you to bogart all to yourself the look on you know whose face when the big reveal happened," said Max.

Jacob and Max both glanced over to where Creed was seen huddled with the rest of the Harriers all the while eyeing the two boys in the perpetually snidely way of his.

"Maybe I made a mistake attempting this," Jacob wondered aloud.

Max was quick to lend him a comforting nudge of encouragement. "Look, half the battle in making a successful go of this is knowing someone's got as much faith in you as you hope to have when making your jump. You sure as hell aren't going to get it from him," said Max, as he turned his gaze to Eksel who was looking more and more impatient with each passing second as he stood at the cliff's edge.

"I'm not worried about Eksel," said Jacob. "After what happened last time, I doubt he'd be stupid enough to pull the same stunt and risk total annihilation by both Damiel and Gotham."

"Yeah, well, personally I wouldn't trust him with a hose if my skivvies were on fire," Max deadpanned.

From the look on his friend's face, neither did Jacob, despite his tepid words to the contrary.

"As for Beavis and Butthead over there, just know they're not your only lifeline should you need it," said Max, motioning to Acruxel or Betryel.

"You're saying I'm gonna need one?" asked Jacob.

"I know you're not. Just helping you focus all of your concentration on where it needs to be."

Jacob forced forth a smile and extended his appreciation in the way most teenage boys are opt to do without words: with a friendly punch to the shoulder.

"You know, you're likely gonna be in hot water with Zuriel for cutting class this morning," he said.

Max replied with a blasé shrug of his shoulders. "If you can't rely on your mates at times like this to support you, who can you? Besides, whatever punishment's coming my way, at least I'll be in good company," he said, reminding Jacob with a return sock to the shoulder that he was in the same truancy boat.

"Can we get on with this already so we can be done with it?" Creed was heard suddenly calling out impatiently to Jacob. "Those of us with wings would like to get back to our training, if you don't mind."

"Why don't ya shut yer gob, bevan," Max was quick to spat back with his fiery Australian bark.

"What the heck's a bevan?" asked Jacob, who oftentimes wished he had in his reach an Australian slang dictionary to keep up with all the colorful idioms Max used from down under.

"Basically, it's the equivalent of the term 'white trailer trash' you Yanks use in The States," explained Max.

Nice, Jacob thought with a grin of approval,

"He's just itching for me to blow this again."

"Then you're just going to have to make sure you don't give that dog the satisfaction," said Max.

Jacob glanced back over his shoulder at the obstacle awaiting him beyond the cliff's edge and he thought to himself, *Easier said than done.*

~ ~ ~

Jacob stripped off his shirt and, with the bright golden sunlight highlighting the two rounded protuberances where the promise of wings continued to gestate beneath the skin, he took his mark. He eyed the group of Harriers who had lined themselves on either side of where he stood and created a sort of runway. As he studied the roughly ten yards of running start leading to the moment of truth, he did his best to cloak his nerves. The beads of sweat already forming in wet pin pricks across his forehead betrayed the growing sense of anxiousness and apprehension gripping him with increased force. For a moment he thought he might actually be sick, but then he glanced over to where Max had positioned himself at the cliff's edge near Eksel and the nod of confidence he received in return was enough to make him force down the creeping bile with a hard swallow.

"We only have several more hours of light left," Eksel remarked in his usual manner that was anything but encouraging.

Jacob did all he could to block out both Eksel and the scowl he could feel coming from Creed. Taking several deep breaths, he instead imagined himself standing atop Penuel Point at the spot he and his buddy Ty would venture to regularly for one of their BASE-jumping outings. There, perched high upon the granite cliffs overlooking the lush green valley which cradled Cain's Corner, he was confident and poised, and, more importantly, free of the fear and nausea that, for whatever reason, took merciless hold of him at Broken Earth. With the familiar, friendly image fixed in his focused eyes, Jacob found his feet and made a fierce dash toward it with all the determination he could muster.

The closer the wide vista came at him the faster and harder his sneakers pounded the ground beneath him when suddenly the mirage of Penuel Point Jacob held in his sights washed away and the barrier standing between the ominous Northern Lands and Eden unfolded itself before him in all its daunting and unnerving presence. The cliff's edge was suddenly there for his feet to push off of in one final, grand leap into the nothingness awaiting him and, in an instant, the wind left him, and the adamant look steeling his visage was cracked by a sudden surge of wariness that swept in suddenly and took hold of him by the nape of the neck. He attempted to put the brakes on his charge, but it only caused him to stumble forward, and at the last moment as he felt the final step of mountain beneath his feet before the abyss suddenly upon him, the fear in Jacob's eyes was accompanied by a fluttering of movement. In a flash, the image of a sparrow that emerged from deep within the color of Jacob's pupils swallowed the boy from sight as his body left the cliff.

"Well then, that was a unique, if not pathetic method of garnering one's wings I've ever come to witness in all my days at Broken Earth," Eksel was heard to remark with an almost haughty purr. "It would seem your newfound credence was, in fact, just a bad case of indigestion."

Max pushed past the angel in an attempt to deflect the barbs of mockery aimed at his friend.

"No cry, no foul. You just got a touch of the willies, that's all. It's happened to the best of us. We'll just give it another go," he said.

Jacob was quick to bat away his friend's arm of support. "Forget it. There's not gonna be another go," he said.

"Come on, you can't give up after just one attempt," pressed Max. "Trust me, half these dills choked more times than not before they got their wings. They just didn't do it with as much flair as you just did."

Jacob wasn't having any of Max's attempts to assuage the mortifying sting he was feeling from yet another public failure atop the mountain.

"He's right, you know; this whole thing's pointless, not to mention pathetic," Jacob muttered with a sulking nod to Eksel.

"Whatever it is that's needed to do this, it's been made abundantly clear I don't have it."

"Balls to Eksel!" Max snapped back, though in a low enough tenure to keep his disparaging comment from tweaking the angel's ear. "And balls to you for thinking like that. Now get back in position and put an end to this nonsense before you force me to reach into your back and yank those wings of yer's out in the more painful fashion."

With a subtle shake of his head, Jacob snatched back his t-shirt Max had been holding for him. "I appreciate you coming here to support me, really, but you best get back to Crescent Scar before you get into any more trouble with Zuriel."

Max opened his mouth to argue further, but he knew from the defeated look in Jacob's eyes it was pointless.

"So are we done here?" asked Eksel, stepping forward. "Or do you plan to regale us further with more bird imitations?"

"I'm done," answered Jacob, ignoring the imploring look coming from Max.

~ ~ ~

The chuckles and giggles continued to follow Jacob as he made his way past the Harriers to begin his hike back down the mountain the old-fashioned way; the non-Nephilim way: by foot. Mired in his own disgruntlement in himself, it was easy to ignore the jeering and ridicule, and even accept it as deserving. That is, until a certain voice found his ear.

"It's amazing anyone here ever considered this joke to be Light Bearer when he can't even live up to being a regular old Nephilim."

It was Creed, and the sound of his voice brought Jacob's feet to an instant halt as surely as he had stepped into a waiting snare.

"Dearest Diary, woe is me! I discovered today the only way I'll ever have wings is by shifting myself into that of a loser bird," the taunting voice continued in a particularly theatrical drone of whininess. "But hey, as long as there's a horse around, I'll be okay."

Jacob's left hand slowly came to form a tight fist around the t-shirt balled up in his grasp as the chorus of laughter that erupted from Creed's deriding parody of himself rang in his ears. It wasn't so much the goading words and manner in which they were spewed that made everything in Jacob's eyesight slowly take on a crimson tint; it was the mention of his journal. And suddenly he found himself back in the Hall of Light revisiting the anger that boiled up inside him seeing Creed pawing through his personal belongings, and the embarrassment of hearing his personal thoughts read out loud for all to hear in such a blatant and violating way. It was that renewed anger that made Jacob turn suddenly, and with a fierce look of intentness he moments earlier had fixed on Broken Earth ablaze in his eyes he stomped readily toward Creed, drew back his fist, and with all the hatred he had for his failure once again to come into his wings he let loose a devastating punch that instantly obliterated the smirk on Creed's face while sending him clean off his feet.

Jacob complained not once about the punishment levied upon him by Anahel when he returned to Havenhid.

CHAPTER TWELVE

I *knew the minute Gotham asked me what it was I was most fearful of when I met him for today's training session that it wasn't going to be a good day. We were at one of our usual spots downstream where the River drowns out the world of all distractions and interruptions by its murmurous churning as it heaves itself forth over rocks and ledges in a lively rush to reach the Big Lands further ahead. Today's lesson was on fear. Specifically, Gotham was schooling me on how to overcome any such fears I might knowingly and, more importantly, unknowingly be harboring inside myself that could prove detrimental to my well-being at a moment I come face to face with danger.*

He explained there were three ways mortals, like myself, react when they find themselves threatened: They flee, they succumb, or they attack. Whichever of the three options a person chooses to embrace in the face of such danger will determine if that person is given the opportunity to see the rising sun of a new day. He was also pointed in saying every Nephilim will at some time in his life be faced with those three options, and more often than not it will be much sooner than he anticipates than later. He then had me take my sword in my hand and face a nearby section of the River where several mid-sized falls created by the rushing water helped to form a relatively calm and tranquil pool, and as I stood staring at the ripples made by the cascades of water Gotham asked me the question: What is it you are most fearful of?

The question took me by surprise, and frankly I wasn't sure how to answer. Maybe it was because I had never really thought about it before that nothing immediately came to my mind. Sure there are things in life I've never been really crazy about. Spiders, for instance. Nor am I much of a fan of creepy old houses despite my love for old horror movies. And don't even get me started on closet doors left open, even a crack, after the lights go out at bedtime. But none of my answers seemed to be accepting to Gotham. Dig deeper, he continued to press me; look deep within yourself and find what really makes you feel fearful. Again, I stood there intensely combing my brain for an answer, and as I did I noticed a faint stirring in the water where I had focused my attention. At least, I think I did. Naturally, I dismissed it as being just a fish, or frog, or any number of the hundreds of critters that make the River their home. But then the sporadic movements became more pronounced and I realized it came from no fish, or frog. Suddenly, a portion of the surface of the water near the center of the pool began to bend and rise upward, as if it were a sheet covering someone—or something. Then I watched as the water shed itself from the form it covered until, to my amazement, I found myself standing face to face with the familiar, dark figure of an Infector.

I looked with alarm to Gotham, who seemed completely unfazed by the sight, and yet, by the look on his face, I knew instantly I wasn't in the state of some hallucination that had managed to creep unexpectedly upon me. I turned back to the Infector and my heart instantly took off in a gallop inside my chest. It was a sight I had hoped never to see again, and yet more terrifying than I remembered it. The dark shape looked as sinister as I remembered it to be, standing motionless in the waist-deep water looking like a mirage made of black smoke; its face was hidden from sight in the blackness of the shroud draped around it, but it didn't keep the memory of its hideous self from reflecting back in my mind in the one memory I wish I could purge from within myself. And while I couldn't see its eyes except in those lightning quick images being flashed inside my head, I knew it was looking straight at me. Even worse, I could feel it. And then it came toward me.

Stay mindful your sword, Gotham advised me as calmly as if he were suggesting I take a sweater along with me before stepping out into the cold chill of an autumn day. But trust me, my hand had already begun to strangle the grip of my sword.

The Infector continued toward me looking like something freshly charred in a blaze with wisps of smoke shaping its black hooded cloak coming off the figure and mixing with the air. My first instinct was to run away and as fast as I could; my feet, in fact, demanded it. But something kept me and my feet firmly planted where they were.

Don't give in to your fear, no matter how strong it might be, I heard Gotham say somewhere in my ear, as if he sensed my strong desire to flee.

The Infector was suddenly upon me, coming at me in a barrage of movements too quick for my eyes to follow fully. All the time I kept my sword at the ready, swinging it now and then at the threatening blur circling and lunging toward me, but I was always just a hair off from striking my target. The Infector, however, always managed to meet his as my wincing whimpers of pain proved each and every time I felt the sting of its knife-sharp claws dig themselves into parts of my body left open for attack.

You're not staying focused, Gotham barked as if I needed the obvious pointed out to me.

Finally, as my aim became worse the more my frustration grew, I abandoned my sword and when the Infector saw an opportunity to come at me again I met it with a swing of my leg and scored a direct hit with a hard kick delivered by my foot. The Infector raged with a high-pitched wail that was like steel scraping against steel as the force of my kick sent it reeling through the air. Quick to recover, it came at me again with a vengeance and again I was ready, only this time I delivered several sharp blows to its smoky hide with my fists before sending it sprawling across the ground with another sharp kick. Without a moment's hesitation, I grabbed up my sword once more and quickly pounced upon the Infector, planting my foot squarely on the demon's chest and my blade against its throat before it had a chance to rise back up. But to my utter shock, I saw the force of my blows had knocked away the shroud of the Infector's hood bringing into the light its face and what was staring back at me was not the hideousness I remembered seeing close up above the waters of the Van Gölü. Instead, I was horrified to find myself staring down at Wray—or at least what appeared to be a perfect likeness of Wray.

"What are you waiting for?" I heard Gotham say to me. "Finish it."

I gave an unsure glance his way and it was clear by the look in his eyes what he meant by "finish it." But I found myself frozen at the sight of Wray at my feet. She looked hurt and wounded, and my first instinct was to reach down and comfort her. And then she spoke.

"Please, Jacob," she said in her gentle voice in which could be heard a quiver of pain, "you're hurting me."

The sharp point of my sword slipped from her neck as my grip on it loosened. Again I looked to Gotham. For the life of me I couldn't find my voice, but I knew he could see in my face my great distress and yet he seemed to ignore it.

"Don't go weak on me now," he growled at me. "End it."

"It"? This wasn't an "it". This was someone I cared a great deal for, and you're demanding I kill her in cold blood?

"Please, Jacob, help me," I heard Wray's pleading voice call out to me.

But when I looked back to her I became even more horrified to find not Wray staring up at me, but my mother.

"You would actually kill your own mother?" she questioned me in a voice that was at once both sorrowful and full of disappointment.

I knew what I was seeing couldn't possibly be real, but a very sick and twisted hallucination being played upon me. And yet it was as if I had been bit by some snake whose venom had suddenly and fully paralyzed me leaving me frozen and shaking like someone caught in the biting cold of a brutal winter storm.

"Do it!" Gotham was again ordering me, only this time screaming in an overflow of frustration. *"End it!"*

It became too much, so much so I felt myself wanting to turn my own sword on myself and run it through me just to put an end to the overwhelming push of pressure I felt begin to compress painfully all around me threatening to crush me out of existence. Instead, I managed to find movement in my limbs; enough, at least, to throw aside my sword. As soon as I did, my *"mother"* shot me a strange smirk and the vision of her wrapped in the smoky frock of darkness suddenly transformed into a shape of molded water that collapsed under the weight of my foot and spread in all direction across the ground before gradually sinking its way into the dirt.

For the longest time, I just stood there in silence. Whatever had just happened—whatever had transpired—I didn't have a clue, and frankly I didn't want one. Nor did I care to endure the berating that would surely come from Gotham, but come it did. Immediately, he was pacing all about me barking a barrage of insults at me at how terribly I had performed. He lamented with disbelief how someone could go from victorious to defeated faster than it took an eye to blink, ridiculing what he saw was weakness inside me, both physically and mentally, and advised me to thank my lucky stars what had taken place was just a test otherwise I would now be a very still and cold corpse.

"It wasn't fair," was all I could manage to argue back once I managed to find my tongue again. *"What kind of sick test uses someone's friend—or better yet, their own mother—and tries to force them to kill them?"*

At first, Gotham stood staring me at me with an oddly confused look, as though my question was an incoming fist glancing the side of his head and leaving him momentarily dazed.

"Not fair? You honestly think the Darkness plays fair?" he asked finally with a sneer as he walked slowly toward me all the while keeping his ember-like eyes burning into me. *"There is no fair in this war we are in. If you think your enemy*

won't use every dirty trick at its disposal to weaken what strength of will you believe you have harnessed then your failure here today is truly more profound than what I have just witnessed. It will use every instrument it can manage to get its wretched hands on to add to its arsenal of weapons to use against you in this fight, and what better a weapon than a Trojan horse? Your friends, your loved ones, your own family—they're all fair game," he said.

"If you think for a moment there is some moral code of honor on this battlefield, then prepare to become its earliest casualty," he told me in as no-nonsense a way as he could. "To beat a demon, one has to get down in the foul sewage with the demon."

If that was the case, then this was an enemy I not only didn't wish to fight, but didn't think I'd ever be able to fight—though I dared not say such a thing out loud for Gotham to hear.

"What about the hunter?" I asked, instead.

Gotham's face went blank until I refreshed his mind about the hunter we came across at the start of our journey to Eden who watched in horror as the dead deer in the back of his truck suddenly became undead and proceeded to make scrap metal out of his ride.

"Do you remember what you told me? Thou shalt not kill," I reminded him. "There is no footnote of exemptions to that commandment.' You told me that."

"Is it even possible, after all the time you've spent thus far under Eden's guidance, that you fail to recognize that the sin of murder is encumbered upon willfully extinguishing from either man or creature a pulse of life?" Gotham argued. "Then let me impress upon you in no uncertain terms even you will understand: there exists no life where light is extinct, and nowhere is the presence of light more absent than in darkness. What you draw up your sword against are but lifeless shadows, but alive nonetheless, not with life, but death.

Naturally, Gotham's explanation made simple enough sense to me, but I was still too angry to offer him much more than an ongoing glare.

"Not everyone has the stomach to go to battle against the populace of the Underneath, and I see now you are amongst that company," Gotham continued on with his rant. "The only way you will ever survive if you choose to do so is to harden your heart like a shield and develop a taste for vengeance. It's obvious with you I still have a lot of work ahead of me."

"You can train me as much and as hard as you like; it's not going to change *who I am," I finally spit back heatedly after having to endure listening to him dump on me as if I was the biggest disappointment to set foot in Eden since Adam. "The fact is I'm not like you. And I hope to God I never am."*

Even as I said the words I regretted them. But they came spewing out of my mouth before I had a chance to clamp down on my tongue. Just one look at Gotham and I knew I had hurt him, try as he did to camouflage it. I wanted to apologize, but my anger at that moment wouldn't allow me to.

If only he knew my frustration came, in fact, from actually wanting to be like him, and knowing it was a bar far out of my reach.

~ ~ ~

Jacob's eyes were already beginning to close as his pen scribbled the last word of his entry into his journal. While still sitting upright in his bed he quickly succumbed to the canopy of peace that had settled itself upon the Garden like a snug blanket and gradually drifted off to sleep. However, all was far from still within the tree-limbed walls of Havenhid.

Since arriving in Eden, Jacob had been spared a visit from the troubling nightmares which had long-stalked him. Yet, as mysteriously as they had gone absent, on this night they suddenly made an unwelcome return. While his roommates slept soundly in their beds nearby, Jacob found himself in the grips of a restless slumber that accompanied him to the middle of a barren desert upon which an engulfing shroud of night had settled. The punishing heat that scorched its desolate hide day in and day out had been replaced by an equally wicked cold night made unbearable in the way it penetrated one's very bones. Unsettling movements of unseen creatures could be heard moving about in the black sky overhead. Now and then one would swoop down and pass by uncomfortably close to Jacob's liking while marking their presence with a blood-curdling shrill of a cry. In the few glimpses Jacob managed to catch of them, though brief and blurred by their fast movements, he could see they were unnatural and ungodly creations. It was, however, the curious figure silhouetted against the darkness and lying upon the ground some distance away—one he'd seen before in numerous visits to this place in previous dreams—that held Jacob's attention. He could see it moving, writhing ever so subtly on the parched, jigsaw-fractured desert floor, and from it seemed to come a low, deep growling of an angry, wounded animal. And though it was not his wish to do so, Jacob found himself taking a step toward the mysterious figure. Then another.

"Dessstinyyyy..." a nefarious hiss of a voice emerged from within the growling.

Jacob stopped and looked down to his right hand which, to his surprise, he saw to be clutching tightly a sword, one that was not his own. It was only when he lifted it into the murky moonlight for a closer look did he recognize it as being the unforgettable sword Gotham had once shown him at the foot of the Tree of Life: The Sword of Destiny. Strangely the sword felt alive in Jacob's grip. He could feel coming from it a strange surge of power pulsating from the weapon, like a heart beating inside a human chest, pumping blood through branches of veins. And he found himself wondering how the sword had found its way into his hand, this Sword of —

"DESSSSSSSSTINYYYYYYYYY..."

The voice came again with greater urgency and again Jacob found his feet moving him forward. And as he drew nearer to the ominous shape, the figure beckoning him still closer lifted its head and Jacob found himself straining with a desperate need to see who—or what—had brought him to this desolate nightmare of a place. In a quick moment, horror revealed itself in Jacob's widening eyes when the moonlight managed to lift the darkness cloaking the figure's face. It was as if Jacob suddenly found himself looking into a mirror, for the face belonging to the darkened figure was the same as his, only with eyes aflame by an inferno of a slow-burning wrath.

~ ~ ~

Jacob was suddenly awake desperately gasping for the breath held captive in his chest by a jolt of fear. His eyes were wide and fixed with fright on the nighttime shadows surrounding him in all their imagined shapes and movements as one might well expect after being abruptly ripped from the clutches of a bad dream.

"DESSSSTINYYYYY..."

A faint echo of the serpent-like voice had followed him back into the conscious world repeating its mantra until it quickly dissipated and fell silent against the familiar sound of snoring coming from the slumbering figures sprawled haphazardly across the other four beds in the room. Yet while the voice had extinguished itself, another soon took its place.

Jacob threw back the covers and swung his legs over the edge of his bed. The floor beneath his bare feet creaked ever so slightly as he stepped carefully past where Mist was lying curled up peacefully nearby. Ever vigilant, her eyes opened and, reflecting like two miniature white moons in the darkness, they followed Jacob to the large open arched window. There Jacob stood quietly peering out over the moonlight-drenched Garden taking curious notice of the strong stirring of wind that had replaced the usually gentle, lapping breeze. It came through the window moaning loudly as it blew past Jacob and swept through the room kicking up papers and ruffling the pages of books in its path. At first Jacob thought he was imagining hearing the voice until the wind's presence drew a low, threatening growl from Mist.

"You hear it, too?" asked Jacob.

Then came another breath of wind and with it the voice became louder and clearer. It was that of a lady, soft and whispery, and while it did not speak Jacob's name, there was no mistaking it was calling to him, beckoning him as its disembodied presence circled around the room. Jacob looked out to the far reaches of the Garden from where the voice seemed to be hailing and he found himself staring in the direction of the Silent Forest, its wooded presence folded inside a silhouette of an eerie shroud that even the silvery-blue light of the moon seemed unable—or unwilling—to cast from it.

It had been some time since Jacob and Max broke one of the

monumental rules governing the Nephilim of Eden and allowed their acute curiosities to lead them by the nose into the forbidden woods. And while their one snooping crossover into the Silent Forest had also been their last, the mysterious woman they witnessed emerging from the pool of water hidden deep in the brush of the Forest had remained fresh on Jacob's mind, and he couldn't help but wonder if somehow it was her voice he was now hearing calling out to him.

Jacob glanced over to where Max was snoozing peacefully and thought to rouse him awake. Instead, he left him to his sleep and returned to his corner of the room where he quickly dressed. As he was about to leave the room and venture out into the night in the hopes of satiating his growing intrigue, his eyes spied a gleaming glint of silver flash from the shadows. It came from his sword leaning against the wall near his bed. He stood looking at it while recalling the sword in his dream and debated whether or not he should take it with him. And, when another gust of wind once more blew the inviting whispers around the room, he reached for it.

With his weapon in hand, Jacob turned and tiptoed to the door, and Mist dutifully rose up to follow. Before she could cross one paw over the threshold leading out into the darkened hall, she was motioned back much to her displeasure and ordered to stay in a hushed command. Sitting back on her hind quarters, Mist watched as the door quietly closed behind Jacob and whimpered unhappily.

~ ~ ~

It wasn't without guarded steps that Jacob approached the darkened footprint of the Silent Forest. Not only did its eerie presence leave him unsettled and nudge awake what valor of courage he could muster, but he remained ever mindful that the Forest was a strictly forbidden place to all the residents of Havenhid to enter. It was bad enough he chose to blatantly disobey Anahel's edict once before, but now he couldn't help but feel as if he was trying his luck by retracing his steps across the barred soil at the risk of what he—and all Nephilim—

had been warned would be severe repercussions. Still, the voice urged Jacob forth, and since it was the only sound he'd heard come from inside the unnatural void of stillness holding court amongst the hovering trees and ragged brush, the intrigue of finding out who was summoning him—and why—eventually won out over the threat of his willful disobedience being discovered and the punishment it would render. And so, clutching his sword tighter in his grip, Jacob moved deeper into the woods.

Whether it was his imagination or not, the Forest felt to be a much more unsettling place to wander through alone than with the company of another, and Jacob had taken only a couple dozen or so steps when he cursed himself for not waking Max and talking him into coming along with him. Not that it would have taken much—if any—cajoling to coerce his friend out of bed for the purpose of venturing out once more into this forbidden pocket of the Garden in search of some phantom voice. Max breathed for such adventures, dangerous or not. It was a boldness Jacob oftentimes found himself in envy of, especially as he stood scouring carefully the haunted darkness surrounding him which made the Forest, for the first time, appear to be a place holding deep inside it an untold curse. What's more, Jacob sensed a strange movement coming from somewhere amongst the trees, as if impossibly the Forest was managing to close in around him. At first he took it to be a cruel trick being played on him by his imagination brought about by the lurking shadows. Then, from the shadows, came sporadic, unnerving sounds of movement unseen and undetected even by the enhanced sight given him by his eyes, which glistened brightly in the smothering darkness like two glittering stars piercing the night-soaked heavens. Was it some unknown creature using the cloak of darkness to stalk him? Or could it somehow be the very trees themselves? Jacob had no idea, nor was he especially eager to find out.

He quickened his pace, and his feet carried him deeper into the woods with the ease of a bounding deer moving swiftly and gracefully over the decaying, hollowed-out shells of trees long- felled and the gnarled, serpent-like roots of those still at attention slithering for great distances across the surface of the damp earth of the Forest floor. He was given little guidance by the immense moon looming somewhere high overhead in the velvety black expanse of sky, which the towering army of trees banded together to blot almost entirely from sight. Yet, enough if its silvery glow managed to sneak its way through the thick foliage to light forth a path which carried the rhythmic pounding coming from the muddied soles of Jacob's sneakers.

Suddenly the voice fell silent, as did the wind upon which it had been set adrift. Jacob came to an abrupt halt. Motionless, he strained his ears to listen, but only the heavy gasps of his own breath could be heard against the cemetery-like hush which had settled itself over the Forest. Had he been too slow in seeking out the source of the summons and left it to slip mysteriously back into the folds of the darkness? His eyes searched all about him and they were not blind to an uncertain familiarity surrounding him. Almost immediately he caught the subtle sparkle of light dancing upon water coming from inside a small clearing just a short distance away, and he knew instantly where he was.

CHAPTER THIRTEEN

LILITH

Jacob made his way through the patch of dogwood and carpet of fern until he neared the water which he found to be as still and lifeless as that of the forest surrounding it. The surface was like that of obsidian; black as pitch and shiny smooth with nary a ripple to reveal even the minute presence of minnows skimming for food, or the eyes of a solitary frog one would expect to see floating just above the water before falling from sight with a singular plop. What life there was in the pool resided in the reflected imprint of the woods circling it and the moon-lit sky above resting upon the mirror-like waters.

And yet an inkling of life was there—or some semblance of it—as Jacob felt its presence stirring close by as unmistakable as a breeze accompanying a cool, spring afternoon. His eyes searched the perimeter of the pool, yet he found not a soul lurking, and quickly he began questioning himself whether he had imagined the voice that had plucked him from his sleep and led him deep into this thicket of trees under the cover of night. Or perhaps, he suddenly found himself beginning to wonder, he hadn't left his bed after all; maybe he was wandering inside one of his dreams from which he had yet to awaken.

"Hello?" he called out not too loudly, but loud enough for his voice to reach any ears in the immediate vicinity who might be listening for him. "Anyone here?"

Not expecting an answer, he was also not surprised when one was returned. It came out of the night in a fleeting gasp, carrying the most inviting of feminine tones.

"I was beginning to think my summons had fallen upon deaf ears. Or that you thought better of crossing twice into the domain of the Silent Forest."

"Twice?" Jacob muttered to himself. "You know I was here before?"

"I know of everyone who passes into the shadow of this Forest," replied the voice. "Only last time you were not alone as you are now."

Jacob squinted his eyes which strained to see across the distance of water to where the voice came and focused themselves on a veil of darkness draped across the mouth of a small cavern formed in a glut of rock hugging the edge of the pool. There, in the hollowed out opening, the faint outline of a figure could be seen lurking.

"So, is there a specific reason why you've chosen to lure me out here in the middle of the night?" he asked.

"Lure?" returned the voice with a faint chuckle. "What an odd choice of words."

With that the figure emerged slowly, like that of a shadow passing across the ground in the twilight hours, from within the cavity of rock. And when the subtle blue tint of moonlight straining through the tree tops to reach the Forest floor drew back the cloak of night that had wrapped itself snugly around the figure, Jacob saw that it was indeed the lady he had first laid eyes upon with Max, and he instantly became entranced by the sight.

"It *is* you," said Jacob.

"You seem both surprised and expectant to find my presence waiting here," remarked the lady. And in truth, she was correct on both counts.

Standing in the ankle-deep shallows of the pool just outside the cavern's entrance, she appeared to be wearing no clothing, yet the flowing tresses of her long hair cascading down across her long, slender body was like that of an exquisite gown created in the color of midnight and carrying the sheen of cold glittering stars plucked from the heavens. Her skin glowed with a radiant translucency seen only in the moon, and for a moment Jacob questioned if the vision of loveliness before him had in fact been sculpted from a block broken free from the heavenly orb. His unblinking eyes followed her slavishly as she waded out into the open pool like some dreamlike vision where much to Jacob's dismay the dark waters swallowed her from sight to mid-torso. She crossed slowly out toward the center of the pool, not so much swimming as she appeared to float, moving with the delicate grace of a swan while leaving nary a ripple to disrupt the glass-like surface.

If this is a dream I find myself in, Jacob silently contemplated to himself, *I really hope it's one I don't awaken from too soon.*

The lady's eyes, as haunting and as dark as the pool into which she waded, remained fast on Jacob's while at the same time taking captive his which never left her. He found himself stilled by the beauty framed in her face like some newly discovered work of art dredged up from the ruins belonging to an age long-lost to the world.

"Who are you?" he finally asked, unable to keep his growing curiosity quiet any longer.

"Who do you think me to be?" the lady responded with a coy smile.

Jacob pondered silently his answer for a moment, though he already had his suspicions.

"Well...even though I don't see any wings on you—at least from here—I'm guessing an angel?"

"And this is how you come to greet an angel," the lady replied, "with the end of your sword leveled at her?"

Jacob glanced down at his weapon he had forgotten was clutched in his grip. The steel of the sword held chameleon-like the cold silver-blue glint of the night in its steel-forged skin. The bewildered look that crept upon his face brought an amusing giggle from the lady which she attempted to shield in a most adorable manner with the back of her hand. And Jacob knew right then if this mysterious stranger possessed any weapon herself it was her disarming smile; so delicate and pleasing were the supple, blood-colored lips, and yet powerful enough to enslave the mightiest army of men in its entirety, much less an adolescent teetering on the brink of manhood, yet still very much a boy.

"No, I am not an angel," she said. "Though I am flattered you would mistake me as one."

"May I ask your name?" inquired Jacob.

The lady's eyes wandered suddenly skyward, but it was from somewhere deep inside the darkness congregating amongst the trees and not from her mouth that a voice —yet her voice, still—pervaded like a gust of wind as though the Forest, itself, released a deep breath.

"*LILITH...*"

As the gentle breeze swept past, what felt like a ghostly finger grazed the back of Jacob's neck making him flinch subtly yet enough so for the lady to readily take notice.

"The Forest brings you great unease, I see." she said.

"Why do you say that?""

"With every passing minute you've stood in its presence, the grip on your sword has grown tighter and more desperate."

Jacob glanced nonchalantly down at his hand and the sword it held and sure enough the lady was right.

"Yeah, well, let's just say there's something about this Forest that doesn't sit right with me, although I'm not quite sure what it is," said Jacob while doing his best to conceal any outward appearance of the jittery nervousness he was feeling. "It's one of the only places in Eden where it is explicitly forbidden to step foot inside, and I don't doubt there's a sound reason for the existence of such a rule."

Even though he didn't have a clue as to what that reason might be—except, that is, for the odd explanation Thaniel had offered regarding the water—and his eyes at that moment were blind to any kind of outward threat, he could feel something most unwelcoming resided amongst the trees, even as he stood there; something armed with the ability to unhinge the courage of those far braver than he could hope to be."

"Yet here you stand, Jacob Parrish, in the thick of its presence without the hollow of an old tree or patch of fern in which to hide yourself," the mysterious figure in the water said. "And the phantom menace of which you seem to believe lurks somewhere in these woods has yet to show itself."

Jacob looked to the lady with renewed surprise. "You know my name?"

"Why wouldn't I?" said Lilith. "Just as I have come to know of you by a more noted moniker for which legend hopes to forever hold a place for you—that of Light Bearer."

~ ~ ~

Jacob noticed movement from within Lilith's long mane of hair as she spoke to him. It came from several of the thick braids woven tightly into the dark tresses, wriggling ever so subtly like the fingers of a hand. He made no mention of it, figuring it was the deceptive light of the night playing tricks on his eyes.

"You seem to know a lot about me."

Again the lady smiled. "It's not every day, or even once in an existence, that a Nephilim is witnessed to breathe life into that which Azrael had stilled with eternal black sleep. Certainly, you didn't think the whispers of such a surprising and unexpected revelation carried to the far corners of Eden would go unnoticed or fail to somehow find an echo in all this surrounding peace."

"To tell you the truth, I haven't really given thought to it one way or the other," said Jacob. "Nor was I aware there was anyone who dwelled in this Forest who would hear such, uh...echoes."

As the boy spoke, an inquisitive look came to Lilith.

"Come closer, if you would," she instructed. "One thing about the Forest, it tends to refuse the company of the light, moon or otherwise, and I wish to have a better look at you."

Jacob inched his way a couple steps closer to the water's edge, and even in the faint silvery gleam of moonlight able to permeate down through the thick overhang of branches above he could feel the lady's gaze strain to strip back the forest shadows gripping him with their shadowy hands.

"It's true...Gothamel is not your father," said the lady.

"No, he's not," said Jacob.

"Then what is the name of the angel who calls you his son?"

Jacob shrugged. "Your guess would be as good as mine, maybe even better."

Lilith, however, seemed to only grow more frustrated by Jacob's answer.

"There's something about you, something quite...familiar, and yet..." said Lilith. "Curse these shadows for playing games with my eyes."

The lady watched intently as Jacob took a couple steps closer toward the dank, soggy bank of the pool, noting the curious manner in which he craned his neck in an attempt to peer down into the dark water, from which his feet remained mindful of keeping a measurable distance.

"You seem to find more interest in the water than with my company. What is it you see that steals your attention away from me?" she asked, watching carefully his searching eyes.

"It's not what I see, but what I don't," said Jacob.

"And just what is it you are looking for?"

"I'm not sure. A passage, I suspect."

"Passage?"

"A tunnel, a gateway...I dunno, maybe even a faint glimmer of light," said Jacob as his eyes narrowed in their labored search.

"I haven't the faintest ability to make sense of your rambling," said Lilith, though the cool tone evident in her voice revealed otherwise.

"It's okay," said Jacob. "You don't have to pretend. I already know."

"What is it you claim to already know?"

"That this pool is not really a pool...at least not solely," answered Jacob. "It's a Through, right?"

The beauty that glowed in the lady's face instantly became a dark, vexing mask.

"Who revealed this to you? It would not have been spoken by one of the winged guardians watching over you. For I know in their ever-vigilant protection of you halflings that they are steadfast in ensuring the existence of this pool be not known to the Nephilim residing inside Eden."

"And I would most likely have gone on not knowing the secret of this Forest had I not asked Thaniel about it," said Jacob.

"Thaniel? He was the one who told you?" asked the lady, growing visibly more perplexed with every spoken word coming from the boy's mouth. "But I am confused. What did he tell you that would find your presence returning here so willingly and without fear?"

"Fear? What is there to be fearful about of a gateway leading to another Heaven?" asked Jacob as he stared almost hypnotically into the water as if imagining the wonder its dark depths might hold. "I have to admit, though, there's this strange, uncomfortable chill nipping at my body and it's been growing more unbearable the harder I try to steal a peek inside, even though I know I'm looking at a door leading to a place promising to be as beautiful as Eden. Maybe it's because these waters look to be anything but heavenly, much less leading to a Heaven. They might be murkier than any I've ever seen before. Then again I'm reminded of the Through leading to Eden was just as unwelcoming and dark before giving way to beauty I've never seen before, not even in my dreams."

"Thaniel told you this pool was a Through to one of the other six Heavens, did he?" asked Lilith.

"Yes."

"And that is all?"

"Yes," Jacob repeated again. "Why, is there more to know?"

The look on the lady's face softened upon hearing these words, and had Jacob's attention not been swallowed whole by the water held in the pool, he might have noticed there was something noticeably different in Lilith's slow-returning smile; it's warmth and charm that once cast a fixating spell upon him now took a cold, sinister shape.

"Very clever, Thaniel," she remarked quietly to herself so that her words escaped being heard by the boy. "It is a cunning bend you have laid in the path leading this Nephilim to me with such ease."

~ ~ ~

As Jacob continued to search the water, he couldn't ignore the weight of the lady's gaze studying him with intense scrutiny. He could almost feel the layers of his flesh being pulled back to offer her keen eyes a porthole to the very center of his being.

"Quite surprising," he heard the lady to mutter.

"What is?"

"Your discomfort with what has been gifted you. One would think it would carry you high upon the back of pride, allowing you to walk a little taller and with your head a bit higher. Yet strangely, I can see just the opposite is true. I would venture to say you have yet to utter out loud that which you have been declared, am I right?"

Jacob said nothing, but stood staring quietly at the lady who somehow had an uncomfortable ability to peer straight through him as if he were a crystal ball holding the gaze of a gypsy fortune-teller.

"It's a lofty thing that has been set square on your shoulders," continued Lilith. "It wears on you, like the weight of an anvil shackled to one's ankle before being cast in a cold, dark sea. So unlike the one who reigned as Light Bearer before your time; he who briefly blazed bright in his anointment before the wick carrying the short-burning flame of his glory was snuffed and left a smoldering ember before going cold."

"You say you're not an angel, and yet you can read minds?" asked Jacob.

"One does not need to possess the power of mind-reading to unlock that which one wishes to keep quiet. More often than not, what is carried in the palm of silence speaks louder and betrays the truth more so than what is revealed by one's tongue," the lady replied. "But in your case it is your reflection that is most telling, just as it was to the boy whose footsteps once marked the path in which you now walk."

"My reflection?"

Lilith lowered her gaze to the water and the image it carried of herself staring back. She grazed it with the palm of her hand in a gentle petting sweep bringing for the first time a rippling disturbance to the mirrored surface surrounding her that sent her reflection scattering.

"The water cupped within this pool has the ability to reveal much about those who venture close enough to cast their reflection upon its surface," she said. "For veiled within its darkness is a pane of liquid glass of remarkable clarity serving as both window and mirror."

A look of great intrigue came to Jacob's face.

"Window and mirror?" he echoed under his breath. And it was then that he noticed a faint movement of shadow and light coming to life in the ring of ripples moving along the surface.

"For those who choose to look—and only a faint few have—the water churns with shadows of things that were, with things as they are, and with things that are yet to be," said Lilith. "But be forewarned, the water in revealing these things does so by dwelling into the soul of the one whose reflection lays upon its surface. And as such, it can also reflect that which has burrowed the deepest beneath one's hide and then deeper still, hidden and unknown, even to the one whose gaze commands it, and for good reason."

"Such as," asked Jacob curiously.

"Love, loss, desire, weakness. One's deepest fear," answered Lilith. "Not all is bad, but like most things secreted to the core of one's being, there is a reason it has been buried. For many, what lies in these dark recesses is like a stranger whose existence had never been known, or welcome."

As Lilith spoke, her hand once more skimmed the surface of the pool and the water suddenly became clear while still, somehow, retaining its murky darkness, and from it, images at once familiar and vividly alive began to reveal themselves to Jacob. The first showed itself in a vision of a wood of trees which quickly gave way to a green, grassy meadow. And in the meadow there was seen a small boy running through the tall, feathery grass while holding in his hands the string to a kite which soared higher and higher in the sky above him.

"That's me," Jacob remarked with wonderment.

The meadow quickly vanished yet the boy remained—only slightly older—and he was now in a garden surrounded by several colorful butterflies which seemed to follow the faintest command coming from his fingers. It was the sight of the woman seen watching from nearby as she pruned her beloved flowers, however, that drew a loving yet pained look from Jacob.

"My mom," he muttered quietly.

She was young and beautiful; a vibrant soul not yet touched by the ravages of sickness, displaying a glowing smile that would eventually dim and grow more forced in an effort to hide the pain the coming years would bring. Jacob almost called out to her, but she, too, faded away and was replaced by an image of the frail, shell of a woman she would eventually become, sitting at the window of her room staring down with sorrow-filled eyes at her neglected garden which once bloomed with the same beauty stolen from her very self. Jacob fought back the tears he felt begin to well in his eyes and to his relief, as well as sadness, the image soon passed from sight as well. It was quickly replaced by more visions.

There was his grandmother seen busy around the house, a house that looked strangely empty and lonely around her. Then came the familiar sight of Penuel Point as he and Ty, his best friend from home, were seen rushing toward the edge of a rocky overhang and flinging themselves out into the vast emptiness framed in picturesque beauty. And as they tumbled toward the valley below them before the chutes strapped to their backs opened to catch them from their free fall, the image again shifted. This time he was seen standing alone at Broken Earth, staring down into the yawning gorge at his feet. Yet despite how many times Jacob could recall standing in that familiar spot, the vision seemed strange and almost dreamlike to witness as he watched himself in the watery image adorned with a most unfamiliar keen and determined look flickering brightly in his eyes along with the reflected radiance of the golden amber sunset coloring the sky.

There was something else Jacob found curious about the image; it showed him holding in his hand a necklace carrying a familiar vial-shaped pendent made of black rock, the same necklace he had long-ago spied hanging from around Gotham's neck. What was he doing with Gotham's necklace, he wondered quietly as he stared at himself pondering it in his palm while wearing a most sorrowful expression. And he watched as he took the necklace and threw it with all his might out into the ravine before turning his back and walking away only to turn around and rush in full run at the waiting ledge. Jacob felt his breath quicken in his chest as he witnessed the vision reveal himself doing what he had yet to find the strength to do: surrender himself with a forceful hurling of his body to the mouth of the gorge. The sight made his toes clench tight inside his sneakers as though to ensure the ground of the Forest floor was still there beneath his feet. He took not a breath as he waited to see the sight of wings unfurl themselves from his back, but the vision of his descent into the gray mist of the gorge quickly gave way to darkness and as it did Jacob nearly cried out for its return, if only for a moment.

"I have no control over the water and what it chooses to reveal, or what it does not," Lilith noted calmly.

The water stirred again and from its depths another vision unfolded itself. Like the others, it appeared dreamlike, but even more so. For this particular image that showed itself was in fact a dream; the same that had stalked Jacob through countless restless sleeps, including earlier this night before waking to the voice calling out from the Silent Forest. He recognized it instantly—the desolate landscape forming a barren wasteland shrouded beneath a cape of night. The sight made Jacob draw back at first, until he caught sight of the familiar dark figure laid stretched out across the sun-cracked ground in the not-too-far distance.

Just as it was unveiled in his dreams—or rather nightmares as he preferred to call them—he found himself standing over the figure. It was bound tight in an endless rope of vine like some unfortunate varmint imprisoned in the coils of a merciless constrictor while slowly being strangled of life. And like his dream, the face of the figure was hidden in shadow, and a voice that had become so familiar to Jacob was suddenly heard coming forth from it. *"Dessssstiny...."*

The image Jacob had so longingly desired to shirk from his psyche now managed somehow to take hold of him, and unbeknownst to him, his feet crept closer toward the pool's edge as he found himself filled with a strong desire to peer past the shadow and into the face hidden from him. Closer he moved toward the water, hand outstretched toward the vision. It was as though he had surrendered all control of himself.

And then the voice called out again, in an ominous whisper, "Come to me, my child."

And with those words the momentary trance which had taken hold of Jacob broke apart as his eyes suddenly caught sight of a strange movement near the water's edge of which he was now only a short distance away, and to his shock he saw a hand with long gnarled fingers fixed with sharp threatening claws slowly coming up from out the water and reaching toward his ankles. He quickly scurried backward to a safe distance while drawing back his sword. When he looked again the hand was gone. As was the vision on the water's surface.

"There's nothing to be fearful of," Jacob heard the lady offer in a tone that was at once soothing and comfort-filled. "They are but visions, and as visions they cannot hurt you."

"Tell that to my eyes," Jacob replied with an edge of annoyance. "They're choosing to play tricks on me."

He stood for some time with his sword poised and ready to strike whatever chose to once again emerge from the water, trick or not. Only when nothing showed itself did he gradually relax his stance and lower his weapon.

"You see?" said Lilith with a smile most pleasing to behold.

"I should go," muttered Jacob, but the lady beckoned to him to stay as he was about to turn away from the pool and her.

"Please don't," she said. "Instead, why don't you put down your sword and come join me in this soothing water? As you can see looking around, we are in no threat of any dragon for which you will be called upon to slay with your weapon."

"I'm sure you are correct about that," said Jacob, an awkward grin returning to his face as he looked about the tree tops splayed across the sky above them. Her charm was quick to work on him, though not completely. "I just can't. But believe me the offer is very tempting."

"Are you accusing me of trying to tempt you?"

"Well, this is the Garden of Eden," teased Jacob, though he was not entirely joking. "It certainly wouldn't be the first time."

Lilith sent a splash of water in his direction. "I believe you just called me a snake."

Jacob quickly shook his head in disagreement. "Oh, no, a snake you definitely are not."

She spied the infatuated look which filled completely his eyes and smiled coyly at him.

"Come then," she said once more making the attempt to lure him into the water, "and I will show you what lies beyond the gates of the Through your eyes were so intent on finding inside this pool."

"You can do that?" asked Jacob with a renewed spark of curiosity that was impossible to hide.

"It's why you came here, isn't it?"

Jacob's eyes came to rest on the lady in the water as if for the first time and trying to spy a glimmer of an answer that would unlock the thick fog of mystery surrounding this strange, yet most intriguing vision of beauty.

"Who are you?" he asked in an almost surrendering tone of befuddlement.

"I already told you," answered the lady.

"You told me your name, that's all," said Jacob. "It's not exactly an everyday sight to find a beautiful woman standing in the middle of a pool in the middle of a forest in the middle of the night, even if she was an angel, which you already said you were not. So, then, who are you exactly?"

"Someone who can show you what lies behind the black, watery mirror of a door before you."

Jacob's gaze fell to the water, and he could not deny his curiosity was stoked like a fire taking to a turned log in a hearth. The blissful look put upon his face by the lady's beauty, though, quickly faded as he began to recount the images the pool had revealed to him only moments earlier. Suddenly, the lure of another heaven hidden only mere steps away was not as tempting as it was when he first approached the water.

"Maybe another time. I think I've seen enough for tonight," he said.

Lilith was swift, and persistent, in her attempt to reclaim him under her spell.

"Then we shall forget the Through and just swim, for in the end the water in this pool is just that; water. And it's such a beautiful night for a swim. You do know how to swim, do you not? Even if you don't, as you can see by where I am standing in the center of this pool the water isn't at all deep."

"Of course I can swim," said Jacob in a slightly defensive tone. And there was a part of him which came close to laying down his sword, stripping off his clothes and jumping into the water to prove it. "But I really have to get back before I am missed. I'm not all that anxious in finding out first-hand what the punishment is for breaking the rules concerning this place."

His reply brought a pronounced pout to Lilith's face. There was something most hypnotic about her, beyond her mesmerizing beauty. It seized upon Jacob's gaze and refused him the ability to look away, not that his eyes fought to shift their focus toward anything else except the vision of loveliness now crossing the pool in his direction. Slowly she moved, gliding through the water with the weightless grace of a lily pad set adrift and somehow leaving not so much as a ripple upon the surface in her wake. And with Jacob's attention firmly fixed on her, he was oblivious to the roots of some of the nearby trees slithering out from deep beneath the ground and slowly creeping along the forest floor toward his unsuspecting feet.

~ ~ ~

"Then would you at least care to prove yourself a gentleman by giving me a hand out?" asked Lilith. She held out her hand for him, but noticed his reluctance to take it. "Perhaps the sight of my nakedness fills you with the same discomfort the looming threat of being reprimanded by your winged overseers brings you."

"Uh, hardly," answered Jacob with a nervous chuckle while attempting to steel himself.

Lilith smiled while her seductive eyes maintained their intense fix on Jacob and stretched her hand further toward him. "Well then, I'm waiting."

Keeping hold of his sword in his right hand, Jacob stretched forth his left arm, but the gesture came with a slowness marked by an inexplicable indecisiveness he very much was aware retained a grip of caution on him, even as he looked deep into the hypnotic eyes staring back at him which seemed to hold a power to pull him forward no matter his will.

"That's it," she cooed as his hand drew nearer. And just as their fingers were about to graze one another, and the smile on Lilith's face widened, a booming cry rang out through the darkness.

"NO!"

The familiar voice was the only thing powerful enough to immediately tear Jacob's gaze from Lilith's, and he turned to find Gotham standing at the far edge of the clearing. The baffled look that instantly swept across Jacob's face came not from the surprise of Gotham's presence, but by the angel's battle stance and the glint of his sword as it was unsheathed from his wing with a blinding swiftness.

"My hand, take it!" urged Lilith with a growing impatience. "HURRY..."

Instead, Jacob slowly recoiled his arm and drew back from Lilith with rising alarm, and when he did, a contemptuous look of disdain revealed itself in her face and the pupils of her once seductive eyes became ink wells of blackness mirroring an intense flame of rage. She lunged viciously forward with frightening speed while sounding a demonic roar, and as she did the vision of bewitching beauty that she encompassed disintegrated instantly and transformed into a horrific, nightmarish sight.

Reacting with speed surprising even to himself, Jacob instinctively swung his right arm into action and let loose the biting forged steel of his sword. It cut through the air with a venomous whoosh before slicing through the unmistakable feel of flesh and a deafening wail of pain shattered the silence entombed inside the Forest. Jacob held what courage he was able to maintain in the defensive posture he retained, but his eyes were wide with terror in the face of the creature before him. Its grotesque features, reptilian in nature and framed within a wild mane of black hair housing at least a dozen deadly hissing vipers much like Medusa of Greek lore, were almost too hideous to behold. Clutching its left shoulder where a stump oozing black blood revealed Jacob's quick reflexes with a sword, the creature thrashed about the edge of the pool in an incensed rage looking as though its only desire was to emerge from the water and come at Jacob. And yet something of great power held it back.

The arm Jacob had severed free with his sword rested nearby on the damp bank near the water twitching with movement. The long gnarled fingers of the hand from which grew sharp, pointed claws curled toward the thumb like it was about to form a shadow animal upon a wall against a bright light. Then to Jacob's shock, the digits morphed together and the hand began to change its shape. At the same time, the arm—gray skinned and scaled—started to grow in length as it wriggled and writhed upon the dirt. Coils began to form and, before Jacob could fathom what was happening, he found himself face to face with an eel-like serpent some twenty feet in length rising upward like a cobra with its eyes blazing red and revealing a jaw lined with razor-sharp teeth.

Jacob instinctively directed his feet to guide him from the hissing monster before him, but, as he attempted to back away, he found himself unable to move his feet and he quickly lost his balance and toppled backward onto the ground. He looked and found to his surprise a tangle of roots and vines wrapped tight around his feet and ankles tethering him firmly to the ground. No matter how hard he pulled with his legs or twisted his feet, he could not free himself of their tight grip. And the sword he needed to cut through them now rested out of reach on the ground where he dropped it during his tumble. He strained his arm to reach for it but the eel quickly darted over to block his attempt and filled Jacob's nose with the putrid stench of its rotting breath when it hissed loudly. A chilling chuckle came from the monstrous figure in the water.

"Grab hold of him, quickly," it ordered the serpent in a voice no longer sweet in its lilt, but possessed. "Bring him within my reach."

Jacob fought harder to kick himself free of the roots binding him, but they had too firm a hold, and seemed to grow tighter the more he struggled. And as the viper leaned in bringing its gnashing teeth uncomfortably closer, Jacob's desperate eyes searched for Gotham and found him just as the angel hurled his sword mightily in the boy's direction. It tore through the air across the clearing in a blinding flash. At first it appeared the sword had missed its target. Everything grew still and silent, even the monstrous reptile hovering over Jacob. It glanced in the direction of Gotham and the momentary stupor filling the hellish creature's gaze disappeared when its eyes rolled back into its head just as its upper body fell away from its bottom half and careened onto the ground in two cleanly amputated parts. There they thrashed about wildly as each end bled out pools of black and innards before finally succumbing to the stillness death brings.

Gotham then came to land at the foot of his kill with his wings outstretched and postured defensively between Jacob and the serpent-haired creature in the pool, and into his hand his sword, guided by the quillon which had momentarily taken the shape and motion of a pair of steel-forged wings when it was flung forth through the air, returned itself like a faithful dog guided back into its master's grip.

"Dare you make one more attempt to lay hands on this boy, Demon, and I promise you will find yourself relieved of your remaining limbs for your efforts," he seethed.

"Well, isn't this a familiar sight," the creature hissed. "The fruit of the great prophesy requiring the aid of an angel to come to his rescue. And a Fallen no less."

"It may be my threat, but it comes backed not by my sword but his, whose bite marks you now wear beneath your coddling hand."

The creature retained its safe position in the water while continuing to clutch the bleeding stump which was all that remained of its arm. Feverishly craning its neck to peer past Gotham with black, soulless eyes glaring from behind its hideous face, it struggled to keep in its sights on Jacob who remained rooted to the ground at the angel's heels and rabidly schemed of some impossible way to get at the boy.

"You know as well as I there's no path for you beyond the water's edge," said Gotham. "And if by some chance there was, you can trust there would be no way around me, nor through me. So give rest to your insistent plotting, Demon, for it seeks to lure you to an unfortunate end."

"You present a challenge in need of pondering. For I see the protective fervor you lend this one is the same, if not more, than that which you gave your own son; not that your boy had much of a need or use for your heroics. As I recall, he acquired quite the disdain of ever wanting to be shaded by your shadow," the creature cooed as the mane of slithering snakes hissed about its head, and as black as its eyes were, a flicker of pleasure could be seen in them when the mention of Gotham's deceased son instantly brought a darkness at once cold and fierce across the angel's face.

"Your son, David—quite the hardy stock as I remember. Certainly not the kind to be left shackled helpless on the ground by tree roots," taunted the monstrous figure while eyeing Jacob as the boy peered out from the footprint of Gotham's silhouette cast over him like a protective blanket. "Then again, after all his training to make him invincible against the dark, unsavory things slithering about in the world, who could have prepared him for the end that would come from his own father's hand, as his unfortunate short life proved."

A look simmering with unbridled hate engulfed Gotham as he took a step followed by another, without the slightest hint of hesitation or fear, toward the pool until the toes of his booted feet barely graced the black, swampy water.

"Your unsightly existence is one well-earned, Demon," seethed Gotham in a low voice straining to contain all of its thundering rage straining for release. "Now back yourself into the foul muck in which you soak and out of my sight. Or so help me I will gladly hold the boy under foot in order to steal from him the pleasure of dissecting your retched carcass, starting with your head."

The creature said nothing in return, but a cringe-worthy smile of glee gradually spread across its face revealing a row of overlapping fangs, unsightly and discolored. Then slowly it receded to the middle of the pool sinking deeper as it did into the midnight-colored water, all the while keeping its sights on Gotham until finally submerging from sight.

CHAPTER FOURTEEN

"**W**hat mischief-making have you taken up, Fledgling?" seethed Gotham as he stood staring down at the water where the creature had disappeared while struggling to keep his rage to a controllable simmer.

Before Jacob could sputter forth an answer, the angel turned away from the pool, and when his fiery eyes settled upon the boy, Jacob silently wished his presence had somehow been forgotten. For one look at Gotham was all it took to see the embers of his anger, that even the nighttime shadows streaked across his face couldn't hide, continuing to smolder and flame. And it was then that Jacob braced himself when Gotham, sword in hand, descended upon him with a blurred swiftness and raised his arm high over his head. As it came swooping down in an arching blow, Jacob clutched tight his eyes and braced himself. A loud slicing crunch followed, and with it, Jacob felt the unyielding binds gripping tight his legs instantly fall slack. A wounded wail, high-pitched and shrill, sounded and seemed to come from the surrounding trees, and when Jacob opened his eyes he saw the roots that had entwined themselves around his legs were now severed and thrashing about in pain momentarily before retreating from sight back into the soft, damp mulch of the earth. Before Jacob could give his newly freed limbs a thankful stretch or wriggle his toes, he felt a hand roughly clasp a fistful of his shirt and yank him upward from off the ground to bring him within inches of the most unhappiest of expressions arrested in Gotham's face he'd yet to witness.

"What part of strictly forbidden about this place did you and your fool mind fail to comprehend?" the angel hissed through clenched teeth.

"I can explain—" sputtered Jacob.

An explanation was the last thing of interest to Gotham.

"Why I didn't let that viper have its way with you is beyond me."

"If it makes you feel any better, right about now I'm wishing you had," said Jacob, forcing forth a strained and unnatural smile.

"You dare to make light of this?" scolded Gotham, his eyes narrowing while tightening uncomfortably his hold on the boy.

Jacob began kicking harder his feet, desperately feeling for the ground that had been pulled out from under him.

"I realize at this moment you probably don't care, but I can't breathe," he managed to croak. And the angel seeing the boy's eyes begin to bug as his chest struggled for air mercifully released his hold and sent Jacob sprawling hard onto the ground.

"Do you have any idea what you almost caused to happen here tonight?" questioned Gotham in a hushed yet serious voice turning his gaze once more to the water while Jacob struggled to compose himself.

"I'm sorry...I know I shouldn't have come here tonight," said Jacob, hoping an apology might somehow work to help quell, at least somewhat, the angel's wrath.

"And yet you did so willingly," said Gotham. "Are all civilians so hard-pressed to follow in the footsteps of the woman Eve?"

Jacob was quiet for moment. "It was the voice."

"Voice? What voice?"

"A woman's voice. It was speaking to me... calling for me," said Jacob as his eyes dared to shift past Gotham to the dark water. "Or, at least, I think it was."

"And so you went to seek it out, in the darkness of these woods, even though you knew it to be forbidden to do so."

"There was something about it...I couldn't ignore it."

"Your life—make that your very soul—from this point forward will depend that you do. Especially now that she knows who it is you are," Gotham said in a most ominous tone which stirred an unsettling look from Jacob. "She knows the Apocrypha telling of the Light Bearer no longer lies in state, doesn't she? More importantly, she has laid her eyes on the one in whom it has chosen to reside and take a renewed breath.

"I didn't tell her...I swear...she just somehow already knew—she knew my name...and she called me Light Bearer," said Jacob before remarking in a much quieter, reflective voice, "She seemed to know everything about me."

Jacob found himself growing dizzy from all the questions spinning around inside his head, when suddenly a look of alarm came over him. "You called her a demon."

"Do you have a better word to describe what your own eyes looked upon and let us hope seared forever in your mind?" asked Gotham.

"She was so beautiful. I thought for sure she was angel," said Jacob, sounding almost mournful.

"Angel? That would be outright blasphemous, if it wasn't so ridiculous."

"It didn't seem so ridiculous to me," argued Jacob. "I mean, what else would I think seeing someone as beautiful as that floating over a Through…you know…before she turned into a hideous, serpent-morphing monster? We are in Eden, after all; you know, the land of angels."

Something the boy said made Gotham cock his head ever so slightly with a strange sense of intrigue.

"You know we stand at the threshold of a Through?" said Gotham, sounding a tad puzzled. "Now you've managed to stoke my curiosity even more as I'm not sure whether I find myself to be more troubled, or impressed, by your lack of trepidation in standing so close to what you know lies on the other side."

"That's exactly what the lady—er, demon—said. What exactly is there to be scared of? I mean, it's a doorway to another heaven," said Jacob. "Sue me for being intrigued by it, like most people would."

"Heaven?" echoed Gotham with growing confusion.

"Although I'm not sure I would want to know what kind of heaven exists where a creature like the one we just saw is running loose," continued Jacob as his eyes scoured the murky water before him.

The expression on Gotham's face gave way to one of utter perplexity. "What nonsense is this you speak? How did a fool notion make its way into your head that this was a Through to one of the other

Heavens?"

"Well, that's what Thaniel said it was."

A stricken look came to Gotham at the sound of Thaniel's name. "Thaniel spoke to you of this place?"

Jacob immediately heard a marked shift of seriousness in Gotham's voice and realized too late he had opened his mouth just a little too wide.

~ ~ ~

"Look, just forget I said anything," Jacob was quick to beg.

"I wish I could forget this night in its entirety, but trust that is not going to happen." said Gotham. "Now then, tell me exactly what conversation you had with Thaniel which led to revealing to you about this place."

"But I promised I wouldn't say anything."

"Then ready yourself for confession, for you lied."

Jacob released a heavy sigh, knowing Gotham would be like a dog with a bone until he was told what he wanted to know.

"Late one night a while back we went to the Library hoping to find something that would tell us why the Silent Forest was off limits," Jacob began.

"We?"

"Me and Max. While we were there we ran into Thaniel and decided to ask him instead since we weren't having all that much luck."

"And?" pressed Gotham much to Jacob's discomfort.

"And...," continued Jacob with a frustrated sigh, "he told us inside the Forest there was a Through which led to one of the other six heavens, just like the Gate we swam through coming to Eden."

"That makes no sense," argued Gotham looking beyond puzzled with every word the boy spoke. "Obviously you misheard the words he spoke."

"How do you mishear something as unbelievable as that? I might daydream now and then during one of his lectures at Study, but I promise you what he told us concerning this Through went in both ears," said Jacob. "Thaniel told us the reason it was kept so is because our curiosity would likely get the better of us and we'd be too tempted to come have a look for ourselves which, after tonight, I guess I helped to prove him right."

Gotham's silence was as grave as he looked, and while his eyes remained fixed on the boy, his gaze penetrated far past him.

"Now, you have to promise me you won't tell Thaniel what I told you," pleaded Jacob. "We gave him our word we would keep it to ourselves."

Gotham didn't agree or disagree to any such promise. In fact, for some time he stood encased in a troubling silence in what seemed a long while, and when finally he did speak it was in the most sobering of tones.

"What you have been told of this place is a complete and dangerous untruth for which all reason is lost on me at the moment. And so it has befallen onto me that I shall tell you before we are to leave here in very pointed terms which will serve no further misunderstanding: there is nothing heavenly about what lies beyond this doorway of water," he said. "And when you see what it is of which I speak you will know without question the reason such a strict edict was put into place, and you will quake when you come to realize the grave error you came so very close to making."

"Obviously, that has been made pretty clear to me now," said Jacob.

His remark drew a chilling glare from Gotham.

"No," the angel responded, shaking his head in disagreement, "I don't believe it has."

He then motioned to the sword which had been knocked from the boy's grip and rested nearby on the ground. "Back onto your feet with yourself, and reclaim your sword."

Once he had, Jacob looked once more to Gotham, who stood staring out across the pool, and immediately he sensed from the look on the angel's face whatever it was that was to be told him would not be of a pleasant nature.

~ ~ ~

"Her name is Lilith," Gotham began, and a faint echo of the name breathed earlier by the Forest pricked Jacob's ears and he knew the angel was referring to the woman who became a nightmare right before his very eyes. "Little has been written of her, and most of what has is threaded in fable and myth. In life she was a woman, as beautiful as the vision you beheld this night. Her beauty, however, masked a dark and powerful wickedness which even angels found inescapable. Many would find their Fall through her seductive ways, and in return she bore their sin in the form of Nephilim, not as you are standing here or those now sleeping away inside Havenhid, but unnatural creations nursed from the teat of a deep unholiness. Many had she when I was sent down to deliver God's punishment, and when I began to silence all of them it was her cries which rang loudest and most vengeful above all the other stricken women."

Gotham gave a pause, as if the sound of the cries he described reached back to him from the distant memory, and in that pause Jacob was certain he saw a fleeting flash of sorrow in the angel's eyes.

"Her wickedness eventually led her here, to this spot where God found in hiding the serpent who had twisted Eve," continued Gotham. "The Through and the waters which cloak it were formed when God rendered his curse upon the serpent. It is here where Lilith was eventually banished, imprisoned in these waters where she serves as mother to the Furies, guiding them in an unquenchable thirst for retribution against the Nephilim who walk the earth today."

"But this Through...," questioned Jacob, "if it doesn't lead to a Heaven as Thaniel said it did, then where—"

His face whitened suddenly as the answer shoved its way forward from the pit of his brain before he could even finish his sentence, and a chilling discomfort settled upon Jacob in a way that urged his feet to flee the forest as he heard Gotham ominously mutter a proverbial scripture:

Her house sinks to death,

And her course leads to the shades.

All who go to her cannot return

And find again the paths of life.

With marked caution, Jacob moved to Gotham's side mindful to keep the distance warned him between his treading feet and the water. Casting his gaze down onto the pond, he saw his image standing beside Gotham reflected upon the water's black surface with a crystal-clear, mirror-like clarity. There then came a surge of light, and Jacob found dancing upon the fingertips of Gotham's left hand a flame of pure white.

"The Light of all light," murmured the angel extending his hand in a slow sweeping motion across the pool. As he did, Jacob peered down into the impregnable murky blackness and, as it was touched by the light's glow, he caught sight of something moving just beneath the water's surface near where their feet were planted and an uncomfortable chill passed through him.

"Only by way of this guiding beacon can the darkness before us be pierced," said Gotham.

Suddenly, Jacob had no desire whatsoever to see what resided within the darkness of the water that only the warming light reflected so brilliantly in his eyes could illuminate. The choice, however, was no longer his, for with a cast of his hand, Gotham sent the light from his hand out over the center of the pool where it seemed to implode on itself and disappear from sight before exploding like a starburst of brilliant white.

What looked to be a death shroud laid upon the surface of the water instantly began to disintegrate and fall away revealing the mouth of an eternal cavern of rock. And to Jacob's horror he saw perched upon the jagged wall of rock hideous monstrosities. They numbered in the hundreds, perhaps thousands, and they looked to be lying in wait, ready to pounce, including one Jacob found to be much too close for comfort near where he stood at the rim of the pool. It was staring up at him with its unnaturally large, black-filled eyes, and with moves too fast to comprehend it lunged upward breaching the surface of the water and took a swipe at Jacob's leg with its claw-shaped hand before it came in contact with the light. Releasing a most unpleasant sound, it fell back into the water with a splash and with that Gotham quickly clenched the air with his hand snuffing out the light and with it the cavern and its inhabitants.

~ ~ ~

"That was...that was...," stammered Jacob as he attempted to subdue the jolt given him. "It was, wasn't it?"

"The passage leading to the lair of the Dragon. The Underneath, it is called," said Gotham with unusual calm, as if he were describing a path weaving its way through a meadow. "Or as it is more commonly known to you—"

"Hell," Jacob's voice echoed the angel's. "And those things...those creatures...they're demons?"

"Feeders, they're called," said Gotham. "Foul creations much like your modern-day vulture. When an Infector has drained what light it can from a mortal soul and rotted it through, the remains are left to the circling Feeders, who descend on such carrion with a ravenous, insatiable hunger. But, yes, demons they all are."

"There must have been hundreds and hundreds of them; too many for even your sword alone, let alone mine, to fend off," said Jacob, still sounding unnerved by what he had just witnessed. "Why are they not coming up out of the water and attacking us like that one...Feeder...who took a swipe at my leg?"

"Because they are unable to," Gotham stated simply. He could see, though, the boy's comprehension was slow in coming. And understandably.

"A Through serves as a door," he began to explain. "And like all doors, they come with locks. Those creatures on the other side can only trespass to the water's edge and no further."

A look of relief swept over Jacob's face.

"Well then," he said breathing with more ease, "what's there to worry about?"

The grim look on Gotham's face remained fast in place without any glimmer of the relief momentarily given the boy.

"What's there to worry about indeed, Fledgling?" he replied. "Except to say that with all locks there is always in existence a key."

"What do you mean by key?" asked Jacob, looking back to the pool. "What kind of key unlocks...water?"

"Any entity residing on the other side of this Through needs no more than to come into physical contact with one on this side, even just the slightest unsuspecting graze of the skin, and it has succeeded in unlocking the door. All it takes is one to cross the threshold and Eden would soon be at the mercy of all of Hell's deep and the darkness it belches from its foul pit," said Gotham in words more unnerving than any Jacob remembered coming before from the angel's mouth. And it was in that instant he understood without question why the Silent Forest had been deemed forbidden, and rightly so.

"The lady in the water...," he began suddenly alarmed. "I almost...I mean, she tried..."

"And she most certainly would have succeeded had I not happened upon you when I did," said Gotham. "I'm only glad to see by the horror marking your face that my mistaken suspicions about what I first witnessed here this night—or thought I was witnessing—were just that—mistaken."

"What do you mean by that?" asked Jacob with a frown. "You didn't actually think I came here knowing what you just told me and was willingly going to...unlock the door to Hell, did you?"

The angel offered up a weak semblance of a smile that couldn't begin to hide from sight the more burdensome troubled look behind it and he quickly turned his gaze to the thick canopy of branches and leaves formed by the trees that allowed only a glimpse of the night sky beyond. "The light of the moon grows dim and the stars are beginning to retire. I think it prudent you be found in your bed before Eden awakes."

"Does that mean you're not going to rat me out to Anahel?" asked Jacob with plea-filled hope both in his voice and eyes.

"Rat you out?" The phrase at first seemed foreign to Gotham, who stared hard at the boy before shaking his head with a certain resignation.

"No, I have no plans to rat you out, as you so put it," he said much to Jacob's relief. "I don't see how it would serve you any benefit. But rest assure, should I again find you in contempt of any rules in the future, you will pray for your fate to rest in Anahel's hands rather than mine, of that I can promise you. Are we understood?"

And to that Jacob readily agreed with a nod of his head. He then took one last glance at the pool gladly knowing he planned to never set eyes on it again before following Gotham's lead through the Forest.

~ ~ ~

The two walked without speaking for some time, accompanied only by the slinking shadows shaped by the night and left to roam amongst the trees, and the sound of dry forest droppings scattered along the pathless ground crunching loudly beneath their treading feet which was accentuated all the more by the noticeable stillness that held constant vigil through the woods.

Strangely, Jacob noticed the trek out of the Forest seemed to stretch much longer than he recalled going in. Even the snaking direction they took through the trees seemed unfamiliar to him. Yet his attention to such things was short-lived as his mind was unable to rest very long on anything other than the mysterious pool, the beautiful lady who attempted to seduce him into its waters, and the shudder-inducing vision of the Underneath's welcome mat he witnessed within its depths. His quiet preoccupation did not go unnoticed by Gotham.

"You've been particularly silent," said the angel as they came upon the massive carcass of a felled tree lying on its side blocking their way like some snoozing woodland giant. "Do you care to share what has quieted your tongue?"

"Just thinking," answered Jacob as his eyes followed the angel's movements in scaling the downed beast with the ease of someone unhindered by the laws of gravity.

"How was it you knew where I'd be tonight?" he then asked when Gotham's feet landed firmly on the other side of the tree.

"I was standing on the terrace of my room when I saw you venturing out into the night well into the hour when you should have been fast sleep," answered Gotham. "Your feet were guiding you swiftly in the direction they had no business being pointed toward, and I saw you had in hand your sword. It was a combination from which I suspected no good could come."

"So you followed me."

"And you should be thankful it is I who has come into possession of your lead instead of one of the Guides, or Anahel himself. Your mood at this moment would be much darker, I can promise you that."

Gotham then noted the way in which Jacob maneuvered his way from the top of the tree trunk down its vine-draped side and to the ground below in three, showy steps absent of any hesitation. It was obvious the confidence lent the boy from his earlier tangle at the Through in which his lightning-quick reflexes had deprived the demon Lilith of an arm had begun to sunk in, and a faint smile of pride formed itself on Gotham's mouth. Yet proud as he was, Gotham was quick to dispose of it, not wanting to further encourage the boy for his disobedience, no matter how successful he had managed to prove himself in the face of real danger.

"Now then, if you are through showing off, let us be off and be quick with our steps," said Gotham. "We are each not doing ourselves any favors with each passing minute that finds us still in the clutches of this Forest."

They were off again, moving quickly through the darkness that hovered about them like an unsavory stranger. Soon there was heard the hooting of an owl in the distance, and Jacob knew they were close to the Forest's edge where it's deathly silence ended and the sounds of life-filling Eden returned.

"You move as though you are the one risking Anahel's wrath should he catch you here," Jacob remarked between heavy breaths as his feet struggled to keep up with the Gotham's.

"In a way, I am. But his wrath causes me less concern than that held within the boundaries of these woods," said Gotham. "For the dangers which lurk amongst these trees are not without peril to angels, in some instances even more so than they are to Nephilim, and trust me when I say they stalk us even at this moment. That is why it has been well understood by all Eden's angels that none would cross the threshold of this place except under the direst of situations. And even then, only by first securing permission from Anahel."

"Direst of situations," mumbled Jacob to himself under his breath. The angel's words struck him curious, but not so much as the sudden thought of Thaniel and the image of him conversing with the lady in the pool which suddenly thrust itself to the forefront of his mind. And after a couple dozen more steps were taken in silence he asked somewhat hesitantly, "So, what reason exactly would an angel have to enter the Forest?"

"For starters, we can begin with retrieving straying Nephilim who find it impossible to abide by the simple rules placed upon them," answered Gotham.

"I mean besides that," said Jacob. "I know I was wrong in breaking the rules coming here. But after seeing first-hand why this place is forbidden, I'm just curious what reason an angel would have to come here, particularly absent a dire situation."

The pounding upon the damp earth by Gotham's feet slowed suddenly, and when they finally came to a standstill he glanced back over his shoulder at Jacob with growing suspect.

"What is it you're attempting to ask?"

"Nothing particular. Just out of curiosity."

"Why do I suddenly find myself ill at ease by your idle curiosity?"

"Uh…how about paranoia for starters?" answered Jacob.

Gotham had come to know the boy very well, from the tiniest facial tics to the subtlest body gestures, and the slight hint of nervousness caught in Jacob's voice did not go unnoticed.

"I told you o n c e y o u do not do very well in your attempts at lying," said Gotham. "The furthest thing from the mind of one such as yourself who just moments ago bore witness to what you have tonight would be the rules governing angels."

It was clear to Jacob they would not be proceeding any further until he had revealed what was swirling about in his mind.

"Fine," he said with a defeated sigh. "I will tell you in confidence only because I can't make any sense of it. But you have to promise to keep it to yourself."

"Do I look like someone who barters?" said Gotham sternly.

And most certainly he did not, at least not at this late hour.

"It has to do with Thaniel," blurted Jacob finally with a distasteful look.

"Go on. What of Thaniel?"

"He's been here," said Jacob. "In the Forest."

"What do you mean he's been here? When?"

"A while back. Right before Illumination."

"You're saying you saw him enter these woods?"

"Well...not exactly," said Jacob clearly struggling with even the most basic of answers.

"What then, exactly?" pressed Gotham with growing impatience.

"We saw him at the pool."

"We? Who's we?"

"Me and Max."

And with those words Gotham's brow narrowed and his face darkened.

"Are you standing here before me telling me this night is not the first time your presence has introduced itself to these woods."

Realizing he had inadvertently dug a much deeper hole for himself with his admission, Jacob's face fell pale and he began stammering like a skipping record in a useless attempt to remedy the disclosure until

Gotham raised his hand to motion him silent.

"I will deal later with both your and Max's clandestine breach," he said in a firm and promising tone. "For now, you will proceed in telling me what you witnessed with Thaniel. And be sure that you are forthright in your recollections, for my patience at this hour has long been exhausted."

~ ~ ~

It took some time for Jacob to recount to Gotham all that he wished to know, and with every word he spoke he felt his stomach tighten itself more uncomfortably around the pit that had formed in his insides. While he was not remiss in knowing the retelling of the night he and Max wound up in the Forest was equal to a signed confession and would likely lead to future punishment, it was the feeling he was somehow betraying Thaniel that made him grow nauseous. After all, in the months he had called Eden home, Jacob had come to form a genuine fondness for Thaniel, and more importantly—trust. He found the angel to be the most intriguing of the Guides, and while most of the other Nephilim found Study to be tedious and boring compared to the rest of their training regiment, Jacob secretly looked forward to the days spent in the Library listening to all the fascinating bits of history and wisdom Thaniel revealed in his lectures. Oftentimes, Jacob would stay after class just to further pick Thaniel's brain, which seemed to be a never-ending well of knowledge and tales no book amongst the countless stacked sky-high inside the Library could begin to match. In return, Thaniel seemed to take an equal liking to Jacob and their time spent talking about all things under and beyond the sun. Now, here he was repaying Thaniel's kindness and friendship by squealing on him like some traitorous sewer rat, and with each word Jacob spewed, the more bitter a taste was left in his mouth.

When he had finally finished, Jacob waited for whatever unpleasant scolding was to follow. At first, Gotham didn't say anything, for a long time; so long, in fact, that Jacob began to stir in discomfort from being the focus of the angel's hard, unyielding stare.

"What is it?" asked Jacob.

"I'm just trying to figure out," answered Gotham when he finally spoke, "what reason under Heaven you would have to speak in such a disparaging manner about an angel like Thaniel."

"What...?" gasped Jacob. "You asked me to tell you what I saw and I told you."

"You actually expect me to believe Thaniel came into these woods to consort with the enemy?"

"Who said anything about consorting?"

"What would you call it?" barked Gotham angrily.

"How should I know? That's why I asked the question," Jacob, growing more confused by the second, answered with growing testiness. "Look...why would I say anything against Thaniel. I like him...a lot. He's been nothing but good to me since I got here. If there's anyone I would speak badly about and not think twice about it, it would be Eksel."

"That's the puzzling question now, isn't it?" asked Gotham. "Why would you?"

What Jacob remained oblivious to at that exact moment was that, for the first time, the angel was looking upon him not as the boy he had grown to love and care for as if his own, but as the son of the dark Fallen he truly was. Doubts had lingered in the back of Gotham's mind where he kept the ever-present secret of Jacob's father locked away. Suddenly, it all came flooding forward like a tidal wave the moment he spied the boy standing at the edge of the pool reaching out to a dark entity. And in the instant he let loose a primal scream of "NO!"—a cry which shook the very Forest itself—it was not at the threat of Lilith being released from her watery prison, but the vision that had terrified the angel of seeing Jacob one day embracing the one thing he done everything in his power to keep out of the boy's reach—the Darkness.

"Look, forget I said anything," said Jacob irritably. "So I broke one of your precious rules about coming into the Silent Forest. Go ahead and punish me. But you're not going to make me out to be a liar as well."

Gotham immediately advanced on the boy and, if not for the growing anger Jacob felt of being accused of lying about Thaniel, he most likely would have attempted a retreat. Yet even as he bravely stood his ground, Jacob still braced himself for whatever pain was about to be delivered to him when Gotham's hand reached for him and found the back of his neck. Then from behind the stern mask he wore, Gotham's eyes came to life in a swirling of golden radiance which held no warmth only ire, and immediately Jacob felt the angel push himself into his mind as if his skull was hinged with a door. Jacob knew at that moment Gotham had chosen to see for himself what had actually taken place the night in question and he did not resist one bit the intrusion. And as he stared defiantly into the shimmering golden eyes staring deeply into his own, Jacob noticed the stone look fixed on Gotham became more grim and crestfallen, and slowly the angel's broad, powerful shoulders slumped and rolled forward as he bowed low his head and exhaled a deep, weighted breath.

"Dear Thaniel, no."

Jacob, however, remained too angry still to wonder, or care, what exactly had brought such great distress to the angel.

"I guess that means you finally believe me," he spat scornfully while yanking himself free of the angel's hold. "Awesome...and all it required was you climbing into my head."

"Where are you going?" asked Gotham as Jacob began walking away.

"Just because you couldn't trust your own son, doesn't give you the right to put your crap off on me," said Jacob. "I can understand now why he turned on you."

The words pierced Gotham like the sharp end of a sword to the center of his chest, and had Jacob not been fueled with such anger to spew such a hateful remark he would have apologized profusely the moment he saw the wounded look fracture its way across the angel's face. Instead, he turned and ran, faster than his feet had ever before carried him. He became a blur of motion moving through the last stretches of the Silent Forest and then even faster through the open lands of the Garden. All the while he heard Gotham's voice behind him calling for him to stop and Jacob knew the angel was following close behind him, but he didn't slow one bit until he reached Havenhid.

Once there he tore up the winding stairways and down hallways until he reached his room where Mist patiently awaited his return while kept company by the snoring coming from his sleeping roommates. Quickly, Jacob crossed the room to the bed where Max was peacefully sawing away at logs.

"You don't want to believe me? Fine by me," said Jacob as he began shaking the lump curled up beneath the covers.

"This isn't necessary," said Gotham, standing on the opposite side of the bed.

"No, of course not," muttered Jacob. "Come on, Max...wake up!"

"This better be good, Jacob," said Max with a sleepy yawn. "I was just in the middle of one incredible dream, and if this isn't important I may just have to kill you."

"It is. I need you to tell Gotham something."

"Gotham?"

Max barely managed a peek through the slits that were his eyes before they flew open as he was jolted awake instantly at the sight of Gotham standing beside his bed looming over him.

"What's going on?" he asked somewhat alarmed. For what reason would Gotham have being in his room when it wasn't even dawn outside?

"Tell him about the Silent Forest?" pushed Jacob, impatiently.

"What do you mean? What about the Silent Forest?" asked Max groggily.

"The night you and I snuck out and went snooping around inside the Silent Forest."

Max stared blankly at Jacob.

"Snooping around...are you crocked? I don't know what you're talking about."

"It's alright, I already told Gotham about it. There's no need to play dumb about it," assured Jacob.

"I couldn't play dumb, even if I wanted to since I haven't the faintest idea what you're talking about," said Max looking more and more baffled.

"You're saying you've never stepped foot inside the Silent Forest?" asked Gotham.

"Can't say I've never had an itch of curiosity to find out what all the fuss was about to make it forbidden to the rest of us, but actually go there and have a poke around? I plead not guilty, your honor," said Max.

Gotham turned a skeptic eye to Jacob who stood quietly stunned at what he was hearing.

"He's lying," Jacob suddenly charged.

"Lying about what, mate?" asked Max. "Look, I'll be the first to admit I've stepped in dingo dung more times than I can count. But having my father find out I broke one of the top commandments in Eden is an aggravation I'm not too keen on suffering this early in my stay here."

"I don't believe this," grumbled Jacob as he found himself becoming more angry. "*You* were the one who woke me up and talked me into breaking that so-called commandment. You wanted to show me the lady in the water—who by the way is no lady...far from it, in fact."

"Lady?" Max looked as though he wasn't sure whether to chuckle or rise up out of bed to make room for his friend to lie down and quiet the spell that had overtaken him. "And here I thought I was the one having the incredible dreams."

From across the room, Ethan stirred in his bed, awakened by the growing clamor of voices.

"What's going on?" he asked sleepily. Any other time the sight of his sitting up in bed staring out from behind slitted eyes with his hair standing straight up on top of his head would have sent Jacob into a fit of giggles. This time it didn't even bring the faintest crack of a smirk.

"Go back to sleep, Ethan," snapped Jacob, and Ethan more than happily fell back into his pillow.

All the while Gotham kept a studying gaze on Jacob who was beginning to wonder if Max was right; had he dreamed the whole thing?

"I really wish I knew what you were talking about, mate," said Max.

When it looked as if Jacob had resigned from pressing his friend any further, Gotham took a seat on the edge of Max's bed.

"Not that I suspect you to be lying, but may I have a peek just to ease my own curiosities?" he asked.

"Knock yourself out," answered Max with a shrug. "I've got nothing to hide."

And Max looked into the eyes gazing down upon him that began to glow golden as Jacob stood quietly by watching. *Finally,* he thought to himself, *now let's see you lie your way out of your own memories.*

"Are we good now?" asked Max when Gotham eventually returned to his feet.

Whatever he saw—or failed to see—swirling inside Max's head, Gotham made no mention of it, either in words or the void that came to settle itself upon his face.

"You still have a couple hours before breakfast," Gotham remarked quietly. "I suggest you use it to get some rest."

Looking even more bewildered, Jacob watched as Gotham turned to leave the room. Before closing the door behind him, the angel looked back at Jacob and held the boy in his steely gaze. And the angel's voice was suddenly echoing inside his head.

"Not a word is to pass your lips about tonight and what you've revealed to me, understood?" said Gotham without moving his lips.

Jacob felt an oddly uncomfortable feeling sweep over him as he began asking over and over to himself, "What has happened?"

And more importantly, why had his best friend betrayed him?

CHAPTER FIFTEEN

DEEDS AND MISDEEDS

The first early breath of morning found Thaniel in the Library. The rows of tables and chairs around him were empty. His first group of students, freshly revived from the night's sound sleep, were still gathered inside the Hall of Light finishing their breakfast, and he knew it wouldn't be long before the sound of their feet would be heard reverberating through the halls of Havenhid, hurrying them to their various study sessions.

He stood motionless, as still as the stillness clutched in the tranquility surrounding him. The only sound to be heard was the constant, never-ending scratching of writing coming from the Witnesses—the four giant books at the center of the Library nearby that took careful record of every breath of creation as it occurred. Thaniel's gaze slowly made its way upward along the great towering walls, searching the volumes and volumes of countless books that filled the most learned and prestigious of rooms in Havenhid. The spines of the books may have been without titles or the name of the authors who penned them, but there was also no need for either, for Thaniel not only knew each book by heart, but also precisely where to find any one he might need at any moment from among the seemingly endless volumes filling the endless shelves.

When his eyes finally found what they sought, his wings appeared, unfolding themselves like the pedals of a flower through two openings smartly tailored in the back of the loose-fitting shirt he wore. They greeted the air with an easy rustling and, with a gentle push upward, Thaniel slowly ascended upward along the wall to where a book had slid itself forward from its spot on the shelf. He took it, then continued to guide his way further upward searching through still more books. Soon another slid forward, followed by another.

When he had gathered the third book from its place, he paused, and while levitating many stories above the Library's parquet floor below, he began thumbing through its pages. As he did, his ears soon pricked to something further above him. Slowly his eyes rolled themselves upward where they caught the curious sight of another book slowly sliding forward from its spot on a shelf several stories higher directly above him. It was hefty in size and bound in a thick, charcoal-colored cover whose wear showed its advanced age, and like the other books Thaniel recognized it instantly—even from a distance—as one of the most important of the books housed in the Library. For in its pages contained not only the history of Eden, but also its closely-guarded dark secrets.

He also knew he had not been the one to summon forth the book. So he watched with growing curiosity as the book continued to slide forward until the weight of it sent it toppling from the shelf upon which it rested. Its fall was in direct line of where Thaniel floated upon the air, but he did not move or shift even slightly out of its path. And as the book plunged downward, it flew open and the speed of its plummet began turning ever so rapidly the pages inside as though an invisible hand was flipping through them in a quick, skimming fashion. Closer it came, its pages still furiously turning, yet Thaniel remained unflinching, and just when it seemed the book was about to painfully strike the angel, it came to an abrupt halt.

Thaniel eyed suspiciously the book hovering above him revealing a chapter titled simply "The Silent Forest" in handwritten text scratched long ago onto the thick parchment-like paper by the tip of an ancient quill dipped in ink as black as a raven's wing. And suddenly he was greeted by a feeling he was no longer alone inside the Library.

~ ~ ~

Throwing a glance over his shoulder, Thaniel directed his gaze to the far side of the Library from where he hovered and was met by the piercing golden glow of eyes belonging to a phantom figure standing behind the wood-scrolled railings of one of the numerous landings meandering through the Library. The figure was hidden, wrapped in a dark cloak tailored from the last remnants of night shadows the morning sun had yet to sweep away.

"Gothamel," Thaniel, instantly recognizing the angel despite the fact he appeared as nothing more than a silhouette, said with surprise in his voice. "By what calling do I find you here at such an early hour?"

"The same which guides any who pass through the doors of this Library—answers," answered Gotham. "Though the answers I seek are absent the pages of the books housed within these walls."

The noticeable weight of angst in Gotham's voice, quiet though it was, did not go unnoticed by Thaniel. "It must be the rarest of questions to achieve such a feat. As you well know, the answers to everything one could possibly have questions about from the dawn of creation until this precise moment are held for all eternity here. I'm not sure a question exists whose answer cannot be found residing somewhere inside this most hallowed chamber of knowledge," he said. "If you'd like, perhaps I can lend you aid in your search. But, at the moment, you must forgive me, for I have students who will be arriving in short order, and I am still preparing the morning's lesson."

He turned his back again to Gotham, and while he settled his gaze once more on the open book cradled in his hands, his attention was not returned to reading the words on the page. Instead, he stood poised waiting; waiting to hear what more Gotham would say or, as he hoped, the sound of him quietly leaving the Library. Instead, after a brief pause of silence, he heard Gotham speak again:

"I fetched one of the Fledglings from the Silent Forest,"

Thaniel's gaze once more slowly shifted upward from the book in his hands to the one still levitating an arm's reach above him.

"The Silent Forest? When did this occur, and who may I ask was so brazen enough to venture inside?"

"Not long before this morning showed itself with its first light," answered Gotham. "Which of the Nephilim it was I'd rather not reveal, for it would serve no purpose at this moment. What is of grave importance, however, is the fact I came upon him with not a moment to spare as he was within a brush of being drawn into the Through."

Even though Thaniel's back was facing him, Gotham could tell his words held the angel's attention in the same way the razor-sharp point of a sword does when it is leveled at a throat tightened with fear.

"Lilith, I presume?" inquired Thaniel.

"Who else could conjure up an illusion of deceit and shape it into a vision of loveliness enticing enough to draw countless men—much less a teenaged boy—to step willingly into a dark lair housing their end?" said Gotham. "Like moths circling a deadly flame."

Thaniel was quiet for a moment.

"Then it was as I feared; the Silent Forest was, indeed, reaching out to the Fledglings," he remarked in a quiet voice of concern. "And the Fledgling whom you refuse to name, he is alright?"

Gotham's head tilted ever so slightly at the subtle note of muted caution held in Thaniel's voice while his eyes remained fixed on his back in careful study.

"Quite," he replied. "The Fledgling, I'm proud to say, showed himself to possess impressive reflexes when suddenly faced with the terror lurking behind the mirage. I cannot say the same, however, of Lilith, who was relieved of one of her limbs before being sent back down into the depths of her black foul swamp."

"Well then, I must say I'm relieved to hear this outcome," Thaniel breathed with relief, though his tone lacked the lilt one would expect to hear upon receiving such news, which did not go unnoticed by Gotham.

"Are you now?" asked Gotham.

Thaniel shot the angel a queer glance over his shoulder.

"You would doubt my concern regarding the safety of a Fledgling?"

"Maybe the doubt you should question is that which can be heard lingering in your own voice," said Gotham.

"I'm not sure I understand what you mean. Perhaps what you detect is puzzlement," explained Thaniel. "Why have you chose to relay word of this incident to myself and not Anahel?"

Thaniel waited for an answer from Gotham, but none was forthcoming.

"If the Nephilim are breaching forbidden boundaries, wouldn't you agree necessary steps must be taken immediately to thwart any further transpirations?" he inquired.

"And what steps, exactly, are you suggesting? Punishment?" asked Gotham.

"Deterrents," corrected Thaniel. "And yes, if need be, punishment, as the Fledglings were clearly warned by Anahel, himself, of such repercussions when it came to the ordinance concerning the Silent Forest. If not for their own safety, then the well-being of Eden itself."

A faint chuckle met Thaniel's ears. Gotham cast off the shadows that had veiled him as he stepped forward to the intricately shaped railing snaking along the ledge of the landing upon which he stood and into the reach of light colored by orange firelight and the pinkish lavender of the early morning hour. However, it was not with an expected grin of amusement Gotham greeted Thaniel, as his fleeting laughter faded, but instead a sober, troubled look fixed upon the angel's face that was at once intimidating.

"You carry within you a great wisdom and knowledge of all," said Gotham. "It is why you have been given governance over the minds of the Nephilim who are brought to Eden and entrusted in your care to arm them with the mental weapons vital to their survival. And so it is I who asks you, if punishments are to be had, who is deserving of them: the Fledglings, or their teacher?"

~ ~ ~

The question brought a mild look of bewilderment to Thaniel's face.

"What an odd remark it is you make, Gothamel. Do you care to explain it?" Thaniel levitated motionless high above the Library floor below him, his wings not fully outstretched, and a look of anxiousness revealed itself upon his face as he stared across the great room at Gotham and waited for the angel to speak.

"You asked me only moments ago why I've come to you instead of Anahel to report this unfortunate incident. I now ask from you an answer to the same question," said Gotham. "Why come to me and not Anahel, with your suspicions of Fledglings breaking Eden's most important rule governing them?"

Thaniel understood immediately the question posed to him. Just two nights earlier, he had come to Gotham to speak privately about a most upsetting matter; while recently standing on the terrace of his chambers taking a breather from grading his students' papers, he caught sight of the shadowy figure of one of the Nephilim stealing away into the night long after curfew. Gotham didn't seem all too concerned, at the time. After all, boys would be boys—or, as he had more often than not come to know them first-hand, inexhaustible wholly terrors fueled by a boundless energy and even greater curiosity for the world around them that no curfew ever crafted in the history of time had yet managed to harness and put securely underfoot. And Nephilim, at the end of the day, were still just that—boys—only with wings to make containment all the much more difficult.

Besides, how much trouble could a Fledgling get himself into in Eden? Gotham had mused lightly to Thaniel's concerns.

How much, indeed, echoed Thaniel, though there was a definite weight of troubled seriousness on his face that was absent Gotham's. And, in fact, he never would have brought the issue to Gotham's attention had his ears not been turned to the faintest presence of a strange sound—a voice, to be precise—slinking its way through the halls of Havenhid like some stray breeze where the Fledglings slept.

What voice? questioned Gotham.

The only one with which the Silent Forest has been known to utter, answered Thaniel.

Only then did the proper amount of concern emerge to shade Gotham's face, and rightly so as his thoughts reflected flashes of his son, David.

Not once did it ever occur to Gotham to question what Thaniel had so delicately brought to his attention.

Not then, not ever.

~ ~ ~

"Why come to me and not Anahel," Gotham asked again when, at first, silence was the only answer to come forth from Thaniel.

"It is no secret between the two of us that I trust you with such delicate matters far more than Anahel," Thaniel finally stated.

Gotham was neither surprised, nor flattered. by the answer.

"If that's the case then why not put the fear of God—or in this case the fear of the Darkness—where it belongs?"

A rare look of puzzlement came over Thaniel.

"I'm not sure I understand what you mean."

"We share a similar philosophy, the two of us, about a great many things," explained Gotham. "One example being we have both of us found fault in Anahel's belief that blindness is best in protecting the Nephilim brought here when it comes to the Silent Forest. Anahel, in all his wisdom, believes a Fledgling is best safeguarded by not having his natural curiosity stoked by the knowledge of what lies within the Forest's boundaries and, on some level, I understand his logic. What I fail to understand is why, if you held high suspicions that some of our younglings were straying into the Forest as you warned me, did you not stamp out their curiosity then and there with the best deterrent of all at your disposal: the truth?"

"As you yourself just explained," answered Thaniel. "It has been Anahel's directive not to stir the imaginations of the boys by breaching the subject."

"Even as they are being led like a cat chasing after a ball of yarn into the very jaws of the dog you think you've muzzled?" Gotham, his voice rising ever louder, argued. "Certainly even you, in this instance, would find it difficult to find blame in a Fledgling's disobedience over something he and his fellow classmates should have been schooled about inside this very room the moment your suspicions were pricked, yet were not."

The angel's words instantly stilled Thaniel.

"Do my ears detect an accusatory charge in your voice?" he asked in a quiet voice laced with offense.

"Hear it as you wish," answered Gotham coolly.

"Strange you would concern yourself with the manner of my teaching." Thaniel's eyes again slowly—cautiously, even—turned to the book hovering above him. "And this wayward book I presume you stirred from its shelf; is there a reason it circles my head like some scavenger bird? Perhaps a subtle way of ensuring it gets folded into this morning's lesson?"

Gripping the railing of the landing, Gotham leaned his body forward while leveling a fierce, yet utter look of uncertainty onto Thaniel.

"That's where we get to the most stupefying part of this whole thing," he muttered aloud. "In fact, you did teach them about the Silent Forest and what resided inside it, didn't you?"

"I did what?" asked Thaniel, sounding both surprised and not.

"Not the entire collective of your students, mind you," said Gotham. "Just a certain two."

Thaniel, at first, appeared taken aback by Gotham's assertion, but whatever momentary discomfort he may have felt was quickly camouflaged by a pleasant smile.

"You'll forgive me Gothamel if I fail to understand quite what to make of your schizophrenic musings," he said in a concerned yet light-hearted manner. "First you find fault in me for being derelict in tailoring my lesson plans to include mention of the Silent Forest while in the same breath suggesting—no...in fact, stating out right—that I've been engaged in educating a select few of this secret history. I must say, if I had more time to spend on this conversation I might be curious enough to look closer at what exactly has happened to muddle your thinking this morning.

His eyes then rolled upward to where the morning sunlight was beginning to filter down ever so gradually toward the Library floor in ever-strengthening shafts of brilliant golden-white, and in its fray his pupils appeared dazzling as two miniature suns. "But, as it is, the hour wastes away the time I need to prepare for my students. So, if you'll forgive me."

~ ~ ~

With his books in hand, Thaniel descended downward to the floor below him, guided by the gentle flutter of his wings. It was a retreat—veiled as one could be, but nonetheless a retreat—as recognizable as an army seeking safety from a blood-drenched battlefield.

Gotham remained on the landing high above watching. And as Thaniel set his books down on his grand desk in the corner of the room, Gotham shifted his gaze to the ancient book of Eden where it remained floating in the air. The book suddenly slammed shut and dropped like a weight, barreling downward until it landed on one of the long wooden tables lined in perfectly formed rows across the Library floor with a thunderous clamor that reverberated to the highest point in the stately room. Startled by the noise, Thaniel spun around and shot a look first to the voluminous book on the table where it had come to rest and then to Gotham whose two feet were already planted on the floor following his long free-fall from his perch above.

"Why is it you choose to knowingly guard your thoughts?" Gotham's accusation was immediately spit forth before Thaniel could open his mouth to speak. "Not just now at this very moment, but earlier, even before you stepped foot through the doors of this Library. It's as though trying to peer through an impregnable fog bank."

"I might ask of you, Gothamel, for what purpose do you choose to read them?" Thaniel volleyed in return.

Gotham continued his approach with slow, yet determined steps until only a couple tables stood between the two angels.

"I am seeking to understand what purpose you would have in leading a Fledgling to believe the Through resting in the Silent Forest would lead anywhere but the Underneath, much less serve as a gateway to another Heaven."

Thaniel's eyes widened and his face gave way a brief moment of unease. "Jacob told you this?"

"I have made mention no Fledglings' name this morn," answered Gotham. "But since you have, and seeing as how the first words from your mouth were absent any utterance of horror or offense at the charge I have just dropped at your feet, I fear my heart will be forced to withstand yet another break before we are through here."

"How ironically fitting that you choose to speak of heartache before allowing me the courtesy of answering the charge, as you deem it, for which you seem to have already sentenced me. Of that, my dear Gothamel, I find to be an immense personal offense coming from you."

Thaniel's words, for a brief moment at least, brought a visible glimmer of remorse to Gotham's eyes.

"So, then, you deny it." said Gotham.

A quiet pause followed in which the two angels stared hard at one another, each searching the other for different reasons, before Thaniel parted his lips to speak.

"It is true I spoke to Jacob about the Through late one evening—the night before the start of Illumination, in fact," he began. "I had found him wandering near the eaves where the Griffiers stand watch. What he was doing there, I wasn't sure, but, as we spoke of this and that, he came to inquire about the Silent Forest and the reason for which it had been deemed a forbidden place. Admittedly, it was a conundrum I was not anticipating at such an hour, and while I respect and even understand to an extent Anahel's viewpoint when it comes to the Silent Forest I could see the curiosity in the boy's eyes demanded the truth, not a further massaging of his naivety. And so, in the little time I had—and it wasn't much, mind you, lest I would keep him up all night and drain him of all energy and focus for the coming day's competitions—I attempted to give an abbreviated answer to the question asked of me the best I could. I see now that it is quite possible I somehow did more harm than good. After all, the proper telling of the Silent Forest and the

Through to the Underneath, which resides within it, does not lend itself well to rushed explanation. And yet how Jacob could have come away with the understanding that the Through led to one of the other Heavens is something that leaves me quite dumbfounded."

Thaniel stopped speaking when he came to notice the questioning look on Gotham's face had done little to shift itself.

"You don't believe me?" asked Thaniel.

"I just find it odd how—aside from the hour of the night and the location inside this Library—the boy holds a memory completely different than your own recollection," said Gotham.

Thaniel began to move about the tables while pondering an answer that might quiet Gotham's puzzlement.

"You mentioned two students I supposedly infected with this preposterous idea," he said suddenly. "I assume the other to be Maximilian, as he was here with Jacob that night."

"That's correct."

"And what did he have to say of the matter?" asked Thaniel before cocking his head when noticing Gotham's reluctance in offering an answer. "Come now, Gothamel, don't tell me it's possible someone as mistrusting as you would refrain from having a gander at his thoughts as well before coming here armed to the teeth in suspicion against me."

"I looked," said Gotham.

"And?"

"And his memory is just as you described happened," said Gotham, bringing a grin of satisfaction from Thaniel. "But," he was quick to add, "it does not explain away how Jacob's recollection could differ so starkly. Even with the ability to mask his thoughts as Nephilim are undoubtedly capable of, he is much too inexperienced to do so at this early stage without me recognizing the deception."

"That much is true," agreed Thaniel.

"Then there was a moment in the Silent Forest when I led him to the edge of the Through to reveal the truth of what lurked beneath the surface of the water," continued Gotham while staring off blankly in thought. "I could see by the look held captive in his face that his perception of it had been twisted, and yet even as he demonstrated a remarkable instinct that guided his feet with caution from venturing too close to the water, his face held no sign of fear, even after bearing witness to the reality that is Lilith. It was then he told me—not as a tattling accusation, but an innocent remark brimming with pure curiosity—that you had specifically told him the Through led to a neighboring heaven as beautiful as Eden itself."

Thaniel shook his head in disbelief. "The only explanation I can entertain is that Jacob, in my short tutorial of the Forest, somehow misheard my words in which they were spoken. Either that, or..."

Thaniel's voice fell quiet, bringing a rise to Gotham's brow. "Or what?"

"I hesitate to even entertain the prospect," Thaniel replied with a burdensome sigh.

"Go on, Thaniel, and say what it is that your tongue finds so difficult to mutter."

~ ~ ~

Gotham watched closely as Thaniel began walking around the perimeter of the tables with slow, measured steps.

"Has it dawned on you—even in a passing thought—that the boy could be deceiving you? Not knowingly, but deceiving you all the same?" asked Thaniel.

"By what reason would he have to deceive me?" spat Gotham in a tone revealing how preposterous he found such a notion.

"Certainly, it is lost on me at the moment. But it cannot be forgotten or overlooked who this boy is—not what the Blackstone or feat over Azrael has conspired to lead us to believe, but who he really is," said Thaniel. "You hail the absence of fear in Jacob's face as he stood looking into the black waters of the Through as evidence of my guilt. But would you expect less from the son of Samael while standing at the entrance to the father's realm?"

"You forget he holds no knowledge of Samael being his father," argued Gotham.

"True. But instinct, even blind, is the most basic and deep-seated shared amongst all living things. Is it not possible that is what is at work now?" Thaniel wondered aloud. "Most certainly by now the Darkness has been stirred by the revelation that the prophesy telling of a Light Bearer once believed dead has taken a renewed breath of life. And do you find it a mere coincidence, Gothamel—whose own intellect rivals my own—that of all the Nephilim to disobey the ordinance concerning the Silent Forest it would be this child who, without hesitation, answered the beckoning call of Lilith to stray into the forbidding darkness where she lies in wait?"

As Thaniel spoke, the honey-sweet tenor of his voice belied his harsh words that fought to stir up Gotham's doubt.

His eyes a dull but simmering flame staring straight ahead, Gotham listened stone-faced while Thaniel continued to speak. "Trust that I recognize the unpleasantness of what I speak. After all, I know how protective you've come to be of the boy. I, myself, have grown quite fond of him as well. Yet are you willing to let your feelings for the child cloud your judgment and blind you to the reality before us, even so much as to bring a shadow of suspicion upon your own brother to make you believe, even for a second, that I would ever be a willing participant in conspiring with the likes of Lilith? As you, yourself, questioned, what purpose would weaving such a dangerous twist of the truth concerning the Through serve me?"

"Trust me, I have spent the last few hours mulling over nothing else but such thoughts," answered Gotham.

Thaniel came to stand before Gotham with just the width of the heavy wood table separating them.

"I see my words are troublesome to you and, if anything, have stood only to leave you with more questions in this place where answers are in abundance," he said in a soothing voice.

"To the contrary, Thaniel," said Gotham with a smile, faint as it was. "You have provided me with much needed clarity."

Thaniel nodded, and his face beamed with an innocence and sincerity unseen so markedly in other angels, which Gotham studied with a keen astuteness.

"Perhaps I will be proved wrong where Jacob is concerned. Perhaps, as is my hope, this has all been an unfortunate misunderstanding of words, as I first noted. For nothing would please me more than to have both our names unsoiled by this incident," said Thaniel.

"Unfortunate misunderstanding," Gotham muttered in an echo under his breath as his gaze narrowed on Thaniel as he turned away.

CHAPTER SIXTEEN

THE DYE IS CAST

"Whoever digs a pit will fall into it, and a stone will come back on him who starts it rolling," Gotham remarked casually as Thaniel started to walk away from him.

Thaniel instantly recognized the words coming from the angel and stopped in his steps.

"Proverbs 26:27."

"It's good to know you have stayed familiar with the one book above all books housed in this Library."

"Is there a reason you choose to recite from it at this particular moment?" questioned Thaniel.

"I just find it more than a little curious that you would defend yourself against conspiring with Lilith when I made no mention, or even breathed a hint of such of a thing," said Gotham.

Thaniel offered no response at first, even as Gotham waited for one.

"And so I did," said Thaniel finally with a resigned chuckle followed by a heavy sigh when he saw clearly that Gotham's face was devoid of all signs of levity.

"Then the boy's memories, as I saw them, are as they were," Gotham spoke quietly, as if the words themselves might cause the floor beneath them to split apart and swallow up everything built upon it.

"Of all sins, the utterance of untruths will prove itself the most deadliest, with the unforeseen power to unseat kings from the highest thrones and cleave whole kingdoms down to its last brick with one swipe of the tongue in the same way a scythe clears a wheat field," remarked Thaniel. "Perhaps we as well should have taken heed of our father's warning to his mortal creations."

"It is not I who stands here at this hour suddenly sounding as someone preparing himself for the confessional box," said Gotham.

"True enough said," agreed Thaniel. "And, as I can see I would have little luck in dismantling your suspicions you have leveled at me this very minute, I hasten to admit it was, in fact, I who conspired in luring Jacob into the Silent Forest last night."

"You?"

"There's hardly a need to cast a look upon me as though I have revealed myself to be Lilith's doppelgänger," continued Thaniel. "I knew the boy would never be in true danger, not with you fast on his heels. Which is why I warned you to be on the lookout for Nephilim sneaking off into the night."

"Explain then what reason you would have in sending the boy into such close reach of said danger?" pressed Gotham who was visibly doing everything in his power to tamp down the anger boiling inside him.

"Admittedly, it was a juvenile move on my part. You see, I was desperate to awaken your lingering fears and unhealed wounds of mistrust you continue to carry all these long years later in regards to your son's unfortunate fate," explained Thaniel. "If anything were to stoke the flame I needed from a dying fire, I knew it would be the sight of Jacob being wooed by a member of the congregation belonging to the Darkness."

The words spoken so casually by Thaniel struck Gotham like some phantom fist, especially the mention of his beloved David.

"What demented game is this you're playing, Thaniel?" Gotham quietly, yet forcefully, demanded.

"One, I regret, that will undoubtedly unleash your ire onto me, prepared as I might be for it," answered Thaniel.

He had barely spoken when the last fibers of control Gotham held over the rage which began its slow simmer inside him quickly snapped like a brittle twig. He lurched suddenly forward, coming across the table in a movement so fast it would appear to the naked eye as nothing more than an undecipherable blur, and he was instantly upon Thaniel. He seized Thaniel's neck in the crushing clutch of his hand and separated the angel's feet from the floor. The two sailed across the Library as if taken possession by the strong gusts of a hurricane, ending with Gotham slamming a noticeably taken aback Thaniel against the wall and pinning him fast.

"By all means, Gothamel, vent your spleen," Thaniel managed to gasp.

"Your visible disquietude is well warranted, brother of mine. For by making me cast undeserved doubt on the boy in defense of my undying belief and love for you, and using the residual burden left me by my sacrificed son to bankroll whatever ploy you have schemed, you have succeeded in awakening this unforgiving fire of mine you so eagerly admitted to wanting to fan. But the question is why; what purpose do you see it serving you? Perhaps beckon me to unsheathe Destiny from its long hibernation?" growled Gotham surlily. "That is, after all, what you seek is it not, Thaniel—the Sword of Destiny? Or will you have me believe Jacob's own eyes betrayed his vision when he observed you several dozen moons past standing at the Through's edge intimately plotting its heist with the dark mistress herself?"

As Thaniel, unable to answer, struggled in the unmerciful hold tightening itself around his neck, Gotham brought his free hand to the top of Thaniel's head and roughly smoothed back the locks of hair which hung in loose golden strands down across his forehead. And as he did, Thaniel became aware of Gotham's flaming eyes searching carefully the skin around his temples.

"I take it by the fire I see in your eyes and more than feel coursing through the hand you have clamped around my throat you suspect I have secretly come to share a membership in your elite brotherhood of Fallen," Thaniel finally managed to gasp strenuously despite the strangling grip on his throat. "Well, then, look closely and you will see you are the only one here who carries the mark of God's curse."

Sure enough his skin was unblemished by the tell-tale brand.

"Is that a glimmer of relief I see in your eye, or perplexity?" asked Thaniel. "After all, what sin do you find me guilty of committing and deserving of such punishment? Practicing the virtue of patience in my wait for you to surface from whatever rock you decided to take shelter under all these years so that I might finally demonstrate a show of brotherly compassion toward you by relieving you of the one possession that has brought upon you so much misery?"

Gotham felt a painful tightening in his chest and his hand loosened its grip on Thaniel and slipped from his throat. Taking several steps slowly backward, he appeared fatigued and deflated in the face of the angel's admission, staring in stunned disbelief at Thaniel, who fell slack against the wall rubbing his neck.

"Then it's true," whispered Gotham as though the words themselves were too horrible to utter aloud. "And do I dare ask why you seek out the sword?"

"Why else has man, angel and demon alike spawned a centuries-long hunt to possess the one coveted relic touched by the hand of our father?"

"WHY DO YOU SEEK IT OUT?" Gotham's voice reverberated in an angry echo throughout the Library.

Thaniel pursed tightly his lips at first as though sealing them to keep whatever the answer a secret.

"I have my reasons," he said.

"And is one of those reasons freeing Samael?" Gotham growled. "For what other reason could there possibly be in your shameful cahoots with Lilith?"

Thaniel knew there was no point in denying what Gotham cleverly surmised on his own, nor did he try.

"You of all should know the power of the sword does not come without a price," he answered simply.

~ ~ ~

Gotham was quick to turn his back on Thaniel, not wanting to reveal the surfacing pain that suddenly unleashed itself from some hidden well deep inside himself and found residence in his tearing eyes.

Please, not Thaniel, he pleaded in silence to himself while confronted with an unsettling foreboding of dread that swept through him like a fast-moving ocean swell. And, for a brief passing moment, he wished for truth in Thaniel's earlier attempt to paint Jacob as a liar. For learning of a Nephilim's deception, even one he cared about as much as Jacob, would be far easier to accept than that of one's own brother. After all, the blood flowing through the veins of a Nephilim boy was half mortal, therefore making them more easily prone to, and in many cases expected to, readily embrace the act of betrayal. And though angels were not immune to this most primitive of weaknesses, as Gotham had witnessed from many of his brethren who now carried as he did the same shameful mark upon their foreheads, Thaniel was the last angel he would ever expect to take this unfortunate turn.

"I hear your conflicted thoughts, Gothamel. I know at this moment I have come to cause you great sadness and disappointment. For this I am truly sorry," said Thaniel.

His words brought a visible grimness to Gotham.

"You dare to offer your apologies, even as you willingly step ever closer to the precipice of your fate?" asked Gotham.

"I didn't expect it would be pleasant when this moment would eventually find itself upon us."

"In that statement, brother, you would be correct. Now come to know this: Destiny is not yours to claim," exclaimed Gotham, his voice once again finding its forceful strength. "Nor will it ever."

"Spoken as someone who has already lost claim to it, but has yet to realize it," said Thaniel in a stern manner rarely heard to pass through his lips. He then approached Gotham, though cautiously keeping a safe distance between himself and the angel whose glare all but burned right through him.

"You'd be wise not to act in haste," warned Thaniel in a voice that returned to its more familiar softer, gentler tone. "My last wish is to bring harm to Eden or the Nephilim in her care, but I will if forced. Keep that in mind if you find yourself contemplating reaching for your sword or taking me again by the throat."

The subtle yet marked threat voiced against the Nephilim made it all the more difficult for Gotham to hold tight to the floor upon which he stood and keep himself rooted in place.

"Behold, for something wicked this way comes in a shape both unexpected and certainly most disheartening," he remarked with a sneer while his fierce gaze of flame not once shifted its sights set on Thaniel. "What cunning voice has met your ear and made twisted your mind? You who has always been so valiant and steadfast in your loyalty and servitude."

"As you yourself were. As you remain, even now as you are left to wander amongst mortals with only the company of your shadow through an endless procession of rising moons and setting suns to keep count of the moments since Heaven cast you from her bosom without a second glance. And I ask you what good has your servitude lent you?" said Thaniel. "No, Gothamel, unlike you I have come to realize there is nothing to reap in wholly placing oneself in the service of another; not for mortal nor angel. The only reward awaiting one who genuflects is calloused knees, and the eternal reminder that they are nothing more than a blade of grass to soften the steps of the feet which tread upon them."

Gotham's voice again rose in an echo of growing anger. "Lest ye forget, we do not exist for the baubles of reward."

"Ah, the thundering pronouncement with what you speak—even now—holds still an unbending air of conviction that is quite noble indeed, Gothamel," said Thaniel. "It does well to shield you from aspersions a most powerful and undoubtedly most coveted of baubles long-held in your possession brings your way."

"There has never been any self-serving purpose in my taking ownership of Destiny, in that you well know, but to safeguard it from falling into hands that should never take it into its grasp. Like the one stretched out for it now," countered Gotham.

"Which makes it all the more noble an effort to behold, doesn't it?"

Never before had Gotham heard Thaniel speak in such a spiteful manner. It made him draw silent for a moment as he realized with great sorrow and angst the perilous ledge Thaniel seemingly was unaware of that lay before him, and an overwhelming sense of helplessness overcame him.

"Oh, Thaniel, you greatly underestimate the currents of the river which you are foolishly flirting to navigate. If ever you were to listen to me, let it be now, and save yourself before you drift too far out into the drink to turn back. For no matter your strength or how hard you beat your wings, trust me, they will overtake you, pull you under and carry you to the fathoms where fire burns eternal," he said. "Listen carefully to the words I speak, for they are uttered with the conviction of knowing. The Fall is long and harrowing, especially for an angel who has soared to the highest of planes. But what's worse is the lonely existence that awaits. In that alone rests a truly agonizing punishment beyond any searing of flame."

In a brief moment that followed, a gleam came to Thaniel's face which made Gotham believe his words had not only been heard, but had entwined themselves around the angel's limbs like life-saving tethers to keep him from journeying any further into the unseen dark abyss looming like a giant sinkhole amid a broken road only a short distance ahead.

"I've long stood in admiration of you, Gothamel," said Thaniel. "At one time, when you still held reign to your place in Heaven, it was as a demigod, in many respects. Your strength, as impressive inwardly as your brawn, was something for which I had always strived yet knew certain I would always fall short of achieving."

Just as it appeared, the light in Thaniel's face quickly dimmed once more.

"It is only now I see how truly weak you are; the same weakness that begets a shackled slave groveling at the feet of his master," he said.

"And before whose feet exactly do you find me in such a prostrate position?" asked Gotham.

"The same one who looked on and watched you spill the blood of your own son to ensure the Light of his kingdom continued to burn, before turning his shoulder to you without so much as an utterance of gratitude," answered Thaniel.

Gotham's face darkened. "How is it possible that all this time you have managed to keep hidden behind such a pleasing smile a forked tongue capable of unleashing such soiled words?"

"Yet you refrain from arguing what I've stated to be anything but true," contested Thaniel.

Gotham looked on with growing displeasure as Thaniel began walking the floor with gentle steps.

"I've come to know a great many things in my existence, Gothamel," said Thaniel. "You can take from any shelf you wish anywhere inside this Library the book of your choosing and I can recite to the word whatever page you turn to. And yet the one thing that has failed my intellect to this day is understanding the nature of your loyalties. How, after all this time, do you still pledge allegiance to the one who refuses you, and in fact, goes out of his way to bring pain to you as a way of enunciating his refusal?"

"My allegiance has always been to what my self knows to be right, to be just, and to be moral, no matter my circumstances," said Gotham pointedly.

"And what has your unfaltering loyalty reaped you?" asked Thaniel. "An existence of deafening solitude...and the comforting shade of the Tree of Life when you lend company to your son who lies forever still inside a stone crypt."

"Silence yourself, Thaniel—"

"A burning beacon of light and power you could have been in your own right, and one you could blaze forth even now while pointing Destiny at Heaven itself," continued Thaniel, ignoring Gotham's warning. "Yet you inexplicably yearn to reclaim your place at the heel of our father like some lap dog. Have you somehow fallen victim to some grand delusion your continuing loyalty will someday be met with the embrace you so long for? Perhaps you've become so simplistic in your thinking that you hold hope in the idea that by saving me you will somehow save yourself."

"You insult me with such words," fumed Gotham with renewed flame.

"And yet here you stand vying ever so valiantly to keep me from straying from the Light, and, as always, so noble in your effort," said Thaniel with a condescending smirk.

The words stung Gotham, and he turned his back to Thaniel and strolled slowly away to keep both hidden and distant the growing look of despair reflected in his face.

~ ~ ~

"True, the effort I make is in hopeful chase of salvation, though it be yours, not mine. But with great sadness I clearly see such an attempt is fruitless," Gotham noted with a sound of great dismay in his voice when he finally spoke. "You who balks at servitude moves ever closer to a new master, and I grow less confident I can slow your drift. The heavens will soon shed yet another of its twinkling jewels."

As he spoke the last few words, his eyes lifted upward to the morning light pouring into the Library in crisscrossing slats of white. And in the golden fiery pools of his pupils resided a great sadness. But it was fleeting, and his demeanor quickly regained its steel before Gotham swung back around no longer appearing wounded to face Thaniel once more.

"Tell me, Thaniel, as you stand hear in mocking judgment of myself, what reward does your new allegiance reap you?"

The question at first seemed to take Thaniel aback, and for a moment he stood silent.

"Come now, Thaniel. Surely you stand to gain a princely sum, you who puts such eminence in compensation for your service," pressed Gotham. "Thirty pieces of silver? Or were you much more shrewd than Judas in your bartering, as I suspect?"

Thaniel's face cracked with a smile. "It may surprise you to hear, but treasure holds no interest for me."

"Then what?" demanded Gotham with a snarl of impatience. "Certainly your promised gesture to free Samael of his bonds does not stem from tidings of friendship and fondness, as I know your disdain for him was at one time as great as my own."

Thaniel glanced around himself, and as he did he lifted his hands at his sides to gesture to the Library surrounding them and said simply, "This."

A curious & peculiar look came to Gotham's face as he glanced about the grand room. "The Library?"

Thaniel appeared more amused, like one in possession of the most intriguing of secrets not yet shared with another's eager ear.

"You limit your gaze," he answered while slowly beginning to circle about Gotham. "I'm talking of the whole of Havenhid, and the trees that hide her from the naked eye. I speak of the Garden and all the animals that deem it home; the neighboring mountains from which pours life into the fabled River that nourishes it all; lands, both sacred and forbidden, that together stretch as far as the eye can see to create this wondrous Xanadu."

Thaniel's gaze moved to a nearby table where the book holding Eden's history had earlier come to rest under Gotham's directive.

"I speak of this book," he continued softly, almost lovingly, as his hand gently caressed its way across the weathered, aged binding, "and all the history scribed inside, to which you so pointedly turned my attention. For all of it—all that makes up Eden—is soon to be my reward."

Gotham at first appeared dumbfounded by the unabashed declaration. But, then, he let escape a series of chuckles followed by a boisterous, hearty laugh let loose to fill the room where his anger once did.

"That's about the boldest of predictions to meet my ears as any I've come to hear in some time," said Gotham.

"It's not a prediction, but a promise," corrected Thaniel. "A promise to make right what has been lost to the whims of rewritten history."

"What craziness do I find you uttering now?" asked Gotham

"You know well of what I speak, Gothamel, or was the slight suffered by me so inconsequential in your eyes it be deemed worthy of nothing more than a passing shrug?" said Thaniel, but Gotham's face still only registered a blank look. "Lest you forget, there was a time not so long passed, and yet separated from us by countless ages, when Eden fell out of sight and mind once Johiel secured its Gate to the outside world. Well before Haniel's footprint would mark these grounds, it was I who served in the position of caretaker to our fair Garden. It was during my long residency that I was tasked with gathering and cataloging all knowledge ever to have existed in a thought. It was I who served as architect of this Library which in turn would become the beating heart within the trees which would eventually give life to Havenhid itself."

"And for your duty you expected to receive the deed to Eden itself like some common landlord?" asked Gotham.

"What I expected," answered Thaniel, his voice rising sharply, "was simple appreciation and consideration. What I did not expect was to one day learn our father had so proudly named Anahel ruler of Eden without so much as ruminating over the work I had labored away so long to perfect."

"Anahel is a governing angel, not a ruler," said Gotham.

"EDEN WAS MINE TO BE HAD!" Thaniel shouted in a moment of inconsolable rage before taking a steadying breath. "And so it finally shall be."

~ ~ ~

Gotham waited until the echo of Thaniel's burst of anger faded into the eaves of the Library.

"How is it, Thaniel, whose knowledge is as impressive as the books held within these walls, that acuity now fails you?" asked Gotham drawing a blank glance from Thaniel. "For what makes you think for a moment God, himself, wouldn't send a legion of angels to lay waste this place and all it holds before seeing you reign over it, especially when your scheme in taking it comes in congress with the Darkness?"

"Even our Creator would think twice before matching Heaven's power against that forged in Destiny's blade," answered Thaniel with unabashed confidence.

"Of course," Gotham sighed as if a light switch was suddenly thrown inside his head. "A blade you speak of as if at this very moment you were in possession of, though I can attest here now, you will never know beyond your warped fantasies the feel of its sway in your grip," said Gotham with equal self-assurance.

"Oh, Gothamel, my dear brother, let's not us quarrel over this," said Thaniel with a smile while moving forward with a hand outstretched which Gotham refused to take in his. "It will only lead to so much unnecessary unpleasantness where there needn't be, traces of which already line your face."

Gotham's gaze remained on Thaniel's hand which remained stretched toward him and his eyes reflected a most solemn of looks.

"It's true you are my brother, and a dear one at that," said Gotham. "It has never been lost to my memory the day I was cast from Heaven's sight in a searing flash of lightning that sent me into the mortal pit. I came to be awakened in the middle of a dusty field and found you standing over me. You offered me your hand then; the only one of my brethren to do so. You lent me comfort when in my rage I rebuked all and everything around me before disappearing into the crush of men. And when my anger quelled enough to allow me to finally emerge from my solitary existence, it was you who offered me welcome and helped to pave the way that I might pass through Eden's Gate and be taken once more into the accepting embrace of the small band of my brothers who reside here. I have always remembered your kindness, which is why this comes to me with such pain and sorrow."

"Then why not take my hand again?" urged Thaniel, clasping Gotham's shoulders. "Give me what it is I ask and in return I will part to you half of Eden; a small token of what you've been denied by our father for your loyalty."

Gotham turned his gaze to Thaniel's, and the sorrow it reflected instantly dissipated.

"Band with me, and a piece of Heaven that was so cruelly denied you will know your rule—*our* rule," continued Thaniel.

His eyes were wide and gleaming bright, almost hypnotically so, making Gotham take a wary step back out of Thaniel's grip as a cloud of contempt moved across his face.

"So, it has come to be after all this time," said Gotham, "that another serpent has slithered its way into Eden."

~ ~ ~

The sound of footsteps could suddenly be heard drawing both angels' glances to a group of boys seen walking down the hall approaching the arched entrance of the Library. The expected students of Thaniel's morning class were just about to enter the Library when Thaniel made a subtle motion with his right hand, and the Library's massive wooden doors slammed shut in their faces with a thunderous clamor.

"The hourglass is almost out of sand and I am losing my patience with you, Gothamel," hissed Thaniel. "Where is it?"

"Where is what?" asked Gotham ever so coyly.

"You know well what I speak—Destiny."

"I do not have it with me."

"Now you dare to insult the intelligence you only a short time before lauded," said Thaniel. "I don't believe for a minute one who possesses the most powerful of all weapons would not have it at all times within his reach."

"Believe what you wish, but as I told you already, I did not take possession of Destiny to possess its power for my own gain, which I now see you would have difficulty understanding."

"I want it!" growled Thaniel, his serene demeanor quickly giving way to impatience.

"Then all my luck to you in finding it. The only clue I will offer you is to tell you it resides hidden away without fear of discovery while leaving even the most ravenous of those looking to claim it to go mad in their search."

A faint trace of pleasure shaped Gotham' mouth as he watched Thaniel pace slowly before him in frustrated silence.

"Oh, Gothamel, how I had hoped to have had more time finessing my plan to fruition. But now here we find ourselves, and Anahel is soon to mark the end of Illumination by officiating over the Blessing of our soon to be beatified Jacob," said Thaniel.

"Is the gnawing I detect in your voice worry that you may fall witness to that which you so rabidly covet passing your wringing hands and into the clutches fate has destined it to be placed?" questioned Gotham.

"No, for the wound you continue to hold close to your heart would prevent the repeat of such a gift, that much I know. But the dawn of a new Light Bearer is not one I can rise up and greet as the curator of this Library for which I've become," said Thaniel. "Unfortunately time is of the essence and so I can only give you until the end of the morrow to allay such concerns."

"And what duty, exactly, do you see me fulfilling, if I may inquire?" asked Gotham.

"You will quietly leave Eden alone without a word to anyone and retrieve that which I seek from you with a swiftness guiding your feet as if lives are dependent upon it because, most assuredly, I now tell you they are. I will be waiting atop Broken Earth for your return with Destiny in hand. Not a minute past the hour when the setting sun grazes the highest peak of Day's Rest will be afforded you. A fitting deadline, wouldn't you agree."

"And if I choose not to comply?"

"Then I will beat our Creator to the punch in turning Eden into a wasteland in his hopeless attempt to stamp out this most incendiary of affronts, and release that which lurks in the black water inside the Silent Forest."

A look of disbelieving horror settled itself in Gotham's face.

"Indeed, such vile words actually escaped your lips, for my own ears heard them," Gotham uttered in disbelief. "But, even after all you've shown yourself to be in this unpleasant shedding of a cocoon this very morning, I cannot for a minute believe them to have been spoken with any measure of merit beyond that used to prop up an idle threat."

"You may choose to underestimate me, but it would be a foolish bet to place. I have not extended my neck this far out into the open to have my head lopped off like some duck being dressed for Christmas dinner. Lose Eden to me, or to the Darkness. It's your choice," said Thaniel with blood-chilling authority. "Either way, trust when I tell you, she will be lost."

Gotham did his best to camouflage the pangs of panic which were quick to envelope him, followed by an even more intense flood of rage stirred up by the audacity of Thaniel's threat. Thaniel was quick to recognize what lurked behind the sudden gloom that came across Gotham's face and what it meant.

"I don't need the power to read your mind, Gothamel, to know what it is you're feverishly mulling," said Thaniel. "But before you allow your anger to arouse from you a foolish reaction, heed what it is I am about to tell you, for it is in your best interest, and more importantly the interest of the Nephilim standing on the other side of the Library door and heading off to various spots of Eden for their lessons, that you hear closely what it is I'm about to say."

He eyed with a casual shift of his gaze Gotham's hands which had balled themselves into two massive clenching fists, and knew all too well the power they wielded.

"Come at me, as I see you are poised to do, and I will be long gone before you reach where I now stand," said Thaniel. "My brawn might be slighter in comparison to yours, but you know as well as I my speed is unmatched, even by you, and it will carry me to the Silent Forest with the swiftness of a bullet leaving the barrel of a gun. And before you have even breached the outer band of trees, the devastating swarm will be unleashed."

Gotham stood silent, for he knew what Thaniel spoke was true. Not only did he lack the speed to overtake Thaniel, he didn't know of another angel who could. And even if one existed, would it be worth the attempt to compete in such a race that carried such dire risk?

"That's the question you would do well in being very careful in answering," said Thaniel to Gotham's unspoken thoughts. "And should the thought come to you as you leave Eden to call upon a legion of angels to aid you, you should also be made aware that I am not alone."

It was then Gotham heard a rustling sound coming from somewhere above him. Turning his eyes upward, he was taken aback to find two angels perched upon opposite landings like living gargoyles with their wings outstretched. At closer look, he recognized them to be two of the three angels who stood watch over the Dilmun Sea and kept a constant vigil of Eden's entrance whose names were Acruxel and Caphel. Their presence both surprised Gotham and left him laden with sorrow, for the blatant desertion of their post could have meant only one thing. And it was always disconcerting to bear witness to an angel's defection from the Light.

"It takes only one of us to open the Through to the Underneath. So, fast as I might be, it is a race I need not compete with you in as Betryel has already posted himself inside the Silent Forest awaiting my word," said Thaniel, referring to the third angel who served as a sentinel at the Gate. "Show yourself foolish in what's been asked of you, Gothamel, and darkness will fall upon the face of Eden. The Nephilim here will be lost save one who Lilith, I have no doubt, will most assuredly come to claim personally herself."

Gotham knew instantly it was Jacob of whom Thaniel was referring. And if Thaniel's words weren't enough, Gotham suddenly found himself bombarded by a flashing barrage of horrific images coming at him showing Eden being consumed by the Darkness Thaniel threatened. With it came the echoes of unimaginable screams of Fledglings succumbing to a frightful and terrifying ending, and amid the smoldering holocaust there came the sight of Lilith, not in the trickery of her camouflaged beauty, but as the monstrous entity she was.

"I'll go," cried Gotham reluctantly in a moment of broken weakness he was pained in revealing. "You will have your sword, if only to ensure the well-being of Eden and the Nephilim in her care."

"A most perceptive decision, and a noble one at that. Anything less would have proven disappointing to me," said Thaniel with a smile of victory before fading to grim hardness once again. "Now, if you don't mind, I have a class that awaits me."

He turned away from Gotham and as he did the Library's heavy doors swung open to reveal a cluster of Nephilim waiting on the other side fixed with puzzled looks. Gotham watched grim-faced as Thaniel beckoned them forward, and as they slowly streamed inside and passed by Gotham on their way to the seats at the nearby tables, the angel looked upward once more to where Acruxel and Caphel had earlier loomed, but he found them no longer there. And he was instantly filled with a sense of dread unmatched by any he had ever before felt.

CHAPTER SEVENTEEN

"Yo, Jacob...hold up —"

Jacob was on his way out of Lions Bite for a much-needed break from training when he heard Max's voice call out to him. Speaking to his friend—or whom he once considered to be his friend—however, was the last thing Jacob wanted and he continued on without so much as a glance over his shoulder. Max ran off after Jacob and finally caught up to him as he emerged through the arena's towering slanting stone wall, and even then Jacob's feet didn't come to a stop until Max came and stood in front of him placing a hand on his chest.

"What's with you? Why're you being a koala's puff?" asked Max. "You haven't said one word to me all day."

Jacob refused to answer. Anything he had to say could be seen in the festering gaze he fixed on Max, and none of it was pleasant.

"Look, I don't know what this morning was all about," continued Max, "but you just can't leave me hangin' like this. We have to talk about this."

Jacob's lips remained sealed.

"If you got yourself into some trouble, all you have to do is tell me about it. Maybe I can help," said Max.

Jacob responded by roughly pushing his way past Max.

"You know if anyone should be pissed here it's me," a suddenly perturbed Max called out after him. "If you needed me to lie for you to help cover whatever it is you did maybe you should have given me a heads-up."

"I wasn't asking you to lie," barked Jacob, turning suddenly on his heel. "I just wanted you to tell the truth."

A strained look came to Max.

"But I *was* telling the truth!" he nearly cried out in frustration. "I've never been inside the Silent Forest."

"Fine, have it your way. We have nothing more to talk about."

Max appeared almost hapless as he watched Jacob begin to back away.

"This is ridiculous, we're mates for cryin' out loud."

"We were mates," corrected Jacob in the coldest of tones. "Not anymore."

This time Max didn't try to stop Jacob who again turned and walked off in the direction of the other Shrikes heading toward the edge of the nearby woods where cooling shade and even cooler water in the form of a bubbling stream veining its way through the gathering of trees awaited them.

When he reached the stream, Jacob dropped to his knees and with great pent-up anger drove the blade of his sword into the soft earth covered in a green carpet of ankle-deep, feathery grass, He then leaned his upper body over the water, dunked his cupped hands into the creek and brought them to his thirsty lips. The welcoming water was cool and soothing to his parched throat. Yet from it came a tremendous surge of warmth, much like the touch or embrace of an angel, and at the same time completely different. It flooded through the body like a slow-moving swell, saturating every muscle and fiber of tissue. To Jacob, it felt as if the very blood pumping its way through his veins was gradually being replaced by whatever mysterious potion churned within Eden's waterways which was then fed upon by even the smallest bits of matter at the very core of his being.

One only needed to take but a sip of the water and one's thirst, no matter how strong it resided upon dry lips, was completely quenched. And even as thirsty as Jacob was from a long afternoon of Damiel's strenuous training at Lions Bite, he found he needed just one drink from his hands to quiet his pleading throat. So when he again immersed his hands back into the water, it was to splash the cool wetness onto his flushed face streaked with sweat, and across the back of his damp neck. A cool breeze brushed past him and skimmed across the water bringing a band of ripples to the smooth, still surface. As Jacob followed the ripples with his gaze, he spied a pair of fish swimming close by—rainbow trout with eye-catching, colorful markings reflecting off their smooth, shiny scales. They swam with ease without any sign of skittishness to his presence, and for the first time that day he smiled; a small smile, but a smile, nonetheless. And as the fish passed, Jacob became aware of his reflection floating upon the water's crystal-clear surface and his smile quickly faded, for it quickly reminded him of the pool inside the Silent Forest.

The Silent Forest.

~ ~ ~

Many hours had passed since Gotham had led him outside the forest's forbidden reach, but for Jacob it had remained a troubling, burdensome presence in his thoughts of which he couldn't seem to shake himself free. The memory of Lilith—both the beautiful and terrifying image that she was—and the recoiling vision revealed to him of what lay beyond the pool's black water shroud had been fighting all day to steal away his concentration no matter how hard he tried to put the previous night's events out of his mind. Even when he proved successful in blotting them out, the relief proved short-lived before the memories reemerged suddenly and at the most inopportune of times.

Such was the case at Crescent Scar earlier in the day when Jacob was summoned forth by Zuriel for an exercise in Mind Bending. He was partnered with a dark-haired, olive-skinned Italian boy named Lucian, who possessed the bluest pair of eyes he'd ever seen on another human being. As they stood facing one another before the rest of the class, eagerly watching from their seats, Jacob attempted Zuriel's instruction to influence Lucian's thoughts. Molding the thoughts held by another, however, was no simple task as the others who also possessed the Grace had come to understand, even for a so-called Light Bearer. It was made even more difficult for Jacob who found himself struggling to fight off the images from the Silent Forest that would burst forth now and then in quick flashes to reveal all their dark horror. And it was when Lucian's sapphire eyes suddenly widened and the face framing them curdled from an unsuspecting fright that Jacob knew he had inadvertently passed on one of the terrible images to the boy, and he quickly pulled back much to Zuriel's confusion.

Jacob's inability to concentrate followed him to Lions Bite. There, where he had shined above all others thanks to the exhaustive training overseen by Gotham, Jacob appeared as someone whose hands had only that day ever gripped a sword. Quietly, Damiel stood off to the side and watched; his troubling, unblinking glare fixed itself on Jacob as he tried to find sense in why the boy's skills had suddenly gone lame.

Heaving heavy breaths and sweating profusely, Jacob struggled to draw back his sword with arms that were burning with exhaustion. And just as he was about to swing forth his blade in a desperate attempt to beat back the unyielding weapon cutting its way dangerously close at the air as it came towards him, he suddenly found Damiel standing between him and his opponent.

"What's going on with you?" asked the angel with a scowl. "That's got to easily be the worst performance I've yet to witness from a Nephilim. He could have ended you ten times over without so much as breaking a sweat."

"What do you want me to say?" huffed Jacob irritably while gasping to catch his breath. "I'm having an off-day."

"Nonsense," said Damiel gruffly. He then took a couple steps toward Jacob, pushing aside his sword and narrowed his piercing eyes on the boy's. "No, there's something else at work here. You're troubled by something."

Jacob quickly back stepped away. "I told you, I'm just having a bad day. Just leave me be."

And before Damiel was able to look closer and spy the source of his troubles, Jacob quickly turned away and hurried off from the center of the arena.

~ ~ ~

Taking a deep restive breath, Jacob remained lost in the soupy fog that had plagued him throughout the day while continuing to stare into the eyes of his reflection in the water, when a chatter of voices coming from directly across the creek from where he knelt caught his attention. When he looked up, he found not a soul in sight. Then, just when he was sure his ears were playing tricks on him, the murmur of voices returned, and this time Jacob knew it was not his imagination. It was two men. Definitely two men; one whose voice was unfamiliar to him, while the other distinctively was not.

"Did you hear that?" Jacob called out to one of the other Shrikes, who was hunched down drinking from the creek a stone's throw away downstream.

"Hear what?" asked the boy seemingly oblivious to what Jacob was referring.

"I thought I just heard ..." Jacob's voice trailed off as he trained his hearing with a tilt of his head, and for a moment all that met his ears was the lulling sound of the trickling stream.

His eyes searched the trees and brush across the water but all he saw was a pair of mockingbirds flitting about with a wild energy along the water's edge where green sturdy stalks of horsetails grew amongst the pickerelweed and iris, as well as creeping spearwort blossoming with its buttercup-like blooms. At first Jacob tried to ignore their distractive bustling about. Then the voices sounded again, and he quickly came to realize they were coming from the mockingbirds themselves.

"Do you trust him?" said one of the birds while cocking its head from side to side.

"Trust who?" Jacob replied with an awkward grin thinking, at first, the question was being posed to him before realizing otherwise when the other mockingbird, who had come to perch itself on a low, nearby branch, spoke.

"My trust in him is of no importance," it began. "Fallen as he may be, there is one thing Gothamel has held tight in his grasp, and that is his virtue. If he bears any weakness, it is that."

Gothamel?

The mention of the angel's name took Jacob aback, but not so much as the voice which spoke it, which he recognized immediately as belonging to Thaniel. Of that, Jacob was certain, the moment it met his ears.

"How can you be so sure he won't return with a legion of our brothers at his side?" continued the first bird.

"Return? Return from where?" muttered Jacob under his breath.

"Because," the second bird replied to its companion, "he has much too delicate a conscious to be forced to live with the weight of another bad augury befalling a single Nephilim—or Eden for that matter—due to his malfeasance."

"Wh-what's going on here? And how are you able to speak with Thaniel's voice?" asked Jacob speaking not so much to the birds, but voicing aloud to himself his growing confusion.

He continued to watch the birds, and the puzzled crook fixed upon his brow gradually receded as he came to realize the pair of mockingbirds were only doing what it was in their nature to do.

"You're mimicking a conversation you've heard, aren't you?" he said bringing a lively response to the birds. "Then go on, what else?"

"Take Caphel and return to your watch over the Dilmun Sea," the mockingbird who spoke with Thaniel's voice chattered on. "The hours given Gothamel to return are not long. Keep watch for him, and when you see him come through the Gate, accompany him to Broken Earth where I will eagerly be awaiting him to bestow Destiny into my hands."

"And then what?" the other bird asked. "You weren't serious when you told him you would give him a piece of Eden in return, were you?"

"Of course I was," came Thaniel's voice. "And what better real estate than lying entombed right beside his son in the peaceful shade of the Tree."

Jacob, who was listening intently to the mockingbirds, let out a noted gasp at what he heard.

"They're going to kill him?"

~ ~ ~

The words themselves were almost too horrible to utter, and at first he refused to believe what he heard to be true. Maybe, if the scheming voice coming from the mockingbird belonged to Eksel, the feeling of disbelief wouldn't have been so jarring. After all, Eksel had made no secret of his dislike and simmering contempt for Gotham. But Thaniel? He had always spoken in such a loving and admiring way about Gotham. What's more, Thaniel never seemed to allow the cursed mark on Gotham's temple influence his respect for the angel or treat him any less than what he was.

Then again, while Thaniel had never exuded the outwardly powerful might Gotham and the other angels in Eden did—at least physically—there seemed to reside inside his muted presence something of unknown and mysterious origin that threatened to be far more dangerous and sinister than brawn if met with an unwelcome challenge. Perhaps because it was so well camouflaged behind kind eyes and even kinder demeanor, it went unnoticed by both angel and Nephilim alike. In brief moments, and to some extent with a certain amount of guilt due to his fondness for Thaniel, Jacob had quietly taken note of it on more than one occasion, particularly now as he sat looking stunned by what he had just heard come from the mockingbirds.

He watched the two birds suddenly disperse into the air as if spooked and retreat into the thick foliage of the trees where they quickly disappeared from sight. Jacob then glanced again upstream to where his fellow classmates had begun to gather in growing numbers to cool themselves by the water seemingly oblivious to the performance put on by the mockingbirds.

"You see Gotham anywhere today?" Jacob called out to them.

"Nope," replied one of the boys.

In a flash, Jacob was on his feet and began asking every one of his fellow Nephilim as they began heading back to Lions Bite if they knew of Gotham's whereabouts, and as he was met with more shrugged responses, the more urgent his inquiry came. And in that urgency he suddenly took off running in the direction of the Tree of Life, even though Gotham had recently refrained from spending any more of his days in mourning at the foot of the tree since returning to Eden. Sure enough, when he finally arrived at the sacred spot there was no one there to be seen leaving Jacob to rack his brains at where Gotham might be. And just as he was about to tear off again in his search something swooped down out of nowhere and stopped him.

"Haniel!" exclaimed Jacob at the familiar sight of the Garden's earthy caregiver.

"I caught sight of you tearing through the Forest halfway between here and Lions Bite looking like you were prepared to mow down anything and everything in your path," said Haniel, placing a stilling grip on the boy's shoulder. "Now, what seems to have set fire to your feet?"

"Have you seen Gotham anywhere around?" asked Jacob.

"I recall catching sight of him earlier this morning."

"Where?"

Haniel noted the boy's impatience to be especially fiery.

"Flying south...toward the Big Lands," said Haniel offering a nod in the direction of Eden's vast presence stretching from just outside the Garden all the way to the Dilmun Sea.

The answer brought a look of panic to Jacob's face, and before the angel could ask him what was wrong, he was off running once more. His feet carried him like a gust of wind from the woods to the River past Havenhid where he followed it down over the sloping terrain through the passage of mountain cliffs forming the entrance to the Garden leading to the wide-reaching Big Lands beyond. There was only one place Jacob could think of where Gotham could have headed—the Dilmun Sea—and the thought made him all the more frenzied. After all, even with the swift speed Jacob's feet could carry him across Eden, he was no match against the wings which undoubtedly had already carried the angel to the sea into which he would dive head-first like some bombardier pelican and disappear from sight beneath the mysterious swells. Yet Jacob refused to allow time and distance to dissuade him and, if anything, it fed Jacob's feet to pound the earth even faster.

Soon, he was out in the Big Lands, tearing deeper into the great expanse laid out before him. Over sloping hills he traveled, nimbly maneuvering his way like a skilled mountain goat along the great jagged rocks protruding from the earth serving as obstacles yet never slowing or hindering his pace. Open grasslands soon followed, and after a long stretch they led the way into the shaded darkness of the Forest. There, with the graceful, bounding quickness of an impala on the run, Jacob wove his way through the army of big trees awaiting him. Now and then, his ears would catch the sound of footsteps running close by mirroring his pace. Glancing about him he saw nothing but forest, yet he could sense a hidden presence lurking somewhere in the brush stalking his moves. Whatever it was, he was not about to let it slow him down, and somehow he found the ability to move even faster.

Soon the trees of the Forest gave way to a great carpet of more green grassland stretching as far as the eye could see and, as Jacob took to it, a familiar high-pitched shriek rang out overhead. Jacob looked to the sky to see the sight of the snake eagle whose presence continued to shadow wherever he went. Its intense piercing eyes searched the lands below while the feathers of his outstretched wings rustled in the wind as it glided across the blue canopy. For a moment, the sight broke the troubled look on Jacob's face and he smiled.

"Beacon, indeed," he whispered to himself.

It was then he felt a slight tremor move through the ground beneath his feet. Glancing behind him over his shoulder he caught sight of a herd of gazelle coming up over the ridge of a slope and running full speed toward him. At first, the sight startled him and he fought to stay way ahead of them. They quickly surrounded him and he found himself in the midst of the stampede. As they sprinted past, bounding forth with the graceful synchronicity of a ballet troupe traipsing across a stage, the initial fear that gripped Jacob gave way to intense exhilaration as he ran with them, and amongst them. And for a brief moment, as his eyes met those who ran beside him and looked upon him with idle curiosity, he felt as though he was one of them.

In unison they ran across the miles and miles of feathery grass unfolded before them until the open grassland gradually shifted direction leading the gazelles eastward while Jacob continued southward, all the while being guided by the River whose tranquil waters served as a knowing path. Winding its way in a bending ribbon of blue across the grasslands, the River flowed forth to where the presence of the Forest suddenly returned and it carved a wide serpentine swath through the vast reach of congregating trees into which Jacob once more disappeared.

~ ~ ~

The sky began to turn.

Blue gave way to colorful swirls of gold and amber. Clouds formed in puffs of gray and lavender, and from within them came a fiery red glow like embers burning hot in a pile of ash held inside a hearth. And for a short while the Forest became chameleon-like as green gave way to a soft rose-colored glow from the light in which it was bathed.

Pressing tirelessly onward, Jacob paid little attention to the brilliant show of color that lent his surroundings a dreamlike appearance. Then, when the light eventually began to fade and a quickening darkness descended onto the Forest, he again caught the sound of nearby footsteps. This time, however, they were closer, and more of them—whoever *they* were—and for the first time since leaving the Garden his feet slowed and came to a standstill. His eyes searched the trees standing like giants all around him, but all he saw was more forest pressing endlessly into the deepening darkness and beyond.

"Who's there?" Jacob called out as the quiet again gave way to the shuffle of steps upon the ground. Whatever it was, it was not human, as the steps treaded too lightly upon the ground. An animal, perhaps, of some kind. Though the question occupying Jacob's thoughts was why was it trailing him for such a long distance, and in such a stealth-like manner?

Then in the distance, a pair of eyes was spied peering out from the shadows like flashes of sunlight reflected off arctic snow. Close by, another pair of eyes emerged in the falling darkness. And while Eden, and the creatures inhabiting its lands, had never showed itself to pose any threat or cause of harm, the memory of the Silent Forest remained with Jacob and instinctively his right hand moved slowly to his left side and lightly came to rest on the handle of his sword.

The patter of steps and rustling of shrubs came from all directions and Jacob's gaze shifted rapidly every which way his acute hearing caught a new sound. Soon his heart began to pound when he realized he was surrounded. By what, though, he had no idea. All he could see were eyes—floating carats of diamonds fixed intently on him.

Then one by one the shadowy figures which possessed the gleaming peepers slowly came forth, and as they stepped into what was left of the fading fiery tint of twilight Jacob could see they were wolves. Jacob turned slowly, eyeing each one as it shook off its cloak and showed itself, and it didn't take him long to recognize them to be the same pack who crossed his path in that very Forest while accompanied by Gotham and Damiel on the day he first stepped foot in Eden. And when his eyes fell on the last wolf there came another rustling from amongst the trees, and still another wolf stepped forward and Jacob's face gave way to surprise to see it to be Mist.

~ ~ ~

"What are you doing all the way over here, girl?" Jacob said both happily and with noted surprise.

Dropping to his knee, he motioned the wolf forward and as she came to him he opened his arms expecting to be inundated by a familiar slobbering licks to his face. Instead, she took hold of his shirt in her mouth and gave it an urgent tug.

"What is it Mist?"

Again she tugged with even more urgency until he rose to his feet and followed her out of the waning light and into the darkening shade of the trees.

"What's wrong?" Jacob, staring into the wolf's face which was now fixed with an intense look he'd never before seen, asked again.

He noticed Mist's gaze along with that of her pack were locked unblinkingly on the sky made visible through a wide break in the tight cluster of trees, and he followed it with his own. There was nothing at first except thin trails of grayish lavender clouds looking like dissipating plumes of smoke. Then there came into view the unmistakable figure of an angel soaring high overhead. The sight drew excitement from Jacob who at first thought it to be Gotham. As he began to rise to his feet, Mist again nipped at his clothing and the subtle growl that sounded from her met Jacob's ears as, "Stay down and close to the trees. It's not him."

Perplexed, Jacob slowly returned to his crouch while continuing to stare up at the sky where he soon caught sight of a second angel. A look of caution filled his eyes as he watched the two winged figures, silhouetted against the dimming sky, circle slowly over the break in the Forest like a pair of scavenger birds. Clearly they were in search of something; something beneath the cover of the Forest. Only after circling above a half a dozen times did they move on and disappear from sight.

"Who were they?" asked Jacob when the two winged figures had gone.

"Acruxel and Caphel," answered Mist. "They were sent to find you."

"Why do I have the uneasy feeling Thaniel sent them?" said Jacob. "He must have somehow found out I've gone after Gotham in hopes of warning him."

One of the wolves whose thick black coat looked to have been spun out of the darkest of nights stepped past Jacob and out into the clearing. His slightly larger size and the way he carried himself made it quickly obvious to Jacob he held the position of pack leader. With his icy eyes trained on the sky he said, "Then we must be quick. They'll keep to the sky until they find what it is they seek."

"What's the point? How can I possibly make it to the Dilmun Sea much less to the Gate with them flying overhead?" asked Jacob with a hint of hopeless resignation in his voice.

"Carefully," answered Mist. "And hidden amongst the rest of us."

At first Jacob was confused by his faithful companion's words.

"Cloaking…of course," he replied with a shrewd grin as he continued to stare into her face. "I guess now's as good a time as any to begin making use of these so-called Graces I've been given, right?"

Sitting back he closed his eyes and took several deep breaths into his body. Once he felt relaxed enough he opened his eyes and fixed them on the dark forest in front of him but made himself blind to all that lay in the path of his vision forcing himself instead to focus intently on the image he held vivid and steadfast in his head. It was of a wolf, majestic and gray with white markings, and from where it lingered inside his sculpting thoughts, it quickly revealed itself in the reflective mirrors of Jacob's eyes. And in that instant, Jacob's body twisted and stretched and hunched as it transformed itself in mere moments into the reflected vision.

With not a moment to spare, the pack was off running following after its black-maned leader while keeping its newest member tightly surrounded. The wolves flew across the forest floor they knew so intimately with immense speed, marking mile after mile with their footprints until they soon approached the mountains standing like a great impassable hurdle between Eden and the Dilmun Sea residing on the other side of its cliffs. As they neared them, the black wolf unexpectedly shifted direction making Jacob stop in his tracks.

"The path leading to the corridor through the mountain is this way," said Jacob, motioning toward the towering leviathan of rock and cliffs looming like resting giants in the distance.

"The Emmaus Corridor is the first place they'll expect a wingless Nephilim to attempt passage through the mountain," argued the black wolf.

Jacob looked to Mist who remained close by his side. "Trust him. You stand a better chance going under the mountain than over it," she said.

Under it? It sounded like an impossible notion, but Jacob held faith in his wolf guardians. It was, after all, their land, their home. Who better than they to know intimately how best to navigate Eden's numerous paths both visible and hidden? And so without further debate, Jacob continued to follow them.

~ ~ ~

Night had finally settled itself upon Eden, and its silvery blue moonlit darkness lent added cover to the pack. They kept an unbroken steady pace in their stealthy trek through the trees, following along the Forest's edge which hugged itself tight to the winding River. Barely a sound was made by their fast-flying paws as they drummed the ground, and even the other wild things residing inside in the Forest were oblivious to their ghostlike presence.

Soon the mighty trees of the Forest began to thin in numbers and a precipitous wall of rock forming the foot of a mountain was suddenly upon them. Like some gray-skinned beast clawing its way from a burrow deep within the earth, it stretched upward forming a cathedral of steep, jagged cliffs that eventually disappeared into a white mist of clouds in its reach for the heavens. The mountain's impregnable presence stood solidly in the River's path. Yet in its ragged armor was formed a deep, cavernous opening into which the River poured forth. At first glance, it appeared almost as if the mountain itself was opening its mouth to quell its thirst from the River's cool water.

The wolves maneuvered their way across the great many rocks and boulders greened with moss and furry lichen which had fallen loose from the cliffs and overhangs above and now encumbered the base of the mountain. A smoldering plume of mist spilling out from within the rock soon left the wolves matted and dripping wet. When they reached the entrance of the yawning cavern, they were met by a great roar which left one wondering whether it came from the River as it surged forth into the gullet of the mountain, or if it was the mountain itself. Jacob shed his wolf cloak and he emerged with his skin gleaming from the wetness of the mist while the beads of water which clung to the curling ends of his damp hair dribbled down across his face like raindrops. With his human eyes, he peered into the darkness held inside the mountain lair that was deeper than the night surrounding them and a slight shudder moved through him, though it was not caused by a chill from the water.

"I think I prefer the Emmaus Corridor," he remarked.

"This way is much safer," said the black wolf.

"It's so dark," said Jacob. He stepped cautiously just inside the cave entrance while straining to look inside. "I don't see how one could possibly navigate more than a few feet before being completely swallowed up by the darkness and left for lost. Even my own eyes which have grown strong in penetrating the dark can barely focus on my own hand when I hold it in front me at arm's length."

"All one needs to safely cross beneath the mountain is an attentive pair of ears," said the black wolf. "Follow the sound the River and it will guide you to the Dilmun Sea which awaits on the other side."

"That might be all well for you," said Jacob, "but I tend to be more comfortable when I can see where it is I plan to step."

"Unfortunately for you, comfort will be in scarce supply on this journey."

Jacob took notice of the black wolf's words. Before he could inquire what was meant by them, another member of the pack came forward carrying in its mouth a branch from a tree it had retrieved from nearby the cavern entrance.

"You can use this to light your way," said the wolf dropping the piece of wood near Jacob's feet before shaking off the droplets of mist clinging to its red-maned coat.

Jacob thanked the wolf and picked up the tree limb. He placed the fingers of his other hand on the end of the branch and even though the wood itself was as damp as everything else in the immediate vicinity of the cavern, it quickly began to smolder before flames ignited in a fiery burst. Once lit, Jacob held the make-shift torch out in front of him making the darkness inside the cavern recoil in the presence of the light and the most dazzling of visions was revealed to him. The walls of the cavern immediately came alive in a sea of sparkles and glittering light. What it was, Jacob did not know. Crystals of some kind? Maybe even diamonds. Or perhaps some unknown mineral more precious than anything known by man. Whatever it was, they embedded every inch of rock in countless numbers. It felt to Jacob as if he had suddenly been jettisoned into the middle of the Milky Way and surrounded by billions upon billions of stars. His unblinking eyes reflected the startling spectacle as the walls twinkled brightly in the flickering of the fire light.

The cavern revealed itself to be shockingly immense forming great fissures and chasms. Above, where the ceiling of the cavern stretched further than the light from Jacob's torch could reach, massive stalactites took ominous teeth-like form. They were complemented by equally impressive stalagmites jutting upward from the cavern floor. After a few moments of quiet awe, Jacob's gaze shifted downward where the sound of rushing water beckoned his attention and he was startled to find his feet perched precariously at the very edge of a steep overhang of rock where the River washed over to form a spectacular waterfall before disappearing into the billowing cloud of mist rising upward.

"Time is waning," said the black wolf.

Jacob nodded and, in a search for some kind of pathway to follow, he thrust forward the torch in his hand in the direction of the darkness to his right. There he saw what looked to be a narrow stairway formed naturally by blocks of rock descending down into the bowels of the mountain and into the waiting pitch. He had taken only a few steps when he turned around and saw the wolves were not following and remained watching at the cave entrance.

"Come along, then," Jacob called out to them.

Instead, one by one the wolves turned and headed back toward the Forest until only Mist remained. Jacob gave her a puzzled look. "Where are they going?"

"This is as far as we can go," said Mist. "We cannot venture beyond the mountain."

"But what if I get lost?"

"You cannot get lost if you follow the River. It will lead you to where you need to go," the wolf answered. "Just be sure to douse the light when you catch sound of the sea. They will be watching for you."

And with that, Mist was gone.

~ ~ ~

Jacob once more faced the path before him, and now that he found himself alone and on his own again it appeared even more daunting. With a deep inhale of breath, he quickly summoned his courage and took the first step of his descent down the steps ahead. They appeared, at first look, to continue steadily downward to what seemed a great depth; just how far, Jacob had a difficult time determining. Silently, he counted the number of the steps his feet treaded; 50 became 100, and then quickly 200. When he reached the 328th step he came to realize the path he followed was indeed taking him underneath the mountain, and by a great distance.

340 ... 341 ... 342 ... 343...

Just when Jacob was certain the steps beneath his feet stretched into eternity, they suddenly came to an abrupt end and Jacob was sure he had finally reached the bottom of the cavern. The deafening solitude that greeted him there was numbingly uncomfortable, and there was nothing he wanted more than to find in quick order the opening that would lead him out of the mountain crypt in which he found himself. He attempted to fend off the choking darkness with a sweep of his torch and the walls came alive with more sparkling flashes. Ahead, Jacob was able to make out for a short distance the narrow path before him and he quickly, yet cautiously, began to follow it. The passage wound its way through a series of turns and bends for quite a long distance—much longer than Jacob thought a mountain could be wide. Dank was the air along the way and the chill it held at brief moments became even more biting from sudden gusts exhaled through some of the many crevices and openings in the rock.

The flame dancing at the end of the torch Jacob held in his hand licked loudly the darkness. It shined forth like a beacon revealing the movement of many shadows shifting about from here to there. All the while, Jacob kept a careful eye on the flame as it slowly ate its way down the branch; for nothing left him as wary as the thought of his illuminated guide consuming itself completely and allowing the lurking blackness to swallow him whole before reaching the end of the passage. Adding to his discomfort was the echoing sounds of things fluttering in the air and scampering unseen across the ground and along the rock walls. He could feel many eyes focused upon him, curious of his presence. Whatever they were, it wasn't hard ignoring them as Jacob found himself transfixed by an endless procession of massive sculptures briefly illuminated in the eternal dark solitude of their subterranean world as he passed them. Shaped by the endless dripping of water inside the cavern over the countless eons, they emerged from the shadows like great museum pieces hanging from the ceiling and standing cemented to the floor, monumental in size and more and more intricate in design the deeper Jacob made his way into the bowels of the passage. It was a spectacular sight made even more dazzling amid the glittering, jewel-like flashes coming from the walls. All the while making its way along the channel it had carved out for itself along the cavern floor mirroring the path Jacob walked could be heard the churning waters of the River. Of that, Jacob was especially vigilant, knowing that as long as he followed the flow of the River he was headed in the right direction—or so Mist and the members of her pack had assured him.

After the passage had stretched on a good distance further, there suddenly came a faint roar of water, much different than that made by the River. Jacob turned an ear to it to listen and, as he caught the sound of breaking waves, a smile of relief came to his face.

"The Dilmun Sea," he muttered to himself. "It must be."

Then, remembering Mist's parting words at the cave's entrance, he took what was left of his torch and quickly doused the flame by grinding the burning ember into the wall of the mountain. Left in darkness, he looked ahead and saw the faint silvery blue glow of what looked to be moonlight in the distance. He was swift in his pursuit of it, and soon he found himself approaching a large arched opening in the rock leading out of the mountain. As he neared it, there came a sound of splashing from his trotting feet as the River and path began to overlap one another. Eager to feel the soft sinking sand of the waiting beach beneath his feet and breathe the cool, salty ocean air deep into his body, he was about to lunge forward across the threshold when his eyes widened with terror and the soles of his sneakers dug themselves into the sleek, slippery stone beneath them in a desperate effort to anchor himself from going any further.

Instead of sand, Jacob found himself fighting for balance upon the edge of a sheer cliff over which the River surged in the form of a waterfall. The passage carved into the mountain had indeed led to the Dilmun Sea, the foamy waves of which could be seen rolling onto the pristine white sandy beach. The only thing, however, that stood between Jacob and the ocean was a couple hundred feet of vertical nothingness. And directly below, illuminated by the silvery light of the moon looming large and ever full in the star-studded sky above, was a small lagoon, into which the River poured itself in a thunderous rain of water, nestled against the foot of the mountain.

Jacob looked all about him for where the path might continue on, maybe shaping itself into another stairway of steps that led down to the beach below, but there was none to be seen; the path had ended abruptly. Even the bold face of the cliff showed no blemishes of jagged rock which Jacob could use to maneuver himself down. No, there was only one way down, and that was either by wing or jumping. And since his back was the same as it was before he stepped foot Eden, Jacob was left with only one option.

~ ~ ~

Holding onto the side of the cavern, he leaned his body forward and studied carefully the lagoon below. How he hoped it ran deep enough, but the dark waters made it impossible for him to tell. For all he knew, a bed of deadly rock fallen loose from the mountain awaited anyone foolish enough to dive into it. He also knew he had come too far to turn back now.

"Nothing to it," he attempted to assure himself while closing his eyes and taking a series of steadying breaths. "Just like jumping off a diving board into a swimming pool, that's all. An exceptionally high diving board."

A long pregnant pause followed before, finally, in a blind lunge Jacob hurled himself into the air with nothing but hope clutched tight in his hands, and he quickly disappeared into the misty deluge of the waterfall. So powerful and overwhelming was the spill from the River, that Jacob found it difficult to tell whether he remained in free-fall or had hit the waters of the lagoon. It soon didn't matter, for something suddenly took a tight grip of him and yanked him free from the showering water. Peering down he saw his feet just graze the surface of the lagoon before being lifted to greater heights. There came a sound of wings and when he looked to see what had taken hold of him, he was surprised to see it was the angel Acruxel.

Angel or not, however, his face held an unfriendly and menacing look, one that let Jacob know at first glance the angel had not come to lend him aid as was his duty at Broken Earth. Instinctively, he began to struggle and fought to free himself from the hands gripping him tight, but the angel's hold was fast on him. Then swinging his lower body upward as if in some circus trapeze act, Jacob aimed his feet at the angel face and sent forth a powerful kick. The hands released their hold and with a yell Jacob realized in a split second it may not have been his brightest move when he found himself falling fast. He came to land hard upon the beach, his body skidding haphazardly across the soft sand which provided some cushion but not enough to fully blunt the pain that exploded in him from such a high fall.

Momentarily dazed, Jacob managed to raise himself up on his hands and knees while shaking the sand from his hair and spitting the granules coating his tongue. Then, looking up, he saw Acruxel come to land heavy-footed on the beach a short ways from him. At Broken Earth, the angel served as a comforting presence to the other Nephilim debating to take the stomach-churning leap in hopes of getting their wings, knowing he would break their fall should they fail. However, at that moment, Jacob found Acruxel anything but comforting as he stood cloaked in night with his wings outstretched and intimidating in both their size and obvious strength. His eyes reflected an inner glow from behind a darkened face, and their weighted stare Jacob suddenly felt upon him proved most unsettling.

"Sorry about that kick, you just kinda took me by surprise," said Jacob with a shaky chuckle. "If it makes you feel any better, it doesn't look like it left a mark."

There came no answer, adding to Jacob's discomfort.

"I'm hardly worth all this bother, really," he continued. "Besides, I'm betting news of you deserting your post to chase after me wouldn't be met with amusement. Not that I have any plans of saying anything to anyone."

Again, no answer. Only the roaring crash of waves. Jacob gave a quick look out of the corner of his eye—first to the left, then right—seeking some avenue of escape and finding none.

"It's only fair I should warn you, I won't be easy to catch," he said, managing to conjure up a tone of confidence.

This time the angel spoke: "We'll see."

It was only two words, uttered in such an ominous way that it was enough to make Jacob bolt to his feet. With nowhere to go but the vast ocean, he sprinted as fast as he could toward it. He did not need to gaze over his shoulder to know Acruxel had once more taken command of the sky, as he could hear the rustling of wings as they furiously beat the air in pursuit of him. Suddenly, the sea whose depths Jacob had traveled so far to reach appeared to lie an impossible distance. The flapping of wings grew closer and he braced himself to be plucked once more from the ground when suddenly he heard Gotham's voice echo inside his head, as it did countless times during their many afternoons of training.

Always be mindful of the Graces you hold at your fingertips, Fledgling.

Despite the growing sense of panic he felt begin to overtake him, Jacob forced himself to dig down inside to a well of calm as he recalled the first time he was in the ocean and the foreign words Gotham whispered into its waters. And as they echoed themselves in his head, he began repeating them. Again, and again, and again.

His feet splashed across the apron of frothy water rolling onto the beach that fast swallowed his ankles followed by his knees, and just as he felt the angel's breath upon his neck Jacob dove blindly into the crashing surf. For a brief moment, there was nothing but a churning calm. When he finally surfaced, his eyes went immediately to the night-colored skies above. At first nothing—not a sign of his pursuer—though the night made it difficult to see much of anything, even with the presence of the moon. Jacob frantically began to swim out to deeper water while again reciting Gotham's words. And in the midst of his mantra, he let out a holler when the angel swooped out of nowhere and once again seized hold of him. Eyes ablaze, Acruxel grabbed hold of a fistful of Jacob's wet locks tight in his hand. Jacob howled with pain as he began to be lifted from the water and, just when he was sure his scalp would tear itself from his skull, a dolphin appeared. Breaking through the surface of the churning sea, it sailed through the air in a fantastic leap and hit the angel broadside with enough brute force to free Jacob from the painful grip and send his winged attacker careening through the air.

Not once during his stay in Eden had Jacob seen any of its creatures take up aggression against their own kind or Nephilim alike, much less an angel. To witness a response to his calling in such a roguishly fearless manner, while startling, only fed further that which Jacob already knew: he needed to flee to safety, and as swiftly as possible.

"Thank you friend," he said to the dolphin as it circled around and brushed up against him. "Now if you can just get me through the Gate, and fast, I'd be grateful."

He barely managed a good grip on the dorsal fin sticking out of the water when the dolphin took off like a shot. Past the rolling breakers it carried Jacob and out toward the open sea where under the night sky it appeared as a sheet of exquisite black silk reflecting the silvery light of the moon. In the distance, the white ghostly presence that was the wall of fog could be seen. Also ahead were the shadowy shapes of the three towering pillars of rock which served as guard towers where Acruxel, Caphel and Betryel held the duty of keeping a constant vigil on the impregnable fog barrier, lying just beyond, and what was given passage through it. Not to his surprise, Jacob saw through the barrage of salty sea water splashing up off the dolphin's fin and into his face that each platform had been abandoned; but why, he wondered.

What was happening?

Now, however, wasn't the time to allow his mind to wander, and even though they were fast approaching the Gate, Jacob couldn't bring himself to breathe easy. Especially when he heard what had become a familiar flapping of wings. Glancing back over his shoulder, his eyes widened not at the expected sight of Acruxel, who had recovered from being rammed by the dolphin, but that of a Caphel, who now joined in the pursuit.

"I don't think we're going to make it," Jacob cried out. "He's coming back at us, and this time he's not alone."

Jacob tightened his grip on the dorsal. Beneath him he could feel the dolphin's strength through its undulations as it propelled itself to an even greater speed. The prowess in which the dolphin moved through the water, while impressive, was matched beat for beat by the angels' wings as they wickedly cut through the air. They were both bearing down fast upon Jacob and his ocean-bred steed, their arms outstretched and hands poised to snatch him with the promise of a grip that would hold him tight in their clutches and deny him any further escape. Jacob fought to hold panic at bay while searching his mind with relative calm for all he had learned over the many months of training he had undergone—not from Zuriel at Crescent Scar, nor Damiel at Lions Bite, or even Thaniel inside the Library walls at Havenhid, but from Gotham in the streams, trees and quiet corners of Eden. For at that moment, it was his voice he heard guiding him. As well as that of the sea itself.

Always be mindful of the Graces you hold at your fingertips...

Jacob lifted his left hand pressed tight against the dolphin's sleek side and he studied it carefully; first the backside and then the palm, its wetness gleaming in the moonlight. And with the beating of wings pounding uncomfortably close in his ears he closed his eyes and exhaled deeply, all the while turning all his concentration onto the water surrounding him. Then, slowly, he stretched his hand skyward. The ocean left in the dolphin's wake suddenly began to stir unnaturally. A great swell, where there was none, rolled itself into view and, as it reared itself upward, a silvery-white froth sprayed into the air from its crest. Larger the swell grew, and from it a liquid form slowly unfurled itself and took the shape of fingers. First one, then two until gradually a water-sculpted hand, massive in size, appeared grasping toward the sky as if some mythical entity was coming up from the ocean's depths.

His eyes remaining closed and hand stretched upward, Jacob swiped at the sky above him. As he did, the giant, sea-formed hand mirrored his movements and took hold of the two angels in its watery grasp stopping them cold in their pursuit. The hand then moved along the ocean surface like a giant wave back towards the shore. The angels struggled, yet despite their strength they could not free themselves from the liquid fingers squeezed tight around them. And just when the hand was close enough to the shore, Jacob made a throwing gesture and with that the hand of water cast the angels hard onto the beach before collapsing into a tsunami of a wave which then crashed down upon them and swept them up in a churning fury of water.

~ ~ ~

When the water finally subsided, the two winged beings were left lying dazed at the foot of the mountains. Acruxel was the first to his feet, though somewhat unsteady, and with a renewed fire of vengeance smoldering in his eyes he hastily shook the water and sand coating his soaked wings and stringy long locks before taking several challenging steps toward the sea that had thwarted his pursuit when a voice called after him.

"Let him go!"

Acruzel turned to find Thaniel standing near the foot of the mountain where he hadn't been moments earlier.

"But we almost had him," argued Acruxel.

"Yes...so I can plainly see," Thaniel, his tone dripping with sarcastic disdain, replied. Though not as much as the look in his eye that he cast briefly down upon Caphel who laid in a soaking heap upon the sand.

"You realize he's heading for the Gate," said Acruxel.

"So he is. But the dolphin he rides upon can only carry him so far before he will be forced to find the rest of his way on his own," said Thaniel.

"Passage through the Gate is as perilous as it is dark. It would prove an impossible task for any Nephilim to navigate his way on his own without our guiding hand. Even for one so deemed Light Bearer."

"What if he does?" asked Acruxel who seemed less sure. "Are you willing to risk underestimating the boy?"

Still somewhat frazzled, Caphel looked up from where he remained stretched on his stomach upon the beach as Thaniel's boot-clad feet slowly strode past him. With his eyes fixed on the furthest reaches of the Dilmuns Sea, Thaniel stood silent for a long moment pondering the question. He then turned his head toward Acruxel without looking at him.

"Perhaps you're right, Acruxel. Rouse the Nekcri," he instructed the angel whose face lit up with an all too eager willingness to comply.

"If the passage through the Gate doesn't send him back, the Nekcri most certainly will," Thaniel remarked quietly to himself as his gaze intently followed Acruxel to the foaming tide of the sea.

CHAPTER EIGHTEEN

"Passage through the Gate is as perilous as it is dark..."

No truer words had ever before been uttered when speaking of the entrance into Eden. Yet they paled as a warning to just how treacherous it was for anyone who wasn't an angel to attempt a journey through the passageway. For to understand even the slightest bit the danger lurking at Eden's Gate, one would have to have some semblance of knowing firsthand the kind of darkness in which it resided; darkness the likes of which few living things have ever witnessed, and of which no word or phrases exists in all the languages ever spoken that come close to describing it.

It came, the blackness did, at the dawn of the Old Testament, when a vengeful deluge of rain unleashed from the heavens joined all seas of the world to form one wrath-filled ocean whose swells would sweep clean the earth and silence the wicked who had so offended God. The waters of the drowned world would eventually recede, but the sediment of the rage it held came to rest just inside the Gate. There it remained, to ensure the entrance into paradise would stay hidden from the entirety of the mortal world for all time. And hidden it had remained, for unlucky was the soul who accidentally stumbled upon it lest they be greeted by the waiting darkness like a deadly moray eel lurking in the dark crevice of a rock waiting to strike.

There was no wading into it. Once within its grasp, its presence was immediate. Suddenly, it was upon you, and all about you, thick and swallowing, consuming whole all who were swept up in its merciless presence. The thought of retreat, when it came—and come it always did, even if only in brief passing—was always too late, and all that was left was an immense amount of nothing confined in a world brimming with absolute nothingness. And it was then the unimaginable imaginings of what the universe was like before it breathed its first gasp of life in a blinding flash of light were suddenly conceivable.

~ ~ ~

It was the anticipation of this black abyss which made Jacob tighten his grip on the dolphin he rode as they dove beneath the surface of the sea and made for the far depths beneath them. The vast reef they came upon was at rest. Its spectrum of colors displayed in brilliant fashion under the light of day had now been replaced by a monochromatic landscape of deep slumbering blues and undulating highlights of bright silver moonlight. The schools of fish usually seen darting about in spawning numbers had retired with the sun. The water held great clarity, even under the blanket of night, and soon a massive chasm which had gnawed its way into a mountain of rock rising up from the ocean floor and covered in coral came into sight. The dolphin swam quickly toward it. Once inside, Jacob's hold grew tighter still, not out of fear and yet coaxed by fear at the same time; for lurking deep in the gullet of the massive, yawning cavern just beyond the opening could be seen the darkness, unmistakable amongst all neighboring shadows, and Jacob knew there was no turning back. Down into it they went, and in a quick instant boy and dolphin vanished completely from sight.

It instantly felt to Jacob as if he'd been stricken blind, and he suddenly felt immense sympathy for those forced to live all their days inside such a desolate void. His only comfort came from his seeing eye guide. Interestingly, he could feel by the dolphin's movements the impregnable blackness caused the creature no trepidation or moments of hesitation as it continued forward at a swift, steady pace. And whenever Jacob felt his chest strain from holding his breath, all he had to do was place his mouth over the dolphin's blowhole where he was fed air bubbles to refill his lungs, which in turn put him more at ease— at least, somewhat.

After swimming for what seemed to have been quite a bit of distance, Jacob felt the dolphin slow, and then come to a stop. At first, he felt gladness at the thought they had reached the other end of the darkness, but the blackness remained all around with no break or sign of ceding to even the dimmest of light. The dolphin sounded a series of clicks and squeals and Jacob soon knew the reason why they had come to a halt; the waters of the Dilmun Sea were thinning and converging with those of the lifeless Van Gölü into which the dolphin could not tread and expect to survive.

"You will have to continue on by yourself," the dolphin clicked.

The thought alone was frightful to Jacob. How could he possibly navigate his way successfully through this black soup that left him worse than blind? he wondered to himself. And without the aid of the dolphin to lend his lungs air, surely the odds of him drowning in his attempt were with him. Sensing his angst, the dolphin sought to lend assurance. The entrance to the Gate was just up ahead, it squawked; a short enough distance for Jacob's lungs to carry him should he swim swiftly. "The dark looks to keep at bay those not welcome to enter Eden, not to wither the fruit harvested inside the Garden. Steer a straight path, and only a straight path, and you will soon be returned to the mortal world."

Still, Jacob could not shake the overwhelming sense of trepidation embracing him. At the same time, he also held great trust in the dolphin, just as he did the wolves who earlier directed him into the unknowns of a mountain cavern. And so he leaned down and placed his mouth over the small opening at the top of the dolphin's head from which a stream of air bubbles was released. Once he had bloated his lungs to bursting, Jacob readied himself.

"Go now, quickly and without pause," the dolphin clicked with urgency.

With every ounce of courage he could muster, Jacob let go of the dolphin's sleek comforting hide and fought to keep himself from not instantly grabbing hold again from sheer panic. Immediately, Jacob began kicking his legs and swimming into the black abyss as fast as his limbs could carry him.

"Steer a straight path….Steer a straight path….Steer a straight path…"

His head held the echo of the dolphin's parting words. Yet in such darkness it was difficult, if not outright impossible, to know how straight one's trajectory was. For all Jacob knew he was desperately swimming in circles, or veering off course toward some unfortunate destination. Such thoughts made him want to reach out and feel out any clues, but he quickly came to the conclusion that anything cloaked inside the darkness would likely be better left hidden and unknown to his touch.

~ ~ ~

What had been assured to be a short distance ahead seemed to Jacob much further than promised. The more he swam, the faster his strokes became, and still more darkness unrolled itself in front of him like some unending carpet of blackness. Perhaps he had unknowingly faltered from the straight line he mentally tried to follow, and yet he did everything he could to keep such thoughts from mulling inside his head. He couldn't risk panic setting in, even as he began to feel the air inside his lungs begin to dwindle.

He continued to swim fast and hard, and from the way the current washed over his face it felt as if he was moving like a spirited fish. If only, he thought, he could take on the form of some such aquatic creature, but he was mentally attuned enough to know doing so in these dead waters could likely prove a fatal mistake. Not that a fatality had yet been averted. With no sign of the darkness ending, and the last bit of the dolphin's air escaping in tiny bubbles from his nostrils, Jacob could no longer ignore his heart thumping louder and louder in his chest, and he suddenly found himself entertaining a terrifying notion: *I'm not ever leaving this blackness; it's going to consume me alive, never to be heard from or seen again.*

Then suddenly, it showed itself to him—a light. As dim as a light can be, but in such darkness one never shone brighter. Jacob raced toward it, not wanting to risk it somehow disappearing from sight, and as he came closer to it, he saw it was the Gate entrance with the night-illuminated waters of the Van Gölü just beyond. Kicking his legs as hard as he could, Jacob passed through the opening in the rock leaving the darkness behind him with a tremendous sense of relief. Then, with his lungs screaming inside his chest, he began clawing at the water in a desperate rush to reach the surface looming uncomfortably far above him, while oblivious to the large dark shape which passed stealthy beneath him as he left the lake depths fast behind him.

When he finally broke through the surface, his mouth was already agape for the precious air awaiting him. He inhaled it loudly and greedily, and the most contented and delighted of smiles formed itself on his face. Loudly he whooped, punctuating his joy by slapping his hands against the water. He did it. It didn't even matter that he was in the middle of the Van Gölü, with not a sign of land to be seen in any direction he looked. He had made it. And he basked in his victory by floating on his back upon the water beneath the starry sky with his eyes closed while breathing deeply the cool night air.

For some time Jacob remained adrift on his back, arms floating limp at his side, and a smile fixed on his face. If the soft rocking of the gentle waves upon which he rested managed to lull him asleep, it was only for a brief moment before a dream—or what he thought to be a dream—of something moving beneath him forced his eyes open with a start. He found himself staring up at the sky blackened with night and sequined with countless pin pricks of twinkling starlight. The air was unseasonably clear and crisp, and the chill it held gave a wispy shape to Jacob's breath. Yet cold was the last thing Jacob felt, and his skin showed not even the slightest of trembles.

Slowly he began to spin in circles looking off to the distance surrounding him for some direction of where to head next. Unlike Eden, the night was moonless and any sign of land was lost to the darkness. Even Mount Arafat with its bright snow-capped peaks was nearly swallowed up by the night, but enough of its mythic silhouette remained visible to point Jacob roughly in the direction of where the island of Carpanak lied. The only question now was, could Jacob make the long swim to its shores?

Many watery miles stretched itself between the center of the lake where Jacob bobbed and Carpanak and the non-stop journey he had made crossing from one end of Eden to the other—not to mention the strenuous race to and through the Gate—had finally left him worn out and exhausted. Now, with his elation ebbing, his body was crying for rest. Yet even if he wanted to give in to the plea—which he did not—

the middle of the Van Gölü was not the place to do so. And so he readied himself for what promised to be a lengthy swim and started eastward.

He had taken no more than a dozen strokes when he again felt something move beneath him, this time brushing against his leg. It stopped him fast and his eyes immediately searched the water which mirrored the same blackness draped across the sky above him. Then came a swish in the water a short distance ahead that stole Jacob's gaze. It was followed by a plop behind him. And then another off to his right.

Jacob became as still as one could be while gently treading upon the water. A light shiver ran through him, though it was not caused by the cold. Something shared the water with him, of that there was no doubt. But what? Even the dolphin who led him halfway through the Gate knew entering the waters of the lake risked certain death. Then he remembered Johiel telling him during his visit to Akdamar Island of the one lone fish able to survive the highly salty waters.

"Pearl mullet," muttered Jacob aloud to himself. "Of course. Just a harmless pearl mullet. What else could it be?"

But just as his face relaxed with a smile of relief, something took firm hold of his leg and with a quick jerk he disappeared beneath the gentle lapping waves of the lake.

~ ~ ~

His scream showed itself in a burst of bubbles which exploded from his mouth as he was dragged down into the dark depths. Whatever had snatched hold of him, the water proved far too murky to see. Where it was taking him, Jacob wasn't about to find out and, with all the might he had, he began to kick and buck and fight until he felt himself slip free. Without pause, he paddled his way furiously back toward the surface. He emerged heaving for air and, as he choked up the water he had swallowed, he noticed the lake around him begin to boil. And from the gurgling water came a monstrous tentacle, pale gray in color and appearing slimy to the touch.

Jacob froze with fright, his eyes growing ever wider as the sinuous limb uncurled itself many stories high into the air. It was then Jacob was grateful that the water shielded this monstrosity from view; for the tentacle alone was enough in itself to stir terror from the most unflinching of men. One couldn't begin to fathom—nor care to at that—what nightmare was attached to the other end of the worming arm, and Jacob had no intention of finding out. He took off swimming, arms chopping their way wildly at the water in his desperate retreat for safety, but it was a futile attempt at best. He had only managed a short distance when the tentacle slithered toward him in pursuit. It quickly took hold of Jacob again, snaking itself tightly around him like a jungle python. Though, instead of being pulled underwater once again, Jacob was plucked from it and lifted high into the air where he was whipped about violently. At the same time, several more tentacles rose up out of the lake.

Jacob fought to free himself from the vice-like grip squeezing around his body, but the more he struggled, the tighter the coils became until he was certain his fate was to be crushed within them. He reached to his side and grappled for the familiar hilt of his sword. Once it was unsheathed, he gripped it tight in both hands and plunged the weapon into the fleshy appendage squeezing him. The wounded tentacle thrashed about in apparent pain and released its claim on Jacob with a vengeful discharge into the air. Jacob plunged back into the seething waters with tremendous force, and as he did his sword slipped from his hand and was lost instantly to the night-colored lake.

Feeling more vulnerable than ever without the stinging bite of his blade to offer some semblance of defense, Jacob looked to see the implacable arms were not through terrorizing him. Again they came at him, like monstrous sea serpents poised to strike in unison, and just as they did, something took hold of Jacob roughly and stole him away from their approaching clutches.

"You are either very brave or very stupid to have found yourself in these waters under the cloak of night, Nephilim."

Jacob looked to see the deep commanding voice belonged to an angel in whose hands he dangled. Though just one look into the fierce strength radiating from the face, which looked at once ageless while holding a bounty of untold years, made Jacob question whether his fate was better served in the hands of this so-called savior or back in the water fending for himself against the monstrous creature still reaching for him.

"I wouldn't exactly say bravery is responsible for me being here," replied Jacob.

"That, then, leaves just one other option," the angel countered.

Below, Jacob spied the darkened figures of three other angels. Their swords were drawn, but to Jacob's surprise they were not using them to slay the tentacled beast. Instead they were vigorously trying to drive the flailing arms back down into the water. As he watched them, Jacob guessed rightly these angels to be the Powers from Carpanak Island he had seen only briefly before over these same waters and under much similar circumstances, and a slight sense of timidity came over him as he recalled the ruthless nature of which they had been described by Gotham the first time he was told of their existence. Now, suddenly, he was in the clutches of one.

"How is it you manage to find yourself on this side of the Gate?" asked the angel.

"Gotham," Jacob answered, first in a quiet utterance under his breath and then again more vociferous as though he'd suddenly remembered the purpose of his mission. "I can't even begin to tell you how important it is I find him, and fast. Tell me you know where he might be."

The angel didn't answer. Instead, he quickly circled around the open air before soaring with great speed into the waiting darkness.

~ ~ ~

"You're sure he's here?" asked Jacob when they finally touched down on a ragged perch of rock overlooking the lake on Akdamar island.

The angel's eyes gleamed brightly from behind the nighttime mask cast upon his face from the unusually dark moonless night. He said nothing but pointed downhill where the silhouette of the Church of the Holy Cross could be seen, its arched windows, wreathed around its tell-tale dome, glowing with flickering firelight coming from inside. When Jacob turned back to the angel to thank him for his rescue, he was already gone, vanishing without further words into the night sky and replaced with the lonely stirring of a chilling wind coming up off the water.

"I really need to get me some wings already," Jacob quietly mumbled to himself.

He then proceeded to navigate his way through the darkness across the island's rocky hide and managed to circle his way around the church to the entrance of the zhamatun. Inside, he heard the murmur of voices marred by a high-pitched clanging of metal coming through the doorway at the opposite end of the darkened hall leading to the cathedral from which a dancing of light could be seen. Quietly, Jacob stepped his way across the stone floor while carefully listening for the indecipherable hum of voices that abruptly fell silent as he approached the doorway. As Jacob craned his neck forward to peer inside the lit church, the unmistakable ring of a steel blade being unsheathed sang loudly and he froze at the feel of the cold sharp edge of a sword suddenly being pressed uncomfortably and pointedly against his throat. His wide eyes slowly followed the length of sword to its owner.

"Jacob!" gasped Johiel, whose youthful self was visibly shocked at the sight of the boy.

Inside the cathedral, squatting beside a large stone block beneath the dome, Gotham watched motionless through an opening in the stringy strands of his long hair falling across his face which also took on a look of unwelcome surprise at the sight of Jacob. Rising to his feet, he let fall from his hand onto the stone floor with a heavy thud a forge hammer gripped in his hand. He was shirtless and his torso gleamed with power both from the ring of suspended fire licking the church walls, and a fire that burned white in the center of the dome floor. Cast upon the walls, his winged shadow loomed like that of a great giant.

"How on this God-given earth did you come to be here, Fledgling?" asked Gotham, and at first Jacob hesitated in answering as he was unsure whether the angel's quiet, measured tone held unexpected surprise or anger.

"Through the Gate, naturally," said Jacob, puffing out his chest somewhat at the sense of pride he felt over surviving what he thought was not survivable.

"By yourself?" Johiel, sounding even more shocked at such a prospect, asked.

"Well, not exactly…that is, yes and no. To be truthful, it's a long story."

"Then be quick in telling it," demanded Gotham with an edge of impatience. "We've much yet to do and time is waning."

Johiel, however, was more hospitable in his manner. Putting away his sword he ushered the boy into the cathedral where Jacob found a welcoming warmth. "Your journey shows on you, as you look quite the fright."

Once Jacob had managed to shake free the chill that made his skin tremble, Jacob began to tell Johiel and Gotham of his journey; how he crossed Eden's forests with the guidance of the wolf pack, passed beneath the great mountain walling Eden from the Dilmun Sea, and how the dolphin led him as far through the darkness of the Gate as it could before filling his lungs and urging him to complete the final stretch on his own.

"And naturally you went," said Gotham, sounding none too pleased.

"I'm sitting here, aren't I?" replied Jacob.

"Stupid child," muttered Gotham to himself as he shook his head with disapproval.

Now it was Jacob who was becoming agitated. "Maybe I am stupid. And maybe you'd be interested in knowing why I chose to take such a risk in the first place," he barked while turning a fiery eye to Gotham. But Johiel was quick to step in.

"Do not mind him. His reaction is understandable considering. It is a dangerous trek one attempts when going through the Gate without an angel to guide him through. You could well have perished."

"No joking. And not because of the Gate either," said Jacob.

"What do you mean by that?" inquired Gotham.

Jacob then proceeded to tell about the monstrous tentacles that came up from the unseen depths of the lake and took hold of him.

"The Nekcri," said Johiel.

"What's a Nekcri?"

"That which has become the mythic monster of the Van Gölü. But as you have come to find out, hardly a myth. The tales spun—both true and exaggerated—by the many souls who live in these parts claiming to have witnessed its presence have made it the stuff of legend. It is, for lack of a better comparison, their own Loch Ness Monster. Quite the harmless creature, the Nekcri is, despite its appearance."

"Harmless? Tell my ribs how harmless it is," said Jacob with a wince as he rubbed his still-tender side. "If it weren't for the Powers coming to my rescue, I'd probably be fish bait right now. What I don't understand is why they didn't just kill the thing instead of driving it back into the lake."

The remark brought a thoughtful glimmer to Johiel's eye. "Why should they want to do such a thing? It's existence in these waters goes as far back as mine upon these shores. Surely it has a right to reside in peace in this place it long-ago decided to make home," he said. "If the Nekcri attacked you as you say it did, I assure you it was by command of a nefarious whisper that managed to find its ear. It's been a loyal creature, one whose presence has kept the curious from stumbling upon the Gate."

~ ~ ~

Once again, the high-pitched ping of metal filled the church. The ghostly weathered biblical figures filling the mural-covered walls were huddled and whispering amongst each other while their collective attention became fixed on Gotham. The forge hammer was back in his hand and pounding away vigorously at the stone slab cradled between his knees.

As curiosity directed Jacob's feet closer to see what it was he was doing, Gotham raised what he was hammering upon up toward the light. It was the blade to a sword, which Gotham closely studied with an unforgiving eye. And as he slowly turned it in his hand, it caught the light and gleamed brightly and Jacob saw instantly that it wasn't just an ordinary sword.

"That's the sword you showed me at the Tree of Life, isn't it?" said Jacob. "It's the Sword of Destiny."

Gotham's gaze remained firmly on the sword, carefully scrutinizing every minute detail to the point of obsession.

"Give me a few more hours and it will be," he replied.

As Gotham returned to working on the sword, Jacob looked to Johiel with growing confusion in his face. Why, he wondered, was Gotham creating a replica of the legendary weapon?

"Thaniel has demanded—or rather I should say threatened—Gothamel to hand Destiny over to him," explained Johiel.

"Threatened? I don't believe it," Jacob mumbled under his breath. Not that he didn't believe what Johiel had stated but, rather, he was now slowly realizing what had sent him through the Gate in search of Gotham was not a figment of his wild imaginings.

"Alas, neither did I when Gotham first told me the upsetting news when he appeared here out of the blue," said Johiel, looking almost wounded by the words he spoke. "Yet it would seem Thaniel has made a most disturbing and heart-breaking decision to follow in the footsteps left behind by many of our brethren down a path from which unfortunately there is no chance of returning."

"But…what would he want with the sword?" asked Jacob.

"Have you forgotten all I told you about Destiny that day you came to sit with me at the roots of the Tree of Life?" Gotham, his gaze briefly leaving his work, griped. "There is only one reason—and one reason alone—why the sword stirs desire."

"It would seem Thaniel—quite unexpectedly—has come to acquire a delicacy often reserved for the palate of man: a taste for power," Johiel interjected with his calming voice, even as he spoke of something most unnerving, "and he seeks to satiate such hunger by taking reign over all Eden with the one weapon which would extend to him the power to achieve such an unconscionable feat."

"I don't believe it," Jacob repeated to himself with a soft mumble.

"Believe it," said Gotham with stern insistence. "He admitted it himself, and much more, when I confronted him early this morning in the Library."

Jacob was visibly flummoxed. Thaniel—the angel he found to be the most angelic of the Guides, and one he held an unraveled trust for—a traitor?

"My greater concern," Johiel's voice suddenly sounded to break Jacob's drifting thoughts, "rests in not knowing what bargain Thaniel struck at the black pool inside the Silent Forest to ensure that power over Eden once Destiny is in his hands. I suspect there was only one demand sought by Lilith in return; the use of the sword to sever the Herrinsu vine that has bound Samael. But most likely there is another, which I fear far more."

"Which is?" Jacob asked somewhat hesitantly, especially when he saw the grim look which came and settled itself in all its heaviness upon Johiel's face.

"The possession of Destiny itself," answered Johiel.

Jacob's eyes shifted to the cathedral walls from where he heard a collective gasp escape from the huddled images as they continued to watch and listen from inside their murals.

"But if he did that—"

"Then the Darkness would hold reign over everything under Heaven," said Johiel in the most forbidding of voices. "Including Heaven itself.

The thought sent a bone-deep chill through Jacob, especially when the vision of the black pool inside the Silent Forest, and specifically the nightmarish creatures hiding behind its veil, flashed in front of his eyes.

It was then he felt an unpleasant weight suddenly come and settle itself on top of him as his thoughts were quickly tugged in what felt to be a million different directions. And, as he tried to make sense of the chorus of voices ringing loudly inside his head, he watched Gotham continue in his work of crafting the sword where all attention was intensely focused. An unusually beautiful sword it was—mighty in size, with a blade thicker and longer than any normal sword in which was housed its heart in the form of an aged spearhead. It was hard for Jacob to believe one weapon could harness so much power, and that such power could find its way into the grip of someone capable of indescribable evil.

"I must have missed something along the way," noted Jacob, after sitting quietly with his thoughts while watching Gotham. "I thought Destiny was in your possession."

"That it is," muttered Gotham. "And so I intend for it to remain. But not for the reasons others wish to claim it."

"Then why make one that isn't?" Even before he finished asking the question, the answer came to him.

"Certainly you didn't think I was going to place Destiny in Thaniel's hands, did you?" asked Gotham.

"Why hand him anything, real or fake?" inquired Jacob. "Why not just have the Powers go in and sweep him and his three accomplices out of Eden. In fact, I don't really understand why Heaven doesn't just sic a whole army of angels on him. End of problem, right?"

An amused grin came to Johiel, but a dark, earnest look remain fixed in his eyes.

"Kill the Nekcri, gather a legion of angels and rush Eden. You show an impetuous spirit, Fledgling," he said. "Have you forgotten already your friends that remain behind at Havenhid? You should be made aware, unbeknownst to them, they are now hostages. In fact, let my voice carry clear that all of Eden has been quietly taken hostage, as Gotham has so informed me, threatened by Thaniel to be swept up and consumed by the Darkness he promises to usher in by opening wide the Through in the Silent Forest if his demands are not met."

"This has to be a mistake," Jacob remarked with a nervous chuckle.

"All of us boys have come to really like Thaniel. In many ways, he's like a big brother we've never had. No way would he harm any of us. I know he wouldn't."

Much as he argued, he knew in the unsettling silence that followed that neither angel was spinning tales, nor did they have reason to do so, and a sudden surge of anger stirred inside him at the thought of his friends being threatened in such a manner, and by someone he had come to trust and consider a friend no less, until he found himself blurting out in defense, "He's bluffing, then."

"Can you be so sure, young Jacob?" asked Johiel whose own voice lacked any semblance of certainty. "The possibility of such a thing happening, where the sudden cries of Eden, pitched in terror, ring out before being forever extinguished in silence..."

His voice trailed off, quivering ever so slightly, and Jacob noticed the bold, invulnerable strength that sculpted Johiel's face briefly succumb to despair.

"Would he really do such a thing?" Jacob pondered quietly.

"Are you willing to risk that he won't?" replied Gotham.

"But he's an angel."

"Oh, Fledgling, please tell me after all this time you don't still carry the same naive view you held in your head of what an angel was before I brought you to Eden," said Gotham with noted exertion. "We are as flawed and weak as civilians, though we'd first be damned before admission of such a thing. It's that weakness that sent a third of my brethren to be cast from Heaven like falling stars and sentenced me to a nomad's existence. And it's that weakness that will continue to thin the ranks of God's mighty army.

"Angel! Yes, Thaniel is an angel! What of it? So was the Dragon, at one time; lofty in his rank in God's eyes than any one of us could hope to soar. But at the end of the day, we walk upon the same feet attached to the same two legs as man does, and as such we are not immune to being spoiled like a bowl of rotting fruit by the same maggots of sin who find sustenance beneath the weak man's skin. As much as it might pain me to say it, I've looked into Thaniel's eyes and saw clearly as I see you before me now the beginnings of such rot, and I remain steadfast in my belief that, yes, he most definitely would bring about Eden's ruin and everything in it to gain possession of Destiny."

"Then if he is weak as you say," said Jacob sadly, "there must be something that can be done to stop him."

"It's being done," said Gotham, pulling the sword from where he had briefly laid it within the flames of an unusual white fire burning big and bright on the stones of the church floor. As Gotham again began hammering upon the blade, Jacob noticed the fire was not being fed by wood or any other fuel, but seemingly the air itself upon which it floated several inches above the ground. Not only that, his clothes which were soaked-through when he arrived at Akdamar were now completely dry, as was his dripping hair.

"What makes you think Thaniel will be fooled by this fake you're making?" he asked.

The answer came from Johiel.

"You're right to voice such skepticism, young Jacob. Thaniel, as we all know, is quite intelligent. More so, he has proved himself to be shrewd and cunning and is not one to easily be taken a fool. On this point, Gotham and myself have debated at great length when scheming this plan," he said as he roamed the perimeter of flitting light gathered beneath the dome. "Thaniel has become one more in a long line who have fallen in amorousness of a deceitful temptress. If history has shown anything, it's that such self-aggrandizing ambitions have a tendency to fatally compromise one's ability to think clearly. It's an unfortunate predilection both mortals and angels share, as Gotham so stated, resulting in falls neither repentant plea nor beat of wing can lend escape."

Gotham remained quiet, kneeling upon the floor. So lost was his attention in the sword he so closely studied for the tiniest of flaws that he showed a brief moment of resistance when Johiel came up alongside him and, embracing him warmly on the shoulder, took the sword from his hand, allowing Gotham momentary relief to his tired-looking eyes made weary from such a taxing undertaking.

"When Thaniel takes this sword in hand," continued Johiel, "he will only see the glory he has long-envisioned for himself, not the sleight of hand that has been so masterfully forged by the white fire of the Begend. Or so we can only hope."

As he spoke, Johiel held the sword up in the air while turning it in hand for his own inspection. And as he did, the steel blade that had been polished to a mirror-like shine caught brilliantly the surrounding firelight and reflected it in myriad flashes of color throughout the church. It was the fire Jacob's eyes turned to instead, drawn there by a singular word uttered by Johiel: Begend.

~ ~ ~

"You're planning to kill him?" asked Jacob as the white flames illuminated his dual-colored eyes.

Johiel's gaze bent from the sword to the boy. "What makes you ask such a thing?"

"You said the sword was made from the fire of the Begend," answered Jacob.

"That is correct," answered Johiel with some reluctance.

"The same fire you carry around your neck?"

As he spoke, Jacob's gaze shifted from the white flames to settle on the simple silver chain Gotham wore from which hung a pendant in the shape of a vial carved from what appeared to be a chunk of dense, black rock. Obsidian? Onyx? Jacob couldn't be sure. Yet dense and dark as it was, it couldn't conceal fully the white illumination of whatever mysterious thing it carried inside. When Jacob finally questioned Gotham about it during a break from their daily training routines, Gotham explained the pendant held the last flickers of the Begend fireball. To mortals it was better known as the "Big Bang"; the explosion of light marking the beginning of the universe and life itself. It also, Gotham noted, held in its blinding flare the power to just as instantly cease all life, both mortal and immortal alike, hence its name.

It was this last unnerving detail that suddenly pushed its way to the front of Jacob's thoughts when he suddenly came to realize the flickering white fire burning in front of him had not only been ignited from the remaining breath of the Begend embers captured in the vial hanging from Gotham's neck, but that its life-giving and stealing powers had been forged into the steel of the sword unto which he was slavishly working.

Again, the church fell silent as neither angel felt particularly inclined to continue forth the conversation. Gotham, though, was quick to recognize the boy's pressing stare would likely not leave either one of them until his hunger for answers to a situation growing more confusing with every passing minute had been fed.

"I told you on the train to Tatvan about the nine Archangels of Heaven, before there were seven," said Gotham finally, bringing a nod from Jacob's head. "Before two of those Archangels forever fell from the ranks, they were brought before God and entrusted with a most important duty. They would, at a future time known only to their creator, be called upon to serve as Messengers of what the Apostle John foretold in his Book of Revelation. Each Archangel was gifted a vial, and inside each vial held a final judgment from God to be poured forth upon mankind when the time came to usher in the End Days.

"The two Archangels who would never see through their duty each took with them the vial entrusted in their care on their long fall from Heaven," continued Gotham. "One would hold an impregnable darkness filled with hidden swarms of horror; the other would carry inside an unspeakable brightness of the light of all light, equally as horror-filled to those who would come to shun its existence."

As he spoke, Gotham grasped the pendant to the necklace he carried.

"Not before this day has the light from the Begend served me other than comfort me with its warmth," said Gotham, sounding almost regretful.

Jacob looked again to the fire and an inexplicable wave of remorse came up from inside him.

"Talk about stupid...how is it I suddenly feel a need to come to Thaniel's defense, even in light of knowing what he's planning?" he asked. "Maybe it's because for so long I've come to look upon him as a friend. I guess I just don't wish to see him dead, even as despicable as he's become."

"Many will come away from this with heavy a heart by Thaniel's betrayal to embrace avarice as he has so chosen to do," Johiel remarked glumly.

Johiel returned the sword to Gotham and, for several quiet minutes, Jacob sat watching while the angel resumed polishing the already perfected shine coating the blade.

"There's more than avarice at work. I think..." Jacob began hesitantly. "I think he plans to kill you."

Surprising to Jacob, the words he uttered caused Gotham not even the briefest of pauses, only a quick unspoken glance toward Johiel before returning his gaze back to the work at hand.

"How do you know this to be?" the angel eventually asked in a quiet voice.

"Wouldn't you rather just look inside my head and see the answer for yourself to make sure I'm telling you the truth?" quipped Jacob sarcastically.

Gotham turned his glare at the boy, but it quickly softened.

"I see you still continue to carry a particular bee in your bonnet." he commented.

Any other time Jacob would have enjoyed needling Gotham over his painfully dated phrasing of words. This was no such a time.

"It doesn't matter," said Jacob with a shrug.

"Actually, it does," said Gotham, turning suddenly even more serious. "You've never given me one moment's cause to call into doubt your truthfulness, yet I have—and on more than one occasion. And for that I am sorry."

The sincerity of the angel's apology, particularly at this most tense of moments, took Jacob by surprise, as he was sure they did not come often.

"The worst thing about experiencing the betrayal of someone as close as one's own son is losing completely the ability to trust anyone else around you," continued Gotham. "Perhaps my distrust was always there—a parting gift given to me by my own father the moment Heaven chose to cast me from its embrace. And in some ways I'm inclined to wonder if maybe I somehow gifted to David his own fate that led him into the arms of the Darkness, as you yourself speculated."

Jacob felt a fist of regret suddenly take aim at his face as he recalled the harsh words he leveled at Gotham in the Silent Forest.

"Yeah, about what I said—" he began before Gotham quickly held up his hand and motioned for his silence.

"Don't now wax over the truth as I sit ruefully in front of you for questioning it," said Gotham.

Only it wasn't the truth—at least truth Jacob held belief in—but rather words aimed to hurt in a fit of anger, and it sickened Jacob to know he had succeeded in spades.

"Mockingbirds," he suddenly muttered after a moment of awkward silence.

"Excuse me?" asked Gotham.

"You asked how I knew of Thaniel's plan to do you harm when you returned to Eden," explained Jacob. "Mockingbirds told me while I was having a drink from the stream near Lions Bite. Thaniel's voice came out of one, while another voice I didn't recognize came from the other. I assumed they were echoing a conversation they had overheard. Then again the more I think about it the more preposterous it sounds. It easily could have just been my imagination making it all up."

"And that's why you came here?" grumbled Gotham. "To warn me?"

"You think I risked going through the Gate for kicks?" answered Jacob.

The polishing of the sword stopped and Gotham focused his piercing eyes dulled with noticeable sadness onto Jacob. And for a moment Jacob was certain the angel was about to reprimand him all over again for venturing through the Gate just as he had earlier when the boy first arrived at the church.

"Stupid child," said the angel remarked as he had when the boy first arrived, only with the faintest of grins and the kindest of voices. "Risking your own life so that danger to mine might be averted. Even in your anger toward me for casting doubt upon you."

There came from him a look that spoke a quiet gratitude that no words could convey.

"Well," Jacob said with a deep sigh, "if it makes you feel any better, I was beginning to wonder myself whether or not I was liar when we went to question Max."

He then frowned deeply as he thought back to the incident that had left him more puzzled every time he revisited it in his mind.

"I just can't make any sense out of it. Why would Max lie about something like that? I mean, I thought we were friends."

"I can answer that for you," offered Gotham, returning to his work at hand. "He wasn't lying."

The statement immediately put Jacob's back up.

"You're telling me you still believe him?" bristled Jacob.

"I'm saying you both were telling the truth."

Now Jacob was beyond confused.

"Come again. Just how exactly is that possible?"

"Easily," said Gotham. "When I gazed at your memory of the night you and Max snuck into the Silent Forest, it revealed itself exactly as you told me. Naturally, it occurred to me you hold the Grace of Bending, which not only allows you to read and influence the minds of others, but manipulate your own memories in order to throw off others gifted with the same power to peer inside your head."

"So now you think I created what happened to throw you off?" asked Jacob angrily. "That's worse than calling me a liar."

"If you'll let me finish," said Gotham strenuously. "I said it occurred to me you were capable of performing such a trick. I also know it takes much training to pull off such a ruse, at least flawlessly enough to be believable by someone as acute to such ploys as I, but such capabilities are beyond even the reach of a Light Bearer as green as yourself."

Jacob let loose a labored sigh. "I can't even begin to tell you how much you're confusing me, seriously."

"Then let me spell it out in simple enough terms," said Gotham. "Thaniel bound Max's memory of everything that happened in the Silent Forest."

"Bound his mem——. What does that even mean?"

"Just as it sounds: Thaniel altered Max's memory of that night."

"But that's crazy," said Jacob. "Why would Thaniel make it so Max couldn't remember what happened but leave it so I would?"

"To play to my distrust," explained Gotham. "To make it so I would become doubtful of you."

The angel then watched as the pity the boy showed for Thaniel's welfare moments earlier quickly faded and became replaced by a rising tide of seething anger.

"Now are you still concerned about what my plans hold for our dear Thaniel?" asked Gotham with a slanting grin. But it was short-lived, and quickly receded back into the solemness masking Gotham's face.

"Your worry is wasted, Fledgling. This blade was not made with Thaniel's flesh in mind," the angel stated grimly. "It is not for me to render punishment upon my brother, no matter how vile the sin he chooses to commit."

Gotham then rose to his feet before Jacob could say any more, and the figures peering out from the murals on the walls watched silently as he crossed the cathedral. When Gotham came to the doorway leading to the darkness residing in the zhamatun he paused.

"The day will soon awaken. See to it the boy is safely returned before first light," he instructed Johiel with not so much as a glance over his shoulder. "I need not tell you how imperative it is his venture be bound to the Gate."

And with that he was gone, into the dark.

~ ~ ~

"But I don't want to go back. I want to help," implored Jacob to Johiel once they were alone.

The cathedral became still as the whispering from the murals quieted. Johiel came around Jacob and crouched down next to him before the white fire.

"You will be helping by going back. Trust me," he said. And with that he blew sharply at the fire. The flames instantly burst into hundreds and hundreds of burning white embers. They floated weightlessly in the air like a small galaxy of stars before slowly circling above the floor creating a spiral of light that gradually ascended upward into the dome. When they reached the top, the embers began dispersing through the numerous windows wreathing the inside of the dome and disappeared into the night.

When the last ember was gone from sight, Jacob turned once more to Johiel who looked to be in deep thought staring blankly into the emptiness where the fire had burned bright. "What did Gotham mean when he said 'I need not tell you how imperative it is his venture be bound to the Gate'?"

"Thaniel cannot know you made it here to Akdamar, nor that you have warned Gothamel of his intentions toward him," explained Johiel. "No, in order to keep Thaniel's suspicions at bay, he must know you failed in your attempt to make it through the passage of the Gate."

"I didn't, though," said Jacob, sounding confused.

"You know that, and I know that, but Thaniel mustn't."

"So I'll just block my thoughts."

The suggestion brought a faint smile to Johiel. "I've great faith in both your strength and your character, young Jacob, of that you must know by now. But, as Gotham duly noted, you are still in the early stages of exercising your Graces and we couldn't chance you being able to put up a strong enough wall against someone as seasoned as Thaniel," said the angel. "Besides, to block your thoughts would only serve Thaniel's suspicions that you are hiding something."

He then quickly got to his feet and stepped his way to a simple wooden pedestal in the corner of the church upon which sat a large bowl, the same bowl from which Johiel had splashed water across his face and revealed his youthful presence hidden behind an elderly guise during Jacob's first visit to Akdamar. Once he had collected some of the water with a pitcher he grabbed from nearby, he returned to the center of the dome near where Jacob sat. There, Jacob watched with a perplexed look fixed on his face as Johiel stretched forth his arm and slowly began pouring the water from the pitcher. Instead of the water splashing as expected across the stone slabs of the floor, it dribbled outward horizontally in a wide line before flowing downward to form a large rectangular-shaped window of water, from which not a drop dripped upon the ground.

"Now think back earlier to when you were making your way through Eden's Forest," instructed Johiel without mention or explanation of the strange stunt he had just performed. "And once you have the image in your mind reach out and touch the water."

Jacob was hesitant at first, but a reassuring nod from Johiel drew his hand closer to the liquid window. Then with just the tip of his forefinger, he touched the water. At first nothing, and then slowly images began showing themselves. They were ghostly at first, and transparent. Gradually they became clearer until it was like looking through a pane of glass. First came trees. Many, many trees. And brush. It was the Forest, and it was passing quickly by as though something low to the ground was running swiftly through it. Suddenly, the back end of a wolf running ahead appeared, followed by another. Then to the left still another. And to the right, there was Mist.

"Smartly done...crossing through the Forest under the cover of wolf's skin," remarked Johiel, clearly pleased while studying the same images that had transfixed Jacob.

"These are my thoughts, exactly as I see them in my head," said Jacob with just a hint of incredulity in his voice.

"Of which we are going to alter, or in this case bind."

"You mean, the same thing Gotham said Thaniel did to Max's thoughts you're going to do to mine?" asked Jacob with a measure of apprehension.

"It's quite harmless, I assure you," said Johiel. "One's memories are but shadowy remnants of things past. And, like shadows, they are ever-changing depending upon how the sunlight decides to cast them onto the landscape. Most times, the things that occur in our lives are not how our memory decides they should exist. In the same way, we are going to decide how your memory since leaving Eden will exist."

"Sort of like mind-bending," said Jacob.

"In a way. Where mind-bending is the influence over thought, binding taps into one's memory and re-crafts it. The shadows are given a new form to tell a different story to whoever proves to have the ability to peer inside and view them. That which is meant to be hidden, is bound from showing itself in a seamless veil of obscurity. You can look at it as sort of like having selective amnesia."

Despite his explanation. Johiel recognized a noticeable uncertainty that remained on the boy's face.

"Not to worry," he said with a reassuring smile. "It is but temporary. Trust me when I tell you your thoughts as they are now will be returned to you."

Eventually, Jacob nodded his willingness.

"Okay then, how does this work?"

"First we reshape your journey."

Johiel moved around and situated himself on the opposite side of the pane of water facing the boy. He then placed his hand against where Jacob's finger remained touching it while allowing the thick membrane of water to flow between them. In short order, the images suddenly began to shift and change. Some became visions that never occurred, while others, like the tentacles of the Nekcri turned phantom-like and receded into darkness. Yet despite the display of his memory playing out before him, Jacob's thoughts remained elsewhere.

"What about Gotham?"

"What about Gothamel?" Johiel, his concentration firmly fixed on the liquid glass, asked.

"Aren't you worried about what Thaniel might have in store for him?"

"Gothamel has come up against far greater entities of evil and emerged unscathed."

The angels' response did little to allay Jacob's concerns.

"What if this time is different?" he asked. "I can't explain it, but I have been unable to shake this gnawing feeling that something extraordinarily bad is about to occur."

Jacob looked past the watery images playing out before him and focused on Johiel's face, and he could see it held a heaviness of some unspoken burden.

"Even those of us who stand immortal must eventually face the possibility that the specter of death may one day pierce us," said Johiel before meeting Jacob's gaze with his own. "Remember what I tell you here now, Fledgling. Whatever happens this day is willed to be. Shed tears if you must, cry out in anger if it so demands, but you must not lose your faith. Do you understand? Delicate as it may seem more times than not, there is no greater weapon of which you will wield, nor breastplate of armor stronger to encase your safety."

"A life-saving blade," Jacob muttered under his breath as the visuals of his memory revealed him sitting on a stoop of stairs outside the church recalling words Johiel had shared with him regarding faith on his first visit to the island.

"That's right," said Johiel reassuringly.

The angel's words held an ominous ring, so much so that Jacob was hesitant to question them for fear of the meaning residing behind them.

"Why is it whenever anyone warns to stay strong to your faith does it signal the coming of something faith-shattering?" he asked more solemnly than nervously.

If he expected some measure of comfort or reassurance from Johiel, he was quickly disappointed, for the angel offered nothing more. Instead, he lowered his hand from the pane of water and the images instantly dispersed. The water was once more clear, and Johiel announced, "It is finished."

~ ~ ~

"So now what?" asked Jacob, once he had refocused himself.

"Now, you pass through it."

A simple enough request. And yet if there was one thing Jacob had come to find since leaving Cain's Corner it was that whenever something appeared to be a simple task it was usually anything but. He cautiously reached into the water first with his right hand and wriggled his fingers about. It was cold, and felt exactly as if he were testing the waters of a swimming pool into which he was considering taking a plunge. He reached further to just past his elbow, and what quickly proved troubling to him was the fact he couldn't see his hand emerging from the other side where Johiel was crouched waiting. The window itself was no more than half the length of the tip of a finger in depth, and yet all he could feel was water.

"It's alright...keep coming," Johiel coaxed him.

Knowing the angel, who had been nothing but a protective presence, would not lead him to harm, Jacob took a deep, steadying breath while making the conscious choice to not close his eyes as he lunged forward and disappeared into the pane with a gentle splash. In an instant it was as if he had dove into some vast ocean. Everywhere there was water and it was filled with images and an echoing chorus of voices both familiar and strange swirling all around him. As he swam about, he looked desperately every which way for the other side to this looking glass of water he suddenly found himself immersed in, but he could find none. Not even a rippling reflection of Johiel to guide him. Yet it didn't matter even if he did, for before he knew it he was overcome by a tide of unconsciousness that carried him with unnerving swiftness into utter darkness.

CHAPTER NINETEEN

J acob woke first to a soft pillow of sand beneath him, then a hard nudge to his ribs.

Or was it the other way around?

The grogginess that greeted him made it difficult to be sure either way. The only thing he was certain of when he finally managed to open his eyes was finding a pair of large feet planted inches from his face and hearing a voice barking down at him from somewhere above.

"Come now, and get up with yourself."

Jacob's gaze slowly rolled its way upward to see who it was speaking to him. He could not make out the face against the blinding white presence of the day, even when he raised a hand to lend cover to his eyes. Whoever it was, the figure slowly lowered itself to a squatting position. As it did, Jacob saw a flash of wings and finally the white veil of sunlight was pulled back just enough for him to see it was Acruxel who hovered above him.

"You've caused me quite a bit of trouble Nephilim, haven't you now?" said the angel.

His youthfully angular face, however, held no outward sign of hostility, while his eyes—pools of fallow gold that they were—gleamed with an intenseness that was more friendly in nature than malicious. Still, Jacob was quick to wonder whether he was mistaking a hospitable look for one of smug victory often seen in hunters kneeling beside their down prey.

With the roar of the pounding surf in his ear, Jacob lifted his head up off the ground revealing a face half-caked in a dusting of the beach upon which he was sprawled. He gave a quick look around him and recognized instantly he was back on Eden's shore just a short hop from the sea whose foaming waves washed over his feet as they rolled up upon the beach.

"What am I doing here?" Jacob pondered aloud.

"My guess is the sea took pity upon you and spit you back onto the sand," answered Acruxel. "It's the foolish Nephilim boy who thinks he can navigate through the Gate alone and see another rising of the sun. But I cannot deny you own the innards to make the attempt."

Jacob stared out across the water while searching his thoughts. The Gate, of course. It was beginning to come back to him, albeit vaguely at first: the chase, the dolphin coming to his rescue and leading him beneath the waves to the dark passage.

The passage…

Formed from the most daunting shade of darkness—but into it they dared to go forth, yet only for a ways until the dolphin was restrained from going any further. It was left to him to go the rest of the way, but he couldn't bring himself to release his hold of the dolphin and go it alone. No matter how hard he tried, he just couldn't. And in the midst of that recollection, an overwhelming sense of shame overcame Jacob from his lack of courage.

I failed him, he voiced to himself as his thoughts turned to Gotham.

"Don't look so glum," said Acruxel, "for I tell you now you would not have found what awaited you on the other side pleasant, had your luck managed to carry you that far."

Whatever the source of unpleasantness he was referring to, the angel didn't say, but it drew a chuckle from him as he rose again to his feet and beckoned Jacob onto his. "Enough time has been wasted on you, and certain powers that be at Havenhid I'm sure would be more inclined in speaking with you than I."

~ ~ ~

They were soon soaring across Eden. And it was from high up in the air Jacob was allowed to see with some semblance of awe the great distance he had covered on foot the night before as he watched an endless sea of forest trees and winding river sail past below him while hanging in Acruxel's clutches. In a short amount of time, the Garden came into sight and they made for Havenhid. As they neared the tell-tale trees, Acruxel swooped suddenly downward and, when he was just a few feet short of setting foot on the ground, the angel released Jacob, sending the boy tumbling hard across the grass before coming to a dizzying rest on his back.

"You'd be well advised to get yourself inside and stay put," advised Acruxel as he hovered overhead. "Should I be forced to give chase after you again I may be inclined to drop you from a higher distance once I've caught you." And with a loud fluttering of his wings, he was gone.

Jacob sat still for a short while until the throbbing and ringing inside his head subsided. Then with some trepidation, he got to his feet and entered the hollow of the tree serving as the entrance to Havenhid. When he reached the top of the stairwell and stepped into the airy foyer, he was greeted with the unique rustling peace found high in treetops. The voices of the other Nephilim were nowhere to be heard, nor should they have been at that hour. Classes had already long started, including the one awaiting him in the Library. Instead of hurrying there—for it was the last place he wanted to be—he continued to linger about the foyer retracing his steps as he wandered in circles while lost in his thoughts until he heard Anahel's voice. He looked to the landing near the top of the grand staircase and found the angel clutching the rail and peering down at him.

"Just the person I was needing to speak with. Tell me, have you seen Gothamel at all this morning?" asked Anahel.

The sound of Gotham's name was enough to make Jacob's throat tighten, and at first all he could manage was a timid shake of his head.

"That's strange," remarked Anahel as his face screwed itself up into a look of puzzlement. "Last I saw him was early morning yesterday. Today, I've looked everywhere I could think he might be, and yet no sign of him. Strange, indeed."

"I'm sure he's got to be around somewhere," said Jacob, managing to find his voice. "Perhaps he needed some time alone. You know how he is."

"Yes...that's what worries me," mumbled Anahel. The concern etched in his face quickly left him momentarily as he turned a renewed focus on Jacob. "Should I inquire as to why I find you wandering these floors instead of being in class where you belong?"

"I was just on my way," answered Jacob.

"See that you are. Need I bear reminding your pupillage is of particular importance and being closely watched?"

He remained looking down from above watching as Jacob directed himself with some reluctance down one of the winding hallways leading to the Library. When eventually he reached the Library's arched entry, Jacob found its large wooden doors open. He peered inside and saw his fellow classmates hunched over their seats quietly at work. Jacob then immediately set his eyes in search of Thaniel, but thankfully he wasn't anywhere to be seen. Taking a deep breath of relief, he stepped as quietly and quickly as he could across the wide stretch of floor separating himself from the rows of study tables where he accidentally bumped Max while sliding himself as inconspicuously as he could into his visibly empty chair.

"Where'd you come from?" asked Max somewhat glumly.

As expected, Jacob ignored him as if he had sat down next to a neighboring empty chair.

"Earth to Jacob, you're being paged," whispered Leos, leaning back in his chair from the table directly in front of where Jacob was seated. "Where have you been since yesterday?"

"Long story," answered Jacob. "I'll tell you about it later."

"We were worried about you, the way you just took off like you did," Ethan piped in from nearby. And, in fact, Jacob could see there was legitimate concern in his friend's eyes. "I don't think a one of us slept all night waiting for you to turn up. So what happened?"

Before Jacob could hush Ethan there came an echoing slam of a book that commanded all eyes to look up in unison to where Thaniel had suddenly appeared.

"Yes, Mr. Parrish," he said with his gaze fixed intently on Jacob. "I'd be interested to learn the answer to that question, myself."

A sense of dread came over Jacob as he slowly rose up from his chair when the angel motioned to him to come forward.

"Return your focus to your work!" instructed Thaniel over his shoulder to his students and immediately the curious eyes that watched as Jacob was led to a far corner of the Library shifted back in perfect synchronicity to the open books before them. When Thaniel had led the way far enough out of the reach of prying ears, he turned to Jacob, who was surprised to find the angel's face friendly and full of warmth as always.

"I must say," Thaniel began, "I expected you would have found yourself in the belly of the Nekcri by now."

His words brought a look of naivety to Jacob.

"What's a Nekcri?"

The inquiry was wholly truthful in its ignorance, for any memory of his face-to-face encounter with the tentacular creature had been successfully purged from his mind thanks to Johiel.

"It's not important, at this point," murmured Thaniel dismissively as his intense gaze carefully studied the boy's face. "I presume by your obvious presence before me that you failed in your attempt to pass through the Gate?"

The question made Jacob direct his eyes away from the angel as he once more was confronted by the unpleasant memory of his cowardice. It was a look that did not go unnoticed by Thaniel. His eyes suddenly brightened and Jacob could sense the angel was scouring his thoughts. It was both an unmistakable and uncomfortable feeling; like being unknowingly watched while showering by a predacious eye peering through the keyhole of a bathroom door. And while the memories Thaniel perused offered mostly visions of the utter blackness lurking inside the Gate passageway, the overwhelming doubt and fear that accompanied Jacob halfway through before sending him back to Eden's shores in reluctant retreat were more than clear enough.

"Don't mistake cowardliness with the smarts of instinct that redirected your course from that which you most certainly would have perished had you attempted to go alone through the Gate," said Thaniel.

"The question is why would you even consider taking such a risk? And more importantly, what would make you suddenly want to flee the splendor that is Eden and return to the mortal world?"

"Don't pretend you don't know when you know exactly the reason," Jacob replied curtly, turning a look of utter contempt onto Thaniel. "I know what you're plotting."

"Plotting? Plotting!" The word seemed to catch Thaniel off guard. "Sounds most nefarious. And just what exactly have I been scheming that has caused you to aim the unmistakably accusatory tone upon your tongue at me?"

"You're planning to kill Gotham." spat Jacob.

Thaniel instantly became stone-faced and gray in light of the accusation, and Jacob noticed an uncomfortable contraction made visible in his throat.

"Did my ears hear you right?" whispered Thaniel. "You lack the courage to trespass through the Gate, yet you manage to summon the bravery to hurl such a vile falsehood concerning my brother to my face."

"It's not a falsehood. I heard it myself," argued Jacob.

"You heard me speak of killing Gothamel?"

"Yes. Well...not exactly," answered Jacob, his adamant tone suddenly softening. "It was told to me."

Thaniel's eyebrows climbed higher upon his forehead. "Told to you? I grow more intrigued with every word passing your lips. And who may I ask served as courier of this most portentous message?"

Jacob was visibly reluctant to answer at first.

"Birds."

Thaniel's grimace faded behind the growing smirk of someone who'd just been regaled with an amusing joke, and what began as a light chuckle bloomed into a full, hearty laugh that filled the Library. Jacob glanced over to his classmates as, one by one, their studious gazes left their books to see what the ruckus was about.

"Did I hear you correctly to say birds?" asked Thaniel once he managed to catch a breath and stifle his laugh.

"That's right," answered Jacob with a tone carrying an edge of annoyance. "Two mockingbirds, one of which spoke in your voice."

Thaniel became giddier. "And on this most damning of evidence you've come to levy against me this most venomous of allegations with the same unquestionable certainty one puts his head to the pillow at night knowing the morning will rise out of the east. Tell me the fate of so many doesn't rest in the hands of an anointed one who shows himself to be so gullible to the chatter of birds?"

The angel's mocking tone and matching smirk only served to invigorate in Jacob a slow-burning aggravation rather than leave him to suffer the gnawing discomfort of embarrassment.

"Fair enough. But it wasn't a mockingbird that stood in front of me, looked me in the face and told me the Through that exists in the Silent Forest leads into one of the six other Heavens when in fact it's a pitfall straight to the Underneath, was it?" said Jacob clearly and with measured force.

The levity Thaniel enjoyed dissipated as quickly as it had appeared at the mention of the forbidden forest and the dark secret it held.

"Then, it's true," he mumbled in disbelief as he took a step backward.

"What's true?" grumbled Jacob.

He could feel his classmates curiously stealing peeks towards his direction out of the corners of their eyes, but they were quick to return their attention back to their instructed reading when Thaniel suddenly turned and briskly made his way over to the group.

"You're dismissed for today," he announced abruptly.

Before Thaniel could have a change of heart, the boys jumped out of their seats with elation and quickly gathered up their things. Then, once the last boy was ushered out, the doors to the Library swung shut leaving Jacob and Thaniel alone inside. For a time, Thaniel stood listening to the chatter and laughter which lingered behind in the hallways before eventually fading away.

"Believe it or not, there was once a time not so long ago when all of Havenhid was as somber and lifeless as a mausoleum," he said in a quiet introspective tone. "When Gothamel's son David died, so too did a part of Eden. As angels, we rarely look upon the passing of a soul through tears as mortals do. Why mourn that which should not be mourned? Then again, our eyes allow us to see the blanket of light awaiting to warm one crossing over and not the cold dark shroud draped over the brittle shell of the cocoon left behind. But this...this was different. I don't think there was a one of us who wasn't, in some way, deeply wounded by David's death...even Eksel, if you can imagine it."

His eyes turned to the far corners of the Library, and then upwards to its highest point, as if his attention was being pulled by some beckoning voice lost to Jacob's ears.

"I've never quite felt completely at ease inside this most beautiful of sanctuaries Eden has created for us since then," said Thaniel. "When the Darkness finds a way to steal inside the safest of havens and, with such cunningness, quietly leads one of your own down a crooked, thorny path where his end lies in wait at the very last paver, it leaves behind the most unsettling of feelings that never ebbs, especially for us Guides. As guardians, our newfound sole responsibility has been to watch over and make strong you most impressionable sons of angels against such dark tides. For the past fifty years, the Silent Forest has become a telltale scar, serving as a reminder of our greatest failure since generations of Nephilim have come into our care. I knew such torment would never cease shadowing us until we found a way to remove the scar."

"You still haven't answered my question," said Jacob, who had been listening intently to every word the angel spoke, yet finding them void of any answer he sought. "If what you say is true, then why didn't you tell me the truth about the Through in the Forest?"

A pained look suddenly surfaced on Thaniel's face.

"That's just it, Jacob," he answered quietly, "I did tell you the truth about the Through and where it leads."

"Heaven is not the truth!"

"I never told you the Through led to a heaven," replied Thaniel coolly.

The assertion made Jacob's eyes widen and glimmer with golden sparks of rage.

"That's a lie, and you know it!" he growled, and even the split-second thought of being struck down where he stood by a bolt of lightning for speaking in such a manner to an angel failed to make him bite down on his tongue.

"Are you to stand here before me and tell me you can't remember?" questioned Thaniel. "After all it hasn't been that many nights removed I found you wandering about here in this very Library and you asked me about the Silent Forest as we were coming down those stairs right over there."

Jacob's gaze moved to the spiral staircase Thaniel motioned to a short distance away.

"I remember clearly what you told me and Max coming down those stairs, and there's no way I would have mistaken or misheard being told about a Through leading to the Underneath with one going in the opposite direction."

Thaniel became noticeably quiet.

"You and Max?"

"That's right."

"But…it was just you I had the conversation with that night."

"Funny," said Jacob with an unamused slanted grin.

"I'm not trying to be," Thaniel, completely straight-faced, answered in return.

"Max was the one who brought up the Silent Forest in the first place," said Jacob, his voice climbing. "He was the one who asked you about why it was forbidden."

"Again, it was just you and I who spoke here that night. You were the one who breached the subject," said the angel.

Jacob wanted to grab hold of Thaniel and shake him hard.

"THAT'S A LIE!"

"What cause would I have to lie about such a thing?" asked

Thaniel.

"I don't know...for the same reason Max lied to Gotham about being with me inside the Silent Forest," barked Jacob angrily.

Thaniel recognized with a look of sympathy the clear frustration that had managed to grip tightly the boy.

"Yes, I heard all about it when Gotham came to speak to me early this morning," said Thaniel, speaking with an unusual calmness. "And if you calm yourself for just a moment, I may be able to help you make some sense of what I believe may be happening by telling you exactly what I told him after much thought."

And so Jacob took a steadying breath and allowed himself to listen as Thaniel proceeded to repeat his conversation with Gotham—not the truth of how he threatened to unleash the wretched inhabitants of the Underneath onto Eden unless Destiny was handed over to him, but the more believable revelation of the Darkness once more reaching out from the eternal pit to twist to its will the one revealed to be Light Bearer, just as it had so successfully with Gotham's son. And every lying word that passed through Thaniel's lips was made all the more credible by the masterfully unyielding sincerity which lit up the angel's face like a candle illuminating a window at the darkest hour of night, as well as a potent sincerity lacing his voice—a sincerity Jacob had never before once thought to question and often regarded more than any other. Yet Thaniel could wisely see the boy was far from gullible, even about things which easily lent itself to moments of gullibility such as the ways of the Darkness—and Light, for that matter. And Throughs. And mysterious ladies found lurking in even more mysterious pools in the middle of peculiar forests.

"What about Lilith?" questioned Jacob.

"Lilith?"

"The lady in the water," explained Jacob who was becoming clearly agitated. "I saw you speaking to her in the Silent Forest...scheming to get the Sword of Destiny away from Gotham."

"Are you certain about that which you allege?" asked Thaniel. "Just a couple breaths ago you stood accusing me of plotting the murder of my own brother."

"Then you deny you're not after the sword?"

Again, there was nothing to suggest Thaniel was caught off guard by the continuing interrogation—at least, not outwardly. In fact, it seemed from his calm collective demeanor that he anticipated such a question—gladly, even.

"My but your mind has certainly become a tangled knot of suspicion, hasn't it?" Thaniel mused in a most sympathetic of voices. "I can't help but contemplate how many times you've sought my voice of wisdom inside this very room about all the things outside the reach of your knowledge, and yet remained silent about the one thing you thought you knew without question, even as it obviously ate at your insides. All you had to do was ask and I would have explained to you my interest in the sword rests solely on your behalf, and this entire misconception could have been avoided."

"What do you mean my behalf?"

"The Sword of Destiny has always been fated to find its place in the hands of the Light Bearer," explained Thaniel. "When it was discovered you, in fact, were the anointed one, my thoughts turned immediately to Gothamel, and more importantly the sword. It is no secret the death of his son, and what brought it about, remains an obvious and burdensome weight on Gotham. Trust—what little there is of it—is not something Gotham holds in great supply, and I wasn't sure Gotham would ever find within himself the mettle to relinquish yet again the sword into the hands of another Nephilim. Perhaps I was wrong for sticking my nose into such matters, but you see I care a great deal about Gothamel, and I know the longer he assumes the mantle of curator over the object that brought about the death of his boy, the longer that dark day would continue to hang around his neck like some insufferable yoke. All I was seeking to do was free him of such binds. Can you not understand that?"

Jacob said nothing at first as Thaniel stepped closer toward the boy, and as he did he saw the lingering suspicion with which Jacob stood eyeing him was beginning to slowly ebb.

"Look closely upon me, Jacob," instructed the angel as he sought to put out the last glimmer of doubt he spied flickering in the boy's eyes, like some pesky mosquito in need of squashing, by shaping his own into two warm hearths of nurturing kindness. "Have I once in all the time we've come to know one another offered you a moment before now in which to doubt me? Surely, by now, you've come to know how fond I've become of you. That you would cast a look of suspicion my way, and worse, be led to believe such repugnant whisperings that I would bring harm to one of my own brothers without trusting to come to me first hurts me to the most center of my being."

Jacob couldn't help but feel a swell of remorse rise up inside him for allowing himself to so easily believe what he had about Thaniel, forcing him to bow his head with shame. Yet it was quickly overshadowed by fear brought about by an even more overwhelming sense of confusion.

"What's happening to me, Thaniel?" he asked.

"Nothing yet for which you need to feel shame," answered Thaniel. "Unfortunately, now that the Darkness has learned you are no ordinary Nephilim, it's not likely you will find peace from its presence until, like the Light Bearer before you, it has succeeded in using its warping and twisting ways to lead you to a similar fate."

It was not an answer Jacob found to be filled with reassurance—nor comfort.

"When I first came here, Gotham advised me how to handle the reality of being in Eden if it ever began feeling unreal...you know...like as if living inside a dream," said Jacob. "I wish he would've told me what to do if it ever suddenly felt like a nightmare. Because right now that's exactly how it feels."

Thaniel placed a comforting hand on the boy's shoulder.

"You look to the angels in whose safekeeping you've been placed, and you trust them to guide you through the danger," said Thaniel with a smile. "That is why, even before you stepped foot in the Library this morning, I had already put into motion a plan I hope will make it more difficult for the Darkness to stalk your scent."

A gleam of hope illuminated Jacob's face. "What do you mean? How?"

"The Through in the Silent Forest," said Thaniel. "Since the day of David's demise, the mere existence of a passageway linking Eden to the Underneath and the threat it served to the one Nephilim who might one day be led by curiosity to stumble upon it has haunted me. It was only when I learned the promise of a Light Bearer we once thought lost to us had returned did I come to understand the urgency of barricading such a gate for good."

"That's what you meant earlier when you mentioned removing the scar from the Silent Forest, isn't it?" asked Jacob. "But is it possible?"

"I believe there is a way," said Thaniel.

Before the angel could explain further, a look of clarity suddenly settled upon Jacob.

"The Sword of Destiny," he mumbled to himself. "That's where Gotham's gone, isn't it?"

Thaniel nodded. "To fetch it from whatever hole in the ground he has had it stashed away in such an unworthy fashion all this time and bring it to me."

It was indeed welcome news to Jacob. But a look of puzzlement was quick in returning to the boy.

"Then...the night I saw you in the Silent Forest—"

"Scheming to get my hands on Destiny?" said Thaniel quickly finishing Jacob's thoughts with a chuckle. "No, it was not a twisted illusion of the Darkness' doing. Neither was it what you believed to have witnessed. A scheme yes, but only on my part to draw down Lilith's defenses. One doesn't just walk up to the threshold of the Underneath with the Sword of Destiny in hand and not expect all the powers of the Darkness to rise up in defense."

Thaniel then watched with the most cloaked look of contentment as Jacob's body relaxed itself into the bedding of lies he had been tucked into unknowingly. Still, as Jacob's gaze wandered about the heights of the Library as his thoughts continued to swarm him, he couldn't fathom Gotham relinquishing Destiny to anyone—even Thaniel.

"I'm not so sure he could just give it up after paying the ultimate price to ensure its safekeeping—even on my behalf."

"I had my doubts as well," agreed Thaniel. "Then again, Gothamel was always partial to reason, especially when the fate of those he loved most depended upon it. And now with your inevitable Blessing upon us, I think he realizes we must be ever vigilant in your safety.

Not entirely convinced, Jacob realized all he could do was wait and see how well Thaniel had managed to reason with Gotham. When he turned to leave the Library, however, he was quickly halted by Thaniel.

"Where do you think you're going?" asked the angel.

"You let the rest of the class go."

"That I did. But they were also here in their seats and fast to their studies first thing this morning and not snoozing away on some beach," Thaniel replied sternly yet with pleasant grin.

Jacob was then instructed to take his seat amongst the empty chairs surrounding him and before he could argue further, a book summoned from one of the shelves fell from the upper reaches of the Library and landed with a loud thud on the table before him. Jacob's eyes caught a quick glimpse of the title—"Summa Theologiæ" by Thomas Aquinas— before the book suddenly opened and the pages fluttered one after the other in rapid succession before stopping at the beginning of the third chapter.

~ ~ ~

For much of the day, Jacob was found hunched over the book reading page after page, and chapter after chapter, and for the first time he was less than fully enthralled with being in the Library and the knowledge awaiting discovery inside its numerous books. Instead, he found himself unable to focus his wandering attention and the philosophical musings about the existence of God and man's ultimate purpose became a blurring of words as reading became a more and more strenuous struggle. With each passing hour, his body slumped ever lower into his chair as the sunlight filtering into the Library from high above danced about him with the soon emerging shadows. Finally, just when Jacob was certain he couldn't read another word, relief arrived in the sound of Thaniel's voice.

"Gothamel should be returning soon," he said.

The sound of Gotham's name brought a light to Jacob's dour face. "Do you mind if I go with you to meet him?"

"I think it would be most appropriate that you be there to greet him with me," answered Thaniel.

Beaming, Jacob sprang over to Thaniel who took hold of the boy and unfolded his wings. They ascended upward to the Library's domed roof past the Greffiers guarding the cache of sacred tomes and writings. And just as it looked as though they were going to smash through the massive arched panes of one of the etched-glass windows, Jacob closed tightly his eyes. Only there was no glass; just a hallucination formed from empty space through which they passed without injury. Instantly, they burst through the top of the trees and were soaring high over the Garden where Thaniel abruptly veered northward toward the waterfalls spilling their way with picturesque beauty down the sheer mountain cliffs behind a rising ghostly veil of mist.

When they finally touched ground again, it was at Broken Earth. No one was there except for a noted peacefulness which almost seemed to be a presence unto itself. Jacob immediately assumed watch to the south searching carefully for any sign of Gotham to appear amid the vastness of Eden that went on for as far as the eye could see. Thaniel, however, stood silently at the edge of the wide cloud-cloaked gorge where the Nephilim bravely leapt for their wings. His eyes were closed and a stillness masked his youthful beauty with just the slightest of breezes giving life to the wisps of his hair hanging across his forehead. Thinking the angel was praying, Jacob refrained from talking and continued with his search of the skies. Still, he couldn't help but wonder what the voice coming from above who Thaniel silently conversed with must have sounded like.

For a long time they waited. The sun, which had burned so brightly, began to grow weak and in its last bid to dazzle, it began to slowly spin the brilliant blue sky into gold as it bended deeper to the west. Thaniel's shadow stretched itself longer across the earth, and after what seemed as though hours had ticked by during his silence, he turned his face skyward and inhaled deeply the air before his eyes suddenly opened.

"The hour I've long-awaited for finally approaches."

CHAPTER TWENTY

THE HOUR OF SHADOWS

No sooner had Thaniel spoken those words, did Anahel suddenly appear, dropping from the sky and landing with a graceful strength.

"A rather cryptic message you sent asking to meet you here, Thaniel," he said, showing a brief moment of surprise when he spied Jacob sitting on a nearby rock who in turn looked equally surprised at the sight of the angel.

Thaniel stood quietly staring northward at the snow-capped peaks of mountain stretching toward the heavens.

"Beautiful, is it not?" he commented finally. "This has always been my favorite place in all Eden, for nowhere else quite reflects its majesty as profoundly."

"I've never found the Northern Lands to be a particularly beautiful sight myself," Anahel remarked gruffly before dismissively turning his back to the gorge and what lied beyond it in favor of the view to the south.

"Sadly, it's been a while since I last cast my gaze from these cliffs," continued Thaniel, moving to stand beside Anahel. "At first I thought it was because the beauty seen from here proved at times too overwhelming to rest one's gaze upon. For who can bear witness to such creation and not be rendered truly humbled, even angels who have witnessed so many humbling creations? But then I came to realize it wasn't the weight of humility that made my visits here infrequent, but the envy."

Anahel's brow dug down into the bridge of his nose. "Envy?"

"Envy of you, Anahel, and the rule you've held over this wondrous Heaven."

"There is only one who rules over Eden, and it is certainly not I," Anahel said brusquely. "My role is nothing more than guardian, custodian and procurator of its well-being as well as its inhabitants. You of all know better than to infer otherwise."

"So I am rightly corrected," said Thaniel apologetically to the sharp reprimand.

Jacob was suddenly on his feet and pointing to the sky in the distance.

"The other Guides are headed this way," he announced, "and what looks to be all of Havenhid."

Sure enough Damiel, Zuriel and Eksel could be seen fast approaching Broken Earth from the valley below with the rest of the Nephilim flapping their wings behind them, and a pleased look slowly came to Thaniel.

"Tell me, Anahel," he said, "have you ever come to ponder what it would be like should your rule—forgive me—that is your guardianship over this paradise were to ever be lost to you?"

Anahel narrowed his gaze on Thaniel who wandered out onto a buttress of rock overlooking the Garden, and a bothersome, unwanted feeling crept over him.

"That's a strange question coming from you, Thaniel," noted Anahel unable to keep the tinge of suspicion from being heard in his voice.

"Is it?" said Thaniel in a most off-handed manner. "I guess then I'm alone in mulling such things about in my mind."

The fact such thoughts even found a way into Thaniel's head immediately struck Anahel as odd and even off-putting, and for the first time that he could ever recall doing so, Anahel found himself casting a questionable eye Thaniel's way.

"For what purpose, may I ask, did you summon me here, Thaniel?" inquired Anahel. "The longer I stand here the more certain I am it was not to awe at the view."

"Patience, Anahel," answered Thaniel.

"Patience is a virtue I am in short supply of today, as I have a great many tasks I still need to complete. Or have you forgotten tomorrow marks the end of Illumination?"

"And the Blessing of young Jacob here. On the contrary, it is at the forefront of my mind," said Thaniel. "But bear with me, if you will, for I guarantee you what is about to occur here will be the most illuminating thing you will have witnessed in quite some time."

There was an unfamiliar ominousness in Thaniel's voice never before heard by Anahel, and its foreignness made him turn a cautious eye to the approaching sound of beating wings as numerous fluttering shadows were seen passing across his face cast by the band of Nephilim accompanied by the three remaining Guides gliding overhead before coming to rest their feet on the ground.

~ ~ ~

"I thank you for being so prompt in answering my message," Thaniel said to the group now assembled at the top of the mountain.

"So...what's with all the mystery?" asked Damiel.

"I'm not entirely sure," answered Anahel. "Thaniel here is promising a most illuminating revelation. Already, he has reflected a most curious light in his musings concerning an Eden absent my guiding hand."

Thaniel gave Anahel a sideways glance and smiled. "Ironic, it is, to hear a tone of suspicion in your voice when just seconds ago you so modestly—meekly even—bowed away from being called ruler of Eden. And now suddenly your back is slowly beginning to arch like that of a cat whose territory has been threatened by an approaching canine."

"And is there someone you have chosen to cast in the role of dog in your analogy?" asked Anahel as the look on his face became more austere, even as Thaniel's smile broadened.

Jacob felt a growing uneasiness as he stood quietly off to the side listening, while at the same time trying to ignore the other Guides' own suspicious looks shift his way as they suddenly took notice of his presence.

"Now that I have all of you gathered, I will keep this as succinct and to the point as possible as Anahel has already made clear he'd rather keep his attention focused on what will undoubtedly be a most marked moment in your young lives," said Thaniel, addressing the gathering of Fledglings before him. "As it should be, as well as it should be for all, for who amongst us could have foreseen the journey we began so many months ago leading to and through the days and weeks of Illumination would end with the most surprising and unexpected presence of our once thought to be lost Light Bearer standing in your midst?"

Jacob immediately felt a surge of heat envelope his head. His ears, especially, felt as though they had inexplicably been set afire as every set of eyes fixed themselves on him. This was not what he had in mind when he agreed to accompany Thaniel to Broken Earth, he thought while smiling in a most awkward and bashful way.

"Illumination by its very definition means to bring forth by light; here in Eden it's come to mean enlightenment both spiritually and intellectually," continued Thaniel, drawing the attention back his way much to Jacob's relief. "I think you would all be in agreement the last several months you have spent here training have proven to be a most learned—and I dare say, enlightening—experience you will remember for some time. From Zuriel, you have come to hone the special gifts of your given Graces while Damiel has helped turn you into untouchable warriors. And as I watched you all climb the wind with ease on your way here just moments ago, I see Eksel has made the sky as comfortable to you as the ground is beneath your feet."

Thaniel's uplifting words only served to dampen Jacob's spirits as he was reminded, all too well, of his back as bare as the day he came to Eden. It didn't matter that he held the distinction of Light Bearer; if anything, it only seemed to enhance for him the wingless failure he remained amongst his winged classmates.

"Myself," continued Thaniel, "I hope I succeeded in filling your minds with untold treasures of knowledge that will serve you in as equal a manner as your sword, your wings and your Graces."

Yet despite his hopeful words, a sullen, broody look quietly settled itself on the angel, and the look in his eyes became noticeably darker.

"I wish I could say the many Illuminations that have passed here with the shedding of years have served me with as much clarity," said Thaniel. "But this garden paradise holds silent an unspoken history that has left such celebrations measurably dim in my eyes."

"What do you mean?" asked Damiel. "What unspoken history?"

Thaniel looked to Anahel.

"I've no doubt Anahel knows of what I speak."

The Guides turned their attention to Anahel, who appeared almost like a statue in his stillness as he stood with his gaze leveled firmly on Thaniel. If indeed he knew what Thaniel was referring to in all his cloaked inferences, he did not say so outright; at first.

~ ~ ~

"Anahel?" said Damiel, finally giving the angel a verbal nudge.

"I thought we had come to peace on this matter," said Anahel softly yet sternly to Thaniel.

"How can there be peace where there exists no reparations?" answered Thaniel.

"Reparations, for what?" asked Eksel.

Hearing the growing agitation amongst the Guides, Anahel finally spoke loud and clear so nothing he said would be misheard by the waiting ears.

"Your brother here apparently remains embittered by a twisted impression which long ago made its way into his brain that I somehow stole something of great value from him," he said. "What he has failed to grasp surprisingly to this day is the realization that what he has long- accused me of stealing from him was never his to be taken."

"Steal? Steal what?" demanded Damiel.

"Eden," came Anahel's voice deep and definite.

The accusation stirred from Damiel a chuckle of disbelief.

"You're joking, Thaniel, right?"

There was no hint of humor to be found, or any expression for that matter, on Thaniel's face except a dripping resentment.

"Laugh if you will, Damiel, but Anahel knows the truth of which I speak whether he chooses to admit it out loud or not. But be assured, it is a wrong I intend to make right this very day."

"Be careful of such threats, Thaniel," warned Zuriel.

"Be assured brother, it is no threat," said Thaniel, looking suddenly less grim and challenging, which left those listening questioning the precise nature of his intentions. "Which is why I wanted you all to enjoy this final sunset of Illumination, especially you, Anahel."

While gesturing to the massive orb of orange dipping lower into the west which reflected itself brilliantly in his eyes, Thaniel smiled pleasantly, like the host of a grand party attending to his guests, which made the next words to come from his mouth all the more difficult to fathom: "For by the time the sun falls dark behind those ridge of mountains, so too will your days at Eden's helm."

Cries of "traitor" erupted from Damiel, Zuriel and Eksel while simultaneously they closed ranks with one another to form a wall of strength as they stepped toward Thaniel ready to meet his insubordinate words with brute force. They were instantly stilled with the raising of Anahel's right hand.

"What shadowy scheme have you allowed to burrow its way into your feverish brain?" asked Anahel in a cool but fire-laced voice. "What's more, how can you stand before me and speak such things knowing I can bring the wrath of Heaven down upon your head?"

"Your power, Anahel, is great; of this we all know," answered Thaniel. "The four of you could easily overtake me like cats batting a mouse with their paws; this I also know. But your intuitive pause just now serves you well, Anahel, for you know me all too well to know such a brash declaration as the one I have just made would never leave my tongue without planning long and carefully for this moment. My days and nights are spent in constant vigil with the leavings of the greatest minds to ever put forth thought. Do you think I would stand here before you with not a sign of fear to be had and proclaim such an ambitious boast if I was not already certain of the outcome?"

The corners of Thaniel's mouth curled like the edges of a leaf made crisp by a hot summer sun as he watched the faces of the Guides struggling to shirk the feel of caution suddenly clasping each of their shoulders. "Think hard the answer as you continue to caress the hilts of your swords with your vengeful anger."

"He's bluffing," Zuriel spat.

"I invite you to test your theory, Zuriel," challenged Thaniel. "Perhaps you will proudly find yourself right. And maybe—just maybe—you will be shown with great horror what the Darkness can do to Eden and all its inhabitants in a blink of an eye when unleashed from the Silent Forest."

The insinuation of such a thing seemed to instantly sap the blood from Anahel and the other angel's faces.

"You would do such a thing?" asked Anahel with great disbelief in his voice.

"That is a question worthy of careful pondering, isn't it: Would I, or wouldn't I?" answered Thaniel. "The even greater question is whether you are willing to risk finding out the answer."

~ ~ ~

An unsettling silence fell upon the mountain top as Anahel stared out over Eden with only a blank look of dismay in his eyes, and then at the Nephilim standing about behind him looking somewhat confused over what was occurring and not completely coherent of the dark threatening hand that had instantly been placed over them.

"This is the boy's doing. He's put Thaniel up to this, I know it!" Eksel suddenly blurted venomously while pointing a damning finger in Jacob's direction.

Jacob was completely caught off-guard and shocked by the anger suddenly leveled his way, as he was just as gobsmacked as everyone else, if not more, with what he was hearing coming from Thaniel's mouth.

"I warned you against allowing this demon seed into our midst," continued Eksel in his rant. "Now, see what has happened? He has poisoned and perverted our brother's mind. You should have allowed me to run my blade through him the night he was first brought here and rid our fair Eden of this blight that has shown itself a cancer."

A look of alarm came to Jacob at the sight of the threatening angel beginning to advance on him.

"Stand back!" commanded Anahel in a gruff bark that stopped Eksel fast in his tracks.

Jacob breathed once more with relief, but it was short-lived when he recognized a keen look in Anahel's eyes that was fixed hard on him. It was a questioning look—the kind one allows to linger on a person they hold suddenly in suspicion of betrayal, and it proved to be as unsettling as it was heavy in weight. And as he then looked to his fellow Nephilim, Jacob saw they all had the exact same look directed his way. It made him want to scream out the utter naivety he shared with them at what was taking place before them, and as he opened his mouth in hopes of finding his voice it was Thaniel's that was heard.

"Don't blame the boy," he declared. "You think so little of me to assume I could so easily find myself under the thumb of a Fledgling? But I hear your thoughts, Anahel, and sympathize with your desperate attempt to make sense of how an angel such as myself could willingly choose to step down from the ranks. And as hard as it might be for you to fathom, sometimes an angel comes to know desires that stem not from the whisperings purred from the Darkness."

"I'm well aware of these desires, Thaniel. And just like you, I've seen those desires take hold of many of my brothers more times than I care to count, and together we have witnessed where it leads them," said Anahel with marked disdain. And despite the fire that had returned to his eyes ever so briefly, yet burned ever so intensely, so too came a noticeable resignation that was upsetting for all who caught sight of it. "For the well-being of Eden and the Nephilim gathered here, I will adhere to what it is you demand. Though it is not mine to pass onto you, I will relinquish my power here. But beware your flagrant disregard for that which looms so large above you. For surely you know, in all your intellect you tout with such pride and arrogance, Heaven will never stand by silently in the face of your attempted thievery."

Thaniel only smiled and put a finger to his lips signaling quiet from Anahel.

"Do you hear that?" he asked as gentle gusts whistled their way through crevices and passes in the mountain and rustled nearby trees. "In just a few moments, when the sun grazes Day's Rest, you will see why Heaven will continue to stand silent and fail you in your needed aid."

All eyes then followed Thaniel's shifting gaze westward where the sun was slowly sinking toward the stately mountain peaks looming in the distance. The sky now looked to be consumed by fire spreading its way in far-reaching flames of glorious color. All was still in those final moments as the blazing ball of light came to rest upon Eden's highest mountain point. Then as it began to slip ever so slowly behind the ridge, the anticipation on Thaniel's face started to dim, and for a moment he began to wonder if the absence of Gotham's anticipated return meant he was being called on his promised threat.

~ ~ ~

Suddenly, three winged figures swooped down from the sky, and a subtle sign of relief came to Thaniel's face when he saw one was Gotham. He was flanked on either side by Acruxel and Caphel.

"You're late," grumbled Thaniel pointedly to Gotham.

"I'm here," returned Gotham surly. There was a noticeable smoldering of contempt in his eyes and they anxiously searched amongst the faces of the boys gathered on the mountain top until they finally found Jacob, and only then did Gotham seem to relax somewhat.

"I didn't expect that you would have assembled an audience."

"And deny myself the pleasure of sharing this most momentous of occasions?" said Thaniel.

"Then you've told them your plan?"

"More or less. Can you not tell from the pleased looks on their faces?

Gotham could see the faces staring back at him were anything but pleased; most notably Anahel's.

"You knew of this, Gothamel?" asked Anahel in a voice that held a tremble of both anger and the sadness of betrayal.

"I'm sorry," was all Gotham could bring himself to say as he looked away, unable to bear the sight of the wounded hurt that had managed to pierce such a vision of strength as Anahel.

Belligerent, hostile words were suddenly spewed forth and the strength of both Damiel and Zuriel was needed to physically restrain Eksel who lunged hate-filled at Gotham who could also see Zuriel and Damiel shared in the same contempt often seen spawned from torch-wielding mobs now aimed his way. While the two angels struggled with all their might to hold back Eksel, it was clear it took an even stronger will within themselves to keep from joining in with their brother.

Anahel bellowed once more for order.

"What of the two of you, as if I need ask?" Anahel, looking with stern disapproval at both Acruxel and Caphel, inquired. "It didn't take you long to begin recruiting from Eden's ranks, did it, Thaniel?"

"You have your army, and I have mine," answered Thaniel.

"And Betryal?"

"Inside the Silent Forest waiting for the command I truly hope you don't force me to give."

Anahel took a deep, grievous breath while glowering with the profound indignation of betrayal.

"You do Heaven a favor by revealing your weak, wavering allegiance," he said with a quiet yet cutting tongue.

Pleased by the defeated look in Anahel's eyes, Thaniel turned to face Gotham.

"I trust you brought it."

He then watched with growing enticement as Gotham brought into view a bundle of burlap which had been tucked protectively beneath his left arm.

"Go ahead," said Gotham with grim resignation. "It's what you wanted. Take it."

For a moment no longer than a deep sigh, Thaniel stood staring at the coveted bundle but he made not a move to take possession of it.

"You offend me, Gothamel," he said finally with disappointment while looking into Gotham's face with eyes full of distrust. "Do you think me fool enough to not know that one cannot simply take the sword from the one who has already laid claim to it lest he be stricken down by death? It must be bequeathed by the hand who holds it into the one who desires it."

A sly grin came to Gotham.

"Surely, you cannot fault me for trying," he said.

Then with noticeable hesitation, Gotham stretched forward his arms, and as he placed the wrapped bundle in Thaniel's hands he could feel a sea of curious eyes anxiously awaiting to see what lay hidden in the twisted burlap. Once it was fully in his grasp, Thaniel breathed deeply, and as he did a faint look of disgust twisted the pleasure on his face as the unmistakable acrid stench of burlap wafted into his nostril.

"That you would swaddle an object of such divine power in this soiled rag proves such a gift is not worthy of your hands," said Thaniel. "Then again, even the finest of spun silk would be inferior for such a treasure."

Thaniel's eyes were wild with anticipation as he held the object in his clutches. Then carefully he pulled back a flap of the burlap and a glimpse of the hilt came into view in a blinding glint of reflected light. Unable to contain himself, Thaniel stripped away the rest of the burlap like a child tearing into a present on Christmas morning, and when the sword in his hand was revealed for all to see there came a collective gasp.

"Lancea Longinus," murmured Damiel.

"The Sword of Destiny," echoed Zuriel.

Anahel stood silent, but his gaze frozen wide in disbelief said more than enough to make Gotham look to the ground in shame. Thaniel, however, showed the uncontainable revelry of one who had uncovered a horde of priceless treasure. He held high the sword with unabashed pride for all to admire, none more notably than himself. The steel gleamed with flashes of radiant light against the fiery tint of dusk as he slowly turned the fantastical weapon clutched tight in his grip before his star-struck gaze. Yet it was not the sword's beauty that held Thaniel transfixed, but the power of which he knew resided in the not-so-beautiful spearhead cradled in the center of the blade.

"What could possess you to even think of doing this, Thaniel?" said Damiel, in a desperate bid to keep his composure. "You were our brother. Eden was your home."

"And so it will continue to be my home," answered Thaniel.

"We most certainly will not remain your brothers," spat Damiel before turning his scowl onto Gotham. "And you...how could you so willingly betray that which continued to embrace you long after Heaven washed its hands clean of you?"

Gotham ignored Damiel, stinging as the words spit from the angel's lips were, and kept his attention firmly fixed on Thaniel.

"We had a deal. I expect you to honor it."

"Deal? What deal?" inquired Zuriel.

Thaniel seemed increasingly entertained in the other angels' growing perplexities.

"No...you wouldn't know about it, Zuriel. But in Gothamel's much-needed defense it should be said he proved most noble to the end in his loyalty to you."

"Loyalty," Eksel spat as if the most bitter of tastes had found his tongue.

"Yes, loyalty...that is, until I offered to give him a piece of Eden in exchange for Destiny. Certainly, you cannot find fault with him in the face of such an irresistible offer."

The revelation brought renewed scorn from the Guides, and they united themselves in an angry chorus to further berate and rage against Gotham.

"You are beneath Fallen," Damiel hissed with the upmost of contempt. "Who would have thought after all this time your soul could be traded with such ease and so cheaply. May God see you to the deepest, most desolate reaches of the Underneath for what you've done here this day."

The hateful words, however, appeared to wound Jacob more so than Gotham as he stood quietly by listening with an ever-growing look of angst and horror at what was taking place in front of him.

"It's not true...it's not true...it's not true..." he repeated to himself under his breath. Whether it was because he truly believed what he uttered, or the hope he could refuse being convinced otherwise, he wasn't sure. What he was certain of, however, was that something wasn't quite fitting together with what he was hearing and seeing; something that filled him with a strong sense of doubt, as if he had somehow slipped into a warped nightmare of reality from which he was awaiting to awaken. Whatever it was lingered in the back of his mind, hidden behind a thick, dark cloak of which he was unable to pull back no matter how hard he tried.

"IT'S NOT TRUE!" he suddenly found himself crying out bringing a moment of distracted pause to the mayhem.

"Keep out of this!" Jacob heard Gotham's voice echo in his thoughts as the angel glanced back over his shoulder, yet refusing to look directly at the boy.

"You know of what deal I speak," muttered Gotham impatiently under his breath as he turned back to Thaniel.

"The Nephilim...yes I know," said Thaniel rather indifferently. His attention was still enslaved by the sword, but Gotham noticed he was now studying the weapon with a more scrutinizing eye.

"Is something wrong?" asked Gotham while calmly watching a troubled frown etch itself deeper into Thaniel's brow.

"Damiel is right...you did sell yourself rather cheaply," answered Thaniel.

"You consider the well-being of forty-eight Nephilim cheap?" asked Gotham.

Thaniel pursed his lips and gave a dismissive shrug of his shoulders.

"They are, after all, only halflings. Certainly not worth the trade of such a priceless antiquity as this sword, even if their numbers were tenfold."

Gotham narrowed his eyes in disgust. "The velocity with which you've come to free fall in your descent is truly numbing."

"What you deem as descent," said Thaniel, grinning, "I choose to see as...evolving."

Gotham couldn't suppress his chuckle. "Evolving?"

"Laugh as you will," barked Thaniel, "but I, too, remain quite aware of whose company I keep this hour. And his shrewdness far out rivals mine."

Gotham stared straight ahead, his eyes hard and steeled as any coat of armor, even as Thaniel slowly circled around behind him while continuing to study closely the sword grasped tight in his hands.

"So, answer me this my fallen friend: How foolish would I be to uphold my end of our deal and allow you to see the Nephilim out of Eden only to find out you've left me a sword that was not the true Destiny?" asked Thaniel.

The only sign of tension Gotham showed came in the form of two knots pulsating on the sides of his face near his ears as he clenched his jaw.

"Paranoia has found your tongue, Thaniel," answered Gotham, his grin covering the unease of feeling Thaniel's presence looming uncomfortably close behind him. "Do you think I would risk these boys' lives over such a ploy?"

"Your hands were once stained with the blood of hundreds of Fledglings," said Thaniel snidely. "I find it hard to believe the sacrifice of a few more would bring a crisis of conscious to come crashing down upon you."

If ever Gotham found himself struggling to retain his control, it was at that moment, with Thaniel's mouth breathing such wicked words in reach of his ears.

"I brought you what you asked," he hissed while attempting to push down the rage he felt rising within himself. "Whether or not you can see what is plainly the Sword of Destiny in your hands is your deficiency, not mine."

"Looks are one thing, and true this sword appears to be Destiny, so much so that even I who have studied and dreamed about it so would be hard pressed to deem it a fake," said Thaniel. "But you know as well as I there is only one way to know for certain if it indeed is what you claim it to be."

And with those words Gotham slowly closed his eyes, for at that moment in a flash of speed no one looking on could see until it had come to be finished, Thaniel snatched hold of one of Gotham's wings and with a glint of steel and a cruel, determined swing of his arm severed it clean from the angel's back.

~ ~ ~

Gotham's back arched painfully and he let loose a howl of pain that echoed its way into the furthest corners of Eden before falling wounded to his knees. The Nephilim looked on with horror but none more so than Jacob, who cried out in protest, and as he attempted to lunge to Gotham's aid, he was quickly grabbed by Anahel and left to struggle with all his might to free himself from the angel's arms wrapped protectively around him.

Horrified themselves, the other three Guides instantly drew their swords, but as they came at Thaniel, he brandished Destiny at them.

"Back with you," he screamed, "or Destiny shall taste your blood as well."

A most feral look had fixed itself on his face and it made the Guides stand back with much reluctance. Each of them suddenly found themselves consumed in an almost overwhelming swell of helplessness as they found they could only look on with utter sorrow as Thaniel turned his sword back on Gotham and savagely relieved him of his other wing, which was then tossed into the ravine of the mountain.

Jacob watched through a stream of tears as Gotham writhed in his suffering upon the ground. Great amounts of what appeared to be water poured from the gaping wounds sliced in his back and it formed large pools that seeped into the dusty ground. *Blood*, Jacob thought to himself as he remembered his first day in Eden sitting with Gotham beside the River and listening to the story of how angels came into existence from water. And now he was watching it flow out of Gotham clean and clear, yet in no less gruesome fashion than if it left the well-known crimson stain of a brutal slaughter on the ground.

"A talisman of power," muttered Anahel as he looked at Thaniel with intense disbelief. "You would do all this...and strike down your own brother in the process...all for a talisman of power?"

"I'd do a whole hell of a lot more for this talisman of power," said Thaniel with a warped glee.

Struggling in his agony, Gotham looked up searching desperately the haze of faces that were staring back at him with pronounced sadness and pity until he found Jacob wrapped tight in Anahel's arms, and he saw the boy's face to be wrenched with the same anguish that had suddenly been unleashed mercilessly upon himself.

"Don't you dare weep for me, Fledging," said Gotham. His lips did not move, but Jacob could hear his voice plainly inside his head.

With all the strength he could muster, Gotham stretched a quivering hand toward Jacob who struggled with a renewed vigor in Anahel's protective arms to reach it. And when the tips of their fingers managed to hook hold of one another Jacob felt a familiar surge of warmth move through him.

"Remember what I told you that day by the Tree," Gotham gasp with pain, "about the lamb."

Jacob knew instantly to that which Gotham was referring, and when he nodded so it seemed to bring a sense of relief to the angel.

"Bring him to me," Thaniel instructed Acruxel and Caphel. Obediently, the two angels pulled Gotham from Jacob. As they did, Gotham looked one last time to Damiel and saw the contempt he had seen only moments earlier in his friend's gaze was now brimming with immense sorrow.

"Remember your promise," he managed to sputter as he was dragged to the cliff's edge overlooking the immense ravine where Thaniel stood waiting.

"I see now by the death slowly creeping over you that I was wrong in questioning whether the sword in my hand was truly Destiny. For that, you have my deepest apologies," said Thaniel as Gotham was held up on his feet before him.

To Gotham's utter surprise, he found there to be tears forming in Thaniel's eyes. Actual tears. "This is your hour, Thaniel; your hour of shadows," Gotham whispered in his struggle to speak. "For whom do you weep: me, or thee?"

The question caused Thaniel's lip to tremble visibly.

"Believe it or not, it is not hate that has brought us to this parting," said Thaniel. Then in a quieter voice he added, "Who knows, one day you may actually thank me for this moment. If nothing else, see it as a last act of mercy from me to free you from your cursed existence."

"May he be as merciful with you," said Gotham, "but I have a feeling he won't."

Thaniel knew exactly who the "he" was Gotham was referring to and he glanced over Gotham's shoulder to where Jacob stood who screamed forth a plea to him to end his attack on his friend. And with his tearing eyes once more cold and vacant firmly fixed on Jacob, Thaniel buried the blade of the sword with one deliberate thrust deep into Gotham's side. Gotham threw back his head but the cry that sounded came from Jacob, loud and untamed in its unbridled sorrow and fury, and no living creature in Eden could escape its sound.

What followed was an absolute stillness as those who looked on helplessly watched the great and mighty angel Gothamel sway and waver on his feet. And the pain etched so deeply in his face slowly receded when he suddenly turned his sights to the sky above him and his eyes grew wide as a voice so long absent to his ears came from behind a rapid gathering of clouds.

"Yes," he whispered with both surprise and ignominy, "I can hear thee."

All eyes turned to the fiery sky, including Thaniel's, but they could not see nor hear whatever it was that had taken hold so completely Gotham's attention. As he continued to stare unblinkingly upward, his face became awash in overwhelming gratitude which gave way to a solitary tear to escape the corner of his eye and slowly stream down the side of his face.

"The sacrifices of God are a broken spirit...a broken and a contrite heart...these, my father, you will not despise..." Gotham was heard to say in a hushed voice. He then seemed to listen while nodding ever so subtly before uttering his final words.

"Deus meus, ex toto corde paenitet me ómnium meórum peccatórum."

And with that, the brilliance that shone forth in his eyes like a rising golden sun slowly dimmed to cold, lifeless orbs.

"Let it not be said I am not a keeper of my word," remarked Thaniel when he finally felt Gotham's body go lax around the sword still buried in his flesh. "I promised you a piece of Eden, and a piece of Eden you shall now have. Go to it."

Then pulling the sword free, he nodded to Acruxel and Caphel who sent Gotham's lifeless body over the edge of the ravine where it disappeared into the cloud-shrouded abyss.

~ ~ ~

It was then the most rarest of sights came to visit itself upon Eden.

A growing plume of dark clouds quickly spread and engulfed fully the sky, and from it thunder began to rumble angrily. Jacob stood staring blankly at the ground where Gotham had writhed in pain after being savagely de-winged and he saw a single raindrop splash down on the dark patch of water staining the ground just a few feet away. He looked to the angry sky and was immediately greeted by a sudden and furious downpour unleashed by the heavens.

"Let all doubt now be put to rest," cried Thaniel, turning to the visibly shocked and grief-stricken Guides and their horrified teenaged charges. "You have all been made witness that I possess both the true Destiny and the unapologetic determination to wield its power."

"So help me, Thaniel, I will see to it by that sword you perish," seethed Damiel with a simmering hatred.

"Let he who itches to put to the test his strength against mine do so now, and you will lend company to Gothamel in consecrating Eden's growing graveyard," challenged Thaniel.

The sky grumbled once again with an angry thunder and Thaniel turned a furious gaze to the darkening sky and leveled at it the sword in his hand which dripped Gotham's blood.

"Well? What are you waiting for?" he cried out with a loud ferociousness. "I'M WAITING!"

He had barely finished with his outburst when there came from above an earth-quivering rumble. The clouds were illuminated with bursts of light and from them a blinding flash of lightning in the shape of a gnarled skeletal hand appeared to reach down from the heavens to violently strike Acruxel and Caphel fully on the forehead before taking aim at Thaniel.

Thaniel seemed stunned at first, his senses stolen from him. Then bringing a hand to his forehead, he instantly felt the unmistakable mark known to all Fallen angels freshly seared into his flesh. At first, it sounded as if he had begun to sob. But it soon became clear he was not crying, but laughing; light chuckles at first, and then hearty, uncontrollable laughing. And as the rain came down with ever-increasing force, Anahel directed the other Guides to begin guiding the boys back to Havenhid. Quickly they made their way down the mountain as the laughter continue to ring out behind them.

CHAPTER TWENTY-ONE

The Nephilim were swiftly returned by the Guides to the safe walls of Havenhid, where they were ordered confined to their rooms.

"Lock all doors, keep all lights doused, and dare not pass one toe across the threshold of your room until you hear otherwise by me," was all the instruction Anahel gave before he and the other Guides—sharing the same tensely unsettled look—disappeared without further word into the night. It was all strangely reminiscent of the night preparations were put in place for Azrael's visit to Eden, and yet it went without saying by the traumatized looks shared by every last boy the anticipated presence of the Angel of Death was beyond preferable to what had visited itself upon them this night.

Never had the halls of Havenhid reverberated with such empty lifelessness, and for the first time Eden failed to provide the young teenagers with the safe embrace they had come to know. The shock of what they had witnessed earlier eventually began to fade from the faces of the horrified boys. Yet it was quickly replaced with an even more painful crashing wave of grief, and no one was hit harder by it than Jacob. Stretched flat on his back atop his bed with Mist curled protectively beside him, he stared unblinkingly through the darkness filling his room at the intricate coming together of tree branches that formed the ceiling above him. However, all he could see was Gotham, mutilated and bleeding, being cast helpless into the ravine that held his demise over and over again. The constant barrage of images that came at him mercilessly brewed tears in his eyes. Still, he continued to beat them back just as he had throughout the night fearing he'd never be able to stem the flow once it started.

Nearby, his roommates also lay quietly sprawled across their beds, like corpses awaiting autopsies in a morgue. They, too, could not find escape in sleep and, like Jacob, were also silently reliving over and again the horror that had befallen Gotham. What sniffles from tears beset any of them was gratefully cloaked by the presence of the rain that continued to drum loudly outside. It was the only sound to be heard that night— that and the intermittent subtle roar of arguing voices which could now and then be heard passing through the stormy darkness like a gust of wind. They came from the fire-lit chamber behind the waterfalls where the boys undoubtedly knew the White Circle had urgently been called forth.

"What do you think they're talking about?" Ethan, unable to bear much more of the silence, whispered.

"I'll give you two guesses, genius," answered Kairo.

"You know what I mean! Do you think they're planning some sort of retaliation? I mean, they have to, right?"

"Man, I hope so," fumed Leos from his bed. "And I'll be right there with them ready to put my sword to use with their's against that traitor Thaniel after what he did."

"Your sword won't do any good. None of ours will. Just like the Guides know their's won't either," said Max.

"They could've at least tried," argued Leos. "Damiel, himself, could wipe the floor with Thaniel any day of the week. Instead, he just stood there and did nothing."

"Didn't you hear what I just said? This is the Sword of Destiny we're talking about," snapped Max. "My father told me about it once long ago and said it was nothing to mess around with. The one who has claim to it literally can bend destiny to his whim. He becomes almost untouchable. There's not an army the sword cannot defeat, man or angel. At first I thought it was some kind of legend, a myth. But after what I saw today..."

His voice trailed off, timid to even mention the course of events that had taken place only a few hours before at Broken Earth.

"That explains why Anahel looked so troubled when he saw it in Thaniel's hands," said Kairo.

"It was more than troubled; it was fear. It was in all their faces. Something I'd never seen before, or ever thought I would," said Max.

"Wouldn't you be—fearful, that is?" asked Leos. "I don't like to admit it, but I'm still shaking over what happened to Gotham. Talk about someone believed to be untouchable."

"I know I'm going to have nightmares about it," admitted Ethan. "I mean, did you see how Gotham's wings were sliced right off him?"

The others sniped at him in unison to stifle such details.

"What's the matter with you talking like that, especially with Jacob right here," cried Kairo. "We were all there...we don't need reminding about it."

Ethan looked to Jacob's bed and the darkened shape made out on it.

"I'm sorry Jacob...I didn't mean to shoot my mouth off like that," he offered apologetically.

Jacob wasn't paying any mind. He was too deeply lost in his own thoughts. Specifically, he found himself continuing in his ongoing struggle to somehow penetrate the dark shroud he felt lurking in his memory. It had felt to him like a dark knot sitting inside his skull holding tight something it refused to give up no matter how hard he tried to untie it. Yet now with each passing minute that had shaped several passing hours it seemed as though it was slowly beginning to loosen. It was almost like a flower blooming. And as each petal unfolded itself from the bud, fragmented images that had been hidden inside began to reveal themselves one by one, and then in continuous bursts.

Pitch darkness.

Monstrous tentacles coming up out of the water.

A white-flamed fire burning.

And Gotham sitting before it fervently hammering away at a shaft of steel.

As Jacob slowly became blanketed in a tapestry of memories unleashed back into his consciousness with all their attached familiarity, he suddenly sat upright in bed and gasped aloud to himself, "It's not Destiny!"

~ ~ ~

"Where're you going?" inquired Kairo when he saw Jacob get up off his bed and quickly shuffle his feet into his sneakers.

"I just need to get out for a minute...go for a walk."

"Walk? Uh, you do realize it's pouring rain outside, don't you?" said Ethan, pointing out the obvious revealed by the nearby window.

Jacob paid no mind. He grabbed for his pack lying on the floor in the corner near his bed and, as he began rummaging through it, something made him stop abruptly. With Mist watching curiously from where she lay on the bed, Jacob slowly pulled out Gotham's long, dark overcoat still folded and resting forgotten at the bottom of his bag since the day Gotham first brought him to Eden. The sight of it brought an immediate and painful pull at his heart momentarily before he gathered every last strand of strength residing inside him to steel himself and slipped into the garment. Instantly, he was reminded of Gotham's large presence when the coat swallowed his athletic frame.

"Okay, forget the rain. How about Anahel's explicit warning that we stay in our rooms tonight?"

Jacob was set to climb through the window when he paused and glanced over his shoulder in the direction of the voice to find Max peering back at him from his bed with a restrained look of concern—but concern nonetheless—fixed on his face. Instead of the rigid look of hostility Max had grown accustomed to from his friend over the past several days, there was instead a noticeable softening in the hardened veneer he didn't expect.

"Don't worry," said Jacob, in his first cordial words to Max in days. "I'll be back before you know it."

And like that, his form twisted and shrank into that of a brown sparrow and flew off into the downpour. It was one of the rare moments Jacob knew what it like to possess wings, but his time to enjoy them was short. Once he had sailed down from the heights of the trees and made the short distance downstream to the pathway on the other side of the River leading to the Tree of Life, he reverted back to his own form.

It was the darkest night he'd seen so far fall upon Eden. The moon and all it silvery brightness had been stolen from the sky without a trace.

Gone, too, was the presence of every last twinkling star, extinguished by an ominous swath of churning blackness of which there seemed to be no end. The rain was relentless, coming down in sheets. It made the River swell, and its usually tranquil flowing waters were roaring and torrential.

Jacob was about to take to the boggy pathway when he caught sight of a raven coming at him from behind. As it swooped down for a landing, its form changed to reveal Max.

"What's going on, Jacob?" he asked.

"I told you it's nothing. I just need to check something out. Now, go back," answered Jacob.

"Look, I know you hate me because you think I've somehow wronged you," said Max, "but we need to squash this thing, at least for the time being."

"I don't hate you," said Jacob. And, as he stood looking at Max, he felt a swelling of remorse inside himself as the recollection of being huddled around a fire with Gotham and Johiel on Akdamar Island and learning for the first time about the binding of memories emerged from the impenetrable fog in which it had briefly been lost. "In fact, I owe you a giant apology...if you'll take it."

The gesture seemed to catch Max by surprise, but happily.

"Well bugger me! What's happened to change your mind?"

"It's a long story, but trust me I'll explain it all later," said Jacob before turning away.

He started off for several steps up the path but stopped abruptly and returned to where Max remained standing.

"It's not Destiny!" exclaimed Jacob impatiently.

Max cocked his head at the same time his face went blank with confusion.

"What are you talking about? What's not Destiny?"

"The sword Gotham gave Thaniel at Broken Earth. It's a replica...a fake," answered Jacob.

"Get your hands off it! And you know this how exactly?"

"Because I was there...at the church on Akdamar Island. I watched Gotham make it," explained Jacob. "It's too complicated to explain right now. The short of it is I heard a mockingbird talking to another in Thaniel's voice about killing Gotham so I went on a frantic search for Gotham only to find out he had left Eden. So I took off for the Dilmun Sea in hopes of catching him to warn him, but he had gotten too long a start on me, which left me no choice but to follow after him through the Gate."

"Wait a minute," interrupted Max. "You mean to tell me you actually had the berries to risk making a go through the Gate by yourself?"

"I wussed out," said Jacob. "Or at least that's what I remembered when I woke up this morning on the beach. But the truth is I really didn't wuss out going through the Gate; I made it through. Only Johiel bound my thoughts to ensure Thaniel wouldn't be able to read them when I was sent back here to Eden and learn of Gotham's plan."

"Bound. Your. Thoughts?" echoed Max with slow enunciation while looking more and more strained in his attempt to follow Jacob's story, much less believe.

"It's a sophisticated way of manipulating one's mind. It's the reason why you can't remember being in the Silent Forest with me," said Jacob. "But trust me, you were there. It was Thaniel who basically erased it from your brain."

Jacob could see his attempt to explain was only deepening his friend's baffled state, and the rain falling loudly was making conversation in the midst of it difficult to have.

"I told you it's complicated, and there's no time to try and explain right now."

Whoa, whoa, whoa...where'r you goin'?" said Max, grabbing hold of Jacob as he turned to run off into the bluster once more. "If the sword Thaniel has is fake, then we have to let Anahel and the Guides know right away."

"The sword might be fake, but it's still dangerous. Gotham made sure of that when he made it in order to fool him. That's how Thaniel was able to do what he did to Gotham. But I have a wild hunch he left me with a clue on a way to stop him that I need to go check out," said Jacob. "Now, you have to go back. There's no sense both of us risking getting in trouble."

"Nothin' doin'," argued Max. "After what Thaniel did to Gotham today, not to mention nearly succeeding in busting up our friendship, no way am I letting you bogart all the satisfaction in taking that winged menace down."

And Jacob saw in the focused flash of light in Max's eyes that arguing the subject any further would be pointless, not to mention a waste of precious time. If nothing else, he was only too happy to feel the bond of friendship he had with Max rekindled as they came together in the clasping of hands with one another.

~ ~ ~

They trudged along as fast as they could, sloshing and splashing through ankle-deep muddy puddles while all about them the rain came streaming down in an almost merciless way. The stormy darkness into which the Garden had been thrown had made everything once so familiar suddenly strange and eerily unfamiliar. They soon reached the clearing where the Tree of Life stood rooted, cloaked like everything else in the deep blackness of the night making it appear more like the Tree of Death. But it was not the tree Jacob was interested in, but the white stone sarcophagus bound tight with ivy which held Gotham's son.

"What are we doing here?" asked Max.

Jacob stood quiet for a moment.

"He made a point at Broken Earth to remind me about what he told me about the lamb," he said with his gaze fixed intently on the sarcophagus. Yet it was the painful image of Gotham wounded and crumpled in a heap on the ground stretching forward a trembling hand that filled Jacob's sight as he recalled Gotham's last words to him:

"Remember what I told you that day by the Tree...about the lamb."

Max gave a defeated shrug. "Okay, you got me...I give up. What lamb?"

"Over there," said Jacob, nodding toward the sarcophagus beneath the Tree. "There's an image of a lamb laying beside a lion carved on the side of the stone."

"And? What about it?"

Jacob didn't answer. He was suddenly too caught up in the more pleasant memory of Gotham, looking strong in appearance, even when dampened by sadness, and possessing his wings, standing beneath the very shade of the blessed Tree of Life. And as he recalled Gotham sharing with him the meaning of the two creatures whose carved presence on the side of his son's plot appeared almost lifelike, Jacob heard the angel's voice:

"By claw and fang, the lion owns a dominion most prized. But the humble steps of the lamb lead to a far greater treasure."

The words repeated themselves over and over again inside Jacob's head until he himself began muttering the phrase aloud.

"Obviously Gotham was trying to tell me something, but what?" wondered Jacob out loud, but the pelting rain made it difficult to concentrate.

"Maybe it holds some deep life lesson he wanted to leave with you before he...you know..." said Max.

Jacob shook his head. "It was more than that...something of great importance; I could see it in his eyes and hear it in his voice. It was almost desperate. He was pointing me back here."

His rain-streaked face became more tense as he continued racking his brain and soon his feet began guiding him toward the burial plot when he suddenly felt Max's hand grab him urgently by the shoulder to keep him from going any further. "Are you off your nut? You can't cross the immortalis blossoms," warned Max.

Both boys' gazes bent their way downward to where Jacob's sopping muddied sneakers were planted just mere inches from where the proverbial flowers carpeted the ground. Even the dark of night did not douse from sight the blood-red blooms whose petals had closed themselves tight to shelter themselves from the ongoing deluge.

"I've got to get across somehow," said Jacob.

He looked to his left, then his right through the blinding rain for some kind of opening or break in the clusters of flowers wreathing the area around the Tree, but he found none.

"I've got to chance it," said Jacob.

"You really are out of your tree. Or have you forgotten Thaniel's little warning to us about the Cherubim?" asked Max.

Jacob, like all Nephilim, was well aware of the biblical creatures that were said to appear and rain down punishment on any mortal-blooded beings who trespassed beyond the unimposing, delicate plants.

"You still willing to believe everything Thaniel has taught us?" argued Jacob. "For all we know, it could be another lie, like the one he told me about the Through in the Silent Forest."

"And on the off chance it isn't a lie?" questioned Max. "I'm not sure I'm willing to take the chance...not when there's Cherubim involved."

Jacob stood quietly pondering Max's warning. "Maybe if I do it without touching the ground."

Before Max could stop him, Jacob sprang forward, leaping high and long as only a Nephilim can do until he cleared the flowers and stretch of grass leading up to the Tree and came to rest atop the stone plot.

"Forgive me. I mean no disrespect," Jacob immediately muttered under his breath to the sarcophagus upon which he knelt, and more importantly to the body of David lying at rest inside.

He ran a hand across the top of the smooth, carved stone and with his heart thumping with anticipation inside his chest he waited wide-eyed for something to sound the alarm of his defiance, but there came nothing but the drumming of rain. Then gripping tightly the edge of the vine-covered stone vault which the rain had made slick and slippery, Jacob carefully leaned his body forward over the side of the sarcophagus which held the carving of the lion and lamb. His eyes carefully studied each image which appeared upside down to him from the way he was positioned, beginning with the lion who was lying with his body pointed in one direction, then to the lamb lying the opposite way, and then back to the lion. And as he studied the details of each carving as closely as possible that the darkness of the night and rain would allow, Jacob heard Gotham's voice echo once more inside his head.

"By claw and fang, the lion owns a dominion most prized. But the humble steps of the lamb lead to a far greater treasure."

"What does it mean? Jacob whispered with frustration to himself.

As the voice repeated itself in his head, Jacob's gaze turned again to the lamb, and more specifically the positioning of its feet curled up beneath its body lying in repose. And when his eyes failed to find anything unusual, Jacob reached down and ran a hand over the carving. It was only when his fingers felt its way about the smooth section near the base of the sarcophagus beneath the lamb did he notice the stone shift ever so slightly.

"What's going on?" Max called out in a hushed cry.

Jacob ignored him. Stretching himself flat on his stomach across the sarcophagus to allow himself use of both hands, he struggled to pry loose the block until finally after a few moments of strenuous, teeth-clenching maneuvering he was able to pull it free. He then hurriedly leaned himself further over the stone plot and, with all the blood in his body rushing into his head, peered upside down into the rectangular-shaped opening that had revealed itself. At first, all Jacob saw was nothing but a dark empty space, but as he stretched his body forward while straining for a better look his eyes suddenly caught a shiny glimmer in the cold blackness that made Jacob's breath catch itself in his chest.

Could it possibly be? Jacob wondered to himself before cautiously reaching into the hidden opening. Before he could manage to grab hold of the mysterious object, there came a rumbling from the ground beneath him. At first he feared his discourteous breach of David's resting place had somehow awaken his wrath. Then there came an unsettling sound from somewhere close behind him, as if the earth itself was being split open.

"I would suggest you get out of there. *NOW!*"

Max had hardly shouted his warning when a horrible shrill cry like that of a lion battling an eagle pierced loudly the night. Jacob shot an alarmed look to where Max stood and even the darkness could not hide the sudden terror that had welded itself to his friend's face. It left Jacob cold and almost too afraid to look and see for himself what had brought such panic to Max's voice, not to mention expression. Yet he couldn't keep himself from slowly turning his head and peering cautiously over his left shoulder. But before he could see anything, something took hold of him and ripped him off the sarcophagus.

With a tremendous force, Jacob was sent hurtling through the air. Thankfully the rain had softened the ground somewhat, though not enough to deaden the shock of pain Jacob felt when his body landed with a hard thump, then rolled several times before coming to a rest. When he looked up, he tried to shake off a momentary dizziness that brought a dancing constellation of stars to his vision. Unfortunately, not so much that it blinded him to the sight of the creature looming over him; though, at that moment, he may have wished for the mercy of blindness to shield him from such a terrifying sight. And he knew then it was a fool he had shown himself to be to have voiced skepticism over the existence of the Cherubim.

~ ~ ~

"Get out of there! Run!" Jacob heard Max yell out to him. Not that Jacob needed to be prodded, especially when he saw the creature start again toward him.

He spun around to make his escape, cursing the drenched ground that left his legs sliding and flailing about awkwardly in their desperate attempt to find footing on the ground beneath him that had become a carpet of slick, slimy mud. Yet even had he the luck of finding himself on the driest of land, Jacob quickly found he couldn't get very far. The Cherub moved with the speed of lightning flashing across the sky. No matter which direction Jacob ran it would suddenly appear before him once more blocking his way.

The Cherub's size alone was cringe-worthy, as it stood more than ten times that of Jacob. However, it was the schizophrenia of its presence which was far more terrifying. It's body was that of a sphinx fitted upon two straight legs with hoofs for feet. Yet its arms were that of a human, as were its hands, one of which clutched tight a sword made of fire. What proved to be most arresting were the four faces—that of a lion, an eagle, an ox, and a man—masking each side of the Cherub's solitary head. As it turned from side to side, each one eyed Jacob in a fierce and unforgiving manner.

"You definitely are not a cute, chubby little angel with a harmless bow and arrow, are you?" muttered Jacob in as calm a voice as possible.

As if to cast aside all lingering doubt, the Cherub swung its sword in Jacob's direction. The searing heat coming off weapon could not be ignored and, as Jacob scurried quickly out of its way, he felt the hairs on his arm become singed from the flaming blade. The beast then let loose into the night another ear-piercing cry while beating wrathfully the four massive wings sprouting from its back. Angrily, it stomped the ground with its hoofs as if it were some enraged bull preparing to charge. It was enough to send Jacob scrambling from out of its shadow, but in his escape the creature caught hold of him again, this time by the ankle.

Desperately Jacob kicked and thrashed to free himself of the Cherub's grip as he was lifted into the air to dangle helplessly upside down like a worm squirming on the barb of a hook before a hungry bass. The creature craned its neck forward offering each of its four faces to study closer the Nephilim struggling mightily in its grasp.

"I could sure use your help right about now!" Jacob called out in a panicky quiver to Max while under the blazing glare of the most unfriendly sets of eyes he'd ever had the displeasure of staring into. "This situation is getting to be a little uncomfortable."

Max had already jumped into action. Taking to the sky, he swooped in on the Cherub from behind.

"You always pick on things smaller than you, you four-faced bully?" he called out mockingly while buzzing past the face of the horned ox and taking the creature by surprise.

Again the Cherub bellowed angrily. Flinging Jacob aside to crash in a heap on the ground, it turned its fury on Max who darted about like an antagonistic sprite just out of reach of the furious swipes coming toward him from the creature's flaming sword. The cockiness Max showed in his flying prowess only served to further anger the Cherub and, in a moment he realized too late that he had strayed a tad too close, the creature batted him with its free hand. The full brunt of the blow knocked more than the wind from Max and sent him flying through the air to fall limp on the far edge of the grassy clearing.

Jacob cried out to his friend but there came no response, nor movement. And when the Cherub turned back to him, it was Jacob's turn to show anger. He made a rush for the sarcophagus, and as he ran toward it he felt the ground once more quiver and shake beneath his feet from the Cherub giving chase after him. He dove forward onto the ground just short of the stone plot when he felt a giant hand make a grab for him. Then, glancing over his shoulder, he caught the frightening sight of the fiery sword being aimed down on him. Quickly, he rolled out of the way just as the flaming weapon delivered its scorching bite to the rain-soaked earth.

With the ground visibly smoldering from its wound, Jacob couldn't help but wonder how there could be in existence any sword more powerful or deadly than the one being wielded by the Cherub. But he was determined to find out. And with a desperate lunge made in the direction of the opening he had revealed in the stone, he reached inside just as the Cherub drew back his sword to deliver another blow. As it came raining down, Jacob swung forth his arm with all his might and bringing to light a sword he now clutched tight in his hand, which met the one shaped by fire. It cut cleanly through the Cherub's flaming blade reducing the weapon instantly to nothing but a shower of glowing, smoldering embers and sparks that quickly dissipated into the stormy darkness.

The Cherub's screeching scream that followed was terrifying as it echoed into the night. Startled, Jacob managed to hold his stance with the sword gripped in his hand held firmly before him as though it were a crucifix he brandished to ward off a vampire. The Cherub, however, showed no further hostility toward Jacob. In fact, it seemed to recoil and show a reluctant submissiveness in the face of the sword being leveled at it. Then, in a flash too quick for the eye to follow, the Cherub vanished.

Only then did Jacob's body relax and breath with ease, but only for a brief moment; for he quickly remembered Max and rushed to where his friend lay sprawled unconscious on the ground. It took only a couple light taps to the face to rouse him.

"That's some left hook that Cherub packs," wised Max while straining to sit himself upright. "So, where'd it go? I was just getting warmed up."

"It just disappeared," answered Jacob.

"What chased it away? Certainly not you from the way I saw him biffing you around. Or myself, for that matter," Max joked as he rubbed his throbbing jaw.

Jacob answered by holding up the sword he pulled from the secreted opening in the stone plot. And it was then they were both given their first good look at the now familiar legendary weapon.

"It's the sword Gotham handed over to Thaniel at Broken Earth," said Max.

"No," argued Jacob, shaking his head. "This is the real one. This is the real Destiny!"

And, indeed, it looked every bit the same as the sword forged by Gotham in the light of the Begend fire on Akdamar. Yet strangely there was something inexplicably different about it. Maybe it was some small unseen detail. Or maybe it was the feel of power and strength it seemed to give off when grasping hold of it. Whatever it was, it was clear to both boys staring at it that it was no ordinary sword.

"The whole time, it's been right here," said Jacob, holding out the sword to allow Max the chance to examine more closely the weapon and feel it in his hands. Smartly, Max leaned away from it with a measured caution, as if he held fear of the weapon.

"Hey, be careful with that thing, will you mate?"

"What's the matter with you?" asked Jacob.

"It's not mine to touch, nor anyone's for that matter, don't you know?" answered Max. "Gotham must have somehow passed ownership of it over to you before he was killed."

Jacob's mind instantly flashed back to the moment at Broken Earth when Gotham took hold of his hand while lying bleeding on ground and reminded him of the lamb. The sword in his hand suddenly seemed to grow heavier. And while he could not deny the exhilarating feeling of power he experienced when he wielded it at the Cherub, knowing the weight of such power was now in his hands proved itself to be much more than overwhelming.

"So now what?" asked Max.

"I haven't the slightest idea," answered Jacob, looking as though he was devoid of a single clue of what to do next.

"The rain doesn't look as though it's going to let up any time soon and my skin has already started to prune," said Max, squinting at the pelting drop of water falling from above. "I suggest we get back while we still have luck in our corner, and figure out our next move."

Jacob agreed. "I also think it's best we keep this between the two of us...at least for the time being."

"No argument here," said Max as he watched Jacob hide the sword away inside the oversized coat he wore. "Having one's backside handed to you by a Cherub is not exactly the kind of thing you want to get around, you know what I mean?"

With the sword tucked out of sight under the cover of the roomy overcoat Jacob wore, the two quickly made their way together through the sheets of falling rain back toward Havenhid. They had nearly reached the River when they were startled by the sight of a darkened figure suddenly standing on the pathway blocking their way. Thinking it might be Thaniel, an uncomfortable shiver moved through Jacob and he clutched tighter the front of Gotham's coat to ensure it stayed closed. The figure slowly approached the two frozen boys, and it was only when a break in the suffocating shadows revealed it was Damiel that Jacob and Max released in unison a breath of relief.

"What the devil has led the two of you to be traipsing around out here in this storm?" Damiel angrily scolded the boys. "Or did the directive that you remain locked inside your room prove too complex for your waterlogged brains to comprehend?"

Jacob and Max both began stammering clumsily over each other's words in search of a believable explanation which Damiel seemed to quickly lose interest in as he focused his gaze past the two boys and deeper into the night in the direction of the Tree of Life. And as he scrutinized the darkness his eyes grew brightly golden.

"What is it?" asked Max with great reluctance.

"I could have sworn I heard the cry of a Cherub," answered Damiel.

"I don't hear anything," said Jacob with as much nonchalance as he could muster.

"I meant earlier, just a short while before the two of you came tearing up this path." Damiel then returned his attention to the boys, slowly looking the two up and down as they stood before him mud-stained and soaked to the skin. "Then again, I highly doubt you would be standing here in front of me like a couple of wandering strays in desperate need of a good wringing out had it been a Cherub, isn't that right? Now, let's get you back to your room where you belong."

He placed a hand on Jacob's shoulder to guide him ahead, but as Jacob took a step forward his foot slipped suddenly on the muddy trail. Stumbling forward, Jacob felt the sword inside his coat almost leave his grip as he struggled to keep upright and firm his footing.

"What have you there?" Damiel asked forcefully when it was more than evident Jacob was concealing something inside his coat."

"Where?" Jacob feigned naively in a bad attempt at playing dumb.

Damiel, however, was in no mood to play games—not this night.

"You're hiding something in your coat," he said pointedly. "Now, do you tell me what is, or shall I seek the answer myself?"

He watched as Jacob and Max exchanged a hesitant glance with one another.

"You're going to have to tell him, anyways," said Max.

"I'm growing impatient. Tell me what?" demanded Damiel.

"Alright," Jacob said with a surrendering sigh. "But we can't show you here."

With Damiel in tow, the boys led the way hurriedly back to Havenhid where they returned to their room as stealthily as they had left.

~ ~ ~

For some time after in the quiet, night-lit privacy of his room, Jacob proceeded to tell the longest and most involved story he had ever before told in his short-lived life; from the night he and Max first broke the cardinal rule concerning the Silent Forest and his later—and hopefully only—encounter with Lilith, to his unlikely race through the Gate and entanglement with the Nekcri leading to a white fire inside the Holy Cross church on Akdamar Island where he learned of Gotham's plan to thwart Thaniel's ambitions.

All the while Jacob spoke, Damiel remained stone-still, the only movement coming from him being the intermittent dripping of water from his wet, tangled hair to dribble across his face and onto the floor. And as he listened with greater intrigue, his eyes remained fixed on the sword Jacob retrieved from the foot of the Tree of Life that now stood on its point resting against the foot of Jacob's bed. So, too, were the attentions of Kairo and Leos, who huddled together with Ethan on his bed to hear about the events they knew nothing about, and Max, who gradually came to learn the details of events that had been maliciously plucked from his brain, or bound as he came to know the angel terminology for the sleight of hand that had been played on him much to his growing anger.

"Then Gothamel didn't betray us or Eden as we so viciously accused him," Damiel remarked quietly when Jacob had finished. "And the last words he heard from our vile mouths before he was cut down was a fervent desire to see him banished to the deepest pit of despair the Underneath had to offer. May God forgive us for being so short-sighted in our condemnation."

"You had no way of knowing," said Jacob in an offering of comfort.

"BUT I SHOULD HAVE...don't you see?" cried Damiel as sorrow laid waste to his face. "He may have been a Fallen, but I knew my brother to be unmoved in his convictions. Yet in a moment of anger I chose to see only the one mark that blemished his beauty—the mark of the wicked and disloyal—while turning a blind eye to that which I knew intimately to be his soul; a soul that chose painfully, yet willingly, to spill the blood of his own child in his loyalty to the Light. And now, apparently, give his own as well."

No one said a word for some time as a darkness deeper than the night settled itself upon the room, and the only sound came from Damiel's pacing footsteps followed by the clamor of a chair he sent flying across the room and into a wall to shatter into a million un-mendable pieces with one powerful kick that made the boys jump in unison.

"I have a question."

All eyes turned to Ethan with looks of surprise that he'd be the one to brave opening his mouth first.

"I get that the sword Thaniel has is fake," he said. "But if, in fact, it isn't Destiny, then how was it Thaniel was able to kill Gotham?"

"Jacob just got through telling you. The sword Gotham made was forged from a special kind of fire," said Leos. "It's called the...the, uh—"

"Begend," Kairo jumped in for the save.

"Alright smarty, then explain how it is Gotham even managed to get this Begend fire. I mean, you said it's the same fire that came from the Big Bang explosion that ended up creating the entire universe. But didn't that happen like a gazillion years ago?" argued Ethan.

"Hello, did you just get here or do you have moments when you're deaf as a doorpost?" answered Max. "Jacob explained pretty clearly how Gotham was given the last remnants of the Begend in a vial which he wore around his neck. After all, he was once one of the Angels of the Apocalypse, ya cluck."

"Oh yeah…I must have forgotten about that part," said Ethan with a slow look of clarity coming to him which drew a direct hit from a well-aimed pillow thrown his way from Leos.

"I should have recognized in his face and the way he spoke that night what he was planning," said Jacob. "He knew someone as smart as Thaniel would be suspicious, and rightly so. The only way he could sell his ploy was prove the sword had the power to strike down an angel, so he literally sacrificed his own life to make Thaniel believe it was the true Destiny."

Damiel stood quietly listening in a far corner of the room and the sorrow weighing upon his face was quickly replaced with a fire of rage as if ignited by gasoline.

"Give me the sword," he seethed as he stepped briskly toward Jacob all the while mindful not to grab outright the weapon within his reach, "and I will end this ruse with Thaniel while delivering justice for Gothamel in one swift strike of its blade."

And for a moment, it looked as though Jacob was about to acquiesce to the urgent request when Max made his friend pause.

"You think that's wise…handing over Destiny like that?" he asked drawing a conflicted look from his friend as well as an unappreciated glare from Damiel.

"What do you mean?" asked Jacob.

"Gotham put the sword in your hands…so to speak. He could have easily given it to Anahel, the other Guides and even Damiel here, but he chose you," said Max, giving the angel a quick glance and adding apologetically, "No offense."

The angel's expression, however, revealed a plenty big enough helping of offense had been taken.

"It just might interest you to know, young Fledgling, that right before I discovered you and your friend looking like a couple of drowned rats wandering about in the rain, Thaniel turned a convening of the White Circle into a coronation...*HIS* coronation, complete with a crown he had the audacity to have placed upon his head until I was too sickened to witness the spectacle any further," spoke Damiel through clenched teeth. "Am I hearing you now to suggest we sit back and allow the sun of a new morning to baptize this unsightly doing?"

Anyone else would have crumpled in the shadow of Damiel's impassioned presence, but Max showed a commendable resilience.

"All I'm saying is the Sword of Destiny has always been fated to find its place in the hand of the Light Bearer," answered Max coolly.

"And we all know how well it turned out the last time such a match was met," said Damiel snidely only to clench his jaw tightly with regret as his words met his own ears.

"That's not what I meant," he was quick to voice with a repentant sigh meant mostly for Jacob. "Revenge bred from the betrayal I feel toward one brother and the deep unendurable mourning for another is twisting me ever more from inside, especially now when I see the wide open avenue in delivering it with all the savory spite lingering on my tongue."

"But there is something to fear," Jacob was quick to point out, "so long as Thaniel holds to his threat of opening the Through."

"Not to mention he still holds a formidable weapon," added Max. "It might not be Destiny, but it can still take out angels, as we all saw."

A defeated look returned once more to Damiel, only heavier in weight.

"Then what, may I ask, do you suggest we do, Mr. Light Bearer?" he breathed deeply while resting fully his piercing gaze upon Jacob.

As if hoping to find an answer to the question written somewhere on their faces, Jacob turned to each of his roommates, but all he got in return was the same blank stare he wore staring back at him.

"Well...as I see it," he began after a moment to scour his jumbled thoughts, "the whole point of Gotham's plan was to give Thaniel a false sense of security by making him believe he finally had what he desired in his possession which he succeeded in doing. Now that his guard is down, the first focus has to be eliminating his ability to use the Through against Eden. The window of opportunity, however, is small. Gotham told me Thaniel planned to use the sword to free Samael in return for the Darkness backing his threat to get the sword. As soon as he tries to cut through the Herrinsu vine holding Samael, he'll know he's been tricked, and who knows what he'll do then."

"Not a problem," said Damiel with not a tinge of doubt to be heard in his voice. "I'll gather the other Guides and we'll regain control of the Through before Thaniel knows what's happened."

"That's exactly the wrong move to make," said Jacob, stopping Damiel as he was about to disappear out the window. "You'll never slip out of Thaniel's sights long enough without rousing his suspicion. In fact, I'm surprised he's let you out of his sight this long already."

"What, then, do you propose we do?" asked Damiel as he studied the boy with a puzzling look. "Because the only alternative we have left would be you swooping down and saving the day."

A slow-forming grim found the angel's face when he suddenly realized he had answered his own question,

"What's so funny? It's not a completely fantastic idea," said Jacob.

"I was being facetious," said Damiel. "Or need I remind you your lack of wings severely hinders your ability to be doing any so-called swooping."

Jacob bristled at the jab.

"Thanks for the vote of confidence," he snapped bitterly. "Besides, it didn't stop me from catching the Illume over the other guys."

"Um...I think you mean we, mate," Max piped in with a raise of his finger in an effort to remind Jacob, and everyone else in the room, of his part in the capture. But he was fast ignored.

"This isn't some competition involving a bunch of Fledglings giving chase after some bird in the woods," Damiel barked with frustration. "We're talking about the very existence of Eden hanging in balance. And in case it hasn't dawned on everyone in this room yet, but that includes your very lives as well."

"Well, I may be just a Fledgling, but how many Fledglings do you know are armed with this?" countered Jacob while grabbing hold of the Sword of Destiny and thrusting it in Damiel's face.

"You act as if you're a wizard brandishing a wand," said Damiel with a quiet seriousness. "Even you are not naive enough to believe that the power of the sword comes from mere possession. It takes training, and understanding of what you hold, to make it the feared weapon it is."

"I've been trained," argued Jacob.

"You mean by Gothamel?"

"And you," said Jacob, making sure the angel understood the value he held in both his teachers.

The angel began to pace about in a haphazard, preoccupied manner.

"I think Jacob's right," said Kairo. The angel stopped and glowered at the boy who swallowed nervously before finding his voice to continue. "It makes sense...at least to me. Thaniel's going to expect you and the other Guides to try and undermine him. I doubt he'll be suspecting any of us to try anything."

"Now it's 'us' is it?" echoed Damiel.

"That's right," Leos chimed in. "I think we can do it...regain control of the Through, that is."

"You think?" mocked Damiel in the complete lack of self-assurance he caught in the boy's voice. "Even if I thought this was a good idea—which I don't—I could never convince Anahel to go along with it."

"Why even tell him?" asked Jacob. "I think it would be a mistake for anyone else to know anything about what we're planning."

"He has to be told," argued Damiel. "Contrary to what Thaniel believes, Eden is still governed by Anahel, and he would never allow Fledglings to be placed in such a perilous position."

Jacob shook his head in disbelief in what he was hearing.

"Why are we even here then?" he balked. "What's been the point of busting our butts all these months training? All we keep hearing is how we have to prepare ourselves and be ready both mentally and physically for the dark days when the Darkness rises up to challenge the Light. Well it's here now, and on our home turf. If now's not the time to put what we've learned to test, then when?"

"You don't understand what you're saying—"

"No, you don't understand what I'm saying. You spoke about feelings of revenge twisting your insides? Then remember Gotham was my friend…more than a friend, actually," Jacob stated adamantly yet with the subtlest trembling visible in his upper lip. "And strong as you might be, Damiel, I don't think even you could keep me from avenging my friend's death."

"Nor me," said Max forcefully while jumping to his feet.

Damiel's gaze then moved to Leos, Kairo and even Ethan as they followed suit showing a unified front, and the unflinching looks of determination shared by each boy was all it took to convince the angel the argument was finished.

CHAPTER TWENTY-TWO

THE SON OF SAMAEL

"Maybe we oughta rethink this whole thing, huh guys?" said Ethan nervously as he stood at the leading edge of the Silent Forest staring into the ominous darkness awaiting him and his fellow companions ahead.

"Don't wuss out on us now, Ethan," said Leos.

Yet despite trying to put forward a brave front himself, Leos couldn't completely hide the nervous look that had seized hold of him in the same manner that could only be described as a deer who accidentally crosses the path of a hungry cougar on the hunt. Neither could Kairo, Max and even Jacob as they felt their already frail courage give way even more while quietly debating whether they had made the right decision in volunteering themselves for such a dangerous and unnerving mission.

"We should probably get moving inside," said Jacob, hating even the idea of such a suggestion.

"Don't you think it might be a good idea if one of us stands guard out here?" queried Ethan.

"And do you have anybody in particular in mind for this deadly assignment?" asked Kairo sarcastically.

Jacob understood Ethan's hesitation and saw no shame in it.

"Look, Ethan, no one's gonna razz you if you decide to go back," he said.

It was more than a tempting offer, but Ethan somehow managed to find the bravery needed to move his feet forward and follow the others across the forbidden boundary. They moved quickly, but quietly through the trees where there was found some relief from the smothering rain, which grew thin beneath the thick umbrella of foliage and became more of a misty drizzle. No one dared to break the notable deathly silence that surrounded them by uttering a single word. Before long, Jacob led them to the exact same spot behind a felled tree trunk where he and Max had hid themselves the first time they secreted into the Forest together.

"Still doesn't look familiar to you yet?" Jacob asked Max. But it was clear from the completely blank look on Max's face as he glanced around what the answer was.

"Not even faintly," said Max.

By now, Jacob was feeling the chill of the rain, and the weight of Gotham's water-logged coat grew burdensome upon his body. Yet it was quickly forgotten when he joined the others to peer cautiously over the top of the tree trunk behind which they were hunkered down to conceal their presence and immediately spied that they were not alone.

"It's Betryel," whispered Leos of the angel seen standing straight ahead in the center of the clearing and, oddly enough, blindfolded.

"Why's he blindfolded?" asked Leos.

Though he didn't say so out loud, Jacob had a sneaking suspicion for the blindfolding, as he turned his gaze to the pool which resided a few short feet away from where the angel stood motionless. Thankfully, there was no sign of Lilith, but just seeing the dark water of the pool itself was enough to fill Jacob with an immediate uneasiness. Knowing the horror cloaked from sight just beneath the surface of the water of which he had regrettably been given a glimpse, it was the one place he had hoped—and even prayed—he'd never have to visit again.

"Whatever the reason," said Max, "it makes what we've come here to do all the more easier."

Jacob, however, shared none of his friend's confidence. In fact, he felt much like Betryel appeared: as though he were standing in front of a firing squad.

"Just remember what I told you back at Havenhid," Jacob mentioned quietly as the boys sank back out of sight behind the tree. "Under no circumstances can we let Betryel get anywhere near the water. Whatever it takes to keep him back, do it. But more importantly, don't let yourself step too close to the pool unless you want an up-close look at the horrors of the Underneath lurking out of sight just beneath the surface waiting for you to take a wrong step."

"That's really the pep talk you're choosing to go with now?" asked a feverishly unnerved Ethan.

They were about ready to step out from behind the tree trunk when they heard an unusual rustling of movement coming from somewhere high above and they quickly ducked back down for cover just as a winged figure was seen descending from amid the tree tops.

~ ~ ~

"That you, Thaniel?" Betryel's voice was heard to call out.

Daring themselves to make even the movement needed to breathe, the boys gingerly braved a look once more over the top of the tree trunk, and to their surprise they spied the figure to indeed be Thaniel.

"What's he doing here?" whispered Kairo.

Jacob signaled him to be quiet with a finger to his lips and watched as Thaniel came nose to nose with Betryel and raised the sword he believed to be Destiny in his hand to the angel's face. Anyone else would have instantly tensed at the feel of the cold steel, but not Betryel. Then with the ease of a knife cutting through the softest slab of butter, the sword sliced cleanly through the blindfold leaving it to fall away from Betryel's eyes.

"She's been impatiently asking for you," Betryel informed Thaniel.

At almost the exact moment, a familiar voice, soft and lilting, suddenly reached out from the direction of the pool.

"What's the matter, Thaniel?" it said. "Don't you trust your own men to be left alone here with me?"

Thaniel did not immediately turn around, but smiled subtly and gave Betryel an affectionate brush of his hand across the side of his face.

"It's not my trust in them that leads me to show caution," he replied.

Turning, he then made his way with slow, casual steps toward the pool, ever cautious of keeping a notable distance between himself and the edge of the still dark water. There, standing waist-deep in the center of it was suddenly seen Lilith, an inescapable vision of beauty if ever there was one. The sight nearly drew the Nephilim from their hiding spot.

"She's beautiful," gasped Max as if it were the first time he had ever laid eyes on the mysterious lady, and in many ways it was. Even Jacob, who knew better of what resided behind the spellbinding facade, couldn't argue his friend's declaration.

"If the ever-growing number of Nephilim coming to Eden demonstrate anything, it's that a great number of my brothers are no more immune to the feminine allure than that of mortal men," said Thaniel. "And if there is one thing I have come to know, dear Lilith, is that your charms have proven themselves more potent and effective than that of any ordinary woman."

Lilith smiled knowingly. "You flatter me, Thaniel."

It was then Thaniel came to notice the absence of Lilith's left arm from beneath the rain of long jet-black hair falling down across her shoulder.

"You've been wounded recently," he said.

The reminder caused a dark shadow to pass briefly across Lilith face.

"Yes, you can say I had an unfortunate accident," she remarked before her face brightened somewhat at the notice of a two-pointed gold crown perched atop Thaniel's head.

"And either I'm seeing things, or you've actually been crowned," she said before her gaze narrowed on a most familiar and damning mark freshly seared into Thaniel's temple. "Twice, I might add."

While Thaniel fiddled with his crown in an attempt to better conceal the painful mark peeking out from beneath the brim, a pleased look came to Lilith as she ran the one hand left her in a caressing fashion across the surface of the pool which rippled with a great many rings cast by the falling rain.

"That would explain the rain then," she said turning her eyes skyward. "It carries with it an inconsolable anger I've not heard in some time now. Or perhaps it's sorrow I detect...I can't quite be sure."

"I reckon it to be a good deal of both," said Thaniel, dismissively.

Lilith paused, watchful and intent. "So, are you planning to tell me what sin you've come to commit that has removed you from your master's grace?" she inquired casually, yet with a rabid curiosity. "And how is it you've managed to avoid being cast clean from Eden?"

Thaniel's answer came without words as he held forth the sword clutched in his hand for Lilith to lay her gaze upon. Immediately, she became awestruck at the sight of the weapon, in particular the unmistakable spearhead housed firmly in the center of the steel blade. Hypnotically, it drew her towards Thaniel, like some worshiping pagan at the foot of a gold graven image, until the boundary of water met land and allowed her to come no further.

"A fall well-earned, winged one," Lilith purred most gleefully. "Finally, we have in our possession that which we have sought, and with it a power unmatched by even Heaven, itself. Now, let me know and enjoy the feel of such power in my own hands."

The Nephilim shared a collective gasp of alarm at the sight of Lilith stretching out the one hand left her toward Thaniel.

"We're too late," said Leos. "If he hands her the sword, he'll open the Through."

The same sense of urgency in Leos' voice made Jacob leap to his feet, but not before Max grabbed hold of him.

"You crazy?" he asked. "What do you think you're gonna do?"
"Just promise you'll stay put," ordered Jacob before he pulled free of Max's grasp and hurried off.

The boys turned back to the pool and, with growing panic, watched helplessly as Lilith stood with her arm outstretched waiting for the sword with an acquisitive eagerness. But as she reached toward him, Thaniel drew the sword close to his chest in a protective manner bringing to Lilith a confused look. "What makes you hesitate? Give it to me."

Thaniel stood quietly, further inciting Lilith.

"I demand that you hand it to me this instant," she ordered with heated insistence.

"Funny thing about this sword," said Thaniel, turning an enslaved gaze to the weapon he cradled, much like a mother beholding the miracle of a newborn bundled in her arms. "The longer I have it in my hands, the harder I find it is for me to part with, if even for a brief moment."

Had Lilith's hateful glare been a dagger it would have staked Thaniel through the center of his chest then and there.

"I suggest then you summon within yourself the exertion needed to relinquish it into my care," she hissed venomously.

Thaniel lowered himself in a squat to the ground so he could be at eye level with Lilith.

"I'm not so certain now that I would exercise such strength, even if I knew I had it," he replied coolly.

A storm of anger swept visibly over Lilith and in that moment the veil of her calming beauty distorted and the terror of her true self burst forth in the quickest of flashes for all to see. Had she not been shackled to the realm of the water, she would have surely leapt forward and pounced upon Thaniel, and yet the angel showed not even the slightest of flinches in the face of her terrifying fury.

"You dare to mock me, angel, knowing a dark army fathoms deep stands crouched at the ready on the other side of this Through?" Her voice took a deep, unnatural turn in its rage that rang out through the Forest and strangled the everlasting silence in a chilling moment that made the blood run cold.

"Fortunately, I stand to suffer greater discomfort from this relentless rain than I do any viable threat from you or your dark army," said Thaniel. The challenging smirk on his face only managed to incite Lilith even more.

"GIVE ME THE SWORD!"

Her cry shook the Forest as if it were caught in the stranglehold of a pair of phantom hands. But then, as quickly as it erupted, her anger was suddenly stolen from her when something just beyond where Thaniel stood drew the focus of her dark gaze. The angel slowly turned his head and a look of surprise found him when he caught sight of Jacob standing several feet away. He immediately motioned to Betryel, who was readying to pounce, to stay put in his place with a wave of his hand and slowly approached the boy.

"This is indeed a surprise," said Thaniel with a note of suspicion. "Then again, you've become quite the regular visitor of this not often visited Forest, haven't you?"

Jacob fought to remain cool and collected, but it was difficult under the weight of the intense look he felt coming from Lilith, whose dark eyes refused to leave him. It was all so strange to him. Even now, after witnessing first-hand the demonic horror that resided beneath the masquerade of beauty she wore like a cloak, he found himself slowly being drawn to her as he had the first time he laid eyes on her. It was only when he forcefully denied his eyes the sight of her did he feel he could breathe freely on his own.

"I had to see it for myself." he said looking back to Thaniel, and more specifically the gleaming halo of gold perched atop his head. "You actually had yourself crowned...as if you're some kind of king."

"Fitting wouldn't you say, at least more so than the coat you're wearing," remarked the angel. "Either the rain has caused you to shrink or you're in desperate need of a new tailor."

"It was Gotham's," Jacob replied bitterly while hugging himself tighter inside the oversized coat.

"Of course it was," said Thaniel slowly eyeing the damp garment. And as he did, Jacob was surprised to catch what he thought to be a grim look of remorse reveal itself briefly in the angel's otherwise blank expression.

"I must admit I'm happy to have this time alone with you, despite this awkward venue we find ourselves at this hour," said Thaniel before leaning himself closer toward Jacob as if to converse in secret out of reach from the other nearby ears. "I can only imagine the feelings of anger and hate you feel toward me at this moment. But hear me as I can only say to you that what I did I had to, hard as it might be for you to understand now."

Jacob glared at Thaniel with a look that could only serve to confirm the angel's suspicions of the boy's feelings toward him.

"Damiel taught us never to give ourselves to hate, and especially anger," said Jacob. "Anger is a wasted emotion. All it does is cloud one's focus and good judgment."

He then glanced down to the angel's right hand and saw that it clutched the sword given to him by Gotham and it calmed him somewhat knowing the replica remained successful in its deceit.

"Damiel is quite wise. But I also saw the look in your eyes just after I...parted ways with Gothamel," Thaniel said in a careful choosing of words, "and what I saw reflected back was nothing less than hate-filled."

"Maybe...at that moment. What I'm left with now is not hate, it's pity." said Jacob. "I pity you."

The boy's words, and the contempt with which he spoke them, seemed to both wound and offend Thaniel in the same breath.

"Pity? How may I ask have I come to earn your pity?"

"All the time I've been here I've heard nothing but how superior angels are and how inferior humans are. Ironic, isn't it, that you've shown yourself to be just as inferior, if not worse? Because you know with all certainty all the things which humans have struggled and fought to learn and know, yet can only rest their faith in. And still you willingly sold it all for the price of your own brother's blood. And for what? Greed. Dirty, stinking greed for power," Jacob spat.

The sullen look captured in Thaniel's face suddenly darkened. "You'll understand when I tell you that the day I'm in need of being schooled in a lesson about the perils of the flight of faith, I'll refrain from taking it from a Nephilim who stands before me wingless."

Thaniel abruptly turned his back on the boy and made his way back to the pool, leaving Jacob a fixture to Betryel's scowling glare. While Jacob did his best not to show any intimidation of the angel, it was far from an easy task. Unlike Acruxel and Caphel, Betryel had a far more unsettling air of danger to him, but nowhere did it appear more prominent than in his eyes, which had a way of burrowing themselves into whoever they fell upon.

~ ~ ~

"I warn you Thaniel, be careful what game it is you are thinking of playing with me," Lilith made herself heard once again as she and Thaniel resumed their sparring. Yet despite the threatening manner in which she spoke, her voice had once more retained the soft, feminine tone to match her beauty. "There's no measure to the wrath that has fermented inside Samael during these long years of his imprisonment; so much so that I question whether even Destiny itself could fend it off once it's unleashed. Therefore, you would be wise to be mindful of the pact you made. Break it and the next mark you incur, I fear, will be beyond your imaginings."

"It's no game I play, nor do you need question whether I will hold to my end of the pact. But the Sword of Destiny is mine, and mine it will stay," said Thaniel with unwavering finality. "I did not come to be branded like some common head of cattle to walk away empty-handed."

"Eden was your price, or have you forgotten the deal you yourself designed?"

"And Destiny will ensure it remains mine."

"You promised to retrieve Destiny for Samael," Lilith argued fervently. "With it, he would finally unleash fully the war against the Light that has long been coming."

"I promised to set him free from the Herrinsu vine with which he is bound, nothing more," corrected Thaniel. "The war will come as expected, and I have already pledged to you my allegiance in it as you have pledged yours to me. Does it really matter in whose hand Destiny is wielded when the path it will clear-cut to victory remains decidedly the same?"

"You expect me to believe you?"

"Believe whatever it is you wish," answered Thaniel without care. "However, I have a sneaking suspicion, when all is said and done here tonight, it will be you who rethinks the plan of freeing Samael."

"What would make you say such a ridiculous thing?" asked Lilith incredulously.

Thaniel's lips tightened themselves noticeably. "All in good time, Lilith."

~ ~ ~

While Jacob remained quietly in the background listening intently, he peered out of the corner of his eye towards the carcass of the felled tree behind which his companions were huddled a short distance away. A line of foreheads and eyes could be seen peeking over the top of the trunk, and in the special way Nephilim had in communicating with each other without their mouths, Jacob told them to stay put and out of sight. At the same time, he clutched tight the real Sword of Destiny hidden beneath Gotham's oversized jacket, drawing from its presence some semblance of peace knowing it was not in Thaniel's hands, as the angel continued to believe. And as he continued to hear the disturbing conversation taking place just a short distance away, the sadder he became. But the sadness was quick in turning to a festering anger, both at what Thaniel had already done, and what he was further scheming.

"It's clear your trust in me is slight at best," Thaniel remarked to Lilith after a quiet moment had passed.

"At best," echoed Lilith.

"Then if need be have your doubt in my words," said Thaniel. "But you cannot find question in my actions; for the blood I've already drawn—the first with this blade I hold here—should speak unquestionably my intent as clearly as the mark on my forehead.

"The angel's words drew a halting look from Lilith. "Blood? Whose blood?"

"Is it really necessary I speak his name when I can already see in your eyes the one you suspect."

"Gothamel?" Lilith gasped. "You killed him?"

"Not at first," answered Thaniel with a cold smirk. He then opened wide his eyes and the vision of Gotham having his wings brutally severed from his back was reflected back for Lilith to see until

Surprisingly, she withered at the sight of the horrible images and quickly turned her back to them.

"What's this? Tears for Gothamel? Tears for the one responsible for your being vanquished to this watery prison?" Thaniel sang with an unabashed glibness. And indeed Lilith felt the rare warm tickle of a tear as it escaped the corner of her eye and left a wet trail of sorrow across her cheek. But as it dribbled its way to her jaw, it suddenly ignited like gasoline to a match and vanished.

"You were not asked to kill Gothamel," screamed Lilith angrily as she turned once more to face Thaniel.

"Neither was I instructed not to kill him," said Thaniel. He watched her with a particularly icy coolness as she moved about the pool like some enraged pacing caged animal in desperate need to lash out.

"If I didn't know better, I'd think you were fantasizing about clipping my own wings—only with the aid of your own hands and not the sword I hold," said Thaniel.

Lilith shot the angel a look inflamed with hate and anger that no words from her tongue could dare to match.

"I must say, Lilith, you are a difficult wight to fully grasp," continued Thaniel as he turned his face heavenward to the cool drizzle of rain, "It has always held a peculiar fascination for me as to how such an impressively dangerous patchwork of beauty, strength and cunningness stitched from the darkest remnants of wickedness that would ultimately give shape to you could be so completely undone by something so simplistic as the whims of the heart."

"What nonsense are you babbling?" groused Lilith with a scowl.

"Just thinking out loud about Gothamel and Samael, the only two souls who managed to prove there exists a heart in that cold mine of a chest of yours," said Thaniel, "and yet render you completely blind to their eventual betrayals."

Lilith immediately became defensive. "Samael has never betrayed me!"

"She exclaimed, while feeling her way through the dark," uttered Thaniel with a secretive smirk, "even as she's stood staring into the face of such betrayal."

An utter look of blank confusion swept over Lilith by Thaniel's cryptic words until without further provocation, her gaze shifted suddenly to where Jacob quietly stood and he saw the expression on her face eventually turn in a way that made his heart instantly quicken.

"You don't mean..." Lilith managed to gasp.

"That Jacob here is Samael's son—conceived with the daughter of the woman who bore Gothamel's son David—well then, yes, that's exactly what I mean," said Thaniel. "Personally, I found it rather hard to believe you didn't recognize the spooky similarities the first moment you laid eyes on the boy."

Lilith swiped at the air with her hand and the nearby trees slowly shifted slightly in unison to allow what light existed in the stormy night blocked by their tangle of branches to find its way to the forest floor where Jacob and Thaniel stood. She then focused her gaze again to the boy, only this time it was as though she was seeing him for the first time, and in many ways it was out in the light. And as she studied hard through the shadowy darkness creeping in from all around his hair, cheekbones, mouth, and eyes—ah yes, particularly the eyes—a more familiar shape that had been elusive to her—or perhaps readily ignored—seemed to emerge before her, and she soon came to share the same horrified expression as Jacob.

"I believe Anahel put it best when he said—and I'm paraphrasing here, mind you—how ironic it was that the Darkness would birth an heir in the form of a Light Bearer which would help oversee its ultimate demise," said Thaniel.

"You're a dirty liar!" Jacob snapped angrily.

"Am I now?" purred Thaniel. Then with a contemplative roll of his eyes he admitted: "True, you've witnessed from me a bit of web-weaving recently. But of this I most assuredly proclaim to be the truth."

"It's a lie!" Jacob repeated adamantly. "I can prove it too, or have you forgotten there exists a little thing called the Descendants Archive."

"So, you've seen the Descendants Archive, have you? Not that I'm all that surprised, being the sleuth you are," said Thaniel. "Unfortunately, an old saying comes to mind: Don't always believe what you read. If I were you I'd revisit that entry of your birth with a more scrutinizing eye. *Weed!*"

Jacob recoiled at the sound of the offensive slur, not because of the derogatory nature of the insult, but that it left Thaniel's mouth in the sound of Creed's deprecating voice.

Enraged, Lilith turned on Thaniel.

"And you knowingly kept this from me?" she seethed through clenched teeth.

"What can I say? I had to make sure to hedge my bets when this moment was finally upon us," said Thaniel with complete disregard for the anger aimed his way.

And with that, Lilith threw back her head and let loose a piercing scream that made the nearby trees tremble with fright.

"YOU'RE LYING!" Jacob spit forth with all the venom his tongue could secrete. "Just as you've lied about everything else."

Yet even in his steadfast denouncement, there was terrible and noticeable doubt fixed in his eyes.

"Gotham would never have kept something as important as who my father is from me," he continued to spew forth every ounce of denial he felt retching itself upward from deep within the core of his being, though more to himself than the angel, "even if there was truth to what you're saying, which there isn't."

"Are you really as certain as you pretend to sound?" asked Thaniel. "If so, then take my hand."

Jacob hesitated at the sight of the angel's hand as it stretched itself toward him knowing it wasn't being offered to lend him comfort.

"Go on, take it. I most definitely can prove the words of which I speak!" The unflinching look in Thaniel's eyes seemed to serve as a willing dare, one Jacob couldn't find the strength to back down from and expect to ever know a moment's peace. So he begrudgingly took hold of Thaniel's hand, and the second their fingers touched the trees and darkness surrounding them began to wash away like a chalk drawing on a sidewalk attempting to survive a spring downpour. In an instant, Jacob found himself in the corner of a warmly lit cozy room—Anahel's room—and to his shock he found Gotham standing a few feet away looking alive and well.

He was in deep conversation with the other Guides, and the nature of their discussion washed over Jacob in overlapping fragments: the rebirth of the Tree of Life, the death of Gotham's son, the fight between Gotham and Samael that ended in Samael's imprisonment in the Infernal Desert. But it was when the topic focused itself on him that Jacob felt a gurgling of nauseam begin to rise from the pit of his stomach as his worse fears slowly began to materialize in front of him. Like a bad dream—no, far worse...a nightmare—Jacob listened in disbelief as Gotham made truthful everything Thaniel, with devilish delight, had unveiled, and the truth was beyond any pain Jacob had ever before suffered, revealing itself in tears that formed in the corners of his eyes.

"I would prefer if what has been said here tonight in regards to Samael remains in this room," Gotham said to Anahel as Jacob looked on.

"He doesn't know Samael's his father?" asked Anahel.

Gotham shook his head. "For some reason he hasn't inquired yet about who his father might be, but I can sense the question on the edge of his tongue."

Overcome with the feeling he was going to be sick, Jacob yanked himself free from Thaniel's grip and instantly the Forest returned swallowing from sight the horrible memory Jacob wished he had never visited.

~ ~ ~

"I'm so sorry, Jacob," Thaniel's voice somehow managed to pierce the shell-shocked grief that had come to envelop Jacob. "If there was one time I wish I was being untruthful, believe me I wish it were now."

Surprisingly, the angel actually seemed to show a genuine concern and sympathy for the boy, but Jacob wanted none of it.

"Keep away from me!" he barked angrily while stumbling as he desperately backed away from Thaniel's consoling reach like some wounded animal. "JUST KEEP AWAY FROM ME!"

His heart was pounding so loudly in his ears he was certain blood would begin seeping out from them. Suddenly, it was all beginning to make sense to him: the uncomfortable looks he got from the other Guides when he first came to Eden, as though they had caught a glimpse of a ghost in need of vanquishing; the ongoing contempt Eksel openly displayed toward him; even Creed's unwavering assertion that he was Weed. Only he wasn't just any Weed, just as he wasn't any ordinary Nephilim as he had come to believe. The panic reeling inside him at such thoughts became almost too much for any one person to bear, and it gave way to an indescribable fear from which he was sure he'd perish. But it was all quickly lost to the anger that surged through him and sought to consume the gnawing feelings of deception like an unstoppable lava flow advancing upon some unfortunate village nestled at the foot of an awakening volcano. And for the first time since Gotham's passing, the overwhelming grief that had gripped Jacob was incinerated into a pile of ashes.

~ ~ ~

"The boy," Lilith was suddenly heard crying, and when Jacob looked back toward the pool he found her dark eyes fixed intently on him. "I want him."

Thaniel drew a deep breath, but he said nothing. Nor did he make a move toward the boy.

"A son of Samael—if indeed that is who he is—has no place in Eden. Nor do you have any right fostering him in secret as you have," said Lilith.

"And what reason would you have for his company?' asked Thaniel. "Certainly not a sudden maternal need to experience the joys of step-motherhood."

Lilith was not amused, even slightly, by such quips.

"I am warning you, Thaniel, do not toy me with on this matter, or I will see you suffer for it," she threatened quietly. "I will not allow you to leave here with both the Sword of Destiny and this supposed Light Bearer in hand."

"Fair enough," said Thaniel after pondering Lilith's words. "But I want your word here and now that if I give you the boy you will continue to pledge all your dark power should I need it in backing my hold of Eden."

"Agreed," barked Lilith impatiently. "Now hand him over to me."

Jacob stood stunned at what he was hearing, and before he could fathom what was happening he found himself in Thaniel's surprisingly firm hold to the back of the neck.

As Jacob struggled, the angel lowered his face to the boy's ear. "I like you Jacob, really I do. And what I do is of no personal ill will toward you, please know that," he whispered. "Under different circumstances I'm sure I would have enjoyed having your company for some time. You bring a rare spirit to this place. But the truth is a Light Bearer is the last thing I need around here, particularly one who harbors such ill will, deserved or not, toward me."

"You're not going to send me in there," Jacob cried defiantly through clenched teeth while trying to push back against Thaniel's strength.

"It won't be so bad. True, it's not Eden, but on the positive side you will finally be united with the father you so longed for," said Thaniel with all the comfort of a thorn pricking the skin.

Jacob eyes were now wide and wild with fright. No matter how hard he fought back, he could not keep from being forced closer to the pool's edge as his feet slipped and slid along the ground made muddy by the rain. He began imagining the arms of the demonic creatures— the Feeders—lurking just out of sight beneath the surface snaking up out of the water, their clawed hands poised to grasp his flailing legs once they were in reach and drag him down into the murkiness with the rest of the damned. It made his feet kick and dig harder and deeper into the slick, rain-soaked earth in a desperate search for leverage to cease the advance, but to no avail. All the while he looked on with terror at Lilith, who stood waiting with an enthusiastic, if not creepy, smile fixed on her face that was anything but welcoming, and it grew wider and more sinister the closer he was guided toward her.

Then, just as he braced himself for the worse, a most thankful sight dropped down from out of nowhere. It was Max, Leos, Kairo and Ethan, and with their swords in hand they formed a human barrier between Jacob and the dark waters of the pool into which Thaniel was intent on tossing him. The sight of them spurred Betryel into action and he came charging like a bull at the four boys until Thaniel simply raised his hand and the pounding of feet immediately stopped.

"Well now, this certainly is unexpected," said Thaniel but showing little concern of worry while eyeing the obstacle standing firmly in his way.

"Let him go!" demanded Leos when it was clear Betryel had heeded Thaniel's non-verbal command to stand down from his attack.

"While I admire your spirit, it might serve you to rethink your stance if you knew exactly who it is you're so boldly stepping up to defend," said Thaniel.

"We know," said Ethan, glancing sheepishly at Jacob. "We heard every word."

Jacob felt a weight of shame suddenly upon him, and he almost wished Thaniel at that very moment would give him the shove to allow the pool to swallow him from sight.

"Then you know you stand with your swords brandished in defense of the Darkness," said Thaniel.

"Pig's arse! We stand in defense of a friend, and a good one at that. Everything else is just meaningless minutiae," said Max offering Jacob a firm and much-needed look of loyalty. It was the same look Jacob found in the faces of all four of his friends, and it sparked a warmth inside him to know the ugly thing that wrung his insides so painfully didn't seem to have any bearing on those closest to him.

"Well, well, that is a touching show of camaraderie you have shown, really, I must say," said Thaniel with clear mockery. "Now unless you really want to put the true bounds of loyalty to the test, I'd advise you to step aside unless you'd care to join your friend for a swim."

Not one of the boys so much as blinked, except for Ethan who peered nervously over his left shoulder at the pool and the mysterious figure of beauty in it waiting with an eager, dark look of delight draped across her face like a funeral veil. Still, Ethan dug his feet into the ground upon which he stood and put on his bravest, most determined face.

"So be it," remarked Thaniel when he saw the boys had no intention of backing down.

He stretched his wings out wide on either side of him to help mow down whatever stood in his way and stepped forward, and when it was obvious the two sides were about to clash Jacob cried out to Thaniel to stop and the angel paused.

"Step back," Jacob then ordered his friends. But they were reticent in following his orders.

"I said step back!" he repeated more forcefully. "I appreciate your help, but really...I can handle this."

Even though the shaky tone of his voice noted otherwise, there was an undefeated glimmer of fire in Jacob's eyes, and it was convincing enough that Max, Leos, Ethan and Kairo, against their better judgment, conceded to clearing the way to the pool.

"A move both smart and dare I say nobly brave," whispered Thaniel in Jacob's ear.

The edge of the pool was now uncomfortably close to Jacob's feet. His breathing became sharp and jagged. Less than a half dozen steps and he'd be struggling against different pairs of hands grabbing hold of him and dragging his body away from the world and into a darkness he'd rather not imagine much less experience.

"He's playing you, Lilith," Jacob blurted suddenly and forcefully. "Thaniel's lying to you about the sword. It's not Destiny."

"What ridiculous nonsense is this you are trying to pull, Nephilim?" asked Thaniel.

Jacob's desperate eyes found Lilith, her face unsmiling and stark

"I can prove it!" he said in the sincerest of voices.

"You're wasting your breath," said Thaniel. "And may the water drown silent your lies."

Jacob's body grew suddenly tense and his heart thumped in a sheer panic inside his chest waiting for the final shove that would send him into the water.

CHAPTER TWENTY-THREE

"Wait," Lilith called out to Thaniel, and Jacob experienced an overwhelming gladness he never expected from the sound of her voice.

"What do you mean the sword is not Destiny? And pray a flight of angels comes to your aid and rescues you from my reach if you perjure yourself to me," she said to Jacob in the coldest—and most promising—of threats.

"It's not me who's lying, it's him," said Jacob breathlessly. "He's tricked you into pledging your loyalty and support to him and that stupid crown on his head. You heard him yourself...he was making sure to hedge his bets. So what did he do? He's made you turn on Samael so in your jealous anger—justified as it might be—you'd rethink freeing him as punishment for his indiscretions. But that's only because he can't free Samael, because the sword he holds is no more Destiny than that tree over there. He's taking you for a fool, and doing a pretty good job at it."

By the look slowly creeping vine-like over Lilith face, she did not take well to such a suggestion. Thaniel noticed her suspicions as well.

"You're not actually buying this absurdity, are you?" he asked, turning an incredulous eye to Lilith.

Then when he saw the boy's allegation had already begun churning inside her head, he thrust forth the sword he held for her to study.

"Does this sword not look to your eyes to carry the spearhead all of history has clamored to possess?" he asked bristly.

"It does," answered Lilith coolly. "But looking and being are two completely different things. I would expect you of all to know that."

Thaniel was becoming visibly more incensed as he himself couldn't keep at bay the possibility of truth in Jacob's pronouncement.

"I'm telling you it's a lie," he denounced angrily. "Then again what would I expect from the son of Samael, standing here spinning words of untruth in a desperate attempt to keep his footing in Eden. Well, you can take your forked tongue where the rest of the serpents nest. Enjoy your time in the Underneath."

He grabbed hold of Jacob once more and, in the last moment he had to make his voice heard before being plunged into the water, Jacob cried out, "Make him prove it!"

There came a moment of intense silence. Jacob waited for the splash of water, but none came. When he opened his eyes, the invisible hand clutching his pounding heart squeezed painfully tighter. He found himself hovering just above the water at an angle even he with all his gifts couldn't right had gravity not somehow been removed between himself and the water leaving him floating.

He turned his fear-filled gaze to Lilith whose outstretched hand seemed to emanate some unseen power that froze the boy in mid-fall from the vanquishing push Thaniel had given the boy.

"Prove how?" she asked.

"Herrinsu vine," Jacob gasped, managing to find his voice, croaky as it was. "Make him cut through a strand of Herrinsu vine. If it's Destiny he will have no trouble doing it and I will voluntarily dive into this pool. But if it doesn't, you will know I wasn't lying."

Lilith studied him for a moment. Then, with a pushing gesture of her hand, Jacob was sent forcibly backward to land on the bank at the pool's edge, which he quickly scrambled away from like a spooked crab.

"Fine then, if it's proof you want, so be it," said Thaniel, looking scornfully at Jacob. "My thanks to you, Fledgling. Here my conscious was weighed down with the moroseness I was feeling having to part company with you in this manner of which you've now managed to free me."

He then looked to the trees searching the cluster of giants in the immediate surrounding area until his eyes found what it was they sought. With an eager confidence, he strode over to one where the unmistakable vine grew plentiful, spiraling tightly around a massive trunk in its slow climb skyward. Thin and string-like, the leafy vine appeared all the more delicate when Thaniel grabbed hold of a strand in his hand. It was hard to imagine anything more than an effortless tug was needed to snap it free from the tree, much less a sword of any caliber. The idea such a vine could serve as eternal shackles was implausible at best.

"To once and for all render silent all doubt that this is Destiny," Thaniel declared loudly as he brought the gleaming blade to the vine. To his consternation, the slender vine resisted the hair-splitting sharpness of the sword. He began sawing desperately at it, and then in his growing frustration he hacked furiously away at it digging the blade deep into the trunk of tree with each powerful blow of his swing but leaving the vine intact without so much of a nick to its delicate snaking stem or loss of even a single leaf.

"I don't understand," Thaniel gasped in disbelief when finally he surrendered any further attempt.

"Then the boy was right, you were attempting to deceive me," Lilith remarked with simmering anger. "And in deceiving me, you attempted to deceive Samael."

"It's not true!" argued Thaniel adamantly, and in that brief moment of denial a rare fear in his voice revealed itself. But it quickly dissipated as he turned suddenly on Jacob and in a blurring flash of movement was standing over him with a gleam of anger in his fiery eyes.

"How is this possible, Nephilim? This sword has not left my hand since Gothamel placed it in its grasp. I drove it deep into his side and extinguished his life with one twist of the blade. You saw it yourself."

Jacob jumped to his feet and for the first time Thaniel witnessed in the boy's stance a combativeness at the ready that gave him a moment of pause.

"That's right I saw it, right after you mercilessly mutilated him, and before you threw him over the edge of the cliff and into the clouds to his death," Jacob spit with a pent-up hatred finally unleashed. "Go ahead, look into my thoughts and see for yourself how Gotham suckered you. It's okay, I won't block them this time. I want you to see every detail that my words couldn't possibly do justice in describing how you've been taken for an utter chump by someone laying dead at the bottom of Broken Earth."

"I've already seen your thoughts," said Thaniel, dismissively.

"You sure about that, like you were about that sword in your hand?" argued Jacob with a sly smirk.

Thaniel kept his eyes firmly on Jacob, but instead of looking at the boy he was looking through him. Jacob could feel his thoughts being perused, like someone mistaking his brain for a swimming pool and diving head-first into it, and he watched with a warming glee the changing expressions slowly wash across the angel's face as the extent to his being duped played out undeniably before him.

"You did make it through the Gate...and past the Nekcri..." There was disbelief in Thaniel's voice, and his eyes narrowed as if he was peering through a small keyhole to spy on what was on the other side of a door. "The Powers...they came to your rescue and took you to Akdamar. Gotham was there...hunched over a white-flamed fire and working fastidiously on a sword. Wait a minute...the fire..."

A painful recognition came to Thaniel's face, not so much from the image he was seeing but that such a possibility had escaped him in the first place.

"The white flame of the Begend," he muttered quietly. "Of course...that's what he used to forge this sword."

He didn't need to see any further, nor did he choose to do so. "Let me guess, they bound your memory with that of a false one knowing full well I'd be suspicious enough to look upon your return," said Thaniel.

Surprisingly, Jacob found the angel wasn't suddenly engulfed in rage by this unveiled trickery. In fact, Thaniel couldn't help but smile as he turned his gaze to the sword clutched in his hand, though not with the same coveted possessiveness as before.

"Admittedly, you are quite the resourceful one, Gothamel, both in craftsmanship and extraordinary sacrifice of life. That is one boast I won't deny bestowing upon you," the angel said quietly. And it seemed at that moment Thaniel recognized clearly—and graciously accepted— the destiny imagined him had been lost. Or rather stolen.

"To see you standing here foolish and defeated as you are right now would be a small consolation to him," said Jacob.

Thaniel peered at Jacob out of the corner of his eye and the rage that had filled his face moments earlier was nowhere to be seen.

"Foolish yes, Jacob; don't be so sure about defeated," he replied. "For you see I warned Gothamel I would open the Through and unleash upon Eden a storm of darkness to be carried to every corner of its lands on the wings of dragons. If he thought such a threat was an idle one I wasn't willing to carry out then he has proven himself equally the fool, even in death."

Jacob proved unmoved.

"You won't do it," he said, raising Thaniel's brow.

"You sound unabashedly certain in your assumption, Fledgling."

"Because I am," Jacob contended. "You won't do what you threaten because you can't. And you can't because you are no longer confident the Darkness you threaten to unleash will leave you unscathed. If anything, after your failed attempt to secure Destiny, and even worse your ruse to keep it for yourself after promising to hand it over to Lilith, I wouldn't be too sure whatever is eagerly waiting to crawl up and out from inside that pool won't come seeking you out first."

Thaniel looked to Lilith and the piercing glare that met him was enough to give thoughtful credence to the boy's words, though he tried to remain straight-faced to keep such mulling ideas to himself.

"And if you're wrong?" he asked.

"Then I will stop you before you even come close to reaching the water, and your fate will join Gotham's," answered Jacob with an unwavering conviction.

The corner of Thaniel's mouth crooked upward slightly. That a Nephilim would levy such a declaration to an angel with such a brass tongue was at best intriguing. Yet any amusement Thaniel held over such a threat soon faded and his face turned ghostly white when he watched Jacob reveal from deep inside the folds of the coat hanging tent-like on his frame the sword he had longed to possess as his own; the true Sword of Destiny.

~ ~ ~

"How have you come to have this?" asked Thaniel in hushed astonishment.

He didn't wait for Jacob's answer, choosing instead to once more delve into the boy's thoughts while he had the chance. "Oh, Gothamel, how you are clever in your utter simplicity. All this time and it was right here, lying completely unguarded right under my nose."

"It's over, Thaniel," declared Jacob. "And now you're going to come with me to give Anahel and the others the good news."

"Over?" said Thaniel with a questioning glance at the boy.

"Do something, Thaniel," cried Lilith urgently. "We can't lose that sword after all this, especially to him."

"Relax, my dear. All is far from lost," said Thaniel in a voice free of worry that made Jacob anxiously tighten his grip on Destiny. "Yes, it appears our little Light Bearer here has smartly seized the upper hand and will reap the rewards of Eden's everlasting gratitude because of it. But appearances, as he should have well learned by now, can be quite deceiving."

With that he threw forth his hand and, before Jacob could even draw back his sword, a great unseen and tremendous force ripped his feet from the ground and sent him flying backward through the air. It slammed him fully against the trunk of a tree knocking Destiny free of his grip. Reeling from a blinding pain, Jacob fell slumped and dazed in a heap on the ground. An explosion of white spots mired his vision which he fought to see past in a desperate search for Destiny. He quickly spied it lying several feet away from him. When he went to crawl for it, however, he was stopped by a booted foot that kicked him over onto his back before planting itself hard against the center of his chest pinning him firmly onto his back at the base of the tree.

"I would have thought one of the first things Gothamel would have taught you is never afford the enemy a second chance to catch you beneath their heel," said Thaniel with his wings spread open while looking down smugly upon Jacob.

"Then you admit you're my enemy," gasped Jacob while feeling a sadness creep over him at the sound of the words. Even now, with Thaniel looming over him with the stain of Gotham's blood unapologetically on his hands and the tread of his foot now painfully pressed against his chest, Jacob couldn't help but mourn the kinship he knew had been lost with the angel, strange as it was. It was not, however, the kind of mourning that came with tears, but with anger—the kind of anger brought about by the taste of betrayal. He could feel it turn over upon itself and pummel his insides like a wave beating against a ragged sea cliff trying to hold back the tidal surge. It found its way to his arms and then his hands, and they in turn found their way to Thaniel's leg, and in a powerful rush of strength that surprised even himself, Jacob somehow managed to cast the angel from off him. How he did it he had no idea, nor did he pause to question it. All that mattered was returning Destiny to his hand.

Rolling onto all fours, Jacob half ran, half crawled his way toward the sword. Just short of reaching it, he was snatched up again by the unseen force that moments before sent him careening viciously into a tree. This time, though, it didn't send him crashing into anything; it held him suspended in its grasp, leaving him dangling upside down above the ground like a human piñata by some invisible snare strung around his ankles. Jacob fought and thrashed about in a pointless effort to free himself until he felt an uncomfortable pinch at his chest coming from the end of Thaniel's sword.

"Now, then, there are two ways we can remedy this situation," said Thaniel as he stood nearly face to face with Jacob, albeit in inverted positions. "One, you will bequeath the Sword of Destiny to me as it appears it is now your right to do so. Or two, I drive my sword through you and Destiny automatically becomes mine the moment your last breath leaves your body. I'm perfectly happy with either scenario, but gracious as I am I leave the decision in your hands."

Suddenly, out of the corner of his eye, Jacob caught sight of Ethan slyly making his way toward the sword laying on the ground and he instantly became alarmed.

"No, Ethan, DON'T..." he yelled.

Ethan stopped dead in his tracks drawing the attention of Betryel who then quickly lunged forward and, ignoring a second warning from Thaniel, he snatched the sword up into his hands.

"I've got it. I've got it!" cried Betryel, first with disbelief, and then with the powerful realization of his feat. There erupted from his eyes the wild glimmer that comes when a treasure of untold worth is unearthed. As his hands gripped tight the sword that gleamed bright with the power it held, the angel's face brightened with illusions of grandeur. Then, just as quickly, his smile faded and his wide idolatrous-filled eyes flooded with an unknown horror. From the center of his chest exploded a burst of flame, and in that moment Betryel managed to set free one final wail of doom before his body spontaneously combusted in a burst of an inferno that rendered him instantly a cloud of ash left to scatter and dissipate into the wet, dank air. And with a marked thud, Destiny was returned to the ground.

The sight pitched fire in Thaniel's eyes.

"Idiot!" he growled before turning his anger onto Jacob. "I shouldn't bother extending you a choice now that you've cost me a brother. So I ask you now, what's it to be...life or death?"

"I'll never hand Destiny over to you willingly," answered Jacob with unwavering defiance.

As fearless a face as Jacob attempted to put forth, his insides were brimming with the stuff that makes hands tremble, lips quiver and foreheads become awash in flop sweat, especially when he recognized to his great distress that Thaniel held no qualms in seeing through his threat.

"Then death it shall be," stated Thaniel as simplistically as looking through a window and noting the kind of weather the day would bring.

Jacob felt his heart throw itself against his chest as if seeking desperately to escape the aim of the blade pressed against his skin. But just as the angel drew back his sword a ceasing cry came from the pool.

"Kill the boy and not even the Herrinsu vine will keep Samael from delivering his vengeance upon you," bellowed Lilith.

Thaniel turned and fixed a wild eye on Lilith. "You are a most difficult creature to make out. I would think you of anyone would relish the sight of seeing the boy's insides. Or did I misconstrue the sight of your outstretched arm earlier when I was about to hand him over to you as something less innocent than a warm embrace in waiting?"

Lilith's silence was all the argument Thaniel needed.

"Better the boy die than Destiny be lost to us. Surely, even you, Lilith, would agree with that summation," he said. "And if given the choice between an heir or freedom, then I surmise most certainly Samael would agree as well."

"That is not your prediction to make, nor is it your decision to render," Lilith challenged heatedly. "Graze even the boy's skin with your blade, and you can rest assure a most pointed reckoning will be due you."

"With Destiny in my possession, I say let it come," said Thaniel with bold contempt in his voice and an even bolder glint in his seemingly possessed eyes.

He turned back to Jacob and just as he drew back his sword the howl of a wolf pierced the long history of silence that had hung over the Silent Forest. Strange enough was it to hear such a howl stray to a place where life and all it mothered refused to tread that it broke through Thaniel's trance-like state and bent his attention to the surrounding trees. But to Jacob's ears, the wolf's cry proved to be most familiar and welcoming.

~ ~ ~

It was while Thaniel scoured with his eyes the stormy darkness filled with a gauzy mist from the falling rain that Jacob, with the vantage of his face pointed toward the ground, caught sight of several roots from the nearby trees slowly beginning to slither up from out of the muddy earth. He looked quizzically to Lilith who stood still in the pool and placed a quieting finger to her lips. Jacob then watched as the roots snaked their way around the unsuspecting angel's ankles.

"Now then, where were we?" Thaniel, turning back to the task at hand when any sign of a wolf presence eluded him, said. "Oh yes, your unfortunate demise."

Barely had he managed to finish his words when his feet were forcefully pulled out from beneath him. At the same moment, the hold on Jacob dissipated and he fell to the ground.

Thaniel was dragged across the damp forest floor for some distance until he managed to right himself at the waist, and with his sword began hacking away at the roots that had taken a tight hold of him. When he finally managed to free himself, he turned back to Jacob but he saw it was too late; Jacob now held once more the Sword of Destiny, and from the look of the double-handed grip he had on it, nothing was going to pry it free from his grasp.

It wasn't enough to stop Thaniel.

He strode toward the boy with a determined step and even more determined look emblazoned on his face. Max attempted to step in between Thaniel and his friend and stop the itch, long in need of scratching, of crossing his sword with the angel's. He was quickly followed by Leos and Kairo and Ethan, all ready to take down the one responsible for filling their heads with enlightening things of the earth and beyond, yet who would hold an everlasting despairing blot in their memory for the one great betrayal he committed.

"No!" Jacob yelled to them. "This is my fight."

There was a desperate selfishness to his cry the boys heard that made them reluctantly give up their stance and clear the way for Thaniel and Jacob to face off with one another.

"Vengeance is mine, I will repay, saith the Lord," recited the angel. "So saith the Light Bearer before me."

"Personally I prefer 'Even though I walk through the valley of the shadow of death, I will fear no evil,' " said Jacob. He gripped tighter the sword he held at the ready in front of him and, firming his footing on the ground beneath him, a true avenging flame flickered in his eyes as the angel made his way toward him.

"For you are with me; your rod and your staff, they comfort me," Jacob whispered the next few lines of the bible verse his mother had so well ingrained in him.

It was only when Thaniel caught sight of the eyes peering out from the darkness of the Forest just behind Jacob that he paused. Not just one pair, but several. They glowed bright, though not like those of an angel. And as they moved slowly forward and stepped into the murky light of the clearing, their shape was revealed: Wolves. The same pack which had served as both guide and protector of Jacob in his race to the Dilmun Sea and the Gate within it. Led by their black-maned leader, they came up and around, positioning themselves on both sides of Jacob seemingly daring the angel to further advance.

"I said I've got this," muttered Jacob, who was surprised as anyone at the wolves' sudden appearance. "I don't want you involved."

But the wolves paid him no mind.

"So...the beasts have decided to turn on their master," said Thaniel.

"That's where you're wrong. The beasts, as you call them, don't recognize masters, but companions...as it should be," said Jacob. "I would have thought you of anyone would be educated about the simplest of nature's equations."

"Well then, are they willing to die for their companion? For their presence here is their death warrant," said Thaniel, "and I shall not hesitate to cut down every last one that attempts to keep me from that sword."

The answer came in a threatening growl from the black wolf who hunched low to the ground and raised high his back.

"I shall start with you, then," said Thaniel, returning the wolves challenging stare. "And when your carcass lies limp on the ground we shall see if the rest regain their good senses."

He started to come at the wolf with his sword when a white blur burst through the trees and came charging from behind. To Jacob's surprise—and horror—he saw it was Mist.

Before he could call out to her to stop, Thaniel at the very last second turned and caught sight of the white wolf just as it leapt at him. There came a bright flash from his blade as Mist hit Thaniel's torso with all four of its paws causing the angel to lose his balance and stumble backward into the forbidden waters of the pool.

Thaniel's face became immersed in panic-filled terror, especially when he saw the creatures from below coming toward him. He immediately began to furiously beat his wings in a desperate attempt to lift himself and retreat to the sky, but it was too late; they had him, and he became just like a hapless seabird caught in an oil seepage bled from a stricken tanker.

"Call them off!" he called out desperately to Lilith, who was standing just a reach away, and remained quietly so.

"You can't let them take me," he cried when the horrifying reality finally took hold of him. "We had a pact."

Lilith remained still, watching with the coldest of stares the hopeless struggling in the seething water which looked to be boiling from the frenzy. Thaniel then turned a most pleading of gazes to where Jacob stood frozen and bearing painful witness to his demise. But Jacob knew there was nothing he could do, even if he had so wanted.

Seemingly surrendering to his fate, the angel uttered one final word in a voice almost too quiet for Jacob to hear: "Zophiel!" Then suddenly he was gone, succumbing to the darkness that swallowed him from sight. And an unsettling stillness returned to the water, and the Silent Forest became silent once more.

~ ~ ~

For some time, Jacob stood in silence staring at the pool imaging what horrors were now greeting Thaniel, and knowing even the darkest corner of his imagination could never fully lend itself to the true extent of those horrors. Yet despite Thaniel's sins—of which, undoubtedly, there were many—Jacob couldn't deny the feelings of sympathy he felt bubbling up inside himself. Yet whatever pity he felt, it was soon forgotten when he suddenly heard the sound of whimpering. He looked to where the wolves had gathered themselves in a tight circle and noticed almost immediately that Mist was not amongst them.

"Um...Jacob...?" It was Max, who was standing near the wolf

congregation with Leos, Kairo and Ethan. "I think you better come over here."

There was a restrained sense of urgency in Max's voice. It matched the same wretched look of despair he found his friends to be quietly sharing; a look which made Jacob's chest suddenly tighten in a most uncomfortable manner. The wolves made way for Jacob as he rushed toward them, and, as they did, his heart instantly sank when he saw Mist sprawled on her side upon the ground. She was panting heavily and her snow-white coat was marked with a bright red fist-sized blemish where Thaniel's sword had punctured itself deep into her side. Grimacing at the sight, Jacob dropped heavily to his knees beside his faithful friend and gently stroked her head.

"Why would you do something so stupid?" he whispered. " I told you it was my fight. I had it handled...I had Destiny."

The wolf whimpered in pain as she struggled to move, and in the painful realization that his brave companion was wavering in her last breaths, Jacob suddenly found his thoughts turning to the River, though not flowing with life, but stagnant and dark in the one moment of its existence when death stilled it.

"Not to worry, Mist, old girl...I refuse to let anything take you," he said in a quivering yet reassuring voice. "I'm going to make you good as new, I promise! Then maybe you can show me how to be as fearless as you."

He could see the pain in the wolf's face and there was nothing more he wanted at that moment than to see it erased. To do so, he needed water, though he wasn't sure why. All he knew was in the rare few times he had exercised the one gift he possessed that made him so unique, water seemed to aid in his success. It was then he wished they were nearer the River. And since there was no earthly way he was willing to venture to the edge of the nearby pool he looked to the sky. Holding out his hands, he allowed the rain to fill his cupped palms, which he then poured over the blood-stained patch of fur. He then was about to bring his hands to the wolf's side when Max grabbed him.

"What are you doing?" he asked.

"What does it look like?" asked Jacob.

"I know how you feel…really…but you can't!" argued Max. "You know the rules when it comes to…you know…"

"Screw the rules!" spat Jacob. "You think I'm just going to sit here and watch her die?"

Then before anyone else could further the argument, Jacob placed his hands one on top the other over the gaping wound feeling Mist's body shudder beneath his touch. He could also sense the worry and impatience coming from the other wolves watching unblinkingly with their intense gazes his every move.

Taking a deep breath, Jacob closed his eyes. The warm stickiness of the blood oozing from the laceration was not lost to him. It was the blood's warmth into which he burrowed his concentration until he could feel the pulsating beats of the heart that pumped it forth and, just as it happened when he placed his healing hands on the River, the veins in Jacob's arms gradually revealed themselves through his skin. Soon, Jacob could feel the flow of the wolf's blood reverse itself, and Mist's heavy panting and whimpering gradually eased.

"You did it!" Ethan exclaimed when Jacob finally removed his hands from Mist's side.

True enough, the stain of blood matting Mist's hide, as well as the wound itself, had vanished completely from sight, and the worrisome look shared by Kairo, Max and Leos who had quietly looked on in stunned disbelief was slowly replaced with unabated gladness.

"Now that's some trick, mate," said Max, giving a nudge to Jacob who looked to be more stunned than anyone at the small miracle that had just taken place in their company.

"Yeah…some trick," said Jacob, releasing a burdensome breath of relief.

It wasn't long before Mist was back on her feet moving about as if she had never been touched by Thaniel's sword. And once she had sufficiently expressed her gratitude to Jacob with a rambunctious licking of his face, and the five boys had traded well-deserved, congratulatory pats on the back for surviving such a draining ordeal, it was suggested they quickly return to Havenhid to ease the worry of the Guides and their fellow Nephilim with news that the threat gripping Eden was no more.

Just as they were about to begin after the wolf pack, which had run on ahead leading the way through the woods, a voice called after them.

"Know that peace will never be yours for as long as Destiny is in your possession." It was Lilith, who strangely enough for the first time looked like the prisoner she was in the solitude of her watery cell.

"Forget her," Leos urged Jacob for whom the threat was clearly intended.

Jacob ignored his companions' prodding to keep going, and he turned to face the deadly beauty who, for the first time since discovering the true nature of her being, didn't send a tingle of alarm or dread through him.

"Maybe you're right, Lilith," he said in a voice absent of fear. "But I've a sneaking suspicion it is you who will never know peace as long as Destiny is my possession."

He held up the sword in his hand so the sight of it in his grip gleaming in all its legend would forever brand itself in Lilith's memory as an unpleasant reminder—and firm warning—of who now possessed the mystical weapon and, more importantly, what it meant. And a snide smile couldn't be helped from creeping across his mouth as a rare look of defeat settled itself like a dark shadow upon Lilith's face as it was made clear his message had been heard.

Jacob turned his back on the pool and was about to continue on with his friends, all sharing the same hope of never having to lay eyes on Lilith or the inside of the Forest from which they were gladly retreating, when suddenly another voice followed after them.

"Jacob..."

It came like a breeze, tickling the back of Jacob's neck in a way that made his blood turn to ice as it spoke his name; for he recognized it instantly. And it made him stop cold in his tracks.

~ ~ ~

"What is it, Jacob?" asked Max.

Jacob said nothing as he stood stone-still with a look of muted terror seized in his eyes.

"Don't leave me like this, Jacob..."

Despite every fiber in his being resisting to do so, Jacob couldn't keep himself from slowly turning around when the voice called out to him again. Then, as if his bodily functions were no longer his to control, he found his feet walking him back in the direction of the pool with small, timid steps. And as he drew closer, his eyes widened at the sight of a familiar image reflected on the water's surface. It was the same vision that had haunted him over the course of countless nights' sleeps; that of a harsh, barren desert swallowed in night, and a massive rock to which a darkened shape was tightly bound.

Ignoring his friends' pleas of caution, Jacob made his way towards the pool's edge for a closer look. "What is this?" he quietly and cautiously inquired of Lilith who was spied lurking on the far edge of the vision.

"Do you really need me to tell you what you already know to be?" she replied.

Jacob opened his mouth to speak, but before he could the voice belonging to the figure tied to the rock sounded again.

"You can't leave me here."

"I don't know who you are," muttered Jacob nervously.

"Of course you do," the voice replied. "It's in accepting the answer with which you are finding difficulty."

The figure then turned its head toward Jacob so that what faint light there was found its face. When it did, Jacob felt an unfathomable chill move through him; for the water of the pool had somehow found a way to play the same deceptively cruel joke with his own reflection as that of his dream.

"It's not possible," mumbled Jacob.

"What do you find so disbelieving? That what you thought to be a dream is suddenly anything but? Or that a father and son could share such a striking resemblance to one another?"

In seeing this most unwelcome vision, as well as hearing this voice that had haunted him for so long, Jacob wondered at that moment if, in fact, everything the night had brought to him had indeed been just a dream. If so, he was never more eager to awaken.

"I SAID IT'S NOT POSSIBLE! EVEN IF IT WAS, I WON'T BELIEVE IT." Jacob was shouting now, not so much to the figure in the vision, but to himself; because slowly this vision that had long-stalked him was becoming harder to disbelieve. And the more his disbelief faded, the more real this figure became. This angel beyond Fallen. The one called Samael, and more notably the one revealed to have fathered him. One only had to glance at the face to see the truth, and for the first time Jacob saw what the other angels saw when they first looked into his face.

"I implore you not to turn away from your father. Not now in his most despairing of need," the figure pleaded when Jacob turned his back to the pool.

"If you know what's good for you, you will never refer yourself in that way to me again," seethed Jacob as he felt both uncontrollable rage and a surge of burning tears fighting to overtake him.

"I understand your resentment of me. But know it stems from lies...lies you and the world of man long ago were made to believe by the Guides and the Light within which they reside."

"I don't want to hear anymore," cried Jacob. But the voice persisted in his ears.

"You cannot abandon me this way, Jacob. Not when the key to my freedom resides in your hand, and yours alone, my only son."

Jacob spun around. His face red with anger and anguish, and Destiny tight in his hand. "Look at it now. It's the closest you'll ever get to it."

"You speak in anger. You don't mean that, my son."

"For the last time, I AM NOT YOUR SON!" Jacob yelled in a

voice that continued as a roaring echo through the trees.

He then charged the pool leaving behind him any semblance of fear or caution he carried whenever he ventured too close to the water's edge. Lilith saw clearly the intent in his eyes and this time it was her face that mirrored fear as she cried out vehemently for him to stop. Jacob paid her no mine, as his feet proceeded beyond where the water licked the ground. There, with Destiny clutched in both hands, he dropped to his knees, and with a defiant anger coursing through the sinewy muscles of his arms he raised the sword high over his head. The last thing he saw was Samael's face contort in a grotesque manner as he witnessed the sword being brought down with a vengeful thrust and a monstrous roar was unleashed. Hideously clawed and mangled hands came up out of the water in an attempt to grab hold of Jacob. But the blade of the sword pierced the surface of the water first, and in that moment the water became like a sheet of obsidian and it shattered in a violent eruption sending jagged shards of pulverized blackness into the air.

When the last of it had settled on the ground, Jacob opened his eyes. To his surprise, the dark water that had occupied the pool was now clear and blue. Even more welcoming was that Samael, and Lilith, were nowhere to be seen, and his presence at the edge of the pool was no longer threatened by fearful creatures lurking beneath the surface. And from within the cavern of rock at the far end of the pool which had served as a place of refuge for Lilith, water once again began to flow.

Max, Ethan, Leos and Kairo rushed to where Jacob remained kneeling in the shallows, his face a blank slate of expression except for the subtle presence of tears held firmly in check from spilling over the rim of his eyes as he listened to the sound of the bubbling water as it cascaded over the rocks from the cavern and into the reborn pool.

"Now, we can go," said Jacob, finally.

CHAPTER TWENTY-FOUR

*T*he *unpleasant task of recovering Gotham's body began early this morning. The weather remained miserable. For the first time—at least since I've been here—the dazzling sunlight that's always lit up Eden so spectacularly without fail was nowhere to be seen. Instead, a blanket of dark, billowing clouds looking like angry beasts stretched as far as the eye could see. Anahel could have wiped the sky clean of their existence with an effortless sweep of his hand, but he recognized Eden itself had fallen into mourning with the rest of us and he left it to its sorrow. Even the waterfalls, always so vibrant and charged, seemed to hang like funeral veils in front of the face of the mountain we passed as we left Havenhid. And yet nothing could compete with the grey and somber mood that had taken hold of all us in what felt like an unrelenting vice-like grip.*

Anahel initially thought it best if the Guides go alone on the search. No doubt he meant to shield us from any further grief. But despite his good intentions, Anahel quickly realized none of us—myself, in particular—wished to be saved from this grief, and reluctantly he gave in to our wishes, but not before handing down a strict stipulation that none of us were to take part in the recovery efforts.

No one spoke a word when we finally reached Broken Earth. The place that had long-served as a pinnacle of hope and excitement where young Nephilim took hold of the essence of their being in a tight embrace and blindly stepped where nothing but faith waited to catch their fall, had suddenly become laden with a dank grimness. Our eyes immediately shifted as one to the same spot of ground that in all our minds carried the stain of blood seeped into the earth, even though there was nothing but puddles of rainwater. I'm certain many of us stood wondering if we'd ever again be able to come to this spot without being assaulted by the haunting image of Gotham writhing in the suffering of being de-winged and defeated on the ground.

There was, however, no pause in Damiel's step. I'd never seen a more hardened look fixed to his face. It was like armor, and instead of taking a moment to acknowledge the painful memory waiting to greet us, he immediately charged the edge of the overlook and dove into the waiting emptiness with the pent-up aggression of someone tackling a hated enemy. In an instant he was gone, disappearing into the ever-present grey soup of mist swamping the gullet of the gorge. Zuriel and Eksel followed after him, though in a much subdued fashion. Wings outstretched, they slowly glided their way downward while slowly circling about the air looking unfortunately like a pair of vultures on the descent until they, too, fell from sight into the churning grey fog. How long they were gone, it was hard to tell; minutes seemed like hours, hours felt like days. The longer it took, however, the more my mind began to play tricks on me as I stood motionless with my eyes impatiently watching for the angels to reemerge from the empty gulf beneath my feet. Perhaps Gotham wasn't dead. He was after all an angel, Fallen or not. Granted, an angel cruelly deprived of his wings, but an angel just the same, and a great one at that. Maybe he had somehow— miraculously—survived the fall. If anyone could, it would be Gotham. Perhaps, I found myself thinking, he just needs the aid of Damiel and the others to help him back up to the safety of those of us waiting for him.

I suddenly felt watched, and for a brief moment I allowed my gaze to stray from the pit of the ravine to find Anahel standing nearby staring back at me with a pained and dismal expression upon his face. It was as if he had been eavesdropping on the plausible thoughts of hope I had been quietly entertaining inside my head. But his own eyes were devoid of any hope, and without words he seemed to strongly discourage me of holding out even the smallest glimmer of such possibilities. I felt my eyes begin to tear as I forced my gaze back down into the yawning chasm—not because I refused to accept his skepticism, but because I doubted my own optimism, hard as it was.

The rain which had been falling with a drowning relentlessness seemed to begin pouring even harder from the dark skies. I took no notice that I was shivering inside my soaked-through clothes, or that I remained alone in my steadfast vigil at the edge of the cliff. The other boys had scrambled to find refuge from the drenching downpour in crooks of rock and beneath the few lone trees nearby. When Anahel overheard those gifted with the Grace to bring forth the sun being urged by the others to dry up the rain, he quickly silenced them with a biting admonishment: "Stand down and bow your head when Heaven weeps, but dare not think it's for you to wipe away its tears."

Finally, after what seemed like forever, Zuriel and Eksel could be seen emerging from the misty blanket below followed close behind by Damiel. As they rose upward, navigated by the soft, gentle row of their wings against the air, I immediately saw in their gloomy expressions and downcast eyes their return was not accompanied by welcoming news.

Did you find him? asked Anahel impatiently before the Guides even set foot on the ground, though it was obvious the answer.

Damiel gave me a quick passing glance as if he wished my presence to be anywhere else but there at that moment before turning to Anahel. "We searched the entire stretch of bottom, even farther than it would have been possible for him to..." He paused sharply for a moment, swallowing back his words to quickly reshape them. "To come to rest."

"The mist runs thick down below, as you well know. It is quite hard to see," Zuriel jumped in.

"You're saying you found nothing?" Anahel questioned as if such a prospect was virtually impossible. And when an answer to his inquiry was not immediately forthcoming he barked with growing impatience, "Answer me!"

It was then Zuriel revealed clutched in his hand the familiar shirt last seen worn by Gotham. It had become somewhat frayed by what could only be imagined as a violent, battering fall, and the rich green fabric was dulled and stained by dirt and what was no doubt blood—angel blood, which appeared like a stain of clear oil. In his other hand were Gotham's pants, while Eksel showed himself to be holding a pair of boots.

So then where is he? I asked calmly, though I was anything but.

Anahel overshadowed my question. "And this was all?"

Damiel said nothing, but extended his left hand which was clenched in a tight fist. When he revealed what lied in the crook of his palm, I felt my breath instantly stolen from my chest at the sight of the vial-shaped pendant attached to the rope of silver chain now absent of the neck from which it had hung.

Very well, Anahel said solemnly. "There is nothing more to do here but bathe needlessly in this wet chill. Let us return to Havenhid."

"Whoa, wait a minute...what do you mean return to Havenhid?" I protested. "You have to go back down and keep looking for him. Take some of us with you. We'll help you find him."

"He's not there, Jacob," Damiel said somberly to me.

"He has to be. You saw him fall as clearly as I did. He couldn't have just disappeared into thin air." My voice was rising to match my nearly panicked state. "You said it yourself...it was hard to see down there. So why don't you burn away

the clouds that are hindering your search. You have the power. Why aren't you using it?"

But none of the Guides seemed to be paying much mind to what I was saying. Even my so-called fellow Nephilim standing nearby looking soaked and miserable as they stared at me with the same blank expression seemed more than eager to make their way back down the mountain to Havenhid where a change of dry clothes waited.

"Fine then," I fumed angrily. "If you won't do it, I'll do it myself."

And I raised my hand high above my head as if to snatch the sun out from behind the shroud of clouds cloaking its presence, and just as I was about to wipe it across the swath of gorge below me and sweep away every trace of blinding grayness standing between us and finding Gotham a hand grabbed me firmly by the wrist. I looked to find myself staring into Damiel's rain-streaked face which, dark and hard as it was, still failed to fully conceal the empathizing sorrow and compassion reeling beneath the surface.

That's enough, he said to me.

You can go ahead and abandon him, but I refuse, I cried.

"I said that's enough, Jacob!" Damiel barked louder. "He's gone. Let him be at rest."

Only then did the unsettling finality of his words I tried so hard to resist finally penetrate my skull and I felt myself go limp as the momentary rage that overwhelmed me began to recede. The others gradually left the mountain back to Havenhid, but I refused and stayed behind staring into the depths of the ravine while my body trembled in my soaked clothes. All the while Damiel's voice remained a constant echo inside my head.

"He's gone...he's gone...he's gone..."

Gone.

But how?

And, more importantly where?

Where does a Fallen angel end up when death comes calling?

Eventually the unrelenting rain won out and forced me to give up my vigil at Broken Earth. Because I still remained without wings, I was faced with the task of making my way back down the mountain the old-fashioned way: by foot. The return trek was made all the more daunting without the guidance of the moon that had been snuffed out of sight by the stormy blackness overhead, leaving me to step mindfully and carefully along the narrow path turned to slippery mud by the deluge of water running in streams down the mountainside. It didn't help being jolted now and then by the intermittent, earth-shaking rumblings of thunder.

The hour was late when I finally reached Havenhid, and the deafening silence that greeted me told me everyone had retired to their quarters for the night. And while my own eyes were heavy with exhaustion, I continued to deny myself the one thing my body longed for at that moment: to shed the cold, soaked clothes clinging to me and slip into the warm, comfortable softness of my bed waiting for me upstairs. Instead my muddy, water-logged shoes sloshed their way along the winding halls to the farthest northern point ending at the threshold of large, arched doorway leading into the chapel.

The heavy, wooden double doors were open and I stepped inside. There was no one there and the only sound that could be heard came from the hundreds of flickering flames absent candles, which burned in clusters along the walls. Their light filled the chapel with a warm white glow and brought to life shadows which danced in silhouette against the numerous statuary positioned all around. The air was filled with a sweet pungent mix of roses and incense, and resting in state upon a small catafalque in front of the altar at the head of the chapel was the carefully folded remnants of Gotham's clothing along with the vial-shaped pendant and chain which had been placed on top. A shaft of soft light shone down from above and illuminated the belongings in a haze of brilliant white. But to look upward failed to reveal the source of the light.

Quietly, I slunk my way to the farthest corner of the chapel and took a seat in the last row of wooden pews where the quiet serenity enveloped and embraced me with its needed stillness. Despite never being much of a church-goer at home, I have always had an unusual fondness for this chapel, even more so than I do the Library. There's a beauty here—both seen and unseen, strange as that may sound—that's absent the rest of Eden. I found myself staring at the spiral staircase of stained glass winding its way upward through the opening of the chapel ceiling and into the night sky beyond. I couldn't help fantasizing where these steps might lead me as I schemed of a way to get a foot on the lowest rung.

As I let my thoughts drift, the sound of footsteps suddenly broke the tranquil quiet and I turned to see Eksel entering the chapel, much to my surprise. Oblivious to my presence, he made his way between the rows of pews to the front of the chapel where he genuflected with his head bowed low. Then, rising to his feet with an uncharacteristic timidness, he approached the altar where the last remnants of Gotham rested. There, he stood motionless and silent for some time before reaching out and passing his hand beneath the shaft of light which bathed the belongings in a gauze of white, yet stopping short of touching any of Gotham's possessions, not even to graze the soft silk of the skirt, or finger the silver chain coiled around the black, hard pendant.

"Dear brother, like this light, you have illuminated a shame within me I don't think I shall ever shirk," I heard him say. His voice came thin and quaked ever so slightly with a surprising vulnerability. "I could gouge my eyes this very moment and still not suffer the blindness that left me unable to see until only now how far more worthy you were Fallen than any one of us who looked down on you from on high. It is a most unpleasant realization that will forever make my heart heavy."

He then turned abruptly away from the altar and made a quick retreat for the door of the chapel, but not before he caught sight of me trying to remain as inconspicuous as possible in my seat.

How long have you been sitting there? he asked sounding somewhat perturbed at my unexpected presence, and yet oddly not as brash as I've grown accustomed to him being when he found the need to address me.

"I don't know...a while I guess. I didn't mean to disturb you," I answered apologetically.

"You surprised me, that's all. I didn't think there would be anyone else here at this hour," he said. An awkward silence followed, and while it seemed to me as if the angel had something further to say, he didn't. Instead, he bid a hurried goodnight and again continued on his way.

"It was a nice thing what you said," I blurted before I had the good sense to bite down on my tongue bringing Eksel's feet once again to an abrupt standstill.

"Then you heard?"

"Too bad he couldn't hear it while he was alive," I said. Was I subconsciously looking to pick a fight with him, I had no idea. Maybe the months and months of enduring his spiteful and plainly unfriendly attitude had finally caught up with me. Whatever the reason I braced myself for him to take aim at me with his acerbic manner. But he didn't. Instead, Eksel appeared uneasy and flustered in a way I didn't think it possible for a great warrior angel like him to become, and again he made for the door only at a faster pace. Then, as he reached the last row of pews where

I sat he stalled once again. Grasping tightly the back of the pew in a way that it looked like he might rip it from the floor, he stood quiet for a moment, though it was clear to me he was wrestling with something churning inside him to get out.

"When I'm wrong, I readily admit so," he suddenly stated in a steely, matter-of-fact voice. His eyes remained fixed on the floor before shifting and leveling his golden gaze on me, and the ever-present keenness for the first time was companioned with a rare humility which caught me momentarily off guard. And in that quiet moment I came to realize Eksel was no longer referring just to Gotham, but myself as well in a way his mouth could never form the proper words. And I knew I had received as close to an apology I would ever get from him.

~ ~ ~

"Awake, Fledgling. It is time."

Jacob slowly opened his eyes to find Anahel patiently hovering above him.

"Time...?" Jacob sighed groggily.

At first he was confused as to his whereabouts until he gave a flitting glance around through the tired slits that were his eyes and saw the glinting flecks of color from the stained glass of the chapel made alive by the morning light. He was sprawled on his back across the church pew, and the pen clutched in his hand was still pressed to the page of his journal laying open on his lap which he last remembered to be writing in before his heavy eyes shut themselves for good.

The church...of course...

"You've been here all night?" asked Anahel.

"I must have nodded off," said Jacob with a groan as he stiffly sat himself up.

"Apparently," said the angel looking somewhat concerned as he observed the boy's dirty and disheveled appearance. "Don't take this the wrong way, but you look like something the storm chewed up and spit out."

"Yeah, well, I promise I feel even worse than that," said Jacob, grimacing painfully as he felt the impression left behind by the hard pew he had slept on while trying to stretch and twist the kinks from his sore body. The tight discomfort held in his muscles was instantly forgotten when he glanced toward the altar at the front of the chapel and saw Gotham's belongings were no longer on the catafalque.

"Where did they go?" he asked with alarm.

"Where did what go?" inquired Anahel.

"Gotham's things...they're gone."

"The Guides came for them a few moments before you awoke," said Anahel in his always calm way. "And you have just enough time to unmuddy yourself before we bid our last respects."

A glum look settled itself on Jacob's face. He was never one for funerals, and he found himself wondering if it was natural that someone as young as he to have been to so many: first his best friend, then his mother, and now Gotham. But he had only a moment to reflect on the subject, gloomy as it was, before Anahel was ushering him to his feet to send him off and make himself more presentable.

In quick order, Jacob changed out of his muddy clothes, and as he did he thought better of slipping into a clean version of his usual attire of jeans, t-shirt and sneakers and chose instead to wear something a little less casual he had brought along—just in case. Then after washing clean the mud smudged on his face and running a comb through his matted hair, he hurried back downstairs with Mist faithfully at his heel to join the others already assembled outside. A few snickers could be heard as he emerged from the trunk of the tree, which made the stiff leather shoes and tie he wore that much more uncomfortable. The approving nod he received from Anahel, who was standing nearby, however, reassured Jacob he had made the right choice in his more dressy attire, no matter the discomfort.

Damiel, Zuriel, Eksel and Haniel emerged soon after with Gotham's sacred belongings. They had been placed on a small but beautifully carved wooden platform. Two gold-trimmed rods slid into fasteners on both sides of the platform allowing it to be raised up and carried on the angels' shoulders like a mobile throne of some long-ago

Egyptian pharaoh. With Jacob at Anahel's side, followed closely by the rest of the Nephilim, the Guides led the somber procession along the banks of the River swollen with the rain that had fallen steadily the day and night before but had since stopped. The air was crisp and sweetly pungent from the passing storm, and the presence of the sun began to reveal itself once more in brilliant shafts of its light cast down through small breaks in the grey, gloomy pall of the surrendering clouds. Without a word spoken, the grouping slowly made its way along the descending grassy slopes at the southernmost edge of the Garden where the valley came to a narrow entrance formed by the walls of two behemoth mountains between which the River passed and continued flowing to the wider reaches of Eden.

Waiting for the procession's arrival were the other members of the White Circle: Rabacyel, Jabniel, Dalquiel and Johiel. Their faces were long and drawn with sorrow, but none more deeply than Johiel's. After a nod acknowledging their presence, Anahel stood himself on a nearby cluster of rock so that all gathered might see and hear him. There followed a long pause, as if all ability to speak had suddenly been stolen from him. Eventually, with a steadying clearing of his throat, Anahel found his voice.

"Never," he began loud and clearly, "did I ever touch upon the thought that I might find myself called upon to bid such a sorrowful farewell to my brother...this brother in particular. I will be brief, as words fail me at this moment. For how does one recount a spirit such as this without falling unforgivably short?"

His voice quivered, and in a brief moment the mighty angel fell weak to his overcoming emotion before managing to grip once more his steely resolve.

"Of this I'll say of my brother, Gothamel," he continued. "Fallen as he may have been, he managed to retain his footing on the high ground our own feet shall never tread. For his was a heart that to its last beat pumped with unconditional loyalty and allegiance, even when all of Heaven estranged itself from him. I ask you, how many of our own brothers have we watched get swallowed with such ease by the Darkness? And yet the one who had every reason to cross its threshold refused. And at what cost? The life of his only son, and when that proved not enough, the cruel surrender of his own. I cannot tell you how many times I have been left in the cold hours of night pondering whether I could have remained as steadfast in my faith while in the company of such casualties."

Anahel then turned a sharply focused eye on the young Nephilim boys gathered about him quietly listening to his words.

"Today was supposed to be a day of celebration long-visited here. Instead, it is with great sadness we find ourselves assembled at this spot and reminded in the most grimmest of ways why you, and countless generations of Nephilim before you, have been brought to Eden," said Anahel. "During the past many months of Illumination, my fellow Guides have trained you in becoming noble servants of the Light, and train you well they have. But I can't think of a more viable lesson for a young Fledgling to take to heart than that which lies before you."

Anahel drew the young boys' gazes to the folded belongings placed with care on the ornate platform. "Not the clothing made empty in such a heart-rendering manner, but the unwavering soul who once donned them. Surely, you will find nothing more illuminating than the memory our departed brother leaves behind. And it is with heavy hearts that we have come to say goodbye to one we can proudly say was Fallen—not by the mark scarred into his flesh, but the humbling manner he chose to meet his end so that the Light may radiate another day. Trust when I say you will not find another like him in our ranks, and may we all cherish the memory our presence, unworthy where we stood, ever came to be shaded even briefly by his shadow."

A moment of piercing silence fell upon bowed heads. The Guides then removed the rods from the platform and walked it to the River's edge. They were just about to wade out into the water when Anahel stopped them. Removing the necklace which laid coiled upon the shirt, he turned to Jacob and tried handing it to him but the boy recoiled.

"He would want you to have it," insisted Anahel.

Again he held it out, and Jacob hesitantly accepted the offering.

"Wear it, and keep him close to your heart," Anahel spoke quietly to the boy, "and may the light he so valiantly safeguarded protect you and keep you from ever knowing the darkest of dark."

Jacob stared down at the memento resting in his palm and took note of the faint glow radiating from within the pendant chiseled from the blackest of rock before closing it tight inside his hand. Anahel then nodded to the Guides, who proceeded to step out into the River and set adrift the platform holding the rest of Gotham's belongings upon the water's surface. Jacob watched in pained silence, and as the slow-moving currents carried the remains along its watery path a most strange sound emerged from the surrounding silence.

Music.

It came in a pleasant humming of strings, and as it grew louder it reminded Jacob of Wagner's "Höchsten Heiles Wunder." It was one of the few operatic pieces he was forced to endure coming from his grandmother's phonograph while growing up that he actually enjoyed with its unusual ability of stirring from him both happiness and sadness simultaneously with each listen. He glanced over at Max and Leos standing nearby, then to the other boys as inconspicuously as he could, but no one else seemed to be struck by the sudden sound of the music. Then as the glorious yet haunting chorus of voices rose up from the melody, Jacob looked to each of the angels, but their mouths were not moving, and he found himself wondering if in fact the music was a trick of his imagination or a long-ago memory shaken awake by this most solemn of moments to ring inside his ears. He soon found himself fighting to hold back the brimming of his tears until he was forced to turn his face to the sky. When he did he was greeted with a most amazing sight: a snake eagle—his eagle—his guide—soaring into view from behind the mountain peaks. And it was not alone.

Dozens upon dozens of other eagles followed in a tightly knitted formation, and with them were included birds of every kind. In perfect synchronicity they swooped in lower from the cloud-stirred sky and, as they did, Jacob could see each was carrying in its beak a rose. They flew over with a grace even remarkable for such winged creatures, and the sky suddenly began to rain only this time it was with the roses as they were released one by one. Jacob watched as they fell along the banks of the River and upon the water to accompany the platform on its journey.

It was then when the drifting platform passed between the two towering mountain cliffs serving as entrance to the Garden that Jacob first noticed the mass congregation of animals lined on both sides of the River stretching as far as the eye could see. Like the angels and Nephilim, animals of every imagining birthed on Eden's lands had come to pay their final respects, and as the platform slowly made its way past, Jacob watched with astonishment, and even heavier heart, as the animals one by one lowered themselves down onto one leg as if bowing to an embodiment of royalty.

Jacob couldn't believe what he was witnessing.

They were bowing.

The animals were actually bowing.

And in the midst of their genuflecting that slowly continued further on down the River, Mist broke away from Jacob's side and charged her way up a nearby rocky slope until she stood atop a jagged boulder jutting out like a craggily finger poking its way from the innards of the earth. Throwing back her head, she released a cry in a piercing wail of a howl that was carried to the farthest corners of Eden. It was then, in that moment, Jacob realized the depth of loss that had befallen not only himself but everything surrounding him, and the tears he had fought so valiantly to hold at bay began to flow in warm, salty streams down his cheeks as he clutched tightly the pendant enclosed in his fist.

CHAPTER TWENTY-FIVE

T he service ended as solemnly as it began. Gotham was gone, and while the Guides and their pupils were accompanied back to Havenhid by this most blunted of realities, Jacob slipped away unseen and headed in full sprint in the direction of the waterfalls spilling off the shoulders of the steep slate mountain resting at the most northern end of the Garden. There he found a familiar meadow of tiger grass and golden flowers where the pleasant scent of honeysuckle and lavender sweetened the air. It was a spot he had come to a few times before, where the muffled rumbling of the falls as it met the River served as a soothing antidote whenever he found his spooked thoughts trying to flee his head in a fierce gallop.

Beneath the shade-giving branches of a large tree, he sat for some time upon a gathering of rock that had been stacked in a way to form a crude, if not comfortable bench, and stared at the Sword of Destiny in his hands. It was the first time since uncovering it in the hidden space concealed in David's burial vault that he had a moment to actually study the once-believed fabled weapon. Deny it though Jacob tried, there was an uneasiness in handling such a relic while knowing it served as the lone key which would one day open the doors to the last surviving kingdom—Kingdom Come. It was impossible for Jacob not to feel the power of such a sword in his hands; power which seemed to feel almost like that of a human heart beating inside a chest. And like a heart, the pounding of life seemed to come from the very center of the sword— the core—where the ancient spear that pierced Christ's side at his crucifixion, looking as ancient as its years, was firmly fused between the hilt of the sword and its extended blade.

The sunlight reflecting off its hide of unblemished metal illuminated Jacob's face as he looked it over while turning it ever so slowly, and in that reflection of light Jacob was caught off guard to catch glimpses of the spear's violent past revealed in shadowy images of the men who at one time held claim to the spear, and the countless bodies it stilled in the many wars it witnessed. And to Jacob's horror, blood was suddenly seen to emerge from the tip of the sword and ooze its way across the blade in a stream of bright red.

~ ~ ~

"The sudden sense of responsibility placed upon you, I have no doubt, must be an overwhelming feeling to bear."

The sound of the familiar voice startled Jacob. He turned with a jolt and saw it was Anahel, standing just a short distance off Jacob's left shoulder as if he had been there for some time. The look which greeted the angel from the boy, however, was less than inviting.

"Believe it or not I've only had the chance to lay eyes upon this sword once," said Anahel. "And then it was all too briefly to really enjoy the beauty that it is."

Jacob turned back to the sword and to his surprise—or not—he found the blood seen seeping from the blade moments earlier had vanished without a trace, along with the images it reflected. He then stretched forward his hand and offered the sword to Anahel.

"That's quite alright, my boy" said Anahel, recoiling somewhat from the offering. "This is one sword best left to be admired from afar."

Jacob understood immediately as he was revisited by the vision of Betryel grabbing the dropped sword from off the ground in the Silent Forest and instantly being reduced to a smoldering cloud of ash.

"I hope I haven't intruded on your solitude," said Anahel. "You disappeared so suddenly after the ceremony. I thought I'd check in with you and see how you were—"

"I just needed to get away," Jacob cut in curtly.

"I see," said Anahel, taking note once more of the unfamiliar, yet not unexpected, standoffishness coming from the boy. "Do you mind if I sit with you a spell?"

"You can do whatever you wish," answered Jacob with a shrug that was just this side of civil. "It's your Garden."

He slid himself over opening up a spot on the bench of rock which Anahel accepted with a satisfied sigh.

"You've definitely come to the right place to gather your thoughts," said the angel while allowing his studious gaze to follow the splendor nature had unveiled before them in a tapestry of rich colors like that of a painting that refused to run or fade, even by the migrating mist coming off the nearby waterfall as it careened down the mountainside and spilled into the River. "It's the same spot Gothamel's son used to frequent when he was here. I can't tell you the number of times I'd find him out here, looking exactly as you do now. If I hadn't known better, I would have thought I'd laid eyes on a ghost when I first caught sight of you."

Jacob said nothing in return, and in the quiet moments that followed, Anahel stared out over the lush meadow in the direction of the River where the sight of Mist bounding about in the tall swaying grass while at play with other small critters faintly tugged the corners of the angel's mouth upward.

"She seems to be faring along well," he said. "You'd never know she was run through by a sword."

Jacob closed his eyes and shook his head. "I should have known someone would squeal on me. Let me guess...Ethan?"

"No one intentionally squealed, as you put it. It was more a slip of the tongue."

"What was I supposed to do, let her die?" asked Jacob coolly.

"No...of course not. As I understand it, she put her life in the way of harm meant for you as very few would, even a faithful companion as she. It's only natural you would want to return such a selfless act. Nor am I here to admonish you for your decision to heal her, particularly on this day when loss has managed to gain such a choke-hold on us as it has," said Anahel.

"However," the angel quickly added, shattering Jacob's brief moment of relief that he had side-stepped a reprimand he was sure was coming, "it bears reminding that what happens here in Eden is not necessarily permissible outside its Gate. You have been blessed with the rarest and most powerful of Graces—this seventh Grace—and with it the power to heal that which is wounded is readily at your fingertips. It's the one Grace from which all other Graces came to be. But as you know, and as I know Zuriel made sure to impress upon you in the strongest of terms, its use is strictly forbidden for the purpose of denying Death to those for which it comes to claim. So explains why this particular Grace which comes from the virtue of Liberality, or empathy—blessing as it may be—also has the uncanny ability of making the one who wields its power feel as if they have been weighted with a curse capable of wrenching one's very soul."

He then looked to Jacob with a sad and weary eye which seemed to reveal a deep, intimate understanding of the words he spoke. "Unfortunately, you will come to know at a time all too soon in its arrival this painful constraint with which you are bridled when you return to the mortal world."

Jacob continued to quietly stare off into the distance as if he had willfully managed to turn off the function of his ears to drown out Anahel's words. But, in fact, he heard every word the angel had to say, and one in particular—curse—managed to repeat itself in his head and had a most fitting feel to it.

Curse!

"You knew, didn't you?" asked Jacob, finally, after a long pause.

Anahel appeared almost expectant of the question—a question that had been poised on the end of Jacob's tongue but kept firmly behind his teeth for a more appropriate time after Gotham had been mourned properly—and now that it had been voiced a pronounced crease appeared above the bridge of the angel's nose, and he sat back and released a burdensome sigh.

"I saw him last night, you know," said Jacob when the angel's answer was not immediately forthcoming. "In the Through inside the Silent Forest. It was exactly like in the recurring dreams I've been having, only it was real. This darkened figure was all tied up out in the middle of some desert...filled with so much rage. Even though I didn't want to, I couldn't help wanting to see his face...and when I did..."

Try as he did, Jacob couldn't keep his voice from quivering with emotion. Anahel felt an overwhelming desire to lend comfort to the boy by placing a steadying hand on his back, yet knew better.

"It was like looking into a mirror and seeing an older version of myself staring back," continued Jacob once he managed to choke down the mix of feelings churning inside him. "Suddenly, in that one moment, it all began to make sense; why you and the other Guides looked at me as though you had seen a ghost when I first came here; the fact Eksel for the longest time showed such disdain for me; how it was I somehow was the only Nephilim whose father was unknown."

Jacob turned his gaze onto Anahel and for the first time ever his eyes mirrored a simmering anger for the angel that was beginning to boil over inside him.

"But you did know, didn't you?"

"Jacob…"

"This whole time you knew...EVERY ONE OF YOU..."

This time Anahel reached for the boy, but Jacob was fast to his feet, as if the embrace were some approaching plague.

"If you'll allow me to explain..." attempted Anahel calmly.

"EXPLAIN WHAT?" barked Jacob furiously.

Rage. It was suddenly coursing through him like a steady oozing of lava. Just as fiery, and equally as scorching. "That you've been lying to me this entire time...deceiving me into believing I'm someone I'm not?"

He was seeing red. Bright, burning shades of crimson. Pulsating like a strobe light to match the pounding beat of his riled heart. More than that, he was turning red, particularly his face, as though the glow of the volcanic eruption inside him was showing itself through his skin.

"I trusted you...I TRUSTED ALL OF YOU!"

"Jacob—"

"Isn't there something written in the Bible about lying? Something about he that speaketh lies shall perish? I definitely know there's a commandment that states you shall not give false testimony against your neighbor, and that one you managed to break big time," Jacob continued to ramble heatedly. "So where's the lightning to burn its mark into your forehead? Clearly, you've earned it!"

The surrounding meadow grew suddenly and strangely quiet—eerily, in fact—as the offense of Jacob's remark revealed itself on Anahel's face like a fast-moving bank of dark storm clouds swallowing a blue sky. Suddenly, it was the angel who was on his feet looking more imposing than Jacob ever recalled him appearing before, and were it not for the anger which still gripped him tightly Jacob might have immediately regretted his choice of words and begged the angel forgiveness for the insolent slip made by his lips.

"It is only because I feel intimately your distress that you still find yourself upright," said the angel whose voice, despite being cool and collective, held all the bite of a snake whose fangs dripped poison. "But I urgently advise you to rethink the manner in which your tongue chooses to lash forth in my direction, or you shall witness very quickly the well which holds my sympathy run dry."

~ ~ ~

Jacob stood glowering at the angel. Never before had he wanted to strike Anahel, but now his feet were all but bouncing upon the ground like a pair of springs ready to launch him forward with his fists flying. Yet he retained enough control over his senses to tighten his lips and in his frustration he let out a growl of surrender and impaled the Sword of Destiny clutched tightly in his hand into the soft earth.

"Now then, I have no doubt what has transpired between yesterday and now has proven most traumatic for you," said Anahel. "I can only imagine the shock it must have been for you to have it be revealed in the manner it was that Samael is your father."

"He is not my father," Jacob was quick to argue.

"UNFORTUNATELY..." the angel's voice boomed over the boy's interruption, "I'm not sure if an appropriate time would have ever presented itself when you would have been spared from such a shock.

In not recognizing that was a profound, if not fatal error on our part. But it was Gothamel's intention that you pass through this ring of fire while getting singed as little as possible."

"I'm sure he had my best interests at heart. You all did," Jacob spat with as much sarcastic bile that he could manage. "He didn't tell me because he knew I'd never come with him to this God-forsaken place and would instead likely be lying at the bottom of whatever cliff I chose to throw myself off of if I knew the truth."

"You have had ample time and more than ample words to make your feelings on this matter known, and now you will let me have mine—without interruption," Anahel sharply scolded the boy. "And I would heartily suggest you keep whatever blasphemy's you feel the need to spew about the one who put the first breath in your chest clenched behind your teeth while you still have them. Do I make myself clear?"

One look into the angel's face and Jacob could see Anahel was not tossing about idle threats, and he swallowed down with great reluctance whatever remaining spite was itching to leap from his tongue.

"Have at your anger, if you are so inclined, once I am finished," continued Anahel, once he observed Jacob's jaw clench itself tight, "but don't let it blind you to the fact that what Gothamel did he did so because he cared a great deal for you. The night he brought you here to Eden he did so knowing the rebuke he would face from me and the other Guides. But he fought us tooth and nail for what has become your rightful place in Eden. True, he asked that we keep the truth of Samael secret from you. But don't you see he did it not in an act of deceiving you, but rather protecting you? You had already been given quite the shock about who you are. Let him first come to terms with being a Nephilim until he is once more comfortable in his own skin was the reasoning he expressed to me. Then, as you are well aware, it was revealed you were no ordinary Nephilim, and the opportunity to tell you the truth made itself all the more distant; not to mention complicated."

Jacob stared straight ahead as he listened, his face a blank slate.

"How was it expected to be explained to you that which neither Gothamel nor myself—the entire White Circle, for that matter—had yet, even now at this moment, come to grasp or have the slightest understanding of?" continued Anahel. "Being anointed the role of Light Bearer is itself both a burden and immense struggle. This I knew and could not in good conscious add to it. But you rose magnificently to the challenge—much more so than I anticipated or, if I were to be completely honest, expected. You proved yourself exceptional even amongst your exceptional peers. And, as we stood watching quietly from the sidelines at the impressive strides of your growth, this looming secret we knew one day we'd have to share with you sort of made its presence fade into the ether. No longer when we looked upon you did we see the son of Samael, but a most promising future leader knighted by the Light."

Anahel could see he was being heard and that his words, little by little, were having a softening effect on Jacob.

"I see you are hurting, and it is not for me to deny you your feelings, Fledgling," the angel said. "But might I suggest you attempt to see past your ill will, if only for a moment, and take notice of how difficult this has also been on Gothamel."

"Difficult how?" asked Jacob surly.

"Well, to begin with, let us not forget it was Samael who Gothamel held responsible for David's death. True, not by his own hand, but most definitely his shrewd orchestration. Any other angel in Gothamel's shoes would have rightly terminated you the moment you alerted the world of your arrival with your first cries," said Anahel. "Instead, Gothamel, for whatever reason, chose to watch over you. He took you under his wing, and—as you could attest to whether your anger allows you to admit it now or not—came to look upon you as if you were his own. Quite a remarkable and, dare I say, beautiful thing. I came to notice every time Gothamel set eyes upon you his face lit up as I've rarely seen or thought possible, even when your resemblance to your father likely served as a constant reminder of his teeming hatred for Samael, not to mention his own festering loss."

The compassionate look that was slow to settle upon Jacob's face suddenly hardened with a sudden emerging shadow of anger.

"Quite calling him that," he hissed.

"Calling him what?"

"MY FATHER," Jacob snarled.

" 'Tis true, he is not your father in the sense the true meaning of the word is known," said Anahel in a thoughtful voice. "He is, however, the one from whom you were made. Of that fact, we cannot turn a blind eye and wish this history had been penned with different strokes of the quill, no matter how much we might desire it."

"What about the Descendants Archive?" asked Jacob. "Why would it have my father listed as Sacerel?"

Anahel drew quiet for a moment.

"Ah yes, the Descendants Archive. That has been a conundrum which has kept my feet pacing the floors of my chamber since my eyes first looked upon the entry," answered Anahel with a wearisome sigh. "The short answer is it was a fraudulent notation added to the book by sleight of hand."

"You mean a forgery?"

The angel nodded. "When I brought you to my chamber and handed you the Descendants Archive I knew I could no longer remain silent about the identity of who your father was. If I didn't reveal to you the truth, the book most certainly would have. For you see, the Descendants Archive only contains a record of Nephilim born to angels, not Fallen. I knew when you opened the book your name would be missing from its pages."

"So, then, how is it I am. And who's Sacerel," asked Jacob who looked to be growing more confused with each word coming from Anahel's mouth.

"Until just recently, that has been the crux of what has left me stupefied," answered Anahel. "Despite our great multitudes, I know intimately each and every one of my brothers. I can assure you the existence of a Sacerel is not among them. Still, I found myself flummoxed by the name the moment you recited it out loud. Hour after hour, afterwards, I found myself transfixed by this simple yet blatant inscription. Who or what, I struggled to understand, was behind this wicked and spurious act? Then it came to me as I found myself muttering the name over and over to myself: Sacerel, Sacerel, Sacerel...Sacer."

If Jacob was confused before, he now appeared utterly dumbfounded.

"I'm not following," he surrendered with a shrug.

"You have fallen lax in your Latin studies, Fledgling," admonished Anahel. "Sacer is a Latin word that more or less translates to 'accursed one,' a description that fits Samael if ever one did. Whoever was responsible for the entry simply added the 'el' found at the end of every angel's name, meaning 'in God,' and Sacerel was born."

"But who would do such a thing? And more importantly why?" asked Jacob.

"Who, indeed. Though, I suspect, if I were to retrace the footsteps of time, I would discover the culprit to be Thaniel, which is not so surprising a revelation considering the events we have watched unfold," answered Anahel. "As for the why? Your guess would be as good as mine. Unfortunately, I'm afraid whatever his reasoning or motivation, he took it with him into the black eternal abyss into which he was cast."

Jacob turned away, ashamed of the pain he knew he was revealing in spades.

"So what does this make me now...some kind of Damien? If I were to shave my head, would I find I was born with the mark of the Beast or something?" he pondered aloud both sarcastically and with some semblance of very real fear. But he could see his musings were lost on Anahel. "You know, from the Omen movies?"

It was clear by the stupefied look that came over Anahel he was completely oblivious to that which Jacob was referring.

"I know not of this Damien you speak of, but I can assure you your scalp has not been marred by this, uh, mark of the Beast," he said. Still, Anahel could see looking at Jacob he was making little headway in allaying the boy's doubts.

"Are you not exactly the same person you were when you awoke this morning as you were yesterday and the day before that?" Anahel put the question to Jacob in a gentle, thoughtful voice. "What has actually happened between then and now that's changed so drastically except the discovery that you now have in hand a piece of the jigsaw puzzle from which you were created that until now has been missing."

"It's a pretty important piece, don't you think?" said Jacob.

"Is it?" Anahel pondered aloud with a questioning cock of his head. "Perhaps. Perhaps not. I would venture to guess its importance from this day forward will rely on how you allow this one piece to affect the rest of the puzzle. So far, it hasn't seemed to blemish the overall picture of the person I now see before me...at least, not in my eyes. But by all means feel free to shear yourself like a sheep and examine yourself for any tell-tale markings should you continue to harbor any doubts."

Jacob could not suppress the smile, weak as it was, that came when the angel gave him a playful rub to the back of his head. Still, there remained something inside Jacob which continued not to sit well with him and made his smile quick to fade.

"What about this whole Light Bearer thing?" he asked. "That is...you still can't believe there hasn't been some kind of mistake made. I mean, why would God make, you know, someone like me Light Bearer?"

"Someone like you? You speak as if you were not responsible for seeing Eden clear of its most perilous moment since its creation; you who looked into the eyes of your fa—"

Anahel was quick to bite his tongue and think better his choice of words before continuing: "Er, that is, Samael—and when met with a plea to free him from the shackles of the Herrinsu vine, answered in kind with a defiant thrust of the Sword of Destiny bequeathed into the command of your hands; not to mention making Eden all the more safer for future generations of Nephilim by ridding it of the Through to the Underneath, for which I have yet to thank you properly. If that does not a Light Bearer make, then I don't know what does."

"You know what I mean, Anahel," said Jacob. "Why not one of the others? I'm not just the son of a Fallen, I'm the son of one of the most Fallen. It makes no sense."

Anahel drew silent for a moment and heaved a heavy sigh. "Sometimes, there are no answers where there exists questions. God has long-resided inside an ocean of light rolling with dark swells of mystery. His purpose about a certain great many things are unknown—even to us angels. But of this I know: He does not make mistakes. When blood flowed into your veins, so, too, did the prophesy of the Apocrypha. Your role as Light Bearer came to be not by luck or the chance of lottery, but a specifically designed purpose. Whatever the reason, whatever the why, neither of us may ever fully understand, nor is it to be second-guessed, not by myself, not even by you."

"I wish I held half as much confidence in myself as you seem to manage," said Jacob sounding none too reassured by Anahel's words.

"If there's one thing I've come to learn—perhaps too lately—is that one should be cautious in their judgments, as not all things are as they first appear," said Anahel.

The angel turned his attention back across the meadow and, as he watched Mist continue to frolic in the tall grass without a care, a troubled look came over him.

"What is it?" asked Jacob.

Anahel was hesitant in his answer.

"I suspect the weight of Gothamel's passing has finally begun to settle itself upon me," he said finally. He then quickly got to his feet and took a few steps out into the band of shade from the tree in a casual effort to keep the tense expression on his face from being further studied by the boy's narrowing gaze. But it did no good.

"Why should you feel guilty?" asked Jacob.

The question at first caught Anahel off guard and he was about to brush it away as he would a pesky mosquito buzzing incessantly about his head when he realized how pointless it would be.

"Amazingly, I still forget after all this time there are some of you who come to share the same power as angels when it comes to seeing thoughts," said Anahel.

Then, as the angel continued to look off into the distance, Jacob noticed him reach into the folds of his shirt and remove from it something he had tucked away. Jacob couldn't see what it was at first as Anahel's back was facing him. Whatever it was, Anahel stood quietly looking at it in silence until finally he turned on his heel and made his way back to the stone bench and without a word handed Jacob a twice-folded square of paper.

"What's this?" asked Jacob. Before Anahel's lips had a chance to part, Jacob had already unfolded the paper to reveal the handwriting inside, which appeared at first glance to be a letter of some kind.

"Six pages of a diary entry written long ago," said Anahel. "I would surmise to say you would find—were you to look more closely—that they once were part of the same journal I now see you toting around."

~ ~ ~

Jacob followed the angel's gaze as it drifted to the brown leather-bound book he had scrawled his thoughts in earlier resting on the stone bench beside him.

"The journal did belong to Gothamel's son at one time, did it not?" asked Anahel.

Jacob nodded. "My grandmother gave it to me right before I left to come here."

"I thought it looked to be familiar," said Anahel. "Many is a day I used to observe David off in some quiet, secluded corner of Havenhid with his nose buried inside that particular journal, and with the furious scribble of his pen branding the pages with his thoughts.

Quickly, Jacob snatched up the book and flipped it open to the very front section where a large portion of pages had noticeably and mysteriously been torn free. He then compared the serrated edges of the pages Anahel had handed him against the frayed remnants protruding from the journal's binding and it was clear they were the missing entries.

"No doubt you're wondering how they came to be in my possession. Quite by accident, I assure you," said Anahel. "One night, shortly after David's death, I was in the Library in search of something to quiet my mind when I came across a book I'm certain very few hands have removed from its place upon the shelf where it resides. It was only later in the serenity of my room as I immersed myself in reading it that I came upon the journal entry you now hold in your hands, which was most mysteriously secreted away inside. What is most surprising, however, is not the discovery of the missing journal pages hidden inside the book, but what the entry itself has to say."

He then quietly watched Jacob—perhaps more studiously than he had in moments past—as the boy immediately delved into what was contained on the sheets of paper trying to find some clue as to why Anahel's voice sounded as troubled as the expression radiating from his face. What Jacob quickly came to discover instead was something very familiar-sounding in the writing that could have been gleaned from some of his own thoughts he himself had saved to the pages of the journal.

"As you can see, you and David are much alike in more ways than you likely realize," said Anahel. "You both have come to carry the mantle of Light Bearer, you've each traded roles as custodian of a most elusive and coveted weapon, and—as the pages you hold reveal—you both shared in the anguish of trying to figure out how to save the one you've come to love and care about most."

Jacob managed to quickly skim his way halfway through the second page when he came upon an unfamiliar name that stalled him from reading any further and revealed from him a most puzzled frown.

"Isaac..." he mumbled the name pensively to himself before turning to Anahel. "A friend of David's?"

"The son of Abraham," answered Anahel. "I trust you know the story known as the binding of Isaac as told in the Old Testament."

Jacob thought for a minute.

"Abraham was called upon to prove his faith and loyalty to God by taking Isaac to the top of a mountain and sacri—"

Jacob stopped himself from speaking further and looked suddenly at Anahel as if the remainder of his sentence that trailed off had managed to reach out and deliver a stinging slap across his face to wake him to the irony of what he was saying, before the words caught themselves abruptly in his throat.

"There on Mount Moriah, Abraham bound his son to an altar and took out a knife," said Anahel picking up where Jacob went silent. "He was about to sacrifice his son when he heard the voice of an angel call out to him, 'Abraham, Stop! Do not hurt your son.' And the angel said to Abraham, 'I swear by myself, declares the Lord, that because you have done this and have not withheld your son, your only son, I will surely bless you and make your descendants as numerous as the stars in the sky and as the sand on the seashore. Your descendants will take possession of the cities of their enemies, and through your offspring all nations on earth will be blessed, because you have obeyed me.'"

Anahel then leveled a look onto Jacob. "I understand you had a late-night conversation with Thaniel some time ago in the Library regarding Gothamel and whether he could ever find favor with Heaven again."

Jacob nodded though it was clear he remained preoccupied with the eerie familiarity of the story the angel had just told him. "The idea that someone like Gotham could still be loyal to God after being cast out of Heaven, even going so far as to sacrifice his own son, and still be a Fallen…it just never seemed to sit well with me," he said.

"No, I imagine not. And as you've undoubtedly been able to gather so far from his writing, David wrestled mightily with the same such thoughts regarding his father's loyalty, but with a much more personal heaviness," said Anahel before taking a deep breath as if what he was about to say required the same steadying of oneself as wading into an ice-cold lake in the dead of winter. "Often in his lessons, Thaniel was apt to referencing the story of Abraham and his son. He found it to be the perfect parable in teaching his students about faith and allegiance to a power much greater than themselves. And it was in that story that David came to believe he had found the answer to his father's salvation."

"I'm not sure I follow," said Jacob.

"To put it as simply and bluntly as I know how," said Anahel, "there were two sacrifices made the day David drew his last mortal breath: one made painfully by a father out of loyalty and love to the one who made him, and one more poignantly, yet deceptively, made by a son out of selfless love for his own father and the desperate hope in removing the shameful mark seared into his forehead and reuniting him once more with the Light that had long ago been extinguished in his life."

"What are you saying...that David purposefully wanted Gotham to kill him?" asked Jacob half smirking as if waiting for a crack to appear in the serious expression fixed on Anahel's face that would betray the twisted joke he was attempting. But there was not so much as a twitch to Anahel's lip.

~ ~ ~

"I don't believe you," Jacob then blurted.

"Nor must you," Anahel returned without a note of offense. "But surely you couldn't deny such a claim if it came from David himself. Well, then, go on and continue reading. It's all there, told in his own words, put to paper in his own handwriting, on pages that were torn free—for whatever reason, and by whatever mysterious hand—from the journal he once owned and which has since been passed on to you."

Jacob refused to be fully convinced.

"But I've heard the other Guides. I've seen the disdain in their faces whenever David's name is mentioned. If what you're saying is true, why do they consider him a traitor, and worse...especially Eksel?"

"In their defense, they know nothing of what I'm sharing here with you," explained Anahel. "Still, a shameful mark on their part all the same. They chose to put their faith in the prejudices they had long before dealt against the boy just because he was the son of a Fallen, instead of following their instincts of who David would prove himself in unfailing terms to be. Not that I reside on any higher plain to cast judgment, as I myself believed the same before this unexpected discovery corrected my blindness."

"Whoa, whoa, whoa, back the car up...then how do you explain what happened? I mean, Samael was there when it happened. David was going to hand him the Sword of Destiny. He even crossed into the Northern Lands to do it. Gotham told me the whole story," argued Jacob.

"Your naivety comes as a surprise to me, Fledgling. Is it possible you continue to believe solely that as it appears to the naked eye, even now after all this time spent in Eden?" questioned Anahel which only served to confuse Jacob even more. "We as Guides do our best to make the Nephilim who are brought here to us as intense in strength as the sun is unbearable to stare directly into. But even they, no matter their training, are not immune to the whims of the Darkness. David was different only in that he would prove himself to be an especially tempting target for the insidious disease which festers beneath our feet. We should have known it was only a matter of time it would rise up like a worm burrowing its way up from within the ground to stretch itself in its dark ways, and sure enough it did. And perhaps, maybe, there was a brief moment when David found himself being lured by the power that has proven, for most, excruciatingly difficult from which to wriggle oneself free, but the moment, albeit, was fleeting. It was during this test of will that David saw an opportunity for the plan he had been mulling for some time to come to fruition. He had managed to deny the powerful ways in which the Darkness attempted lasciviously to twist him, but he also knew his attempt to free Gothamel from his shackles would be no easy task.

"There are only two things that can draw a father to commit the ultimate crime against a son: anger and love. David believed Gotham's salvation lied in the latter; not the love he held towards him, though of that there was without doubt no shortage, but for his own father who had banished him so long ago. And he knew the only way he'd ever meet the bite of his father's sword, as he believed he must, was to take aim at that love by sacrificing himself as a traitor to the Light in the most believable, and dare I say threatening, way possible."

"But it didn't work," said Jacob. "Gotham's still a Fallen."

"Yes...I know," noted Anahel, looking more grievous than he sounded.

"This doesn't make sense," Jacob mumbled as much to himself as he did Anahel. "When Gotham told me the story of what happened to David when I went to see him at the Tree of Life, he didn't tell me any of this. Why wouldn't he tell me the truth—"

Jacob immediately paused when he saw the angel grow noticeably sullen-looking and an unpleasant feeling slowly bubbled its way upward from the pit of his stomach.

"He never knew the truth, did he?"

The pained look that tightened its hold on Anahel's face became more pronounced and Jacob immediately knew the answer.

"I can't believe it...you never told him...never told him the whole thing was a sham...that David never had any intention of giving the sword to Samael," said Jacob. "That's the reason you're feeling guilty now, isn't it?"

"It was never my intention to keep such a thing secret," Anahel, his voice rising defensively before he took a steadying breath, rebuked. "At least, not at first."

At first?

"Before you take aim with your stones, keep in mind Gothamel vanished from Eden the moment the lid to David's sarcophagus was sealed, and long before that fateful visit to the Library where I made this unsettling discovery," said Anahel. "When an angel chooses to disappear and go into hiding, it's an extremely difficult task, even for those of us with our heightened senses and powers, to seek them out inside a crowded world from which they wish to not be found."

He stared off into the distance as if imagining such a self-imposed life of exile and his eyes shaped themselves into sad portals in which the sun seemed unable to reflect itself with its usual brilliance.

"What reason, you might ask, made me keep my vigil of silence when eventually he did resurrect himself and return to Eden, this time with you tow?" he then asked. "Believe it or not, there was a moment I came very close to telling Gothamel the truth. It was on the night he came to inform me he was parting ways with Eden once again; the night before Illumination. He showed up at the door to my room looking more tortured than I thought such a burden was able to be visited upon a living thing. The years he had spent trying to outrun the painful memory of his son's fate had caught up to him with a vengeance and settled itself upon him with a crushing weight. In his eyes, Eden was not the vision of paradise that it appeared to everyone else, but a dark, ugly stain, as unsightly as the punishing mark seared into his temple. This heaven had become in many ways his hell, made all the more unbearable in the knowing that his son laid in repose just a reach away inside the confines of a stone vault from which he could never be awakened."

"That's what I don't understand," said Jacob. "Why not tell him the truth and ease his suffering? You owed him that!"

"The night Gothamel came to me, he had resigned himself from wrestling further the ghosts that continued to haunt and torment him," continued Anahel. "And as I listened to him explain his reasoning to flee once more from all that had at one time been comforting to him, I took notice of the journal pages peering out from inside the book in which I found them residing on my desk where I happened to be sitting. I had been revisiting them ever since his return to Eden struggling night after night in deciding what the best course of action to take. I casually reached for them—actually had my fingers on the pages—and was about to give them to him. But then Gothamel said something right at that exact moment, and I found myself pushing the pages out of sight back inside the confines of the book."

Anahel grew quiet, but in his head reverberated the hollow echoes of Gotham's voice lamenting the cruel fate dealt him of never having the chance to reunite with his son, even in death. It made him tighten his lip to keep from showing its quivering with emotion as he recalled the pain heard in Gotham's voice.

"Here was one of the most formidable angels ever to be formed by God's hand, a loyal servant and fierce warrior of the highest order who could stare into the horrors illuminated inside Hell's fires and flinch not the slightest bit, nor wail in pity when made to suffer the consequence of his own making. Yet it was the love he had for his only son, a love he protected more fiercely than his own life, that would prove to be his one grave weakness," said Anahel somberly.

"You questioned why I didn't just come out and ease Gothamel's suffering with a simple revelation of truth. But I ask you, would it have...eased his suffering, that is?" Jacob opened his mouth to answer but quickly stifled himself as the angel looked straight and deep into the boy's focused, if not confused, gaze. "Knowing Gothamel as closely as you came to know him, can you in all honesty say you believe he would have found relief—peace, even—in knowing the truth contained in the confession you now hold in your hands? True, he would find comfort in knowing his son was not the traitor he has been long-believed to be, but at what cost? For Gothamel, the time he had with his mortal son was beyond priceless; for an angel such time is painfully fleeting and dissipates as quickly as it takes an eye to blink. I couldn't imagine his reaction in knowing his son cheated him of such precious moments, no matter how selflessly. In fact, I venture to say the pain would be all the more unbearable in the knowing that such a sacrifice was made on his behalf, especially when realizing it was all for nothing."

Jacob could almost hear the thud of his heart as he felt it sink like a rock inside himself.

"No...the truth as I've come to share with you is but a knife with the ability of replacing one wound with an even deeper, more painful cut to the flesh. I couldn't in both good conscious and love for my brother bear to witness such an affliction," said Anahel with a resigned sigh. "By the look in your eyes, I think it fair to say you've come to the conclusion much more expediently than it's taken me all these many years at which to arrive."

~ ~ ~

The patch of clouds that had remained at the front of Jacob's thoughts instantly began to part and lift, and as much as he wanted to argue Anahel's words, he couldn't. Nor could he ask the thousands of other questions whirling about inside his head for fear of the answers.

Like where did someone like Gotham go when death came calling, if not Heaven? Was he eventually relegated to the one place made for the Fallen he had so vehemently resisted in life? Or had his resistance earned him the mercy of some empty void in the inbetween—a purgatorial limbo? And what of his mother? Ever since learning the truth of his own coming to be, he had been tortured by the thoughts of what had become of her soul? Had she been forced to be reunited with...with—

"We could change things," blurted Jacob suddenly as he tried to shake clear such unsettling thoughts from inside his head. "Now that we know, we can use our powers to Drift and go back to that moment at Broken Earth and tell the other Guides the sword is fake. Then they would have no reason to be fearful of Thaniel and overtake him and his followers before they have a chance to kill Gotham."

Anahel smiled kindly at the boy. "I would be disappointed if you hadn't mulled such thoughts over in your mind. But you don't need me to tell you such thoughts can be only that."

A grim but understanding look came over Jacob. He looked down to the journal pages still clutched in his hand and strangely had no further desire to finish the rest of what they contained. But when he tried to hand them back to Anahel, the angel refused them.

"Keep them," he instructed. "When your time ends here, take them home with you and share their contents with your grandmother. While I've no doubt they would have only added incrementally to Gothamel's suffering, I'm more than certain they would have the opposite effect on her."

Jacob nodded and as he began to refold the pages he suddenly became aware of how many—or in this case how few—pages there were.

"Where's the rest?"

"The rest of what?" asked Anahel.

"The journal pages. There was a lot more that were torn out of the journal than just these six," explained Jacob while opening up the journal to reveal the shark-teethed remnants lining the inside spine where at least five times the amount of pages had been torn free.

"Interesting," commented Anahel as he examined the journal. "But I don't have an answer for what is becoming a mystery of more curious proportions by the moment. The only pages I know of are these I found in the book in the Library. Perhaps the others are stashed away—for whatever reason—in other books. Then again, if that were the case it would well take you the better part of several lifetimes to conduct such a search for them. That or incredible luck."

Jacob continued to study the serrated void made visible in his journal and as he did his perplexed state quickly morphed into intrigue as he thought to himself, *I wonder what else he was trying to hide.*

~ ~ ~

"The afternoon is wearing away," Anahel, taking notice of the orangish tinting of the sky, remarked after a while. "I suggest we start back, as it won't be long before dinner is served in the Hall of Light. That is, if indeed you have plans of returning to Havenhid."

"What makes you say that?" asked Jacob, throwing the angel an odd look.

"Oh, I don't know," Anahel replied. "Before I came out here, I went by your room in search of you and noticed your things had been packed and your bag waiting for you on your bed. Call me strange, but I've found a packed bag to be a sure sign of someone's coming or going."

"It's true," confessed Jacob, "I had planned to leave sometime after the ceremony. I just couldn't imagine being able to stay on here with everything that's..."

"Had planned?" said Anahel. "Does that mean you've changed your mind?"

It was clear from the conflicted look that swept over Jacob that he was still wrestling with the decision. He glanced all around with an indecisive gaze at the heavenly wonder that was Eden surrounding him. As much as he loved it, and as beautiful as it was, it had changed. In what way, he couldn't quite pinpoint, but it didn't quite look the same to him in his eyes. Nor did it feel the same. Or perhaps it was just him; he certainly no longer felt the same.

Maybe that was it...

"Of course it's your decision to make, but I'm certain Gothamel wouldn't want to see you turn your back on all the hard work the two of you have accomplished over the past many months, especially when there's still so much for you to learn here," said Anahel while not being completely neutral in his diplomacy. "Certainly no one knew better than him the impossibility of escaping oneself, or the ghosts which choose to follow, no matter how far or fast you set your feet to running."

Jacob listened, and the heavy, resigned sigh that left him sounded his inability to deny Anahel's words, despite his desire to do just that. Rising to his feet, he retrieved Destiny and called for Mist, who peered over the top of the tall grass at the sound of her name. As he watched her bound her way toward him, Jacob asked Anahel if he would mind taking her back to Havenhid.

"Of course not. But...where is it you're going?" the angel asked somewhat apprehensively that his words had failed to change the boy's mind

"It's time I deal with something I should have done a long time ago," said Jacob cryptically. "If I return to Havenhid—and I'm not saying I will—it's not going to be as half a Nephilim anymore."

Anahel frowned. "I don't understand...you're as much a Nephilim as any other who's passed through Eden's Gate."

"No...I'm not," argued Jacob, "not as long as I continue to need a Snowdrift to compete in the Illumination, or an angel to haul me around like some baby in need of a papoose."

Anahel's face softened with clarity and his gaze drifted past the boy toward the spectacular waterfalls and then beyond to the highest point of the towering cliffs where Broken Earth resided. Then, giving the boy an understanding nod, he motioned Mist to his side, and both the angel and the wolf watched as Jacob made his way across the meadow in the direction of Broken Earth when the boy paused his steps suddenly.

"There's just one more thing," he said to Anahel.

Anahel smiled slightly and answered with a sigh: "There always is."

"I've been meaning to ask you ever since the day you found me playing hooky at Broken Earth: Why have the demons and whatever else that lurks in the Underneath bothered with some Through in the Silent Forest when they could just come into Eden from the Barrens?"

"You think it would be that easy, wouldn't you?" Anahel answered with a chuckle.

"Isn't it?"

"Not when we don't exist in their eyes," said Anahel. "An inhabitant of the Underneath who stands where you and I did that day looking in the direction of Eden is not greeted with the view of this paradise created by the Light, but an icy wasteland that surrounds them in all directions in endless and inhospitable stretches. Oh, they know we are here, somewhere; and those who have gone in search have been met by a sudden and harrowing end when their feet unknowingly approached the great gorge which separates us."

The explanation appeared to lend Jacob comfort and he continued on is way.

As Anahel stood watching the boy as he grew smaller the further he made his way, the sound of footsteps approaching casually from behind pricked his ears.

"So, now he knows the truth about the Samael."

It was Damiel, looking melancholy as he stared off in the same direction as Anahel and Mist.

"Eavesdropping, were you?" asked Anahel.

"Not intentionally. Like you, I was concerned about the boy after all that's happened."

"He's much stronger than any of us give him credit for being."

Damiel couldn't argue the point, yet his hardened look held a hint of worry.

"Still, do you think it wise allowing him to go up there alone?" he asked.

"Questioning my judgment, are you?" Anahel challenged lightly.

"The boy has a lot to prove, both to himself as well to us; and prove it he will, in his own time, on his own terms.

"Be that as it may, I think it best I trail his steps," argued Damiel.

"I assure you, Damiel, he will not be in need of a lifeguard this day," said Anahel followed by an emphatic, "Trust me!"

He then turned to leave calling on Mist to follow along and, as the two began the walk back to Havenhid, Damiel turned his head and lamented over his shoulder, "I wish you would have told the rest of us the truth about David."

The comment caught Anahel sideways and brought a pause to his steps.

"There's a lot of things I wish I'd done," was all he said in return before continuing on, leaving Damiel fixed to the spot where he stood as he looked on again at the barrier of mountains looming like a slumbering creature of rock before him.

~ ~ ~

Once back at Havenhid, Anahel paid a visit to the Library where he made the long ascent to its highest tier. There he was greeted by the unwelcoming presence of the three Greffiers who focused their perpetual vigilance onto the angel and eyed closely the bundle of burlap he carried with him. It was the same bundle Gotham had brought to Broken Earth to present to Thaniel; that which concealed the fake Sword of Destiny. And while the sword was revealed to be a forgery (and an uncanny one at that), it had also proven itself to be nonetheless dangerous, the latter of which was reflected in spades from within Anahel's gaze when he unwrapped the deceiving replica and gave it last scrutinizing, if not remorseful, once-over.

"Take special care in keeping this safe and most of all secure," Anahel instructed the Greffiers when he finally swaddled the sword once again into the confines of its burlap blanket.

Anahel then hurled the bundle into the gulf of empty space that separated himself from the vast bank of shelves unreachable by any visitors to the Library and fiercely guarded by the Greffiers. One of the large hawkish creatures let loose an ear-piercing shrill of a shriek in reply before leaving its perch and snatched the bundle with its razor-sharp talons before depositing it amongst the numerous books, scrolls and other sacred documents that were clearly off limits to anyone who to ever managed to journey to this rarely visited spot of the Library.

Only when Anahel saw that the sword was safely in the guardianship of the Greffiers did he retire to his room where he took to his comfortable chair beside the fireplace and picked up where he last left off in his latest book choice from the Library. Next to him, Mist lay sleeping at the foot of the hearth where a warm, comforting white fire burned of its own accord without the aid of wood to fuel it.

Try as he did to hold worry at bay, Anahel couldn't keep his eyes from looking up from his book periodically and peering across his room toward the open balcony which held a framed view of the mountain Jacob was last seen heading towards. Several hours had already past, and when finally twilight had arrived and the sky once flaming with the fiery colors made in the last gasps of the setting sun gave way to one of deep hues of blue and lavender, highlighted with soft pinks and the glittering flicker of the first awakening stars, did Anahel set down his book. Stepping out onto the balcony, the cool, clean fragrant air he usually breathed deeply was ignored, as was the sight of the splendid waterfalls appearing as serpents made of sparkling diamonds as they slithered in magnificent fashion over the looming cliffs and down the face of the mountain. The only thing in Anahel's sights was the spot where Broken Earth rested out of sight behind a cluster of ragged rock, but the telltale sign he'd been watching for had so far remained elusive. Had he, he began to wonder, shown misjudgment in allowing Jacob to venture to Broken Earth on his own while his head was filled with so many conflicting thoughts? And had he made an even graver error in waving off Damiel's suggestion to follow after the boy as a precaution?

As his concern gradually took on a feeling of worry, he quietly began to hope Damiel had ignored him and carried on with his instinct, but something told Anahel that was not the case. It was an unpleasant feeling he felt beginning to ripen in the pit of his stomach. Then, just when he was about to unfurl his wings and take to the sky, he was greeted with a most remarkable sight; a brilliant flash of light—the kind of light that could only come from one thing. It belched its presence behind the silhouette of the mountain in a flicker of bright blue, much like a burst of lightning erupting within the billowing darkness of storm clouds. It was only but an instant, but it was all that was needed for Anahel to breathe with relief, and a smile—like that which comes to visit a proud father-to-be upon hearing the first cries of his child's arrival into the world—unfolded itself across his face. Then almost as quickly as the smile appeared it gradually faded away, much like the message of light.

Now, he thought to himself, comes the real test

<u>Tales of the Nephilim Brotherhood</u>

The Crossing Point (Book I)
Released in the Fall of 2020
&
My upcoming new book

The Beloved Exiles (Book III)
Due to be released in the Fall of 2022

www.ingramcontent.com/pod-product-compliance
Lightning Source LLC
Chambersburg PA
CBHW021840010726
47493CB00005B/1488